THE RUNEBEARER CURSE

THE RUNEBEARER CURSE

THE DEMON-SLEUTH SCROLLS BOOK THREE

DAN JOLLEY

FALSTAFF
BOOKS
WWW.FALSTAFFBOOKS.COM

For my partner, my better half, my sounding board, my voice of reason and wisdom, my font of eternal patience. My wife Tracy. Thanks for putting up with me, sweetie.

PART I

THE COURIER

1

The soft silver light from the runes in Camble Delakroy's eyes played off the steam of her breath, turning her last ragged exhale into a specter that danced and shimmered before it died, silent and lonely.

"I can't tell you what I don't know," the Watch Captain said. "He was torn apart, yeah. But it don't look like no wild animal did it."

The members of the Ninth Crucible followed behind the captain as they climbed the broad, slowly spiraling staircase, making their way upward, ever upward. Cam wasn't sure how long they'd been climbing. She didn't care that much. Cam cared about very little these days.

Just ahead of her, Commander Raoul Cullen matched the captain's paces effortlessly. He might as well have been strolling along a perfectly level promenade in the middle of Caulspring for all the exertion it took him, rather than bulling their way into the thinnest, coldest air at the top of a frozen city on the Empire's northern border.

She didn't have to turn her head to know that Percy Bitters, their Keeper, was right behind her. Panting a little but by-the-Dragon's-scaly-nutsack determined to show no weakness, never you mind his long, snow-white hair and aggressively forked white beard. Flax and Jax kept pace with the group as well. The two blood lynxes rarely made a sound at all, and never while they were working.

The felines represented a welcome constant in Cam's life.

The wheezing, grunting chorus from farther down the staircase signaled that Wallace Embry, the Ninth Crucible's new Enforcer, hadn't passed out yet. He'd never passed out, Cam admitted to herself, in open contradiction to his perpetually labored breathing and massive, barrel-like gut that she couldn't help but think of as uncouth. The Thaumetallicon had assigned Embry to their Crucible less than a month after Nysska—

After Nysska *left.*

No one ever found a body, Cam had insisted, over and over. *Nysska Stonegate jumped off the top of the falls at Dragon's Pain and only suffered a few bumps and bruises. She could easily have survived this!*

Except that at Dragon's Pain, Nysska hadn't just been shot with an arrow big enough to have come from a ballista's ammunition stack. Even as Nysska's body had disappeared into the waves, the arrow remained, lodged in the stone wall of Raoul's cliffside home and coated slick with her blood. A fall from a balcony into the ocean a hundred meters below? Surviving that was possible. Doing so with a hole in her chest and all her blood pouring out into the saltwater?

Cam realized she hadn't taken a breath in some time and filled her lungs with the frigid air of Mount Stark. The atmosphere tasted bitter and metallic on her tongue. They passed a window, small and set deep in the tower's grand stone walls, and she got a glimpse of the blizzard settling onto the walled city. The assignment had mentioned the possibility when it came in. Not to give them any choice in the matter. Just as a courtesy.

"All right, here we are," the Watch Captain said. Cam remembered him introducing himself as Porter. The Ninth Crucible gathered behind him, bunching up in a short hallway that led to a massive wooden door. This far from Caulspring, this far from the Empire's all-pervasive influence, not so much emphasis had been placed on bronze. Aside from things such as door hinges and, of course, weaponry, Mount Stark left a vast impression on Cam as a city of white and gray. White for the snow. Gray for the stone, cut from the nearby mountains block by block and stacked high. The citizens occupied much the same space in her brain; white for the overwhelming alabaster skin tones she'd seen so far, gray for the furs everyone wore. She wondered which animals died the most to provide the people of Mount Stark with warmth. Wolves? Otters? She hoped it wasn't bears. Not after what had happened at Solace Canyon.

Raoul adjusted his Thaumetallicon-issued heavy coat as he stared at the splintered wood of the door. The supple, fur-lined brown leather inset with strips of bronze stood out in Mount Stark almost as loudly as the deeper brown of Raoul, Cam, and Embry's skins. He said, "You and your men did this?"

The latch of the door hung loosely, the wood around it splintered. The City Watch had hammered a new bronze band into place and fitted it with a padlock.

Captain Porter nodded. "We had to. The smell—that was what the maid first noticed—it was getting pretty bad, and since the door was bolted from inside, well, we had to bust it open."

Raoul looked Porter in the eye. "That was in the report, but I wanted to hear it from you myself. The door was bolted from *inside* the room?"

"That's right, Commander."

"And there's no other way to access this place?"

"Well—you'll see, sir. When we get inside. Just, ah, give me a second." Porter began picking through a massive ring of keys.

Cam was about to say something to Percy but changed her mind and reached out to turn his face toward hers. Percy frowned and pulled away. "What're you doing?"

Cam said, "Hold still. You've got another aggressive eyebrow hair."

Percy rolled his eyes. "Why bother? I'm hideous."

She put her hands on both sides of his face in a *Hold still* gesture and smoothed the errant hair down with her thumb. "Because it was sticking straight out, and I didn't like it pointing at me." As Percy chuckled, she said, "And you're *not* hideous, what're you talking about?"

Percy gave her a tuned-down version of his normal face-splitting grin, put his hands on her wrists, and gently pushed them away from his face. "It's not as if I have anyone to impress. Or as if I ever *will* have anyone to impress."

Without looking at Cam or Percy, and in a tone drier than dust, Raoul said, "Whether that's true or not, if those eyebrows get any more out of control I'm going to have to cite you for a uniform violation."

Cam and Percy looked at each other, both wide-eyed, and burst into laughter.

"Here we go," Captain Porter said, the padlock clicking open.

The door swung easily on well-oiled hinges, and the laughter died as the lingering scent of decay pushed its way into Cam's nostrils. Flax, the blood lynx, let her jaw hang open, getting a good purchase on the odor, but her brother Jax hissed and backed away from the door.

They entered the chamber single file. It occupied the entirety of the top of the square tower, a single large space cosmetically divided into living room, bedroom, and study. Cities as large and wealthy as Mount Stark tended to have indoor plumbing, but Cam's understanding of the mechanism was limited, so she didn't question the absence of a toilet. The porcelain-covered shit bucket sat behind a torn, blood-smeared privacy screen in one corner. Cam didn't envy the maid who had to climb all those stairs three or four times a day to attend to it.

The chamber looked as if someone had taken a bucket of dark reddish-brown paint and spun all over the room with it, sloshing it everywhere, trying to stain and spatter every surface. Cam placed her feet carefully so as not to tread in any vile, sticky puddles.

"All of a sudden I'm glad for the fucking cold," Percy said, eyeballing the room with his face creased up. "Imagine this kind of scene down near the border." He poked at a broken chair with the toe of his boot.

Every piece of furniture in the place had been destroyed, as if a furious bull had been set loose in it. Cam frowned, looking more closely. The damage rose above and beyond what would result from one man's murder. As if the killer had been trying to make some sort of brutal, chaotic point.

Only two of the walls had windows, both of them stained with dripping red stripes. The windows were a good bit bigger than the functional one Cam had glanced through on the way up, meant to afford the room's occupant a grand view rather than simply allow a soldier to fire a crossbow through it. Captain Porter gestured at the broad panes of glass one at a time.

"There's the only other way anybody'd could've gotten in here," he said with an apologetic note in his voice. "Except nobody did." He put a hand on the back of his neck. "I mean to say, nobody could've. It's, uh…well…it's a lot like the others."

Raoul grunted. "Yes, we'll get to that. For now, let's see if we can make short work of this." He turned to face Cam. "You ready?"

"Ready for more disappointment? Sure."

Cam didn't miss the tight, fleeting frown he tossed at her as he raised his arms. "All right, Percy, Wallace, you know the drill. Captain Porter, have you witnessed a Sensor taking in a crime site before?"

Porter dipped his head. "I have, sir."

"Good, then you'll have no objection to giving ours the room."

The blood lynxes hadn't entered the room yet at all. They moved aside as Raoul ushered Percy, Wallace, and the Captain out into the hallway. Turning back, Raoul asked, "Would you like the door closed?"

"Yes, please."

Raoul pulled the shattered door back into its frame, and Cam moved to one corner of the large room. She wanted to turn back to the door and see Nysska there. Hear her voice, the words singing with her brilliant, alien accent. Listen as she joked around with Percy or teased Raoul.

Cam had dreamed of feeling Nysska's lips on hers again. Of sliding her arms around Nysska's fearsome, powerful body. Of raising her own silver eyes to gaze into Nysska's perfect yellow ones.

Cam had told herself over and over that she and the towering, perfect sethyd could never have worked. She had even made the case to Nysska herself at one point, more or less, when Nysska suggested running away from the Empire's forces to live together in the wilderness. Virtually every human in the Empire hated sethyds. And two women living together the way a husband and wife would was flatly illegal, with punishment up to and including execution. *What kind of a life would that be?* Cam had said. *The two of us, in the middle of nowhere, cut off from the rest of the world?*

It would have been a life.

That's what Nysska had said back to her.

How many nights had Cam lain awake, crying silent tears, wishing she could run away with Nysska? In the middle of nowhere, on some uninhabited island, it didn't matter. Cam had said the words—had told Nysska how much she loved her—but only after Nysska vanished from her life had she realized how inadequate they were. For days upon days, weeks upon weeks, Cam fantasized. If only she could get a second chance, she'd spend the rest of whatever life she had left showing Nysska the meanings of "love" and "devotion."

But fantasies weren't real, and now Cam felt something very close to nothing at all.

She powered up the runes implanted in her corneas.

In the last few weeks, her eyes had begun to sting. Just a little. Not even enough to mention to the rest of the Crucible. But she knew what it meant.

The toxin in the argonium was finally beginning to make itself felt.

The rune poisoning affected every Sensor differently. Some suffered for years, stubbornly refusing to give up the position in the Empire that afforded them respect and security and, yes, a bit of power. Others gleefully used their runes pain-free until the argonium consumed them all at once.

The only constant was that no Sensor had yet to live past the age of forty.

Cam had celebrated her twenty-sixth birthday alone. Silently mourning the death of the only woman she'd ever truly loved was as close as she'd come to a "silver lining"—she'd never have to have that argument with Nysska again. No more defending her everyday use of her Sight Runes, no more listening to Nysska warn her off of them, no more hearing Nysska say that she wanted to squeeze each second of Cam's life for every bit of juice she could.

Cam meant to live the rest of her life to the fullest. Whether she had fourteen years left or ten or five.

Every bit of it aimed at the day when she could confront the bastard who'd shot Nysska and sent her plummeting into the cold, dark, unforgiving sea.

Cam shook her head, dislodging the distractions, and focused on the crime site in front of her. Under normal circumstances—which came along more and more rarely now—Cam could bring the power of her runes up to maximum and use them to see what had taken place, who had done what to whom.

She called her gift "Ruby Tears," since it only allowed her to see the *blood* of recent victims and perpetrators. Not skin nor flesh nor bones, only the arteries and veins, animated in the shape of the human that owned them—bizarre, bodiless laceworks of hot, pumping red liquid, paired with the cool, motionless ribbons of the deceased.

Ordinarily, once she witnessed the commission of the crime, drops of the killer's blood spilled from her tear ducts, scalding their way down her cheeks for Flax and Jax, the tracking animals, to lock onto. That was supposed to be the way a Crucible functioned. The Sensor observed the crime, the tracking animals and the Keeper hunted the perpetrator down, the Commander pronounced judgment by the authority of the Imperial Tribunal, and the Enforcer used a huge bronze headsman's axe to mete out the punishment.

Cam could muster no surprise when the normal process failed.

Ever since the introduction of the new metal, chervoxite, from the mysterious land across the ocean—ever since the face-changing insurrectionists known as the Gemini had alloyed it with argonium, thereby creating an entirely new branch of thaumaturgy—the intended use for Cam's runes had proven less and less useful, or even applicable at all.

She recognized the sensations as they prodded and seeped into her mind. The horrendous *emptiness*, as if a hole in the world had opened that only she could see, and which threatened to pull her in. The excruciating sense of wrongness, tearing through the fabric of everything she had always understood to be the world itself. The *obscene* nature of it—the foul sacrilege—the vile affront to everything the Great Silver Dragon had ever created.

If I believed in the Great Silver Dragon, Cam muttered to herself as she brought the runes back down. When the dancing silver flames had receded, leaving her with glimmering silver eyes that did no more than allow her to see in the same way as a woman who had not been born blind, she went back to the door and pulled it open.

"No luck." She moved out of the way as the rest of the Crucible and Captain Porter came back in.

"Rust?" Raoul asked. They had discovered, to their combined stress and annoyance, that metallic flakes composed of the ruby-red argonium-chervoxite alloy—flakes which had become known as *rust*, for *red dust*—completely disrupted a Sensor's ability to perceive the crime when sprinkled around a crime site.

Captain Porter cleared his throat. "We, ah, we already looked for rust. Swept the entire apartment. Found nothing."

Wallace Embry, who still hadn't quite caught his breath from the climb up the stairs, spoke to Porter. "It doesn't have to be rust now, Captain. We've caught a few people with red amulets—made from the..." Embry spoke carefully, getting each syllable right. "...*chervoxite* alloy. Turns out, if you wear one of those while you're committing a crime, it's just as good as using the rust. Or, uh, or as *bad*, I guess you could say. Would say. It's bad, is what I mean."

Raoul gazed around at the dead man's belongings. "And you've got the body stored?"

Porter nodded. "We went back and forth about it. Whether we should just leave it here, since the storm's coming in and it's prob'ly going to be plenty cold, but I made the call and had him taken down to one of the root cellars. I hope I didn't fuck anything up."

Raoul said, "No, that's fine. We're going to search this room ourselves, top to bottom, but before we do, I'd like to hear about the victim."

Porter's eyebrows lifted. "Oh—you mean from me? I—it's not—I mean, me and him weren't *close* or nothin', I—"

Raoul made a placating gesture with one hand. "Just in your own words, Captain."

While Porter described the murder victim—a bookkeeper who'd been in charge of monitoring and replenishing the food stores for Mount Stark's Imperial garrison—Cam wandered over to one of the windows. It had a broad, deep sill, and Flax jumped up onto it and peered at her with the startling silver eyes that marked her and her litter-mate as seraphic animals.

"All that argonium in your veins doesn't seem to bother *you*," Cam said, barely above a whisper. "Guess it's just humans that have to put up with the not-so-great effects, huh?"

Flax purred and nuzzled against her, and when Cam stroked her head, the big cat pressed her face into Cam's palm.

Rander Borley, the dead man who'd lived and worked here, had had quite the view of Mount Stark. The tower capped off one wing of the Mayor's residence, which could only have been described as a castle, and looked out and down on the snow-covered roofs of the city stretching away below. Cam followed them, structure after structure, until everything brought up short at the massive city wall. She thought of a good word to describe Mount Stark as a whole: *fortress*.

Cam picked Flax up in her arms—something the blood lynxes occasionally tolerated—and scratched her chin as she drifted over to the second window. Unlike the first one, this window did not give her an awe-inspiring view, but rather showed her another tower, twin to the one in which they all stood. Wind howled outside and the snow thickened, but she could still see the other tower clearly enough to gauge its distance from Borley's top-floor flat. A gap of ten meters separated the two.

Something Captain Porter said caught her attention, and she set Flax down on the floor and rejoined her teammates, who stood clustered near the room's cold, empty fireplace.

"That's what I was sayin' earlier," Porter went on. "There ain't no ledges or nothin' on the outside of the tower. So, yeah, somebody could've got in through one o' the windows, but if they had, we would've found marks from the climbing equipment. And every bit o' that stone is smooth as silk."

Percy went to one of the windows, popped the clasp free, and tilted it outward in its frame. "Well, fuck," he said softly.

Raoul joined Percy at the window and closed it again as a frigid blast from outside blew snow and bits of ice into the flat. Raoul appeared as if he were about to say something, but Percy beat him to it. "Could some fucker have *jumped* across? From that other tower, I mean."

Porter made a sound sort of like a chuckle. "Ain't nobody doin' that. For one thing, there ain't room on the other tower's roof to get a runnin' start. For another, even if you had a runnin' start, ain't nobody strong enough or fast enough to make that kind o' jump."

From the apartment's doorway, Nysska Stonegate said, "A sethyd could do it," and Cam's knees buckled and collapsed underneath her.

2

Raoul was at Cam's side in a heartbeat, of course, helping her to one of the dead man's couches, which he flipped over onto its legs. Nysska watched as Cam struggled past the couch, brushing Raoul's hands off her. Watched as Cam's brilliant, heartbreaking silver eyes focused on her again, watched as her feet moved, almost running, headed straight for her—

And then stopped still, as General Boris Cullen and Mount Stark Mayor Steevn Ragwild filed into the flat.

What would Cam have done, had they not been observed by such high-ranking, Imperially loyal officials? Flown to her, leapt upon her, smothered her with hungry kisses? Slapped her face for scaring her so badly, for weighing her down with crushing grief? Nysska's bones fairly vibrated with the need for Cam to do just that. Any of it. All of it. Yet she stood as still as a great tree, and forced her eyes away from Cam, and hated every heartbeat of her own life.

No one knew what to say. Even General Cullen hesitated in the face of the tension filling the room thick as ice fog. Into the silence, the new Enforcer—Nysska had been told his name was Embry—decided to speak.

"You have got to be Nysska Stonegate," he said, and shifted his considerable mass in her direction, one enormous, beefy hand extended as he approached. Embry had skin like oil-rubbed bronze, and the light from the torches in sconces around the room's perimeter glimmered and danced on his broad, smooth scalp. Large, square, brilliant-white teeth lit up his face as he gave her what she took to be his best affable grin.

Nysska took a step back from him. "Yes," she said, and Embry dropped his hand. As Embry faltered—he looked as if he'd just realized how exposed he was, right in the middle of the space between the Ninth Crucible, Captain Porter, and the group comprising Nysska, General Cullen, and Mayor Ragwild—Nysska cleared her throat.

"I know this is strange. I know you've all believed me to be dead for the last three months. I know I owe you all an explanation. But please, please trust me when I tell you that nothing—*nothing*—is of greater priority right now than apprehending the person responsible for this murder." She glanced at Captain Porter, then at the Mayor, but spoke to the group at large. "I have reason to believe the murderer is a sethyd. And that they are also responsible for the other two murders that Captain Porter has been investigating. We must find this killer. Before he has a chance to leave the city."

The weight of the Ninth Crucible's eyes bored into her. Neither Percy nor Raoul had said a word yet. Cam was also silent, and that silence hurt the worst of all—

Until Flax padded across the floor, gazed up at her with her beautiful, clear silver eyes—and *hissed.*

Percy's hand flew to his dagger.

Raoul scowled and spoke to General Cullen. "Father, what the *fuck* is this? What's going on here?"

Cullen opened his mouth to answer but broke off as Jax crossed the flagstones and nuzzled his sister's shoulder. A bit of the silent communication the blood lynxes employed passed between them, after which they both turned and stared up at Nysska. Flax took a tentative step forward, sniffed of Nysska's boot, then padded half a meter away, yawned, and began grooming.

Percy's hand drifted away from his dagger's hilt. "They seem to think she's all right. Just *different.*"

General Cullen said, "I have full faith that what Enforcer Stonegate is saying is true. Finding this killer and bringing him to justice is of the utmost importance. I am also aware of the highly unusual nature of these circumstances, and so—Mayor Ragwild, Captain Porter...and Enforcer Embry, too. If you would. I believe a few minutes in the hallway won't impede our progress unduly."

Wallace Embry took a moment to process what General Cullen meant.

Finally he said, "Oh!" and followed the General, Captain Porter, and the Mayor out of the room. General Cullen pulled the door into its ruined frame as they went.

Immediately Cam took a step toward Nysska, but Nysska held up a hand in an unmistakable gesture: *stop.* Cam's jaw dropped open, and the hurt that flitted across her features felt like a nail in the heart.

"Why?" The word came out half-strangled, choked with pain. Cam said it again. "Why won't you let me touch you?"

"Fuck that," Percy all but roared. "Where the *fuck* have you been? We've stood around with our cocks in our hands for three fucking months! You couldn't have fucking *told* us you were still fucking well *alive?*"

Nysska squeezed her eyes shut. Raoul said, "Please tell us you've got a reason. I hope it's a damn good one, but please tell us there's at least a reason of some kind."

Nysska's legs trembled. She groped for the back of a couch. "I'm sorry," she managed. "I'm sorry you haven't heard from me, and I'm sorry I made you all suffer, and I hope you'll believe me when I tell you that I am so, so sorry for what I'm about to say."

"What?" Cam demanded. "What is it?"

Nysska heard an entire world of pain in that plaintive question. She said, "I can't tell you where I've been or what I've been doing. I can't. Not yet."

Tears spilled out of Cam's eyes. Percy threw his hands up, plainly disgusted, and Raoul's scowl deepened. He said, "You can't? Or you won't?"

"I know what you must be thinking now." Nysska stared the floor. It was easier than looking at any of her teammates. Her *family.* "I know what you must be thinking *of me.* And I can only ask you to trust me." At the tiny sound that escaped Cam's throat, she hastened to add, "And I know how *ridiculous* that must sound. The entire time you've known me, I've kept secret after secret, and now I've got another one, and it's not fair to any of you."

Cam turned away from her, silver eyes flashing to every corner of the flat—looking for some concealed place, some nook to hide their voices and give them at least a façade of privacy. No such place existed there. The tears had increased by the time she turned back to face Nysska.

Words fighting through the tears and the pain, Cam whispered, "Why can't I touch you?"

"It's not you." Nysska didn't move. Kept her hands rigidly by her sides. "It's not any of *you*. I can't—I can't touch *anyone*."

"Yeah, but fucking *why*?" Percy got in Nysska's face, forcing her to backpedal. "What kind of secret would keep you from making fucking physical contact?"

Nysska whirled away from them, throwing her own hands up in as great a gesture of frustration as she could muster. "I *hate* this!" she cried. "Do you think I don't fucking *hate* this?" Lowering her voice, she came back toward Cam, but stopped a meter away. "Do you think it's not fucking *killing* me?"

"I don't know." Cam wiped her eyes with the back of one bronze-inlaid leather glove. "*Is* it?"

Nysska sank down to one of the couches and buried her face in her hands. "I don't blame you. I don't blame any of you. It's the least I could do, the *very least*, to explain *why*. But I can't. Not yet."

A note of Commander's bronze shot through Raoul's voice. "Why *not*?"

Nysska raised her head, tear-filled eyes blinking. "Because I took an oath. The most revered, binding oath a sethyd can take. And because..." She spoke directly to Cam. "Because it's for your own protection."

Percy said, "What the fuck is that supposed to mean?"

Cam said, "It's fine," and something in the depth and finality of her words cracked Nysska's heart in half. "All the secrets she's had, there's always been a solid reason she's kept them. Hasn't there?" Cam sniffed once, her tears drying. "I see no reason not to trust her now."

As Nysska stood, Cam turned away from the group—away from *her*—and the broken stone of Nysska's heart crumbled to shards. "I swore an oath. I promise, I would tell you all everything if I could. I *will* tell you everything, as soon as I can. I have no right to do this, I have no right to think any of you would grant me this wish, but please trust me. Please." Since Cam still had her head turned, Nysska addressed Raoul and Percy. "The sooner we catch this murderer, the sooner all of this can be put to rest."

Raoul heaved a long, massive sigh while Percy tugged on his forked beard.

Finally Percy said, "I don't like it. I don't like any little fucking bit of it. But Cam's not wrong. You've come through for us time and time again. I don't figure it'll hurt me or the kitties any to give you the benefit of the doubt." He stared off, through one of the walls, for a couple more moments before adding, "I'm still fucking mad at you, though."

"I don't blame you."

Raoul made a growling sound in his throat. "We mourned you. We fucking *mourned* you."

Nysska murmured, "I'm sorry, Raoul."

"Shit. Percy's right." He rolled his eyes. "Welcome back, then. Can't shake your hand on it, though, can I?"

"Thank you. Thank you." She paused. "Cam? Can you go along with what I'm asking? At least for a while?"

Cam turned and looked Nysska horns to heels. "Why are you wearing a regular Cathedral uniform? What's the story with this clown hair?" In a slightly less caustic tone she added, "And what happened to your *horns*?"

Raoul gave a snorting sort of laugh. "I was going to bring all that up."

Nysska sighed and smoothed the front of the Cathedral-issue cold-weather coat General Cullen had given her. With zero enthusiasm she said, "It's supposed to be a disguise."

Percy said, "A ridiculous disguise?"

In a development that pleased Nysska not at all, Raoul picked up on Percy's direction, which appeared to be *Let's make fun of the sethyd.* "So you file your horns down a little and stick a red wig on and what, you think you'll disappear in a crowd?"

The mirror above Rander Borley's fireplace, unlike the carnage made of the rest of the flat, only had a single thin crack running along one side of it, such that when Nysska glanced at herself in it she got a clear, unbroken view. *Disguise indeed.* The segments of her horns that pointed skyward, once proudly and dangerously pointed, had been filed down to much shorter lengths and blunted. Now her horns emerged from her forehead, extended a few centimeters parallel to the ground, and turned up into useless little knobs. She reached up and ran her fingertips across them, then pushed a hand into the mane of spiky red hair. She thought of it as "big," as opposed to her natural preference of "long and easy to braid."

"Oh, this is no wig," Nysska said. "I created this monstrosity myself."

Raoul folded his arms and touched his chin with one speculative finger. "All right, but what we're asking is why you would make yourself look like *that*? I mean, you did that *deliberately*?"

"Ha. Ha. I bask in your humor. Ha."

Percy's head tilted down. "All right, hair and horns aside, what exactly is that beautiful thing hanging from your hip?"

Grateful for any change of subject, Nysska threw the catches off her scabbard and drew her khopesh. Percy whistled at the sight of the long, curved bronze sword, and Raoul held out a hand. "May I?"

Nysska handed the khopesh to him. "And that's a traditional sethyd weapon. I suppose neither of you have seen one before?"

"I've never even *heard* of one before," Percy said, the bronze flashing in the blue of his eyes.

Cam turned and moved past Nysska, heading for the door, no trace of humor on her face at all, good-natured or otherwise. "If you're all done playing with the shiny toy—you said we've got to catch this murderer, right, Nysska?"

Any jollity that might have made its way into the flat vanished. Nysska said, "That's right." She took her khopesh back and secured it in its scabbard as she followed after Cam, but brought herself up short as Cam turned and peered up at her.

"All I'll say is…" Cam jabbed a finger at Nysska's nose. "This better be one *mind-blowing* explanation."

After a short rap at the door, General Cullen opened it and stepped inside, leaving Embry, Porter, and Mayor Ragwild in the hallway.

The General had not discussed his son with Nysska on the journey to Mount Stark. As he moved past Cam and Nysska, taking up a place near Raoul and Percy, she expected Raoul to say something. Greet his father in some way, now that the shock of Nysska's appearance had worn off a bit. After all, it had been three months since she and Cam overheard the agonizing exchange Raoul had with his father at Cliffside, their ancestral home. Surely they would've patched things up by now.

Instead, the two Cullen men avoided each other's eyes, and Raoul stayed silent. Without preamble, the General said, "Nysska found me three days ago. I believe her—as she has asked all of you to do as well—that she cannot divulge the details of her whereabouts for the last ninety days, but like you, I am inclined to cut her such slack as is necessary. She asked me to get her official clearance to pursue a sethyd she believed could be found in Mount Stark. It was only after we arrived that she and I both learned of the murders that this unnamed sethyd may or may not have committed here previously, and that this was the case to which the Ninth Crucible had been assigned."

"Wait," Cam said, her brow creasing as she fixed her eyes on Nysska again. "You're saying you didn't come here because we were here? You weren't seeking us out?"

Nysska let her eyelids slide shut before giving her head a tiny, rueful shake. "It was not my intention to turn up and torture you all with my lack of information. I had hoped to resolve every bit of the...the situation in which I've found myself before reuniting with you."

Percy's expression mirrored Cam's. "So, what, you realized we were here, and decided it'd be too fucking inconvenient to try to find this killer sethyd while we were getting in your way? Too much trouble to avoid us, so you'll bust in and give us all fucking heart attacks instead?"

General Cullen let a stern edge creep into his voice. "Enforcer Stonegate has been officially attached to the Thaumetallicon as an independent consultant. She's authorized to operate in Mount Stark under the same aegis as the Argonium Infantry's extraordinary activities squads —under the name Lianne Hardesty." He cleared his throat. "Since *Nysska Stonegate* is still officially wanted for questioning in relation to the disappearance of a large shipment of enemy contraband."

Cam scoffed.

Nysska spread her hands. "I didn't want to get you all mixed up in the...the shit in which I've become mired. Since you are here, though...it would be the height of folly not to ask the finest Crucible in the Empire to help me track down a killer."

Raoul surprised her by saying, "The solution is simple. We could depart. Get out of Mount Stark and leave you to your investigation with no emotional obstacles in your way."

As he'd been speaking, the apartment door swung open, and Mayor Ragwild stepped inside. "No one's leaving, I'm afraid," he said, sounding genuinely upset about it. "I've just had word—the blizzard's come in full force. All the roads are closed. *No one* is leaving Mount Stark until the weather clears up."

3

The air settled heavy around Nysska as she and the rest of the team searched Rander Borley's apartment. Captain Porter watched them work with cool eyes, as his men had already accomplished this task to his satisfaction. A general feeling of things left unsaid clouded and clotted the space between Nysska and the people she loved most in the world, preventing her from asking whether there had been any advances in search techniques during the months she'd been away. Now and then she felt eyes on her, but whenever she turned her head to acknowledge the observer, those eyes darted away, whether brown, blue, or silver.

Hating her life and herself, Nysska bent to the task. There were only so many places things could be hidden in a flat such as this. Raoul stretched out on the cold stone floor on his back, peering up underneath the desk, no doubt looking for hidden compartments or nooks. She agreed with his instincts, since Borley was a bookkeeper. If he was going to hide a secret anywhere, the desk where he'd spent countless hours scribbling notes onto scrolls and sheets of parchment seemed the most logical.

She was still thinking about that when she noticed the bed move.

Not much. It didn't skid across the floor or anything so obvious. But a spot in the center of the mattress lifted for a heartbeat, shifted, and lowered again.

Nysska looked around. She spotted Jax after a moment. The big tom crouched behind the ruined privacy screen next to the shit bucket, industriously chewing on a mouse. Flax was nowhere to be seen. Nysska went to the bed and dropped down to the floor, in much the same posture Raoul had taken at the desk. Before she'd modified them, her horns would have prevented her from getting her head all the way underneath it, but now there was just enough room to slide her skull underneath the frame and get a look at where Flax had gone.

The bed was one of the fancier ones she'd seen since coming to human lands. It had two layers—a mattress soft enough to make her back ache just thinking about lying on it, and a platform underneath encased in heavy fabric. Flax sat in the center of the platform's underside, the top half of her body poked up through a hole in the cloth. Nysska softly called out, "Flax? What're you doing in there?"

The big blood lynx wriggled down out of the platform. She dropped flat to the floor and pushed with her toes to slide over to Nysska, purring as she moved past and climbed out from under the bed.

Nysska turned her body, forcing one shoulder under the bed, and reached up and into the hole from which Flax had emerged. It took a small bit of feeling around, but soon her fingers closed on a rough-bound book.

When she sat up, everyone else in the room had gathered around her in a half-circle, watching expectantly. "Well?" Captain Porter said. She couldn't tell if he sounded impressed despite himself, or simply spiteful. "What'd you find?"

Nysska stood and held the book up in the lantern light. Between two covers fashioned hastily out of scrap wood, a thick sheaf of parchments lay, covered in the same kind of tiny, cramped handwriting that adorned every paper on Rander Borley's desk. The difference was that everything on the desk was written in Plainish, and as she flipped through the pages in the wood-covered book, she recognized exactly nothing.

"What is this?" Nysska asked, holding the book out to the assembled crowd. "Does anyone recognize the language?"

General Cullen took the book from her, frowning down at it. "It's nothing I've ever seen before." He offered the book to Captain Porter. "Some kind of regional dialect?"

Cam's eyes glimmered a tiny bit brighter as she came around and peered at the book past Captain Porter's shoulder. "I don't think it's a language at all," she said. "I think it's a code."

Flax had jumped up into Percy's arms, and Nysska watched as he fished a treat out of a pocket and fed it to her. "You're a good girl, you are," Percy murmured, and then glanced down at Jax, who had reared up and put his front paws on Percy's waist, very clearly to say, *Yes, hello, I would like a treat as well.* Percy scoffed. "I saw you eating that mouse. Plus you didn't find us a mystery book full of mystery codes. No treat for you."

Jax growled as he padded away but didn't sound as if he meant it.

"So is that it?" Mayor Ragwild asked. "I'll admit my men didn't find this when they did their search, but are we done with this room now?"

Nysska glanced at Raoul, and found him looking at her in turn, both of them as if to ask—*Anything else to add?* Nysska dipped her head in what she hoped was a deferential manner. Raoul took her meaning accurately, and said, "I believe we are done with this room, yes."

"Thank the Great Silver Dragon," Mayor Ragwild said. "So I can have people come in and clean? The last thing I want is all this blood growing maggots."

"Yes, Mayor," General Cullen said, "Your people can clean. But we have further business with this crime."

Ragwild nodded and gestured vaguely downward. "Right. Yes. You want to see the body. Correct?"

"Very much so."

"Then allow me to lead the way. I have yet to lay eyes on it myself."

The group filed out of the tower flat. Nysska wondered if the Mayor would be so keen to observe the body once he'd actually shared space with it.

Ragwild led them down the long, winding staircase up which they'd come, through a dim, narrow hallway that Nysska suspected was primarily used by castle servants, and then down another set of more traditional stairs composed of straight flights and landings. By the time they'd reached the bottom, they had to be down inside the bedrock of the city itself, judging by the lack of windows and the presence of ventilation shafts peeking from the ceiling.

"It's just down here," Ragwild said, and led them through a doorway filled not with a door but with several sheets of heavy fabric cut into vertical strips.

The room they walked into might as well have been exposed to the snow and frigid winds, given how cold it was. Shelves and racks lined the walls, all of them stacked with vegetables, trays of eggs, and packages of dried meat. Nysska flashed back to the cellar at Summergray where they'd stored the thirty-two sethyd corpses that had been burned to death in the Church of the Great Silver Dragon's efforts to "cleanse the land" of the "encroaching sethyd menace." That bit of makeshift cadaver storage had been very nearly the opposite of this arrangement, though. Instead of all-pervasive cold, the summer's heat and bathwater-like rain had threatened to putrefy the bodies such that the Ninth Crucible could glean nothing from them.

Here, the body of Rander Borley simply lay on the cold stone floor, covered by a blood-stained white sheet. Nysska wouldn't have been all that surprised to learn that it had frozen to the stone beneath it.

Since no one else seemed anxious to approach the body, Nysska went to it, grabbed a corner of the sheet, and whisked the covering away.

"They weren't kidding," Cam murmured. "This Borley fellow really was torn apart."

Wallace Embry made a gagging sound, turned on his heel, and left the room, staggering through the fabric door-cover. Nysska glanced over at Raoul and said, "He's the one taking off heads for you?"

Raoul shrugged. "Axe strikes are clean if you know what you're doing. You're aware of that." He indicated Borley's corpse. "This shit is anything but clean."

Nysska had seen human bodies dismembered before. She had even done a bit of it herself—but only with the use of a sword or a headsman's axe. Rander Borley had been...she could think of no other way to put it. He'd been *pulled apart*. Both of his arms lay next to the torso, his left leg had been positioned so that the shredded stump touched the equally shredded ruin of his hip socket, and his head, while still attached to his body, had had its neck twisted so viciously that the bones of his spine had turned to powder.

Raoul turned to Captain Porter. "You said this murder made you realize it was linked to two others. How so?"

Porter swallowed hard and approached the corpse. Rander Borley had been dressed for bed, in light gray silk pajamas and bedroom slippers. One of the slippers still clung to his right foot. *It must have been stuck there by the dried blood.* "This right here," Porter said, pointing high on the side of the corpse's chest, near its armpit. Nysska moved around to get a better angle and saw a near-perfect footprint, preserved in the corpse's flesh as clearly as if the foot had stamped its impression into a bank of mud.

Porter turned to the rest of the group. "You already know this, Mister Mayor, sir, from my report. It's this footprint. Boot-print, to be more precise. We found one like it in the blood at the second murder site, and it made me think, so I went back into my notes—I've been taking notes, like we're supposed to now—and one of my men had said he saw a boot-print on the door at the first site. Like somebody had kicked the door open." He ducked his head and spoke to Nysska's collarbone. "It's, uh, if I may say, ma'am, it's because of you—you and your Crucible—that we had to start takin' notes in the first place. The, uh, the Thaumetallicon sent out some sub-decrees. Said we needed to, uh, to *document* everything we seen at crime sites. Now that the, uh—y'know. The red metal's out there. So, that is to say, we wouldn't have made these connections if not for, uh. For you."

Nysska couldn't decide if Porter's stumbling speech indicated an inherently bashful nature, or if he simply felt uncomfortable talking to a demon.

Demon. Nysska turned the word over in her mind for a second or two. She'd decided she might actually like it now.

Flax and Jax had been circling the corpse. Jax moved in closer, sniffing, and his mouth dropped open. Nysska knelt and looked him in the eye. "You think a sethyd did this? Someone like me?"

Jax nodded, which caused Mayor Ragwild and Captain Porter to gasp. At this point, sethyds had become more common in the Valconian Empire than seraphic animals like the blood lynxes, though not by much.

Nysska nodded back to Jax, sat on the floor, and pulled her boot off. She placed it carefully over the boot-print on the corpse's pajama shirt, demonstrating that they lined up perfectly. "Right. As I thought."

"So—so what does this mean?" Mayor Ragwild asked, sounding as if he'd rather be anywhere else on the continent. "The killer stomped on him?"

Nysska put her boot back on and stood. "No. It means the killer braced their foot against the body and used the leverage when they pulled the arm free of the shoulder."

Quietly, Raoul said, "They?"

Nysska let her shoulders rise and fall. "A female sethyd could have done this just as easily as a male."

Captain Porter shivered. "So…we need to find a sethyd…who's a man, or a woman…who has feet the same size as yours?"

Nysska paused. It sometimes still caught her by surprise how unfamiliar with sethyds most humans were. "All adult sethyds are the same size, Captain," she said in what she hoped was a patient, neutral manner.

"Men and women both. The variations between our heights and weights are negligible...as are the variations between our strength levels." She looked down at the corpse again. "We do vary in skill. Quite markedly. But our strength is uniform." She glanced at Cam, who was looking down at the corpse, then over at General Cullen. "*Any* adult sethyd could've done this."

The General blew out a long sigh. "Well. That narrows it down."

Nysska nodded. "Which means—in the absence of the *who*—we have no choice but to figure out the *why*."

Percy spoke up for the first time in a while. "So the only fucking hope of catching this fucker is figuring out how a sethyd thinks."

Trying not to put too facetious a spin on it, Nysska curtsied to the group.

After Cam had tried and, to the surprise of no one, failed to read Rander Borley's corpse, just as she'd failed to read the blood-splattered crime site, a lull had fallen over the group. They needed to find out as much as possible about Borley's life, as well as about the lives of the other victims, and see if they could decipher the mysterious wood-covered book found inside his bed. But when Wallace Embry's considerable gut made a sound not unlike the grumbling of an irritable bear, Mayor Ragwild held up his hands and addressed the whole group.

"It's nearly dinner time," he said. "I'm aware of the urgency of this task, and that a good night's sleep will probably evade us all until the killer is found and arrested. But I, for one, cannot think properly on an empty stomach, and let me just head off any protestations from the Ninth Crucible by saying that I don't want any of you functioning at less than full capacity. Also, my kitchen staff does a roast chicken dish that'll make you want to move to Mount Stark. Let us adjourn to my private dining room, and then we can get back about the business of finding our homicidal sethyd."

Nysska had found herself drifting closer to Cam, and to her pleasant surprise, Cam murmured, "Has there ever been a politician who wasn't in love with the sound of their own voice?"

That sounded so...*normal.*

Such the sort of thing that Cam would have said to her, or that she might have said to Cam, in the days before the incident on the balcony at

Cliffside. Back when their lives were—well. Not normal, no. Nothing about their lives had been normal since they'd met. But back before things were...

Like this.

"Maybe Galena Vachs," Nysska ventured, keeping her voice quiet as she and Cam followed the group of men out of the vegetable cellar. She wondered how the Governor of the Green Needles Territory was faring these days. That sent her mind skittering off down an unpaved path, envisioning how she'd have to relive the same trauma she'd inflicted on the Ninth by showing up, alive and well, after they'd all mourned her death and moved on. Surely Galena Vachs would have the same reaction—the shock, the relief, the inevitable anger. For each person she knew who'd believed her to be deceased, she would need to offer apologies and feel like hammered shit all over again, every time.

Cam brought her back from her self-pitying tangent. "We're at the back of the group. No one's looking at us. I'm still furious with you, Nysska, but the urge to take your hand is almost too much to resist."

Nysska looked down and saw Cam's fingers straying close to hers, and jerked her hand away with a short, sharp, involuntary hiss that she bit off as soon as it left her lips.

She didn't bite it off fast enough. The mask of hurt, of *betrayal* on Cam's face felt like a crushing knee to the gut. "I'm sorry," Nysska said instantly. With a careful look at the rest of the group, still making their way ahead of them, she motioned with her head for Cam to drop back. "It's not that I don't want to touch you," she whispered. "I've been dying to feel your skin on mine ever since—"

"What?" Cam asked in a mirrored whisper. "Ever since *what*?"

"I can't tell you, and it's *for your own safety*. All right? I can't tell you anything, and I especially can't touch you, and I know this isn't fair. But please. Please trust me. Trust me and I swear I'll make it up to you."

Cam's lips tightened into that hard, unwelcome line again. She said, "I prayed. Every night, I prayed to the Great Silver Dragon—a god I only barely believe in—that you would come back to me." She paused. "Now that you're here...Nysska, if I can't touch you, and you won't tell me why—"

"Can't," Nysska said. "Not won't."

"All I'm saying is—it might be easier not to be around you at all."

Nysska could think of nothing to say to that, and trailed along after Cam and the rest of the group as they climbed the narrow stone stairs.

4

A somber bunch sat around a sturdy wooden table eating roast chicken and, if Nysska were being honest, painfully flavorless vegetables. Somber—maybe edging into sullen, except for Wallace Embry, who appeared perfectly content with the heaping plate in front of him.

It looked to Nysska as though the longer Raoul had to think about things, the more unsatisfied he grew. She had no doubt that her presence there, along with her maddening refusal to elaborate on *how*, exactly, a grievous arrow wound and a hundred-meter fall into the ocean hadn't killed her, made up a large part of his discontent. The more she observed, though, the more she thought General Cullen's arrival had just as much to do with it.

She caught Cam looking at her a couple of times, but each time those silver eyes darted away.

Nysska tried to keep food in her mouth as much as possible, in hopes of not being asked to speak, but halfway through the meal a thought that appeared to have been simmering in Captain Porter's brain finally came to a boil.

"Enforcer," he said.

Wallace Embry immediately answered, "Yes, sir?"

Porter had one of Mount Stark's apparently well-known hard yeasty rolls in his hand. He used it to wave at Embry first, then to point at Nysska. "Not you, son. Her."

Nysska took a drink from the badly-blown, bubble-filled glass flagon that had been set in front of her at the meal's beginning, reflecting for half a heartbeat on how much she disliked mead, and said, "Yes, Captain?"

Porter stared at his plate. "I been thinkin' about somethin' you said, back in the cellar." He took a bite of chicken and spent an interminable amount of time chewing and swallowing. She caught Percy looking at her, an expression in his eyes like, *Do you know what this is about?*

Nysska shrugged and waited for the Watch Captain.

Finally Porter said, "You mentioned back there that every one o' your people was the same size."

"That's right."

"Men and women both. And they're all just as strong as each other."

"Correct."

"So, if a man was to come up and try to arm-wrestle you, you'd stand just as good a chance o' beatin' him as he would o' beatin' you."

Nysska took a moment. "Yes, that's accurate. In fact, we tend not to engage in contests of strength the way humans do. Unless one competitor knows a better technique, or is injured, they tend to end in draws."

"It's just hard to imagine. You're *all* more or less just alike."

She cleared her throat. "To an extent, yes. We all start from the same place, you could say. But as I also mentioned, individual sethyds can and do learn vastly different skills. We specialize just as much as humans do."

Porter blinked at her. "Meanin' what, exactly?"

Nysska thought what she'd said was perfectly clear, and in other circumstances might have said so and continued with her mediocre dinner, but with General Cullen there, along with the Mayor and—most important—Cam, she decided to be as polite as possible. "Meaning some of us are miners. Some are healers. Some are artists or musicians. We choose a path, just as humans do, and we try our hardest to be the best at whatever it is we set out to be."

Raoul, Percy, Wallace Embry, and General Cullen all seemed genuinely interested in the conversation, but none of them said anything.

"All right," Porter said slowly, sounding as if he were painstakingly putting thoughts together before he spoke. "But...I suppose...I'm sorry, Enforcer, I'm tryin' not to sound stupid."

Nysska took a bite of bread and spoke around it. "In your own time, Captain."

"Men—human men—we're bigger'n our women. Bigger an' stronger. That's the way it's always been. That's how men an' women learn to get along."

Nysska decided to take a chance. She leaned forward and fixed her eyes on Captain Porter and said, "Do you mean to say that all human women are aware of their inferiority to human men?"

Porter threw his hands up. "Now, I ain't tryin' to say that!"

Barely above a whisper, Cam said, "Nysska…"

Nysska ignored her but did a respectable job keeping her voice even-tempered. "Human men are physically superior to human women. That is true throughout human society. Yes? You said it yourself. Men are bigger. Stronger. And women are small and weak."

Porter couldn't seem to think of anything to say to that. He took a swig of mead with a very slightly trembling hand.

Nysska continued. "In answer to what I believe might be your question, sethyds are raised with no such notions. No sethyd man can intimidate a sethyd woman purely through size or strength." Her voice ratcheted up a notch in spite of herself. "None of my sisters—and by *sisters*, I mean all sethyd women—have ever knuckled under to a sethyd man because we were afraid of what he might do to us. That is a concept I discovered, to my horror, only once I arrived in Imperial lands. None of my sisters have ever feared for their lives when they rejected a man's advances. None of my sisters have ever stayed with a mate for fear of suffering at his hands." A memory flooded into Nysska's mind. A memory of her time in the Forty-Seventh Crucible, when the huge, bear-like Commander, Brux Haller, had forced himself on the tiny, meek Sensor, Morrin James. "None of my sisters have ever refused to report a slight against us committed by a man for fear of physical reprisal."

Cam's head had raised as Nysska spoke. Eyes glittering in the lantern light, she quietly said, "Are you saying—are you saying rape does not exist among the sethyds?"

Nysska blinked. She sat back in her chair and drummed her fingertips on the table's edge. "No. I am not saying that."

General Cullen spoke up for the first time in the conversation. "Then…are we to understand…that the only way for a sethyd woman to be violated is—"

Nysska finished the thought for him. "To be gang-raped? That is not the only way. Just the most common."

Percy's eyes had grown huge. "Fucking hell. That *happens?*"

Nysska's lips twisted into something a little like a snarl. "I should not have used the word 'common.' It happens exceedingly rarely. I...can think of perhaps a dozen recorded cases." She glanced around the table. "Such things are not kept quiet. There is no sweeping under the rug, so to speak."

Cam sounded breathless. "And the rapists—if they're caught—"

"They are *always* caught."

Cam asked, "Then what's the punishment?"

With zero hesitation, Nysska said, "Death."

The meal continued in silence.

It had been months since she'd thought of Brux Haller. Of what he'd done to Morrin every chance he'd had.

Of what Nysska had done to *him*.

She let her eyes close as she slowly chewed. The last night of her assignment to the Forty-Seventh, Brux came to her room at the inn, drunkenly declaring his intention to fuck her, just as he'd fucked Morrin so many times. And Nysska warned him. She said that it wouldn't go the way he wanted it to. That she was not like his human cows.

She kept her eyes closed as she tried to justify to herself the actions she'd taken. The way she'd physically dominated him, the way she'd taken control of his sexuality, taken his power away, taken what he'd used as a weapon over and over and made him a victim of it.

That was before she'd met Cam and Percy and Raoul. Before she'd learned that humans could be noble and pure and full of light. Before she'd fallen in love with Cam. When Nysska had done what she'd done to Brux Haller, she'd still despised humans and everything they stood for.

Did that make it right?

If she'd done such a thing to another sethyd, she'd be facing the death penalty.

Her appetite suddenly gone and her throat dry, Nysska struggled to swallow the bite of food. She tuned out the rest of the scattered conversation, such as it was, and kept her eyes on her plate until meal's end.

Nysska wondered what the citizens of Mount Stark must have thought, seeing the odd procession pushing through the rapidly accumulating snow—a recognizable Thaumetallicon Crucible, known by their armor if nothing else, a General of the Cathedral, two members of the city govern-

29

ment, and a red-haired demon. Whatever they thought, none of them cared to voice it, as face after white-skinned face appeared and disappeared at heavily curtained windows.

She'd spent a good bit of time with that word. *Demon.* It was certainly the source of plenty of heartache. She remembered vividly the tiny wisp of a twelve-year-old boy who had rebuked her in the name of the Great Silver Dragon, telling her to return to the pits of hell along with the rest of her unholy kind. Yet just as vividly lived the memory of addressing the Arch-Pastor of the Dragon Church—of telling him to call her "demon" with a wave of pride behind the word. Watching his face, the mask of smug self-righteousness shattering into sheer terror, as he plunged hundreds of meters into the ribbon of lava far below.

Along with her brother.

Gerrit.

She'd never heard Gerrit voice an opinion, one way or another, concerning the use of "demon" when referring to the sethyds. Not that it mattered. Gerrit had abducted their mother, held her captive, used her to force Nysska to spy on the Ninth Crucible for him, and ultimately taken her life.

Now and then Nysska missed the brother she'd once had. A fleeting feeling, consumed in the bitter flames of her hatred like a brittle leaf in a bonfire.

A memory came to her. She and Gerrit were...seven? Eight? Playing hide-and-seek with two of their friends, Tylar and Randolf. Nysska had found the perfect hiding spot, a disused cistern at the edge of the farm next to her mother's property, and clung to the stone wall inside just below the rim.

Until one of the stones gave way and she fell down into the black, slimy water below.

Tylar and Randolf found her there. Tylar was a healer's son, and when he and Randolf linked hands and reached down and plucked her out, he attended to the scrapes and cuts she'd suffered from the fall. Randolf's mother owned a coal mine. He distracted Nysska by talking about the different kinds of rocks that made up the cistern's walls and made her laugh by giving each type a personality, speaking to her in comically altered voices.

"Please don't tell Gerrit or my mother that this happened," Nysska had begged them. "I'm not supposed to get into things like cisterns and mine shafts. I'll be in so much trouble."

She remembered Tylar's easy grin, and Randolf's assurances that her secret would go no further.

The two of them had been Gerrit's friends, much more than hers, but Nysska had always felt comfortable and safe around them. She wondered where they were. If they'd survived the *Krizo*. She wondered what it might be like to have sethyd friends now.

"This is it," Captain Porter said, bringing the group to a halt in front of one of the hundreds of near-identical stone houses lining the snow-covered street.

"Fuck me," Percy said after a low whistle. "So our killer's targeting rich assholes?"

"She didn't own the whole house," Mayor Ragwild said with what might have been a disapproving tone. "Lura Dovetree was a widow. Childless. Worked in the stables. She rented the attic, which she could barely afford."

"Great," Cam murmured, quietly enough so that only Nysska could hear. "More stairs."

Nysska frowned. "Since when have stairs bothered you?"

Cam ignored that question and followed Raoul into the house. Nysska wondered what to make of it.

It was late enough and the snow outside was coming down hard enough that the residents of what was clearly a boarding house kept to themselves while the group ascended to the attic. The house's exterior and load-bearing walls might have been stone, but the staircase they climbed was made of wood, and Nysska didn't like how loudly it creaked under her weight.

When they reached the top—a narrow landing that ended in an equally narrow door—no one had to say anything. Everyone simply pressed themselves against the walls and made way for Cam to enter the attic apartment. Percy looked as if he might want to make conversation, but Nysska was in no mood to talk, and when she kept her gaze fixed on the floor Percy simply squatted and gave Flax and Jax each a bit of chicken he'd squirreled away in his pockets.

Cam emerged a couple of minutes later, shaking her head. "Same as the other one. Not as messy, though, for which I'm grateful."

The group filed in. Nysska took a moment to let her eyes rove over the space.

The room was about half the size of Rander Borley's tower-top home, a rectangle with a ceiling that slanted sharply upward from both the left and right walls, so that the only place Nysska could stand completely upright was in the center of the room. Unlike Rander Borley's place, a large wild animal did not appear to have been set loose inside it. The only things smashed were a plain, straight-backed wooden chair and a small table that had stood beside it. The broad blood stain on the floor had been half-heartedly cleaned up.

"The maggots have already been and gone," Captain Porter said.

"How long ago was Ms. Dovetree killed?" Raoul asked.

"It's been a month." Porter gestured with his head toward a floor below. "Landlord hasn't been able to rent the place since then. He's plenty sore about it."

Quietly, Nysska asked, "And the third murder took place when?"

Porter didn't need to think about it. "A month before that. That'n was the first one where we started keepin' the kind o' notes your lot was askin' for. 'Cept we wasn't real clear that it *was* a murder. That'n might've been natural causes. Uh—except for the, uh. The boot-print. On the door."

Nysska said, "So we're working in reverse order. The most recent murder first."

Porter's eyebrows rose. "Is that not right? Am I fuckin' that up?"

Nysska caught Raoul staring at her, but she couldn't tell if it was because he found it irritating that she was doing so much talking, or if he felt genuine interest in her answer. She said, "No, no, this is fine. Looking at the freshest evidence first."

Percy bent over and spoke to Flax and Jax. "All right, you both know what to do. Same thing as that other place this afternoon. Anything unusual, point it out to us. Got it?"

Jax stepped forward and pushed his face into Percy's hand for a second, then joined Flax. The two of them wandered off to opposite sides of the room.

General Cullen, Mayor Ragwild, and Captain Porter stayed out of the way as the Ninth Crucible searched Lura Dovetree's room. *The Ninth Crucible and me*, Nysska said to herself. She was no longer a part of the unit. That role had been assigned to the young man Wallace Embry.

Nysska watched Embry from the corner of her eye as she picked through the scant personal items Lura Dovetree had kept in a small chest near the door. His size was a boon when it came to physical intimidation, no doubt, and she had no reason to think he couldn't swing the heads-man's axe with the necessary force and accuracy. At the same time, he seemed...lost. Like a little boy who'd wandered into a game older children were playing, pantomiming the actions as best he could while hoping no one would notice that he didn't know the rules.

Embry caught her looking at him at one point. He turned to her and opened his mouth as if to speak, but apparently decided against it mid-thought and turned away again. Nysska couldn't tell whether his shyness, if that's what it was, stemmed from her being the Crucible's former Enforcer, or from the violet shade of her skin and the horns growing from her forehead. She didn't think he presented the hallmarks of a Dragon Church zealot. She also didn't think she could be too careful about that.

Cam finished with the shabby, paint-chipped wardrobe and came over to her. "Find anything?"

Nysska closed the chest and stood, towering over her. The words Cam had said still rang loud in her ears—*If I can't touch you, it might be easier not to be around you at all*—and a petty part of Nysska wanted to say something like, "If it's so hard to be around me, why bother speaking to me?" Instead she said, "No. Nothing. Nothing out of the ordinary, anyway."

Cam looked over toward Raoul. Nysska followed her line of sight to the Crucible's Commander, standing with his hands on his hips, gazing down at the two blood lynxes, both of whom were sitting in the middle of the floor and vigorously grooming. Raoul shot a pointed look toward Percy, who shrugged and said, "Pretty sure that means they didn't find shit either."

Captain Porter spoke from the doorway. "So there ain't nothin' to point us nowhere, then."

Nysska's grasp of Plainish was excellent, but it still took her a moment to wade through that barrage of double-negatives. Into the silence, Raoul said, "Nothing we can use, no."

Mayor Ragwild sounded discouraged. "So we go to the third crime site?"

Nysska said, "If I may?" Both Raoul and his father nodded assent to her. "Just because there is no evidence to be found among her personal belongings—belongings which, correct me if I'm wrong, could have been picked through in the month since her death?"

Captain Porter frowned, but said, "You ain't wrong."

"It doesn't mean we can't try to piece something together. We're looking at someone—a sethyd, almost certainly—killing a human once a month. The first one could've been mistaken for an accident, correct? But

33

it led to this one, which was plainly violent. Followed by the awfulness at Rander Borley's home."

Raoul said, "I think I see where you're going with this."

Nysska continued. "Right. It seems to me that the killer is getting more savage with each murder. More out of control."

Mayor Ragwild's expression soured. "So. As you've said. We have plenty of reasons to find him—or her—as quickly as possible."

Nysska nodded. "Correct. But we don't yet know what that book means that we found at Borley's. And for all we can tell here, Lura Dovetree was nothing more than a stable worker. But there *has* to be some reason the killer's picking these victims. There has to be some pattern to their murders. So if we can't tell anything from going through her things, I suggest we talk to people who knew her."

Wallace Embry said, "You mean like at the stables? Where she worked?"

"Yes. But in the interest of efficiency, I say we start with the other residents of this boarding house." She turned to Captain Porter. "Would it be possible for you to set members of the Watch at the exits, to make sure no one leaves until we speak to them?"

Porter shrugged. "Yeah. But that don't mean somebody couldn't've left while we been up here."

Nysska's yellow eyes tracked over to the room's single window. "I'm hoping the blizzard will have cut down on that." Facing Porter again, she added, "But it might be necessary, if someone isn't home, for your men to track them down."

Porter huffed and looked to the Mayor for approval—hoping Ragwild would shut the idea down. When the Mayor only nodded, though, Porter squared his shoulders and turned to leave. "As you say," he threw over his shoulder before she heard him clomping down the wooden stairs.

Percy had come over to Nysska. He gazed up at her while tugging on one half of his forked beard. "What if we can't put anything together?"

She leaned back against the closest wall. "Sorry?"

"You said there had to be some reason this killer sethyd's targeting the people he's targeting. But what if there isn't? What if this fucker's just choosing people at random?"

Nysska bowed her head and folded her arms across her chest. "I don't know. We might be fucked."

Captain Porter had already left to organize the men of the Mount Stark City Watch and, now that it had become clear that the Ninth Crucible was not about to pounce on the mysterious killer and string him up in the public square in the next twenty minutes, Mayor Ragwild lost a measure of interest in the pursuit. That disappointed Nysska. She and the rest of the Ninth had had particularly awful encounters with Imperial Mayors in the past, and she'd hoped Ragwild might prove to be of a different, perhaps less inferior breed. *So much for hoping.*

General Cullen addressed the group briefly before he, too, left with Mayor Ragwild. "I've been a soldier my entire adult life, but not once have I ever been an investigator, and I don't want to get in your way. So if you'll excuse me—and my advanced age—I believe it's time I actually slept."

Raoul ducked his head, his face solemn. "Anything you need, sir," he said, and Nysska couldn't decide what kind of sentiment lay in the words. General Cullen looked as if he might shake his son's hand, or perhaps clap him on the shoulder, but instead he nodded once, curtly, and left.

"How do you want to do this?" Raoul asked Nysska, and Wallace Embry's eyebrows shot up. She had to wonder if he'd ever before witnessed his Commander openly deferring to someone who did not outrank him.

Nysska let out a long sigh before answering. "All we're trying to do is find out what these people knew about Lura Dovetree. None of them is a suspect. At least not yet. What I'm getting at is that it's not a hostile presentation we're making, so maybe I should just stay in the hall and listen. Rather than having them cowering and shitting themselves." She cocked an eyebrow at Wallace Embry as she continued speaking to Raoul. "If you think you need intimidation, your new Enforcer has more than enough size and presence for that, does he not?"

If Embry had possessed any hair, his eyebrows might have disappeared into it. Recovering in an admirably short amount of time, he cleared his throat and said, "Yes, yes of course, I'll help out any way I can."

Nysska decided she liked the large, round young fellow. Inexperienced or not.

Once they established that City Watchmen had been posted at all the exits—including a window on the second floor that opened onto the roof of a neighboring building—the Ninth Crucible went door to door, reassuring the tenants that no, nothing was wrong, and no, they weren't in any kind of trouble, and could they please answer a few questions about their former neighbor, Lura Dovetree.

Nysska hovered outside each doorway, along with Flax and Jax, who evinced zero interest in taking part in official interviews. They all became variations on a theme: *Lura was perfectly nice, never said much, mostly kept her own counsel, never made any trouble for anyone, lovely neighbor overall.* The description of a woman who never ruffled any feathers and never let anyone know anything truly personal.

The interviews went like that for an hour and a half. Knock on a door, wait for someone to answer, convince them that it was Imperial business and they had no choice but to talk, then listen to innocuous bearshit that did nothing to further the investigation.

Things changed when they came to the back corner room on the ground floor.

"Who's there?" came a creaky male voice.

"This is Raoul Cullen, Commander of the Thaumetallicon's Ninth Crucible. We'd like to ask you a few questions, sir, if you'd open the door." When nothing happened for a few seconds, Raoul added, "We've got men watching all the doors and windows, so you'll save yourself some heartache if you just open up and let us ask you what we need to ask you."

Nysska caught the sound of feet shuffling from the other side of the thin wooden door.

Raoul glanced around and up at Wallace Embry. Embry nodded, moved to the door, and pitched his voice at least an octave lower than normal. "Open this door, sir, or I'll be forced to knock it off its hinges."

The door unlatched and swung open, and Cam gasped. Nysska had been hanging back, but took a quick step, enough to let her peer around Embry's bulk, and had to stifle a gasp of her own.

The man standing there had a crater for a face.

No—Nysska revised that thought, her horror deepening as she took in more details. He still had a face. But his nose had disappeared entirely, leaving nothing but a gaping black hole, as had his upper lip, so that his top teeth lay fully exposed in decaying gums. Nysska couldn't tell how old he was. Aside from his nightmarish facial damage, he had the kind of waxy-looking hair that hadn't quite finished turning from blonde to white, skin so pale it verged on translucent, and deeply sunken eyes that looked like two pools of inky shadow.

Worst of all, traces of Scent Runes clung to the edges of the ghastly flesh crater.

His speech mangled by the lack of upper lip, the former Sensor said, "What's this about?"

Cam made a tiny sound. A grunt of pain or a sob, Nysska couldn't tell.

Raoul looked around at the rest of the group, eyes wide as a deer's. He cleared his throat and made a show of consulting the sheet of parchment one of the City Watchmen had handed him. "Mr. ...Olivette, is it?"

"That's right. So?"

"So. Sir. Um. We'd like to know if you ever had any interaction with the woman who lived in the attic until last month. Lura Dovetree."

Olivette's brow creased for a second. "I don't know anything," he said, and moved to close the door.

Wallace Embry caught the edge of the door with one hand. "Sir, I'm sorry, but I think you do." Embry still used that rumbling voice, and the way Olivette reflexively shrank from him made Nysska want to cry.

Raoul moved closer. "Mr. Olivette. We are investigating a string of homicides. Anything you know could be very useful. Please don't make us insist."

"You do whatever the hell you want," Olivette snapped. "You're going to anyway. Search the place, beat me, fuck, go ahead and kill me, it's not like you'd be changing my plans."

Cam moved past Raoul and Wallace Embry to face Olivette, the silver in her eyes dimming to the barest glimmer. "Please. Mr. Olivette. You're a part of this. A part of us. Please cooperate."

Olivette's eyes narrowed. "I'm a part of you, am I? Is that why the Thaumetallicon dumped me here? Is that why my only use to them now is to die like a good soldier, so they can come and yank what's left of the metal out of my face?" He leaned toward her, his voice dropping to a rasping whisper. "You take a good look, little girl. A good, long look."

Embry's voice returned to its normal speaking timbre, and Nysska realized the big man was fighting back tears as he said, "Sir. Surely you're not here *alone*? Surely the Cathedral hasn't just—abandoned you?"

Olivette scoffed. "As if any of you care." He glared at the group for a long moment. "My wife was on her way back from Lakefield when the snow started. I'm sure she'll get here as soon as she's able. Not that she can stand to look at me anymore." Olivette cast his eyes up, through the hallway's roof. "Lura. Never meant any harm to anyone. Just doing what she had to do to survive." He folded his arms across his chest. "Like any of us. Like *all* of us. Lura Dovetree worked in a gambling hall called the Echo Box. She entertained gentleman callers. For a reasonable price."

While Raoul continued talking to Mr. Olivetter, Cam turned and brushed past Nysska and moved slowly down the hall, away from the former Sensor's room.

Nysska caught up with her just inside the house's front door. "Are you all right?"

Cam hesitated before shaking her head. She said nothing as she walked out of the house, past the City Watch, and into the frozen street.

Nysska let her go.

5

Booted feet crunched through ever-thickening snow as Nysska followed the Ninth Crucible through Mount Stark's narrow lanes. A vicious blast of wind struck her from behind, and she braced for the impact of a heavy braid that never came. She had no helmet, unlike the official members of the Ninth, and every so often had to shake the snow out of her great shaggy mop of dyed-red hair.

Three streets over from the boarding house where Lura Dovetree had met her fate stood a large stone structure much like every other large stone structure in the walled city. Light gray stone blocks from foundation to roofline. A slate roof, what little of it could be seen in a few snow-free patches. Lantern light spilling out from windows on the ground floor, no light at all from the three levels above that one. Olivette had referred to the place as, "the Echo Box." No sign announcing its name hung outside.

Every member of the group had to raise their knees high to make any headway through the snow. Nysska found it amusing, watching the group march along as if in some kind of parade.

The street had become a kind of snow-lined tunnel. The constricted lanes of Mount Stark already gave her a tiny thrill of claustrophobia, and now, with every door and window shut tight against the snow—and the winter blanket absorbing any bit of stray sound—Nysska had a sensation of being surrounded by an icy grip that grew ever tighter.

When they reached the corner opposite the Echo Box, Cam turned to the group. "So how are we handling this?"

Percy scoffed. "Well, obviously, I'm going in by myself."

Raoul's brow wrinkled beneath his Commander's band. "How do you figure that?"

Percy rolled his head around on his shoulders. "Come on, boss. An entire fucking Crucible shows up? That's what you call a *raid*. But if one Keeper shows up, half-lit, and wants to squander his hard-earned Cathedral pay on a few rounds of slapper, well, that's just a soldier unwinding." He glanced around the group, eyes twinkling, and unbuckled his bronze-inlaid jacket. "Besides, I'm the only one of us who looks disreputable enough to pull it off."

Cam had been scanning the buildings on this side of the street. "There's a shop there that looks abandoned. We could wait inside till Percy scouts the place." She sounded purely business-like. As if she hadn't all but run away from Olivette's room. Nysska had been trying to find a way to approach Cam about that but hadn't come up with anything, so she stayed silent.

Percy grinned. "Right! Scout the place. I'm a fucking *scout*."

Raoul heaved one of his raspy sighs. "Do you even have any money to gamble?"

Percy had been rumpling his normally carefully-maintained beard. "*Pshaw*, boss, when have you ever known me to be anything but frugal?" He knelt in front of Flax and Jax. "Listen, I'm about to go poke around that building over there. I won't be gone long, but while I'm inside, I need you two to protect all these lunkheads for me. Got it?"

Both blood lynxes stared at him with wide eyes. Nysska couldn't tell whether the message had gotten through or not, based on their lack of reaction, but Percy seemed satisfied. He stood and brushed some snow from his thighs. "I'll go see what there is to see. No worries."

"Be careful," Wallace Embry said, and Percy grinned even more widely and punched the young man in the arm. Nysska watched as he crossed the street and disappeared into the shadows surrounding the building's entrance.

She followed Cam, Raoul, Embry, and the blood lynxes as they stepped through a doorless doorway and into a space that did indeed look as if it had once been a small shop. Now the stone floor held nothing but debris. The scents of human urine and feces reached Nysska's nose, muffled somewhat by the cold.

Nysska cut her eyes toward Cam, but whatever fleeting bit of sentiment had allowed Cam to make small talk had left her. She stood at one glass-free window, staring out and across the street, hugging herself and clearly wishing for no company.

Raoul moved closer to Nysska, pitching his voice low. He sounded unhappy, but Raoul Cullen had never been what Nysska would consider cheerful, so that made it nigh impossible to guess the most prominent source of his dissatisfaction.

There was a time, not that long in the past, in which Raoul had been madly, hopelessly, and silently in love with Cam. Nysska knew for a fact that Cam had zero sexual or romantic interest in men. She wondered if Raoul understood that as well, and if he had attempted anything with her in Nysska's absence. Nysska herself, along with every other sethyd, made no distinction between male and female lovers, and it had always been a bit difficult for her to fathom how so many humans solidly, solitarily—and, in her eyes, arbitrarily—preferred one gender over another. She supposed it could have been possible for Cam to consider trying out a partnership with Raoul. He was a decent, lawful, kind man, after all. Still, watching the two of them interact over the preceding day, she'd detected no hint of any entanglement that hadn't been there before her departure.

"So Lura Dovetree plied her trade in a gambling den," Raoul said without preamble.

Nysska inclined her head. The plume of her breath mingled with Raoul's as she spoke. "According to Olivette, yes." An image of Olivette's ravaged face flashed before her. She trembled and shook her head in an effort to dispel it.

"But the third victim—Borley—we have no reason to believe he ever went there."

She shrugged. "Perhaps. Perhaps not. I cannot help but wonder if that book we found in his mattress might be his accounting of wins and losses at such a place."

"The book *you* found, you mean."

"If we're getting specific, Flax found it."

"Maybe Borley did frequent this place. Maybe he even knew Lura Dovetree. Are we thinking that the two of them got wrapped up in something illicit, and that's what got them killed?" He paused for a long moment. "Maybe—I don't know, maybe Borley paid Dovetree to seduce someone wealthy, and then blackmailed them?"

Nysska thought that over. "It's possible. But it doesn't explain why the killer waited a month between murders. If he knew who was involved, why not get rid of them both at the same time and be done with the matter?"

Raoul nodded slowly. "That is a good question."

"We also haven't looked into the first victim yet. There may be something at that crime site that will tie all of this together. Give us an indicator of where to go next."

When he didn't say anything else, Nysska softened her tone further and asked, "How are things between you and your father?"

Raoul looked up at her sharply, and Nysska reminded herself that he had no idea she and Cam had overheard him talking with General Cullen back at Cliffside. His voice on edge, he said, "Why do you ask?"

"Well...when last we were all together, I could tell there was some tension between the two of you. I suppose I hoped it would ease in the months since I've been gone."

Raoul checked to see whether Cam or Wallace Embry were listening. Neither of them seemed to be, and Flax and Jax were busy playing in a drift of snow below one of the broken-out windows, so Raoul motioned with his head farther back in the shop. Nysska followed him a few paces.

"Aside from the time we spent trying to find you—or find your body—I haven't actually spoken to my father."

"Not in three months?"

A flash of something like pain or maybe annoyance crossed his face. "Look, the aftermath of what you did—what we *all* did, at Solace Canyon...it was nothing but chaos for a while, and we decided—well, Father decided—that it would be best if the Ninth got as far away from Cliffside as possible. Dug into work. Made it clear where our loyalties lay."

Nysska rubbed the bridge of her nose. "I'm sorry, I haven't even stopped to ask, stopped to *think*—what have I missed? I see the Thaumetallicon was quick to replace me, but what else has happened? They're taking notes now?"

"They are. They *have* to, if they want to have any chance at all of catching anyone with access to chervoxite." Raoul folded his arms and tapped fingertips on one biceps muscle. "That's probably the biggest thing, at least as far as it's affected us. Everything's gotten a lot more complicated. Gone are the days of *report a crime, send a Crucible, catch the criminal, lop off a head.* Now we all have to..." He chuckled with little mirth. "We have to follow the example you set for us."

"The red dust is *that* common now?"

"It's all over the fucking place, unfortunately. And people are calling it 'rust' now."

"Ah. Yes. I heard that back in Borley's quarters. Red dust. Rust. Saves a bit of time, I suppose."

"So the Thaumetallicon's been sending out sub-decree after sub-decree." He smiled faintly. "Word of what Morrin James was able to accomplish got out in short order, too. Half of the sub-decrees have been coming from her. She's doing well. Very well."

Nysska let her lips curl upward. "I'm glad to hear it."

"I don't know that much has changed with the sethyds. Slocum still keeps to itself. Near as I can tell, Emperor Valco's still interested in bringing them more formally into the Empire's structure. I think he's looking at the Argonium Infantry and thinking, *They're pretty good, but what if I could do that with sethyds?*"

Nysska made a soft choking sound.

"You all right?" When she nodded, swallowing hard, Raoul said, "No, wait. I was lying to you. The biggest change is the Empire's relationship with the Church of the Great Silver Dragon."

"Oh?"

"No doubt. Tongues started wagging about the Arch-Pastor's involvement in the massacre at Summergray, and now the whole Northern Clutch has been...I don't know what the term would be. Disavowed, maybe? They've definitely fallen out of Imperial favor." He leaned back against a dingy wall and slowly kicked it with the heel of one boot. "But now there's a whole other squabble brewing, where the Southern Clutch and the Eastern Clutch have sided with the Empire, but the Western Clutch is sympathetic to what the Northern Clutch was doing, and there's even rumors of some kind of civil war brewing inside the Church."

"Have there been any more, ah, incidents like Summergray?"

Raoul shook his head. "No more massacres, at least not that anyone's heard, but I don't think Valco's anxious to let any more towns fill up with transplants from the Crags, either. Can't be any more mass sethyd murders if there aren't any mass sethyds."

A lull fell between them. After a few silent moments Nysska said, "Your father is here now, though. Are you going to talk to him?"

Raoul appeared to consider his answer for a good while before he spoke. "I don't know what kind of relationship you had with *your* father..."

"Well—the kind of relationship you're talking about—sethyds don't have that."

"Oh right! Right. Cam told me about that. You're raised by your mother and your uncle. Yeah? The siblings are—what do you call it? Pair-bonded?"

"That's as good a term as any. If Gerrit hadn't gotten swept up in the Mountain Bulls' zealotry, he and I would have raised any children that I might have given birth to. But to answer your question, my relationship with my uncle was good. Solid. He was a stern man, but fair, and he had something of a soft spot for me, I believe I can say. His name was Amar."

Raoul nodded slowly, as if processing all of what she was telling him. "I know you're aware of this, but my relationship with my father was... not great. Growing up. He was strict. *Very* strict. Sort of...overwhelmingly so. And I know that he was trying to shape me. Make me into what he believed would be a good man and a good soldier. But the way he went about it all..."

Nysska gave him room to continue.

"When he came to meet us at Summergray, it was...it was as if a different man had stepped into my father's skin. Not like what a Gemini would do—not what a Gemini *did*, for that matter."

Nysska suppressed a shudder at the memory of the skin-shifting man known as Lockridge, who had impersonated General Boris Cullen to devastating effect.

"And, once I got over my shock, I thought...what if this could be a fresh start? What if I could relate to him more now as an *equal*? Or at least as man to man, more than as child to father." He looked up into her eyes, and the depths of the pain that lived there made Nysska want to turn away, as if she had just witnessed him naked and averting her gaze would be the good and decent thing to do. "It hasn't worked out quite like that," he said. "Not yet."

"Perhaps...perhaps, while you're both here...you should carve out some time to talk to him. Just the two of you."

Raoul chuckled. A dry, brittle sound. "It's a funny thing. When I think about my father—when I think about what he put me through, as a child —I become aware of this thing inside me like a well. No—more like a *pit*. A bottomless space...filled with anger. Filled with *fury*. And, over the course of my adult life, now and again I've had occasion to—well, to *access* that pit. Draw on it—draw from it. It's provided me with a jagged kind of motivation. When I've had to scream orders at men during combat...

when I've had to fight for my own life...Dragon's claws, I drew on it at Altamar, and again at Solace Canyon. It kept me alive." He shook his head, looking rueful. "I am genuinely afraid that if I talk to my father, if we bury the hatchet and smooth things over between us, that I'll lose my access to that pit. And I know it's, it's, it's not a *good* thing. That it's there, inside me. I know it's like a cancer. But what if it turns out that the cancer is what makes me who I am? What if it turns out I don't know how to function without it?"

The more Raoul had talked, the more Nysska became aware of how ludicrously unprepared she was to hear this kind of emotional unburdening from her former Commander. Thoughts whirled in her mind like uprooted trees in a tornado.

"I'm sorry," Raoul said. "I don't know why I'm burying you in all this. You didn't ask for it."

"I'm pretty sure I did."

"Still. This is inappropriate. Unprofessional."

"Unprofessional? Raoul—I know I make it difficult, but I do believe you and I are friends. Listen...one of Atiina's teachings is that anger clouds the mind. It, like everything else in the world, must be moderated, because anger taken to excess makes the mind weak, pliable, and prone to error. You are already a good man. I believe, if you decide to let go of this pit inside you, that you will only find your strength and stability *increased* by the decision."

Raoul gave her the ghost of a smile. "Atiina. That's one of the...Exemplars? Am I getting that right?"

Nysska nodded. "Atiina is the Exemplar of Wisdom. There are a number of others. We have Exemplars of Knowledge, of Forgiveness, of Patience. They are role models, more or less."

"But not deities."

"No. We have no deities."

Raoul tilted his head back and gazed without focus at the ceiling. "Given everything that's happened with the Church of the Dragon in the last year...I don't know. I don't have any problem with people believing whatever they believe, but—"

"Percy's coming back," Cam called from across the shop floor. With a mutual glance that said, *This feels like a good place to bring this conversation to an end*, Nysska and Raoul joined her, with Wallace Embry watching from another glassless window frame.

The wind and the snow both had picked up speed since Percy had entered the building, and he hunched against it, shoulders and elbows drawn in tight until he stumbled into the shop, legs caked with snow up past his knees. Beer fumes wafted off of him.

"Got to admire the dedication of the hopeless gambler," Percy said with a smirk. "Whole city's shutting down to see how deep this fucking snow gets, and they're still in there playing round after round of slapper. Bartender said it wasn't quite as crowded as normal, but not by much."

"What did you learn?" Raoul asked, sounding a bit overly formal to Nysska's ears. Returning to his official, Thaumetallicon-sanctioned role as Commander.

"Whooo, you should see the inside of that place." Percy rubbed his gloved hands together, the kind of action meant to stave off the cold. "*Mirrors*. Mirrors fucking everywhere. Mirrors behind the bar, mirrors on the doors, mirrors all over the walls. Mirrors in the fucking ceiling. I mean, I know it's meant to make the place feel bigger, but if I wanted to see my ugly mug reflected from every fucking surface, I'd—well, I'd—huh. I wouldn't go in there, that's for damn sure."

"Did anyone know anything about the murder victims?" Nysska asked quietly.

Percy threw her a lopsided grin. "Well, now, that wasn't exactly my remit, was it? I was just supposed to scout the place out. Even a grunged-up degenerate loner wearing bronze is going to come off like a raid, he goes in and just starts asking questions about dead folks."

Raoul frowned. "So you didn't get any additional intelligence."

"Whoa-ho-ho, that's not what I said, is it?" His grin went from lopsided to decorating his whole face. "All I had to do was mention to the bartender that I was in Mount Stark on business, then make a show of telling him I wasn't supposed to talk about it, and before you know it *he's* asking *me* if I'm here to look into Lura Dovetree's murder."

Cam spoke up. "He knew her? By name?"

"That he did. Said she was an honest whore, plied her trade the way she was supposed to, kicked the proper percentage back to the house for every trick she turned."

Raoul had taken a small pack of quarter-page-sized parchment out of an inside pocket of his jacket, and made notes with a stubby pencil. "Did Rander Borley come up?"

"Not in connection with Ms. Dovetree, no. If they were in cahoots, the bartender didn't seem to know fuck-all about it. But yeah, he was there. Two or three times a week, at least."

"That knocks down our blackmail theory," Nysska murmured to no one in particular. "If Borley and Dovetree didn't know each other." She drifted over to one of the windows and stared out into the snow.

"We can come back to this place," Raoul said, tucking his notes away again. "We've still got a murder site to look over."

Gazing out at the city, a flash of movement caught Nysska's eye. Something dark—something at the crest of a roof across the street. It was there and gone too fast for her even to focus on it, just a flicker at the edge of weak lantern light, an impression, and when the wind parted the white curtain enough for her to see the rooftop again it stood empty.

For just a tiny fraction of a second, though, she *might* have spotted the silhouette of a tall, lean figure sporting a pair of horns.

6

A fter hunting down Captain Porter and getting him to station City Watchmen around the Echo Box—on the lookout for anything unusual in general, and for a sethyd in particular— Nysska went with the Ninth Crucible to the site of the first murder. The sun had begun to come up by then, though it was hard to tell at first. The blizzard had not let up.

As they fought their way through the snow-clogged streets, Raoul said, "Tell me again. Tell me exactly what you saw."

"I'm not convinced I saw anything." Part of Nysska wished she hadn't mentioned it at all, but her more rational side shouted that impulse down. "Little more than a flash in my side-vision. Could have been a sethyd, on top of one of the roofs—or it could have been nothing. A product of my imagination and caution. Something I *wanted* to see."

Cam didn't look at anyone as she spoke. "It seems to me that the chance of there being *three* sethyds in Mount Stark is...what's the word. Negligible? At least implausible. So if you did see one, it's more than likely the one who's been killing people."

Percy shifted Jax's weight on his shoulders, and glanced over at Flax, who padded along on the surface of the snow as if it were cobblestones. "Which means he or she's watching us. Knows what we're doing. Right?"

With a note of vexation creeping in, Cam said, "Why would one of your people be doing this, anyway, Nysska? You've told us sethyds are rational. Yes? We know they can get wrapped up in political extremism—like your brother—but this doesn't even make sense. Why would a sethyd come to a human city and kill what seem like random people? And why do it once a month?"

Nysska's mind raced, going over the oath she'd taken, searching for weak spots or knotholes through which she might pull the truth. Or at least some part of the truth, squirming and squealing. "It is...possible... that the killer is only *here* once a month."

Raoul blinked. "What, you mean he's passing through? Mount Stark is just a waystation on, on, on some kind of route?" Nysska nodded silently, and Raoul stopped in his tracks. "I'm getting pretty fucking tired of you withholding information, Nysska. You know a shit-ton more than you're saying, and it seems to me that not giving us crucial information is going to get more people killed. Maybe get my *team* killed."

Nysska stopped as well and turned to face the group. A gust of wind whipped a spray of snow between her and them, and in that moment she felt more cut off than in the entirety of the three months she'd spent away from them. Her unruly red mane whipping in the frigid air, she said, "I am telling you all I'm able to. I'm—I'm not accustomed to—"

Bitter fire lit Cam's words. "Oh, don't you stand there for one second and say you're not accustomed to keeping secrets."

Tears sprang up, scalding and infuriating, and Nysska fought them back. "When all of this is finished, I will tell you everything. I will give you a day by day account of what I've done in the missing months. Hour by hour if you like. I will tell you everything that happened to me, everything that was done to help me, and every coal over which I was dragged in the process. But right now it seems to me that we have until this blizzard lets up to find a killer before they flee the city and lose themselves in the mountains." She paused, silently cursing the tears that continued to threaten her. "If this has shattered our trust beyond repair, then so be it. I will consider that one of the greatest losses of my life. But I don't have the luxury of considering it at the moment. Now can we please visit this third crime site? Before, as you say, Raoul, anyone else gets killed?"

Only the delicate spray of wind-borne snow reached her ears for several long heartbeats. Then Raoul shrugged his shoulders and said, "It's up here on the next block, according to Porter," and moved around her. Neither Cam nor Embry looked at her as they followed Raoul. Percy met her eyes for half a second, but couldn't seem to think of anything to say, and passed her by.

Nysska came very close to breaking down in that moment, very close to surrendering to the tears entirely, when Jax appeared out of the snow and sat there at her feet, staring up at her. Even through the wind she could hear the deep, rich purrs emanating from him, and in the next second Flax appeared and joined him. Nysska said, "You two understand, don't you?"

Jax yawned. Flax gave Nysska a slow wink and motioned with her head: *Come on. We need to go.*

Nysska followed the blood lynxes as they trudged along in the Ninth Crucible's footsteps.

The first murder victim, from two months prior, lived in a basement room underneath a baker's shop. "All right," Raoul said, looking down the narrow hallway to the victim's door, "This was the owner's mother-in-law. The fellow who first started the bakery died two years ago and left the place to his wife, and the wife and the dead man's mother didn't get along too well."

Cam made a sour face. "So the mother-in-law got banished to the basement?"

"Could've been worse," Percy said. "She could've gotten booted out of the city entirely." He looked around at everyone. "None of you have had to put up with a mother-in-law, I take it?"

"Come on." Raoul led the way toward the door. "According to Nysska, we don't have much time to find this asshole, so let's make every second count."

Nysska sighed but didn't bother trying to make the situation any better. Bleakly she considered what her life ahead might look like without any involvement in the Thaumetallicon. Without the family she'd found in the Ninth.

Without Cam.

Not that I can blame any of them, she told herself silently. She'd kept one too many secrets, one too many times. Would she trust anyone if they'd consistently lied to her? Even if it turned out that they'd had damn good reasons?

She liked to think *she* had damn good reasons.

"Boot-print's still there," Percy said from ahead of her. "Doesn't look like anybody's bothered cleaning it." He pushed the door open. "Doesn't look like anybody's been down here at all since they carted the body out."

"What was her name?" Nysska asked, just loudly enough for the group to hear her.

Raoul didn't look at her. "Mary Fung."

Nysska had to duck her head to get through the doorway, and when she made it into the room she halfway wished she'd just stayed outside. The place was oppressively small. More like a decent-size storage closet than a place where a human could live. The Ninth Crucible stood in the center of the room, bunched up, looking around them, until Wallace Embry said, "This is silly. None of us can breathe packed in like this. I'm going to wait outside."

Nysska stepped away from the door and let the bulky young man pass. He met her eyes briefly and gave her a polite nod. Nysska had no history with Embry. His civil demeanor had a lot more to do with him going along with the sentiments of his unit than with his personal feelings.

Embry was correct, though. Once he'd left, the other members could spread out a tiny bit. Percy gave the blood lynxes the same instructions as at the last two places, and they prowled around the room's perimeter, sniffing and pawing at things.

Nysska didn't think they'd find anything because there was so little *to* find. The room contained a narrow bed neatly made with multiple threadbare blankets, a pole sticking horizontally out of one wall in a corner with a few items of clothing draped over it, a cast-off wooden crate that held up a dented metal wash basin, and the ever-present shit bucket. No privacy screen for this one, though. Mary Fung probably couldn't have afforded one and would have had no reason for modesty in her room, alone. There were no windows.

"How did Captain Porter describe Ms. Fung's death?" Nysska asked, again to no one in particular.

Raoul pulled out his sheaf of notes. "They put it down as old age. Took note of the boot-print, like we said, but they thought it was just somebody who'd come to talk to her, couldn't get her to the door, and kicked it open to see what was going on."

"But no one reported her dead?"

He flipped from one little piece of parchment to another. "Not until the daughter-in-law found her. After the door-kicking."

Nysska nodded thoughtfully. "Well then. Cam?"

Cam tilted her head from side to side, vertebrae popping. "Right." She caught Nysska's eye for a second but looked away. "I'm not hopeful."

"Anyone found anything?" Raoul asked. "Percy? Anything from the kitties?"

Percy held up a slapper chip. "Just this. Confirms that Old Lady Fung went to the Echo Box—at least once—but I don't know that that does us much practical."

Raoul tilted his head to one side. "Boot-print and Echo Box. You're right, it doesn't tell us anything new, but this is no red herring, either. Let's give Cam the room."

Nysska ducked back out of the place Mary Fung had called home and pressed herself against the wall as Raoul, Percy, and the blood lynxes filed past her. She made no attempt at conversation for the few minutes it took Cam to reach her conclusion. Neither did anyone else.

Cam emerged from the room and said, "Same as the others. I, uh...I don't think—no, I *know* I've never dealt with anything like this before. Someone who's killed and gotten away with it, and then just...just *kept killing*. Ordinarily, I'd say 'There's nothing useable here.' But that's not true. The fact that I can't read this site—that, and the boot-print—it *is* him, isn't it? The sethyd. The killer."

Raoul blew out a long, raspy exhalation. The temperature wasn't quite low enough, there in the hallway, for the members of the Ninth to see their breath, but only just. "I don't know about anyone else, but Ragwild's dinner has run out for me, and if I can't sleep, I'm sure as fuck not going to keep bouncing around the city with my stomach growling. So we're going to go and get some food." He raised his head, and his eyes bored into Nysska's. "And decide how we're going to go at the Echo Box."

Nysska nodded and said nothing.

Twenty minutes later Nysska sat slightly apart from the rest of the group and gnawed on a tough piece of ham shoved between two pieces of tough bread. The inn they'd found, along with the dyspeptic innkeeper who hadn't gotten the day's pot of stew ready to go yet, was small and dirty, and the dining room—if it could be called that—contained only one oblong table with a few mismatched stools shoved under it. Nysska perched on her stool at one end of the table, wishing Cam would get up and come and sit down across from her, and talk to her, and maybe caress one calf with her foot.

Of course, Cam didn't do that. Of course, it wasn't reasonable that she would.

The pressing need to find the killer sethyd—the need Nysska had brought with her to Mount Stark, about which she could say nothing— had begun to transform into *hatred*. Hatred for the killer. Hatred for the oath she'd sworn, about which she could also say nothing. Hatred for the circumstances that had planted her here, where resentment and mistrust and increasing animosity surrounded her instead of the love she so deeply craved.

Everyone else had been handed the ham-and-bread as well, and Raoul talked around a dry mouthful. "All right. Let's sum up. What do we know?"

Nysska had just taken a bite and could not talk yet. As her jaw worked, Wallace Embry spoke up, tentative. "The only thing we know is that all three victims went to the same gambling den."

Raoul stared through the tabletop. "And we know that how?"

Embry looked as if he were answering questions on a formalized test and suspected a trick. "Uh...because of the boot-print in common...and the slapper chip...and how the bartender said what's-her-name worked there, and Rander Borley was a customer?"

Raoul nodded, eyes still unfocused. "And the sethyd connection...?"

Embry glanced around. When no one objected, he went on. "It's because that's the only way anybody could've gotten to Mr. Borley. I think. And, uh...because Nysska said we're looking for a sethyd. Because the boot-print was the same size as hers."

"But other than the Echo Box, the three victims don't have anything in common. A bookkeeper, a whore, and somebody's unwanted in-law? Why would the killer have chosen them?"

Nysska put her sandwich down in a hurry and turned sideways, facing the group. *"They all lived alone."*

One of Percy's eyebrows lifted. "That's it? They all gambled, and they all lived alone?"

The thought that had taken root in Nysska's mind grew. "What if that *is* it? What if that's their only connection? They frequented the Echo Box, and they all lived alone, which made them easy targets?"

Raoul lifted his head and focused his eyes, finally. "But *why*? Why single out random citizens? And if, as you say, this is merely a stop on the killer's route—a route I for one would *very* much like to learn more about —why kill someone while they're here?"

Nysska rose to her feet, her ham-and-bread forgotten. "I don't know. But the one link between the three is that gambling hall. If all three of them went there regularly, and that's the one thing they had in common, wouldn't that mean that the killer was there, too? That that's where he saw them?"

Raoul scowled at Nysska and scowled at his meager meal and pushed his stool back as he stood. "Time for a full-blown raid, then," he said, waving his ham-and-bread at her. "But I'm taking this with me."

They undertook the walk from the inn to the Echo Box in silence, but not entirely because no one felt like talking. The snowfall continued and, though citizens and City Watchmen alike had begun shoveling it out of the streets, it was still a struggle pushing their way through the accumulation.

Thanks to the early hour only a handful of gamblers stood around the slapper tables. Raoul managed to calm them all down after their initial surprise and near-panic. "We're not here to cause any trouble," he told the tiny crowd. "But if you could pause in your games for just a few minutes we'd be appreciative. Patrons, head over to that table, and we'll talk to you if we need to. Employees—to the bar. Now."

Percy indicated that it was a different bartender now from the one he'd spoken to the night before. This one was a study in mediocrity—pale skin, medium brown hair, medium height, medium build. Nysska was glad they didn't have to circulate a description of him. He could've passed for better than half the people in Mount Stark.

Raoul seemed keen to do the talking. "What's your name, sir?"

The bartender regarded them all coolly, suspiciously, but kept his wits about him. "Fredrik. Sir."

"Fredrik, have you witnessed anyone coming in recently, or hanging around, that struck you as unusual?"

"Unusual how?"

"Out of place. Curious. Worthy of fucking note."

While Raoul and Fredrik talked, Nysska turned in a slow circle, taking the place in. Percy hadn't been lying—the Echo Box's interior was indeed festooned with mirrors. A long, multi-sectioned one lined the wall behind the bar. Each wall had at least a dozen mounted on it. She glanced up and saw mirrors in the ceiling, regularly spaced in a wide grid pattern, square reflections gleaming down every three meters or so.

Her memory of the building's exterior came back to her. Light gleaming from windows on the bottom floor, but the three levels above all dark.

Her gaze didn't leave the ceiling as her jaw dropped open.

This is where he saw them.

Nysska whirled back to Raoul and Fredrik and, with no regard for who might have been talking, pointed at the ceiling. "What's up there?"

7

F redrik spluttered for a second. "N-nothing—just—"

Nysska was about to grow more forceful in her questioning when Wallace Embry stepped forward, his massive, log-like arms folded, and peered down at the man from beneath fearsomely beetled brows. "She asked you a straightforward question. Give her a straightforward answer."

Fredrik took half a step backward, swallowing hard. "It's where we watch the games," he said meekly. "Come on. I can show you."

Nysska and the Ninth Crucible followed Fredrik to a back room, where a set of narrow wooden stairs led up to an unlocked trap door. He climbed the stairs, pushed the trap open with no hesitation, and beckoned everyone to follow him.

When everyone had emerged onto the second floor Fredrik made an expansive gesture with both arms, but spoke in a dry, resigned tone. "Feast your eyes."

Nysska's vision would adjust more quickly than any of the humans'. She peered into a large, dimly lit, almost completely empty room containing one chair per mirror set into the gambling hall's ceiling. Only two people occupied the chairs at the moment, both of them looking around in obvious surprise at the arrival of a Thaumetallicon Crucible. The chairs, and the two watchers stationed at them, were lit from below by light shining up through the two-way mirrors.

"Cozy," Percy said, as Flax and Jax began sniffing around.

"We have to keep the lights off," Fredrik shot back. "Otherwise the mirrors just turn into windows. Don't want any of the patrons looking up and seeing any of our spotters. Or worse yet, recognizing them." He glanced around, a tentative smile on his lips, as if he'd just made a joke. "Talk about awkward family dinners," he finished, his words trailing off.

Raoul turned to Nysska. "What were you thinking? That the killer was lurking up here? Picking his victims by spying on them through the observation mirrors?"

Nysska frowned. At that point everyone's eyes had adjusted to the gloom, making it obvious that there was no place for a 190-centim sethyd to hide in the broad, empty space. Her eyes settled on an irregular protrusion in one of the far corners—a section of wall that punched out into the floor for a meter and a half before taking a ninety-degree turn and connecting with the adjoining wall. Essentially a large wooden box sealed tight to the floor and ceiling.

Nysska turned to Fredrik. "I saw four floors to this building from the outside. We've accounted for the first two." She raised a finger and pointed upward. "What about the other two?"

"Those are sealed off. You can't see it from the street, but part of the ceiling caved in, so Mayor Ragwild got a bunch of stonemasons to take a look. They declared the top two levels 'unfit for habitation,' but said this one and the main floor were all right." He shuffled his feet. "I might've, uh, persuaded the head stonemason to let us stay open."

Raoul's eyes narrowed at the man. "You own this building?"

Fredrik gave him a sour eye. "What, do I not look like landed gentry?"

Flax had approached the boxed-off area and now sat, staring at it. Her brother joined her and began sniffing around its perimeter. Nysska pointed. "What exactly is that?"

Fredrik shrugged his shoulders. "I don't know. Was a bunch of seamstresses on the third floor until the ceiling caved in. They minded their business and didn't complain, so as long as the rent came in on time, I left them alone."

Percy approached the wooden box, one hand on his chin, with Cam trailing after him. He said, "Based on what I know about carpentry—which, mind you, is *almost* fuck-all—I'd say this looks like the kind of thing that was supposed to be a staircase."

The silver of Cam's eyes grew brighter the closer she got to the corner in question. With a quick flare, they died back down again as she turned back to the group. "It still is a staircase," she said. "Just blocked off."

Nysska passed Cam on the way to the inaccessible stairs. She tried not to meet Cam's eyes, in the way that two strangers passing each other on the street easily mind their own business. It didn't work. Silver met candleflame-yellow for a half-second before Cam turned away, and Nysska's heart ground itself to dust.

Struggling to keep her breathing even, Nysska ran her fingers around the seams of the wooden panels until she found a tiny metal latch. With a soft click, a narrow section of one wall pivoted silently inward, revealing a set of dusty wooden stairs.

Even with the most cursory of glances Nysska spotted the familiar boot-prints in the dust of each step.

"I didn't even know that was there!" Fredrik all but shouted. Nysska turned to see Raoul standing uncomfortably close to the bartender, volumes of accusation on his face.

Nysska drew her khopesh, staring up into the darkness beyond the stairs, but paused when Wallace Embry stepped in front of her.

"I'm the Enforcer," Embry said. "You should let me go first."

Nysska read no condescension. This came from a sense of duty. And maybe, she considered, a need to prove himself.

"You've never faced a sethyd before," she said, pitching her voice low so that only he could hear it.

"Maybe not. But this is my job."

Percy, whose hearing had always rivaled that of his blood lynxes', had moved close enough to glean the direction of the conversation. "Nobody's about to think less of you, Wallace. Nysska's here specifically to find this fucker. If he's up there, let her be the one to corner him." When Wallace hesitated, Percy added, "Speaking as somebody who's seen a sethyd fight —more than once—you don't want to get in between two of them in a scrap."

"I mean you absolutely no disrespect, Enforcer," Nysska said, and finally Embry nodded and stepped back. Nysska threw a glance at Percy. "This is not to say that I don't want any back-up."

Over Percy's shoulder, Raoul drew his Imperial longsword, with Percy and Cam following suit a moment later. Nysska looked down and saw Flax and Jax perched on the bottom step on either side of her, both cats looking up at her as if waiting for a signal. "You heard me," she said, mostly to Flax. "Let me go first."

When Flax winked her left eye, Nysska took a deep breath and mounted the stairs.

There was no trap door at the top. Only a yawning blackness. Nysska's pupils dilated as they sought out every scrap of illumination they could find. When her head came up above the level of the floor she saw rows of widely-spaced window frames along the walls of another huge, empty space. With her free hand, she made a gesture below her: *wait*. Nysska held perfectly still, concentrating. *Listening*. Listening hard enough, she hoped, to hear any faint scrapes or taps or escaping breaths.

Snow had piled up in the window frames and lay in drifting heaps on the floor below them. It still fell outside the windows, the blanketing clouds tamping down the daylight, so that the vast floor lay far more in shadows than in weak gray illumination. Nysska heard only silence. Her eyes still darting around, she said, "Bring lanterns," and listened to Wallace Embry's heavy footfalls retreating.

Nysska crept up the remaining stairs until her feet touched the heavy, wood-plank floor. Half the space, now that her eyes had adjusted even further, looked as though it had taken heavy water damage, and the fourth-floor ceiling above it was clearly what had caved in. The other half, aside from the snow making its way in from outside, contained only dust and cobwebs...

Except for a place in the center of the farthest wall.

The khopesh ready in her right fist, Nysska made her way across the floor, hearing extended as far as she could manage, ready to react at a split-second's notice. Nothing moved. Nothing came at her. Yet her breathing sped up the closer she got.

Part of what lay in front of her was a crude living space—little more than a pallet made of blankets and a small pile of cast-off food remains. Apple cores. Seed hulls. An afterthought. The most basic needs and nothing more.

The other part was much more elaborate. A fine table, no doubt stolen from some citizen's house, stood against the wall between two windows, draped with a rich white-and-gold cloth. Bits of gold jewelry as well as unmounted jewels lay in a circle on the cloth, and in the center of it—

Lantern light flooded the space as the Ninth Crucible came up the stairs one by one, each set of footsteps providing brighter and brighter illumination of the thing inside the circle of gold and jewels.

"What in Dragon's name is that?" Cam breathed.

They all stared at a golden statue, a third of a meter high. It depicted a woman. Tall. Lean. Beautiful. A pair of graceful, curving horns sprouting from her forehead.

"It's an Exemplar," Nysska said, her words hollow.

Raoul stopped beside her, staring at the shrine. "Which one? What'd you say they were—Wisdom, Patience, so on?"

"This one's a recent addition," she said. "It's Yshtarra. The Exemplar of Conquest."

———

Nysska and Wallace Embry sat in a cold, dark, third-floor room across the way from the Echo Box, far enough back from the windows that no one from the street could have seen them, but close enough to peer out at the gambling hall. Other such rooms were occupied by Percy and Cam, and Raoul and Captain Porter, and Porter had stationed his men in discreet locations further surrounding the Echo Box. The plan was to wait until the killer returned to the nest and then move in, surround them, and subdue them at best or kill them at worst.

"I need to question this sethyd," Nysska had told Raoul. "It's imperative."

"I understand that's *your* imperative," Raoul had shot back. "But the Ninth was assigned to prevent any further murders in Mount Stark. If that means this asshole dies on bronze, then that's what happens."

Nysska hadn't argued with him. Now, sitting in the room with Embry, she wished Raoul had decided to put her in the same room with Cam, even though she doubted Cam would have had anything more to say to her than the hulking young Enforcer did.

Outside the snow pelted down. It fell and fell, faster than the citizens could keep up with it, and finally the city gave up. The citizenry huddled inside now, conserving warmth, wrapped in blankets and tending meager fires. Nysska shifted position, rising slightly so that she could see the Echo Box's front door. A lone woman pushed through the snow and slipped inside.

Nysska had never felt the urge to gamble. She found it hard to comprehend.

"One thing I don't understand," Embry said out of nowhere.

"Oh? What's that?"

Embry never took his eyes off one of the gambling hall's windows. "This killer. This, uh, fellow sethyd of yours."

"We are hardly all of the same stripe."

"All right. My apologies. This sethyd. He would've been seen if he'd come down to the floor where the spotters were watching the gamblers."

"Presumably, yes. Unless he was working with one of them."

Embry allowed himself the briefest of glances at her. "Oh! I hadn't even considered that. Is that—could that be happening?"

"Don't know. Captain Porter's men are questioning the hall's employees."

"All right. Well...if he *is* working alone, how would he have been picking his victims? Is he perched up somewhere like some kind of gargoyle, watching people come and go?"

"Maybe. But what I suspect happened is much simpler than that. There are gaps and knotholes in the planks of the floor where the killer was hiding. They could have peered down between those, to the observation mirrors directly below, and spied on the gamblers like that."

Embry blew out a long, faintly visible breath. "Shit. That's two floors down. He could see people well enough that way?"

Focusing on the target window, Nysska said, "Sethyd eyes are sharp."

Embry surprised her by chuckling. "If I may—that's the kind of thing I've been hearing a *lot* in the last three months."

"Pardon me?"

"'Sethyds are strong as bulls. Sethyds are faster than greyhounds. Sethyds don't scar when they heal. Sethyds have a second set of eyelids they use while they're swimming.' Is that last one even true?"

Nysska said, "Hey," and when he turned his head to look at her, she slid her watersight lids closed, the blue of the membrane turning her brilliant yellow eyes a soft green for a couple seconds. The watersight lids retracted as Wallace Embry's own eyes grew huge enough that she could see the whites all the way around the ink-black irises.

Softly, he said, "Holy fucking shit." After a few moments, and what appeared to be careful consideration of his words, he added, "It's been a lot to live up to."

Nysska thought she knew what he meant, but with a subject as potentially sensitive as this, she wanted to be crystal-clear. "What has been?"

"Your reputation. Of course. Which I'm beginning to believe was well-earned. Everyone else in the Crucible talked about you...a bit...incessantly. I've felt like the most brazen impostor ever since I joined them."

Nysska frowned. "The Ninth has a reputation as one of the finest Crucibles in the Thaumetallicon, doesn't it? If not *the* finest?"

Embry gave her a reluctant sort of shrug. "I guess so. Yeah. Ever since you embarrassed the Third last year especially. At Summergray, I mean."

Nysska thought about saying, *Yes, well, a sethyd crime needs a sethyd to solve it,* but elected not to. Instead she said, "My point is that you would not have been assigned to the Ninth if you hadn't already established something of a reputation of your own. Correct?"

Embry rubbed a hand across his scalp, which had begun showing the barest hint of stubble over the last few hours. If his head hadn't been attached to such an oversized, muscle-thick body, he would've looked boyish. "I've done a few things, I guess." He grinned, which only reinforced the youthful impression. "Not won any speed trials, though, that's for sure."

Nysska shifted her position to get more comfortable. "When I first arrived on human lands, I found the colossal variety in sizes and shapes of humans...overwhelming, if I'm being honest. As you heard me telling Captain Porter, all adult sethyds are basically the same size. Men and women. Same level of strength. Same degree of swiftness. It was difficult to comprehend that two humans could vary so greatly. That one could be objectively more physically powerful than another, simply through an accident of birth."

"I sense a 'but' about to appear."

"*But* now I've begun to be, I suppose I might say, impressed. Maybe even a bit envious. Some humans are plainly, objectively, better suited to certain tasks than others. I find that appealing, in a way."

Embry's face darkened as he stared out across the lane. "Hmm. Well. I've given what you were saying to Captain Porter a good bit of thought. And hearing you talk now, maybe it's not much more than a case of people wanting what they don't have. I've been this big since I was thirteen. My parents, my teachers, everyone knew what I should do, just because of my size. I was going to be a lumberjack, according to my grandfather. My grandmother came from what my father used to call a 'shady background,' and hinted that I should be a personal bodyguard for one of the royal families. But only when she was drunk. My parents... well, they both wanted me to end up exactly where I have."

Nysska thought about that for most of a minute. "Is this where *you* wanted to be? An Enforcer, in a prestigious Crucible?"

Embry ducked his head and let a sheepish grin lift one corner of his mouth. "I wanted to be a singer."

Nysska's eyes lit up. "Seriously?"

His face fell. "I know, I know, it's stupid."

"No! No. Wallace. I asked you because *I* am a singer. That's my profession. Well. Was my profession." While he tried to gauge whether or not she was joking, she thought, *All that time discussing me, and my career as a priest-singer never came up?* The only member of the team she'd ever told about that was Cam—which meant Cam had never told anyone else. Nysska wondered what that meant.

His attention drifting badly from the Echo Box, Embry said, "What kind of singing did you do? If I may ask?"

"Maintain watch, please." When Embry snapped back to his assignment, visibly embarrassed, Nysska said, "It would be difficult to explain without demonstrating, and this is not the place." In an effort to make him feel less mortified for letting his duty slip, she followed that with, "I would love to hear about what kind of singing *you* engage in, though."

Embry didn't turn to look at her this time. His voice took on a wistful note, of which he might have been unaware. "I grew up in a village called Stockbridge. A long way south of here. But I guess most places are a long way south of here, huh? I, uh...I sang with a—with—with a friend. His name was Rikk. We performed in a few pubs, here and there, and my parents just thought it was a lark. Something a couple of silly children did to pass the time after chores were done, maybe make a little money while they were at it. They didn't kn—"

Embry broke off. His voice dropped. Grew even softer.

"I've—if I can ask—it's just. It's just that I've heard a few things about sethyds."

"...Oh?"

"I've heard...with sethyds...they say people can fall in love with—with people like themselves." He swallowed hard, and cleared his throat. "That two—two women, for instance, or, or even...two men? They can be together." Embry rubbed his scalp furiously. "I even got the impression that maybe—maybe you and Sensor Delakroy..."

His words stopped, as if they had collapsed of exhaustion and died.

"Anything between Sensor Delakroy and me is very much none of your business."

"Of course, of course. I'm sorry. I overstepped, that was incredibly inappropriate—"

"But...what you heard is true. We can love whomever we wish." When he said nothing further, Nysska ventured, "Is that how it was between you and Rikk?"

Embry swallowed again, and nodded. Once. His eyes glistened, and he blinked quickly.

"And...is that why you're here? And not singing somewhere, with Rikk alongside you?"

"My parents. They found out. It's—it's illegal. You know? Of course you know. Everyone knows people like that end up on forks."

Nysska took a deep breath and let it out slowly. "That doesn't make it *right*, though."

She was about to say something else but the thought snapped off like an icicle when she caught movement on the roof of the Echo Box. A gust of wind whipped snow across her vision, so she couldn't be one hundred percent sure, but it appeared to be a tall, dark, lean shape dropping down into the collapsed portion.

Nysska sprang to her feet, lit a lantern, and waved it wildly in the window, alerting everyone else.

The plan they'd worked out with Captain Porter and Mayor Ragwild, with General Cullen providing advice here and there, kicked into motion. Three dozen crossbowmen charged up onto the roofs of the surrounding buildings, determined to make a pincushion of anyone who tried to flee via the rooftops or the higher windows. All of the building's doors had been chained shut save for the front entrance, and more men of the City Watch boiled out into the streets around the Echo Box, shields and pikes at the ready, prepared to pin anyone climbing out of any lower windows to the building's stone walls.

Nysska sprinted down the stairs. She heard Wallace Embry's thunderous footsteps behind her, the young man already panting. Nysska bolted out into the street, feet crunching frantically through snow, and plowed through the gambling hall's front entrance. The rest of the Crucible rushed in right behind her, Embry bringing up the rear. When Captain Porter himself signaled that no one had come down from upstairs, Nysska drew her khopesh and took the steps two at a time.

The observation floor was empty, the same as the gambling floor below. An abundance of lanterns drove away any bits of shadow, giving no one any possible place to hide. Nysska didn't slow down as she raced across to the previously-hidden staircase and up to the huge room containing the shrine to Yshtarra.

At first she thought she must have missed the killer, as this level appeared just as empty as the one below it. Then she noticed that the

Yshtarra idol was missing from its shrine, and spotted a pair of boots disappearing through a gap in the ceiling that hadn't been there before. Nysska sped to it as a section of rough wood mimicking the surrounding ceiling settled into the gap. She gathered her legs under her and leapt vertically, the khopesh held straight above her. The camouflage lid shattered and splintered. She used the khopesh's backward-curving hook to dig into what remained of the lid and let her downward momentum and body weight pull it the rest of the way out of the gap. With scraps of wood and corroded bronze raining down around her, she leapt again and clambered up through the hole. Across the half-destroyed fourth level, a tall, dark, lithe figure touched a section of wall. It hinged outward like a descending drawbridge, and the figure slipped through the opening with zero hesitation.

This is a practiced thing, Nysska told herself as she barreled after her quarry. *A planned escape route.*

Icy wind whipped snow into her face. A narrow wooden walkway dropped from the Echo Box's fourth floor, bridged the gap between it and the next building, and came to rest on the sill of a window set into the neighboring structure's fifth floor. Like many of the gambling hall's windows, this one was devoid of glass, nothing more than a yawning, ink-black hole into which the killer had fled.

It was the ideal place for a trap. The most cautious and prudent course of action would be to signal the rest of the Crucible and the City Watch, cordon off an area of several blocks, and search each building room by room until the killer was found.

Maybe if the quarry were human.

Nysska's right foot only hit the wooden walkway once as she crossed the space between buildings and flung herself through the window into the darkness on the other side.

She pulled up short in a glassware storage house. Row after row of shelves filled the space, each one packed with crates and boxes, each of which appeared to be packed in turn with canvas-wrapped bottles, jars, and drinking vessels. Nysska heard rapid footsteps on the far side of the room and bolted after them, catching sight of the lithe shape as it disappeared down a wide stone stairwell. Without thinking, she grabbed a heavy glass jar and whipped it at the shape's head.

The jar shattered in a razor-sharp cloud of glass fragments. She heard a high-pitched yelp of pain as the footsteps receded.

Something about that cry of pain didn't sound right.

Nysska slammed into the wall of the stairwell and used the momentum to carrom off it and downward, down toward her prey.

Were the fleeing footsteps coming from out on the third floor? Or the stairwell below? She heard the scrape of leather on wood from the floor and dashed after it. Along the way she spotted a few widely-spaced drops of bright red blood.

"Stop!" she barked. "This will go much easier for you if you just fucking *stop!*"

The footsteps and the drops of blood led her to another door, opening onto a stairwell on the opposite side of the building from the Echo Box. Nysska's breath rattled harsh in her chest and throat as she smashed through the door—but she drew up short at an unexpected sound from below her. A *boom boom boom*, frantic. Like the sound a trapped animal made when it tried to break out of its cage.

Nysska reached a landing and turned, peering below her. The door the killer had intended to use, the door that would lead outside, to freedom, refused to open, no matter how frantically sethyd fists and feet smashed against it.

The snow. The blizzard's packed snow against the door.

Her quarry—the tall, dark, wiry shape that had fled from her with such speed—threw itself madly at the door, mounting desperation and fear building in the trapped-animal ferocity.

Finally the man turned away from the door and stared up at her, ragged breath after ragged breath tearing out of his lungs.

It was a *human.*

He stood as tall as any sethyd, with the same rangy build, violet makeup smeared on his face and his hands. A cap jammed onto his head had two black horns sprouting from it, above his unmistakably human eyes—wide and brown, with bloodshot whites encircling them.

The Yshtarra statue protruded from a pack slung around his shoulders.

He held up his violet-stained hands and wailed, "She made me do it! She *made* me do it, I swear she did, I swear to the Dragon, I swear on the lives of my children!"

Eight minutes later Nysska booted the man out into the snow in front of the Echo Box. She held his horn-cap in one hand and the statue of

Yshtarra in the other. The members of the Ninth pushed through the swiftly assembling ranks of the City Watch, followed moments later by Captain Porter and Mayor Ragwild.

Raoul looked from the tall, lean man—who had insisted through sloppy sobs that his name was Timon—to Nysska and back. She watched Raoul's shrewd eyes taking in the violet makeup and the fake horns. After several long moments he said, "So the killer's been ahead of us this whole time. Watching. Listening, no doubt. *Mocking* us."

Nysska's lips compressed into an agitated line. "That, or they have people like Timon here under their thumb. Or both." She threw the horn-cap at Timon, who had sunk down onto his knees in the snow.

"I'm sorry!" Timon cried. "If I didn't do what they said, they'd kill my family! I had no choice!" His bloodshot eyes darted from Raoul to Nysska to the Mayor and back. "Do you understand? I had no choice! None!" He held up his hands in supplication. "My wife and daughters might be dead already because I got caught! Can you send Watchmen to see? Can you protect my family? Please—can you protect them?"

Nysska knelt in front of him and clamped his jaw in her hand. "*Who?* Who threatened you and your family?"

"Yshtarra!" Timon said, just as an arrow arced out from the darkness and punched through his skull, entering his temple on the right side and protruding from his ear on the left.

Nysska dropped the twitching body as Raoul screamed for everyone to take cover. She didn't move. Just turned to stare in the direction of the arrow.

Cam came to her out of the snow. "What the fuck are you *doing?* Get inside, get out of the fucking street!"

"That was meant for him," Nysska said calmly. "For Timon. If it had been meant for me, it would have found me." She turned and saw Captain Porter taking shelter in the same shop where she and the rest of the Ninth had waited on Percy earlier, and made her way to him, Cam scampering inside ahead of her.

Raoul and Percy came out of the shadows at the back of the shop, Raoul seething. "The fucker's *playing* with us! He could've gotten out of the city clean with this fucking *decoy,* but no, he's got to stick around and laugh at us!"

Nysska faced Porter. "Captain, there is a chance that Timon's family is not dead. Would you send some men to check on them?"

Porter had gone deathly pale, but he nodded, and Nysska watched him turn and speak to a couple of his men, who took off through the snow.

Scowling, Cam said, "So all this was a fucking distraction? To what end? Like Raoul said, the killer could've gotten away clean!"

"There's only so far he could get," Mayor Ragwild said, climbing in through an empty window frame on the opposite side of the shop from the street where Timon had died. He gestured broadly about him. "The snow hasn't stopped since last night, and we were already cut off at sunset. You can't get through the passes when they're ten meters deep with it. Sethyd *or* human. Our murderer literally has nowhere to go."

"Which means this was a distraction." Nysska faced Cam and Raoul. "But distracting us from what?"

Percy had been attending to Flax and Jax. The two cats could prowl along on the surface of the snow without leaving much more than shallow indentations, but now they were springing up and diving into it like winter foxes on the hunt. Percy turned to the rest of the group and said, "Where's General Cullen?"

Mayor Ragwild glanced around, looking surprised. "Uh—he would've gotten the alert the same time I did. I assumed he'd be right behind me." He hooked a thumb over his shoulder. "Last time I laid eyes on him, he was heading into his room, back at my residence."

Raoul's face turned a weak shade of gray. Without a word he broke from the group and plunged outside into the snow, carving a path back up the street toward the Mayor's mansion, assassin's arrows be damned. Nysska heard Cam, her voice filled with horrible realization, say, "Oh no," and then, "Nysska, what're you—"

But that was the last thing Nysska heard, because she raced after Raoul—pursued him, caught up with him, and passed him, her legs tearing a channel through the snow. The only people on the streets were City Watchmen, and they got the fuck out of her way as she bulled past, the bulk of the mansion looming ahead of her. A tiny sound made her look to her left, then to her right, and she might have smiled at the sight of Flax and Jax flanking her, bounding along over the snow's surface, if her entire body had not been saturated with dread.

Nysska and the blood lynxes reached the mansion's front door at roughly the same time. One of Ragwild's servants had spotted her through a small observation port. He swung the door wide, allowing her to burst in surrounded by a flying cloud of snow and ice and big cats. "Where is General Cullen's room?" she barked at the servant, a one-armed man in his fifties, and followed his hasty directions up a flight of stairs and down a hall to the door at the end.

"General!" she bellowed, even before she reached the door. "General, are you in there?" Nysska slapped her hand against the door, hammered against it, hard enough that the wood splintered. When General Cullen didn't answer, she tried the latch, found it locked, and split the door in half with a kick.

Nysska froze, there in the doorway.

The blood lynxes milled around her as she sank down to the floor.

The tears came as she heard the sprinting footfalls of the Ninth Crucible thundering up the stairs and down the hallway. Nysska didn't look up at them. She couldn't.

Inside the room, General Boris Cullen's body lay across the bed, brutalized in a way that would have made identifying him difficult if that were all that had been left.

His blood-spattered head rested on a silver serving tray, carefully placed on a table at the foot of the bed, so that his lifeless eyes would settle on anyone coming through the door.

Nysska pulled her knees up and hugged them as Raoul's screams filled the mansion like the spectral wails of a slaughtered army.

8

"D oor by door!" Captain Porter screamed from somewhere outside. "Block off every street as you finish it! Beat this bastard out of the brush like a fucking fox!"

Realistically, Nysska didn't think the Watch could carry out those orders. The blizzard still raged, rendering Mount Stark more and more snowbound, making it harder and harder to navigate the lanes and byways. Leaving the people huddled in their houses all the more vulnerable because it limited where and how fast they could run.

As far as she knew, there was no protocol for a situation like this. The Valconian Empire had relied on the Sensors' rune-based thaumaturgy to solve crimes for the last three hundred years. It was only since the skin-shifting Gemini had emerged from their subterranean glass-and-metal cocoons that the standard procedures had stopped working. Only since the "rust" had made its appearance. Nysska wanted to be out in the snowfall, out with the City Watch, combing Mount Stark for any sign of General Cullen's murderer.

She also wanted to be there for Raoul. He sat in the next room with Mayor Ragwild. Their voices, low and tense, came to her through the door, but not clearly enough to make out any words.

Nysska stood in a corner of one of Ragwild's parlors. Percy sat on the floor a couple meters away with Flax and Jax both piled up in his lap. Cam perched on the edge of a chair, silver eyes flickering toward and away from the door behind which Raoul and the Mayor spoke. Nysska didn't think Cam was using her runes to look through the door—their icy glow was nowhere bright enough. She wondered if that was because Cam wanted to respect Raoul's privacy, or if she didn't want to see the pain and horror etched onto his face.

That question rendered itself moot when the door swung open. Raoul moved slowly into the parlor, eyes unfocused, inhales and exhales rigid in a Cathedral breathing exercise. Cam rose and went to him. She guided him to the chair she'd been sitting in and knelt beside it, one of his hands clasped in both of hers.

"I don't know what to say," she murmured. "No one should have to go through this. We're here for you, Raoul. Whatever you need."

No tears stained Raoul's face. His eyes still focused on nothing, but his brows drew together. "Did you know the killer was going to do this?"

Nysska, Percy, and Cam all realized Raoul had aimed that question at Nysska at the same time. Cam pulled in a tiny gasp and softly let go of Raoul's hands. Percy didn't raise his head from the cats, but a black scowl crossed his face.

"No," Nysska said. She didn't move from the corner.

Raoul looked over at her, his eyes finally clearing. "You've been lying to us this whole time. Keeping information from us."

Cam said, "Raoul—" but he ignored her.

"You knew the killer was on a schedule, that he passed through Mount Stark once a month, yet you neglected to mention that until we'd already wasted Dragon knows how many hours. Is there anything else this oath you took prevented you from letting us in on? Did you know this murderous fuck was working up to killing a decorated Cathedral officer?"

Nysska kept her eyes focused on the toe of her right boot. "No. I had no idea. I'm sorry, Raoul. I truly am."

Raoul stood. Slowly, never taking his eyes from her, he approached until they stood almost nose to nose. "I don't think I believe you," he said, and the calm, solid way in which he said it hurt worse than if he'd screamed it in her face. "I don't think I *trust* you anymore, Nysska. I think you withheld information from us that would have kept my father alive." He paused, and she drew breath to speak, but he cut her off. "And I feel no need to see you any longer."

No one else said anything. Nysska could see Cam clearly over Raoul's shoulder, and while she looked as if she might have wanted to speak, she visibly chose not to.

Nysska nodded once. "I understand. I shall trouble none of you any further." She moved out of the corner, around Raoul, and made her way out of the room without addressing anyone else.

Nysska had left the parlor and made it a few meters down the hall when Cam caught up with her. "Nysska. Wait." She stopped and turned as Cam glanced up and down the hall, making sure no one else was around to hear her words. "If you level with us, you know he'll forgive you."

Cam reached out to take Nysska's hands, and Nysska jerked them back, stepping out of Cam's reach. "I know no such thing. Raoul was very clear in his meaning. And...I do not blame him."

Cam closed the distance between them again, but kept her hands away. "You can level with me. Nysska—it's *me*. You can tell me anything. You know you can."

Nysska took a deep, slow breath. "I can tell you that I love you. I can tell you that I have never regretted anything in my life the way I regret General Cullen's death. But Cam, I need you to understand. I *cannot* tell you where I have been. And I cannot touch you." She let her head drop back and peered deep into Cam's eyes. "I cannot touch *anyone*."

"But *why?*" Cam demanded. "Do you have some kind of disease? What in Dragon's name could prevent you from physical contact?"

Nysska's throat nearly closed up with the effort of fighting back the tears that burned her eyes. "I...have a task I must complete. This blizzard..." She gestured broadly around them. "I must treat it as a boon, since it has prevented the General's murderer from fleeing Mount Stark. But when the task is complete, I will have to leave. I have no choice. Please believe me—*I have no choice.*" She took another step away. "I hope to see you again. Under better circumstances."

Cam's jaw dropped open. "Are you—are you saying *goodbye?*"

"I meant exactly what I said. Word for word."

Cam started to say something else, but Nysska turned and strode swiftly down the hallway, down the stairs to the front door and out into the snow.

A helpful City Watchman—helpful after he'd overcome his shock and fear at facing a demon up close—told her which streets the Watch had already searched, or at least tried to search. "If you want to join the effort, ma'am, just head straight down this way—" He pointed with an only slightly trembling arm. "Till you get to Captain Porter. He'll pair you up with someone. Every warm body's welcome, he said."

Nysska did head in the direction that the Watchman had indicated, but at the first opportunity she ducked inside a shop, apologized to the owner who was taking advantage of the blizzard to do inventory, and climbed the stairs until she stepped out onto the building's roof. The rafters underlying the slate creaked at the weight of her body, already loaded down with a heavy layer of snow as they were, so she moved carefully as she lifted her eyes and scanned the roofs of the taller buildings.

After a few seconds she spotted the one she needed: one of the city's multiple Churches of the Great Silver Dragon, a tower rising from its center until it disappeared into the low-lying clouds. Nysska moved to the edge of the roof and leapt across the gap to the next building. Then the one after that, and the one after that, until the Church loomed directly ahead of her.

If she recalled correctly, the kite spires that normally adorned the Dragon Churches did not contain internal staircases, so as to prevent the general public from climbing them and interfering with the brilliant shining kites moored at the top—kites that represented the Great Silver Dragon itself. The priests used a series of pulleys and a platform to ascend the spire and removed the platform entirely when not in use. Nysska didn't think their ceremonial kite was flying today. That made no difference.

She clambered up the sloping roof to the kite spire's base and stared up at the dizzying column of stacked stone blocks. The temperature at the top would be even lower than down among the streets and alleys, and might actually get cold enough for her to feel it. For her fingers and toes to grow numb. For frostbite to sink its teeth into her flesh. "Shitty time to take up rock climbing," she muttered to no one, and began scaling the tower.

Ten minutes later, after a series of near-falls and one heart-stopping moment when the bit of stone on which she'd been bracing a foot crumbled to dust beneath her, Nysska reached the top of the kite spire and pulled herself over the edge, breathing hard.

The top of the spire wasn't very spire-like at all, she decided. It looked more like the top of a castle's tower, the kind of structure built for defense, with a flat floor surrounded by a crenelated wall. The bronze mount for the Dragon kite was bolted into the stone on the spire's eastern edge.

Nysska caught her breath and stood upright, stretching—

That breath lodged in her throat like a bone when a sethyd slipped over the wall next to the kite mount.

Her eyes were a shade of orange Nysska had never seen before, a shade so deep and rich that they verged on red, and her horns curled upward into long, dagger-like spikes. Neither of those were what caused Nysska's heart to stumble and almost fall, though. That came from the midnight-blue leather armor the sethyd wore.

The armor of the *araneoj*. The Spiders.

The same elite warrior division to which her brother Gerrit had belonged.

"I am Jinna Marsdown," she said. "Born Jinna Kulkarni."

The clouds above them flared a brilliant blue-white, followed a heart-beat later by a deafening clap of thunder.

"I am Nysska Stonegate. Born Nysska Kaur."

Something in the air changed. The fine hair on Nysska's arms stood on end. Another brilliant blue-white flash turned Jinna Marsdown into the briefest of silhouettes.

"Oh, I know who you are," Jinna said, after another booming roll of thunder. She moved closer. Nysska noted the thick black leather bag slung around Jinna's body, and her heart broke free of the grip that had held it and thundered against her ribs. "I've been watching you," Jinna said. "You and your little conclave. But then you knew that, or you wouldn't have come up here."

Nysska slid the khopesh free of its sheath. "I came up here because I knew none of them could follow me in time to prevent this from happening."

Amusement crossed Jinna's face. Nysska didn't even see her hands move—it was as if they simply sprouted a pair of long black daggers. "Prevent *this* from happening? And what do you think *this* is going to be?"

"I thought it was going to be me subduing you. Killing you if I had to. And taking what you have in that bag away from you. Away from *them*."

"Adorable," Jinna said, and Nysska didn't see her feet move at all.

From one heartbeat to the next Jinna Marsdown simply flew at her like a bird of prey diving out of the sky. The khopesh flashed upward and prevented one of those black daggers from driving through her eye socket. The second dagger tore through the heavy fabric of her coat as well as the multiple layers of shirt and undergarment and skin, laying her open to the bone, but Nysska had moved just in time and the blade only skittered along her ribs. The pain flashed into her as if a red-glowing coal had been pressed into her skin, but she resisted it, fought it, and let the khopesh do part of what it was designed to. The razor-sharp hook near its tip caught the dagger meant to drive into her skull and, with a sharp, hard twist, tore it out of Jinna Marsdown's fist. The black blade spun out into the snow and fell noiselessly from the spire.

Jinna's boot came up and drove into Nysska's breastbone and flung her backward, but she had steeled herself against the pain and rolled, coming up to one knee in time to block the remaining black dagger as it drove toward her heart.

"Fast," Nysska gritted out, and the dagger that had sprung from the sheath on her hip to her free hand found purchase in Jinna Marsdown's flesh. The other sethyd cursed and spat and sprang away as the loudest peal of thunder yet shook the stones beneath them.

Nysska rose to her feet, dagger in one hand and khopesh in the other, and she and Jinna circled, feinting, looking for openings.

"Why?" Nysska threw out. "Why murder humans? Why draw attention to yourself?"

"Practice," Jinna spat back. "I had heard how easy they were to kill. Wanted to see for myself."

Nysska jabbed with the khopesh, its needle-sharp point driving Jinna back, out of range. "You thought an old woman presented a worthy target?"

"Hardly." The orange of the woman's eyes deepened as Nysska watched, turning a full blood-red, red and clear as rubies. "She was just the appetizer. That fool of a military man. He was the main course."

Jinna charged in fast, and the black dagger dug into the meat of Nysska's shoulder. Pain made her fingers spasm, so much that she dropped her own dagger, and she kicked it out of Jinna Marsdown's reach.

"You know what I am," Jinna said. "Because you know what your brother was. They talk about you. Back in the Crags. The sethyd who killed her own sibling. It's…" She shook her head. "It's unforgivable. Merits the highest punishment. A punishment I'm more than happy to carry out."

"Confident words," Nysska said, and wished she hadn't, because she desperately needed all her breath. It spiraled out around her in trails of white as she sidestepped and pivoted.

"You're a *priest-singer*. Not even that. You *were* a priest-singer. And I am a Spider. Come here, little fly."

Jinna charged again, and Nysska lost sight of the world around her.

All she saw, all she felt, was the black dagger in the elite soldier's hand, the way Jinna slipped every thrust and slash of the khopesh, the way the black blade bit into her again and again, deeper and deeper each time. The blade shredded the leather and fabric meant to protect her from the elements just as easily as it tore through her skin. Within seconds the Cathedral-issued coat and shirt and trousers hung from her in blood-soaked tatters.

Nysska screamed and shoved Jinna against the low stone wall, the dagger trapped against Jinna's breast. For a moment Jinna's vastly superior skill didn't matter. It became a contest of evenly-matched strength.

"Nothing you've done here makes any sense," Nysska gritted out. "It's what you're carrying, isn't it? You've had too much exposure. It's poisoning you. Curdling your brain."

Jinna Marsdown's blood-red eyes flashed. A mad grin stretched her mouth as she grabbed a handful of Nysska's hair. "If this is how I go, I am satisfied," she said, and heaved them both backward.

Gravity fell away along with the roof of the kite spire.

A flash of lightning split the sky, glaring off Jinna Marsdown's madness-soaked eyes and pain-lusting teeth.

Nysska remembered this feeling. Plummeting from the balcony at Cliffside, the pain of the arrow that had punched through her chest, the flashing, flickering horror as her consciousness galloped away from her.

But things had changed since then.

This time, as the snow-covered roof of the Dragon Church rushed up to meet them, something very much like peace flooded through her. A peace bordering on euphoria. She twisted in mid-air, easily shoving Jinna Marsdown beneath her, and in the split instant before impact the euphoria culminated in a body-wide, soul-deep *click*.

The piece filling the last empty spot in the puzzle.

A key turning in a lock.

The change reflected in Jinna Marsdown's abruptly terrified eyes as the air around them split with a bone-rattling blast of thunder.

Nysska used Jinna's body as a battering ram and slammed them through the Church's roof. They crashed like a boulder in a landslide into the rows of massive pews below. The impact split an oak pew in half as they smashed through it and struck the broad flagstones of the floor.

Jinna kicked away from her and staggered to her feet, grinning from a bloody mouth. "You thought that would kill me?" she slurred. "They teach us ways. *Techniques*. Methods of hardening the body. Making it like *stone*." She looked down and saw her own dagger protruding from her side, driven there when they struck the roof, and wrenched it free as she took a step toward Nysska—

Wallace Embry bellowed like a furious bull and smashed into Jinna from behind, wrapping his arms around her in a bear hug. The black dagger flew from her grasp, and Nysska screamed, "Wallace! Get away from her! Turn her loose, Wallace, she'll kill you!"

"Like fuck I will!" Wallace screamed back, and Jinna Marsdown slammed the back of her head into Wallace's face, pulverizing his nose in an explosion of blood.

Wallace grunted and swore and hung on.

Nysska shouted, "Turn her loose and get away!" but the stout young man did not, and Jinna flexed and screamed, and Nysska heard both of Embry's arms break. Other voices reached them, shouting, screaming. Nysska saw only Jinna and Wallace Embry as he staggered away from her, dazed and going into shock. Jinna charged at him and threw a kick faster and stronger than that of a bull, and Wallace's right thigh snapped and folded as he collapsed to the stone floor.

Jinna scooped up the dagger and whirled on the next combatant, blade raised high.

That combatant was Cam, the next member of the Ninth to arrive, her longsword in hand and eyes gleaming silver.

Jinna shrieked and leapt toward Cam, black blade aimed at her throat.

Each of the pews in the Church of the Great Silver Dragon of Mount Stark were fashioned from a single oak tree. They were labors of love, transported and carved by dozens of skilled craftspeople. Each one weighed at least four hundred kilgrams.

Nysska picked up the nearest pew, whipped it over her head and brought it straight down onto Jinna. The ferocious impact smashed Jinna Marsdown's skull and drove her body into the stone floor with a wet, sickening crunch of hundreds of splintered bones.

The glare of lightning turned the inside of the Church blue-white as the stone vibrated from the apocalyptic boom of thunder, and the clouds above them, having tired of snow, dumped torrential rain onto Mount Stark.

A column of rainwater fell from the hole smashed in the roof. The cascade fell directly onto Nysska, and she raised her face and let it wash over her.

Nysska stood there, panting, the members of the Ninth Crucible gaping at her. The skin of her arms and legs and chest lit from within by glowing, pulsing, brilliant red runes.

PART II

THE SURVIVOR

9

Three months before...

The cold threatened to take her.

It had already hammered its way through her skin and turned her muscles to shattered ice and cracked open her bones. When it settled into her marrow—

When it settled into her marrow she was going to die. Sink down below the waves and settle onto the ocean floor. A cold, lifeless thing, food for fish and crabs.

Hands grabbed at her. Soft and weak, too weak to haul her water-logged carcass out of the water. She weighed at least a ton because all the air in her lungs had been replaced with ice and mud. All the ice and all the mud came in and settled in her chest because of the hole. Something had punched a hole in her chest and because of that everything was going the wrong way, all the air and blood had rushed out and made room for the ice and the mud and the cold to pack tight inside her.

More hands now, grabbing at her, pulling her, but it didn't matter, she had frozen and needed to sink, that was what dead frozen things did—

When her body slapped down hard on the unforgiving wood she discovered that she had something besides the cold. She had *pain*, and would have screamed if there had been any air in her lungs. Instead she twitched like a fish hauled out of the surf and where her body still had any feeling left, that sensation came to her as agony, sharp and grinding as her limbs bent in places where she had no joints, as her back and her neck rasped inside of her like pouches full of broken glass.

Her vision came to her.

Flash—

The faces of strangers, bent over her, every touch of every hand a new flare of pain, as if making a pincushion of her with ragged blades and

Flash—

Moving, swaying, moving, coupled with the sound of hoofbeats on hard earth and

*Flash—*more hands, different hands, different faces swimming in and out above her and around her, skin changing and warping like

Like cuttlefish

Nysska tried to cry out, but though a tiny bit of air had somehow found its way back inside her chest, making even the tiniest sound caused her to erupt in a fountain of the purest agony, and when the tears started in her eyes she welcomed their scalding heat because the rest of her was still so cold, *so cold.*

The hands came again, more and more of them, clamping onto her wrists and ankles and knees and elbows, lantern light flashing off the blade of a small, wicked knife as someone began flaying her alive.

She both felt and, through wild eyes, saw the skin peeling back in sheets from her right leg before darkness claimed her.

When next she woke, Nysska dared not move. The pain that had replaced all of her flesh and bones and organs had transformed into...something else.

A tingling. A *skittering.*

As if tens of millions of tiny ants had burrowed into her and marched just underneath her skin, marched and marched, carrying out orders with their tiny brittle legs and waving antennae and shearing mandibles.

If I move, they'll sting me.

Nysska lay perfectly still and concentrated on using her eyes, only her eyes. She tried to breathe as little as possible, so as not to upset the horde of ants inside her.

Nysska lay on a bed. Of that much she felt certain. A bed with a thin mattress, covered with clean sheets, some kind of blanket draped across her. She felt naked, as the sheets and the blanket touched every part of her body, but she didn't want to move her eyes enough to check and couldn't risk raising her head. She lay in a room lit by a single lantern, judging by the shadows it cast. The one part of the room she could observe directly and without question was the pine-plank ceiling.

Unpainted but tacked in place by someone skillful, the stripes and swirls and knotholes wove themselves together into a unique field of constellations

Nysska blinked her eyes…

And when they re-opened, sunlight had invaded the room and a woman's concerned face hovered over her.

"Wow," the woman said. "I guess it worked."

Reluctantly, with great caution, Nysska swallowed. It hurt. Her mouth was cotton-dry, her throat filled with rough gravel. In the hoarsest of rasps, she asked, "What happened?"

"My name is Ruth," the woman said, and brought a ceramic cup to Nysska's lips. It contained the coldest, sweetest water Nysska had ever tasted. "Not too much," Ruth cautioned, and took the cup away before Nysska was ready.

"What happened to me?" Nysska repeated. "Where am I?"

"You know, I really should go and tell Master Seeley his patient is awake," Ruth said.

Was that accurate? Was she a patient?

…Or a victim?

Perhaps even the subject of an experiment, judging by Ruth's first words to her.

Nysska reached out to grab Ruth's wrist and was surprised as much by how slow and weak the action was as by how violently Ruth jerked away from her. Nysska frowned and opened her mouth to speak but shut it again when a wave of vivid red washed over Ruth's face from her left ear all the way to her right.

"You're a Gemini," Nysska said. She meant it to sound certain and maybe a little threatening. It came out like a kitten's mew.

Ruth turned without a word and left the room.

Crawling subdermal ants or not, Nysska knew better than to let herself be a victim of the Gemini if she didn't have to. She tried to sit up and, when that didn't work, inched and groaned her way up to her elbows. Nysska shifted her weight and threw the blanket off.

She couldn't tell how loudly she screamed.

Nysska screamed at the sight of the hundreds upon hundreds of sutures running up and down her arms and legs, across her abdomen, atop her breastbone.

She screamed at the sight of the red runes that had been implanted there, the glow of each one turning her skin magenta.

Or maybe she didn't scream at all. Maybe she made no noise before she fell sideways on the bed and slid bonelessly to the floor and lost her grip on consciousness again.

Nysska dreamed. Or maybe not. Maybe she had died. Maybe this was all in her imagination. She couldn't tell.

A man in a black coat with ornate golden patterns sewn into it bent over her. Poking. Prodding. Running rough, blunt fingers along her limbs. He was a big man with the darkest skin she had ever seen, and hair and eyes to match, and she didn't like the way those eyes slid across her, twitching from suture to suture, examining every square centim of her body.

"Good," the man said, straightening up. "So far, good. Hix—keep me apprised."

A voice from somewhere above her head said, "Yes, Master Seeley."

When next Nysska rose to consciousness, lying on the bed again, she became aware of someone moving around in the room with her. It took effort to open her eyes, and even more effort to make them focus, but eventually the blurry double-image united and resolved into Ruth, the Gemini nurse.

Someone had placed an extra pillow under her head and shoulders, which allowed her to get a better look at the room that had become her whole world. It reminded her of the hovels occupied by the suspects she'd tracked down in the Forty-Seventh Crucible. Dirt-poor villages on the Empire's outskirts, filled with millers or sawyers or coopers who spent their entire lives toiling mercilessly, only to die with little or nothing to show for it.

Aside from her bed, a single straight-backed chair, and a small side table, the room contained a window covered over with rough, heavy curtains, a dilapidated wardrobe with one door hanging from a single hinge, and a stand for a wash basin and pitcher. Nysska had always found herself uncomfortably, unreasonably itchy whenever she'd gone without bathing for an extended period. Her body at the moment was saturated with unfamiliar, unwelcome sensations, but itchy she was not, and it made her wonder whether she'd been sponge-bathed and who had done it.

"Where—"

That one word was all she could manage before her throat closed up, slamming tight into an interlocking grit-filled column, but Ruth's head jerked around and she rushed to Nysska's bedside, quick to hold a cup of water to her lips. The water didn't even want to go down at first. Nysska feared it might pour straight into her lungs instead. Eventually she made herself swallow, and the pillar of her throat eased and opened again. After several more sips, Nysska whispered, "Where is the Ninth?" When Ruth only showed her a confused frown, she tried again. "Where is Cam? ... Camble Delakroy? Where is she?"

"I'm sure I don't know," Ruth said, taking the cup away. "Best not to drink too much all at once. You need to pace yourself. Most of all, you need to rest."

Nysska tried to grab Ruth's wrist again, and her arm did move, but only in a weak, aimless motion that did nothing but shift her hand along her ribcage under the blanket. "She must think I'm dead. I have to let them all know I'm alive."

Ruth patted Nysska's shoulder. "There will be time for that. The thing you *must* do right now is recover." A shadow passed across Ruth's face. "You were...if I may say so...you were quite a mess when they brought you here. If any one of *us* had been injured that severely, we would have died. A *human* would have been dead when they dragged her from the water."

The sensation Nysska had been trying to ignore since she opened her eyes grew more pronounced—the now-familiar pulsing, crawling, ants-beneath-the-skin vibration—and when she glanced down at her body she could see the glow of the runes even through the thin blanket that covered her.

"It couldn't have been that bad." Nysska swallowed laboriously, gestured for the cup of water, and after another two sips said, "Sethyds are tough, but we are hardly immortal."

Ruth shook her head. "It'd be easier to count the number of bones that *weren't* shattered. They laid you out on Master Seeley's table and—I couldn't help shedding tears at the sight of you. You were like—like a sack of broken sticks."

It made the vibration beneath the hundreds of sutures flare, but Nysska pulled her arm free and laid a hand over Ruth's. "My Crucible. My *friends*. Unless someone has told them otherwise, they must believe me dead. I have to get word to them that I live."

Ruth gently placed Nysska's hand back on the bed. "There will be time for that, I am sure. But as I have told you before, and I do not lie to you when I say this, you *must rest*. If you do not allow your body to heal, you will die. It is as simple as that."

Nysska said nothing else as Ruth gave her a few more sips of water, tidied up aimlessly around the room for a few minutes, and left. Nysska lay there, staring at the ceiling, trying to take stock of her situation. She had no idea how long she'd been unconscious while the Gemini transported her, so she had no idea how far she'd traveled. All she'd seen beyond the door so far was a flash of a couple trees, so she had zero clue as to her current location. She couldn't see her breath. That was something. That meant they couldn't have taken her that far north, because the room contained no hearth, no fire, no way to stave off the harsh winter's cold. *Somewhere south of Cliffside, then.* It was so little to go on that it might as well have been nothing.

Sunlight shined around the edges of the window's curtains. Setting her jaw, Nysska determined to count her heartbeats until the sun set.

When she opened her eyes again it was full dark.

The ants raged and fought inside her, warring against her ribs and in her spine and along the lengths of her arms and legs, but the frustration she felt with herself at falling asleep, combined with the crawling, spurred her into teeth-gritted action. Nysska pushed the blanket aside to find that someone had put a knee-length night garment on her. With a grunt she forced her legs over the edge of the bed. Pushing herself upright caused her head to sway and wobble, but none of her limbs cracked or folded where they weren't supposed to. Nysska took as deep a breath as her lungs would allow and pushed up to her feet.

The runes flared, their intensity spiking from magenta to pure red as they gleamed through her violet skin. Nysska pulled the blanket off the bed and wrapped herself in it. She didn't seem to have any runes in her face, for which she said a silent thank-you. Moving one foot carefully and deliberately at a time, she shuffled across the floor, opened the door the tiniest crack, and peered through it.

All she could see were trees. The thought flashed through her mind that she'd been imprisoned in a tiny cabin literally in the middle of nowhere, but then voices came to her, male and female. Soft. Careful. Nysska looked left and right, stepped through the door, and made her way to the nearest corner.

She did indeed appear to have been put in a tiny cabin, but not one in the wilderness, or at least, not the pure wilderness. Other cabins dotted a tiny valley, visible thanks to lantern light in their windows, and when she concentrated hard enough to overcome the warring-ant roaring in her ears she could hear the music of running water. *Probably built around a stream.* Good for drinking and maybe fishing.

The first moon rode high in the sky. The second one would be coming up soon, driving down her chances of escape with its near-sun-like brightness, so if she were going to make a go of it, it had to be now. Nysska wrapped the blanket more securely around her—more to hide the light of her runes than for warmth—and crept toward the trees.

At full strength Nysska could come close to flying, her feet were so fleet. She could far outpace any human and even a few sethyds whose adult lives had been devoted to more sedentary pursuits. Now her legs and feet were made of lead. Each step took a concerted effort, and she feared her footfalls were loud enough and shook the earth enough to alert everyone in whatever village this might be. What felt like hours later, she reached the tree line and turned north, parallel to the stream. Eventually she'd hit a highway. There, she could flag down a passing Imperial patrol. Emperor Valco still wanted her for questioning in relation to the massive shipment of chervoxite she'd destroyed at Solace Canyon, but she liked her odds with him better than with a bunch of Gemini. As far as she knew, they'd only saved her to experiment on and eventually torture to death.

The pine needles beneath her bare feet made far too much noise for her liking. Ordinarily when moving through the woods this close to an enemy encampment Nysska would have used an asymmetrical stride, meant to sound more like a forest animal rooting about for food than anything with two legs moving with purpose. Now the choice was made for her. Each step took such an effort of will that she couldn't have moved in a uniform gait if she'd tried.

One of Nysska's feet swayed through open air, and if she hadn't grabbed hold of a sapling she would've pitched forward onto her face. She shook her head in an unsuccessful attempt to clear it of the ant roar, then judiciously bent her knees, crouching to listen. A tiny burble of water let her know that she crouched at the edge of a creek bed. No doubt a tributary to the stream that wound through the Gemini village behind her.

I can do this, she told herself. *If the only thing that stands between me and getting back to Cam is a fucking creek bed, I can fucking well do this.*

Nysska let go of the sapling and turned sideways and slid one questing foot down the sharply sloping bank. When that foot struck a small rock outcropping on the way down, it sent a jolt of pain up her leg and into her spine and skull, a jolt so blinding that she didn't know she was falling until the earth slammed into her.

She couldn't breathe.

Water flooded into her mouth and nose and ears, and some dim part of her mind told her she had tumbled face-first into the creek below, but when her arms flew up to push her out, the right one snapped halfway between her wrist and elbow. Nysska slammed down onto her right shoulder and fell back into the water, strangling and choking. Her left arm found its way underneath her and pushed and pushed—just enough to lift her face above the water's surface and take a great gasping breath— and then her left shoulder failed with a horrible crunching sound and her face plunged into the creek again.

Nysska screamed. Somewhere in her experience, deep in her memories, she knew she shouldn't, but panic finally set in as her broken body failed her. The scream emerged not as the eardrum-bursting cry of pain and frustration she meant it to, but as nothing more than a cloud of bubbles.

The bubbles faded out, growing smaller and smaller, and finally stopped—

Just as a pair of hands fastened around her shoulders and heaved her over sideways, splatting her on her back in the mud, and as her chest heaved and she spluttered filthy creek water out of her nose and mouth, a man she'd never seen before gathered her in his arms and held her to his chest, his own body shuddering.

"You can't die," he said. Amid the pain and the slowly receding panic Nysska heard him speaking through sobs. "Please, you can't die, you can't."

Nysska could barely see the stranger that held her. He was little more than a curly-haired silhouette in the first moon's light. But his scent flooded into her nostrils, warm and rich and deep, a welcome replacement for the creek water, and she turned her head and buried her face in his chest.

Other voices came to her from over the creek bank, frantic, searching, and the man drew in a great breath and bellowed, "Here! I've found her! We're here!"

He held her like that, gently stroking her hair, and his hot tears fell on her cheeks and into her half-opened eyes as she blacked out.

The growling in Nysska's stomach woke her, followed by the scent of bread. Not fresh-baked, she didn't think, but Nysska's senses had always gotten a bit sharper when she was hungry, and she couldn't think of the last time her hunger had been this profound.

A man sat in a chair nearby. He looked about forty, a thin man with a long, narrow nose. He had receding curly hair the color of sand and the kind of pale skin that indicated he didn't work outside for a living. His blue eyes looked kind, if a bit watery. His lips curved in what might have been an involuntary grin when she stirred.

When he moved, Nysska caught a trace of his scent, and the events of the previous night came crashing back.

This was the man who'd saved her life.

"Please don't try to get up," he said, in a voice deeper than she was expecting. "My name is Hix. I'll be glad to answer your questions, at least the ones I'm able to. But first it would make me happy if you'd drink some water and maybe eat a little something."

Nysska moved her arms and legs experimentally. Her shoulder, the one that had failed so catastrophically only hours ago, hurt when she moved it, but she *could* move it. A splint had been applied to her broken arm, but she felt remarkably little pain from the fracture. No restraints shackled her to the bed. She wondered if that was because the glaring debacle of her escape attempt was meant to be seen as reason enough not to try for another.

Keeping her voice as calm as possible, Nysska asked, "Are you a Gemini too?"

He chuckled. It sounded rueful. "No. No, I'm just a human. The, uh, the Cathedral saw fit to pay for my education, and eventually assigned me to the Thaumetallicon. Where I learned my vocation at the Imperial College in Taurus Hill."

Nysska shifted on the pillows someone had placed beneath her head. "I've been to Taurus Hill. Who's the head Runemaster there?"

Hix showed her an easy grin. His teeth weren't quite even, but they were white and looked strong and he was in possession of all of them. "When I was a student, it was Professor Greig. That's been a few years. If there's been a change since then, I haven't heard about it."

Nysska remembered Professor Greig, with all her dusty formality. "So I have you to thank for all the metal shoved into my body."

He lifted his shoulders and let them fall. "Not entirely me, no, though I did assist. Master Seeley was in charge of your procedure. He should be in shortly to check on you. Until he gets here, though, are you sure I can't interest you in some water? A tiny piece of bread?"

Nysska's stomach growled at the word "bread." Hix seemed genuinely non-threatening. That, coupled with the fact that if these people had wanted her dead they surely would already have killed her, finally made her nod. He picked up a cup from a nearby table and tried to bring it to her lips, but she reached out with both hands and took it, drinking under her own power. When Hix took the cup back she didn't want to admit how much of her strength she'd used just on that one gesture. He tore a small bit of bread off a loaf she couldn't see. Nysska didn't object when he gently fed it to her.

After she'd had several more sips of water and eaten a handful of bites of bread, Nysska said, "Why?"

"Why what? …Why did we decide to implant runes in you, or why did we rescue you after you were shot and fell into the ocean?"

She only stared at him.

Seeming to take that as a prompt, Hix said, "Well, one led to the other. We had to do something once we'd hauled you out of the water."

A jumble of memories chased each other across the surface of Nysska's mind. She remembered standing at the top of the oceanside tower at Raoul's family home, talking to Cam. Looking down at the sunset-colored sea and spotting two boats. Hearing the resonant *twung* of what could only have been an Argonium Infantry bow. Feeling the impact as the arrow pinned her against the wall.

"You were in one of those two boats."

Hix nodded. "We'd gotten wind of an assassination attempt on you."

Question after question built up just behind Nysska's lips. "Where is Cam? Is she safe?"

Hix spread his hands. "I would assume so? The boat carrying the archer who shot you fled the scene, and we have heard nothing about any move on the Cullen home. As far as we know, the rest of the Ninth Crucible is unharmed."

"How long was I without consciousness?"

Hix silently ticked numbers off on his fingers. "It's been four days. Sorry, I sort of lost track of time, between the implantation and the follow-up care."

Nysska stared up at the now-familiar pine ceiling. "Who shot me?"

"We believe the Church of the Great Silver Dragon was responsible. They didn't kill you at Solace Canyon, and from what we've heard, they really, truly wanted to, so they hired an Argonium Infantryman to do what they couldn't."

She raised her head and looked down at her body, once again covered by the blanket. With a bit of effort, she pulled an arm all the way out from under the covers and examined the rows of sutures. The glow of the metal beneath. The runes' light shimmered and danced like sparks above a fire. "That tree trunk the Infantryman shot me with missed my heart. Obviously. And I have survived falls from great heights into water before. Why was…all this…why was it necessary?"

Hix leaned back in his chair. "It wasn't the water you fell into that was the problem, Miss Stonegate. It was the rocks right under the surface that did the work."

She let her arm fall back to her side. "For the third time, I ask you— *why*? I understand that you were trying to save my life, for reasons I don't yet comprehend, but what led you to think that turning me into a tarn would accomplish that?"

"Oh, you're no Tarnished One. You are…well. In point of fact, we weren't actually sure what implanting the runes would do to a sethyd. As far as we know, it's never been done before. But it was either take that extreme measure, or watch you slowly bleed out while all your organs failed. We took the chance." Apparently sensing that Nysska's patience was wearing thinner by the second, Hix went on. "The runes have a healing effect. Well, a healing effect in the short term. They do involve argonium, and argonium remains toxic. For a while, the regenerative effect outpaces the toxicity, but it's a fight the healing effect eventually, inevitably loses." He paused. "Or maybe none of that's true, because as I said, this has never been done to a sethyd. So there's really no way to know what will happen."

Nysska slid her eyes closed and thought of Cam. Carrying around the runes in her eyes that let her see and do miraculous things, but which would surely kill her by age forty, if not sooner. "All right," she said. "I'm weak, but I can tell none of my bones are broken. That means you can take these fucking things out of me, yes?"

Hix reached out and put his hand over hers. His skin was soft and warmer than she'd expected, and he gave her a tender bit of pressure as his voice grew just a hair huskier. "I can't. Not yet. Miss Stonegate, please believe me when I say that none of this was my idea. The last thing I want to do is hurt you."

Nysska pulled her hand out from under his. "None of *what* was your idea?"

From the room's doorway a feminine voice spoke out. "I'll take over from here, Hix. You can go."

Staring at the woman—who moved into the room with the confidence of a Cathedral general—Nysska remembered a story she had heard from a human who worked on a farm that raised chickens. One of the jobs he had was to separate the male chicks from the female chicks, and to do it in a hurry. According to the human, the way to learn to tell the males from the females at a glance was to watch an older, more experienced human do it, over and over. Eventually, the man telling her the story claimed, he was able to tell the chicks apart just as effectively as the teacher did—and yet he never figured out exactly *how* he was doing it. Some kind of subconscious clue or series of clues allowed him to make the distinction.

Nysska felt a bit like that human, in that she could tell the woman was a Gemini, even though she couldn't have explained to anyone *how* she knew. The woman had light brown skin, dark brown eyes, and a tight cap of gray hair that clung to her scalp in tiny curls.

And she was a Gemini. Nysska had zero doubt.

Hix stood and gestured toward the woman. "Nysska Stonegate, this is Bronna Smith. She's, uh—well, she's in charge here."

Bronna Smith said, "Our guest already had that figured out, Hix. And as I told you, you can go now."

Hix dipped his head. "Of course." He shut the door behind him as he left.

Bronna Smith did not settle into the chair Hix had left vacant. Instead she stood at the foot of the bed, reminding Nysska very much of Governor Galena Vachs, though with not even half the charisma. Her voice was low and rough, as if she had spent a lot of time raising it to be heard over crowds, scarring the voice box.

"You're wondering why you're not dead."

"I suppose I am."

"Because the last time you encountered one of us, you ended up *screaming his brains out* of his skull in the Tember public square."

"No. The last time I encountered any of you was at Solace Canyon, when a handful of sethyd soldiers carved your people into bloody chunks."

Smith took a moment, her face unreadable. "Hmm. I stand corrected."

"And before that, though I did not meet any of the Gemini personally responsible, at least one of your people conspired with the Dragon Church to kill an entire village full of sethyds."

Smith leaned forward, bracing her hands on the footboard. "Yeah, that brings me to the point I wanted to make to you today. We—the Gemini— we're not a monolith."

One of Nysska's eyebrows twitched up. "Oh? Are you about to tell me that some of you think Emperor Valco is simply misunderstood? That he's a good man, all things considered, and not deserving of your wrath?"

Smith came around the bed and perched on the edge of Hix's chair. Nysska followed her with her eyes, wishing she had her khopesh at hand. Wishing she had the strength to wield it. "Emperor Valco committed an atrocity when he ordered his men to slaughter us while we were waking up. But he didn't know us. He couldn't know our intentions. When he saw what we could do, he panicked."

"That's incredibly gracious of you. By which I mean I don't find it credible."

Bronna Smith folded her arms under her breasts. "Valco wouldn't have given the order he did if he hadn't been scared. Just look at *your* people. He didn't need to be that generous, when you all got turned into refugees. It's because Valco knew who you were. Knew you'd gotten along with humans just fine for five hundred years. He had no reason to fear you, and so he rolled out the welcome wagon."

Nysska shut her eyes and turned her face away, rather than risk Bronna Smith reading any of the thoughts and feelings that crowded into her mind and heart. *Valco knew nothing of the Mountain Bulls then. Of the sethyd plan to overrun and subjugate the human lands. He would have set fire to our ships as they sailed into the Imperial harbors if he had.*

"Do some of us want Valco dead? Sure, of course. It'd be foolish to deny that. But some of us—myself included—see a better path forward."

Still facing the opposite wall, Nysska said, "And what path is that?"

"Assimilation. We've got to educate Valco. We've got to show him that not all Gemini are alike, just as not all humans or sethyds are alike. If we can get him to understand that, he'll grant us amnesty. To the Gemini who want it, I mean." For the first time, Bronna Smith's confidence hitched the tiniest bit. "We call ourselves the Parakeets."

Nysska frowned. "The what?"

"The Parakeets. Because they're harmless. We took a vote." When Smith noticed Nysska politely stifling laughter she scowled and said, "Look, that's beside the point. Valco won't give us amnesty if we just show up and ask him. We—the, uh, the Parakeets—need an advantage. We need an alliance, and the more strategic, the better. Which is where you come in."

Nysska turned her head to face Smith. "Pardon me?"

"We need to ally ourselves with the sethyds."

"You're—" Nysska let herself chuckle out loud this time. "Oh. You're *serious.* You want to get in bed with the same people against whom you orchestrated a mass murder."

"We need an envoy. An ambassador. We need *you,* Nysska Stonegate."

Nysska laughed harder. It hurt. "Oh, Ms. Smith, of all the sethyds you could have chosen, I am the *last* one on whom you should be banking." When she didn't respond, Nysska went on. "Perhaps you don't know this about me—I am an exile from the sethyds. I was banished, along with my mother, for opposing the prevailing political forces. It was either be booted out to live the rest of my days taking care of Simana in the wilderness or face the gallows. I am not even welcome to *visit,* much less to be any kind of, of *advocate.*"

Bronna Smith sighed. "Yeah, I know, all that's true. But you're the sethyd we have. And—it gives me no pleasure to be this blunt with you—you've got no choice."

Nysska summoned up her strength and pushed with the heels of her hands, wriggling up to a sitting position in the bed, her back against the headboard. The motion made her head swim. When that calmed down she said, "Explain."

"As Hix told you, the runes he and his master implanted in you are actively healing you from the arrow wound and the fall. But they're also, over a longer course, poisoning you. We don't know how long the poison takes to make itself felt in a sethyd. You're the first."

"Yes, yes, I know."

"Well. The runes're the only reason your body's able to heal. If we took them out now, your injuries would overwhelm you, and you'd die." Nysska gritted her teeth but said nothing. "Related to that, the only person who can successfully remove your runes…is the runemaster who implanted them. If anybody else tried it—or you were dumb enough to try it yourself—you'd die."

Nysska blinked a few times. She reached over and picked up the ceramic cup from the bedside table, but almost dropped it as the runes in her arm flickered and flared. Nysska took a sip with a trembling hand and put the cup back.

"I don't think I believe you."

"Yeah, I probably wouldn't either if I was laid up in that bed. The thing is, though—can you take the chance I'm lying?"

Nysska glared at her.

"It'll take a while for the runes to heal you completely. While that's going on, your body'll get used to them, and sooner or later it'll learn to accept them. When you're ready to travel, you'll make the journey to the Crags and plead our case to the sethyds. And it's not going to be till you've convinced somebody influential enough to make a difference for us that we'll get those runes taken out." Bronna Smith stood, close enough for the yellow of Nysska's eyes to reflect in her almost-black irises. "You'll keep this mission secret, too. Tell anybody, and you break the deal."

Nysska's chin jutted defiantly. "That makes no sense. I'm going to need allies if I have any hope at all of pulling this off."

"It's necessary, Enforcer Stonegate, because first, nobody can know that a sethyd's had a successful rune implantation. That knowledge could trigger an imbalance of power that'd destroy the Empire and fuck up all of Kainos. Second, our location here is secure—for now. If anybody knows what business you're carrying out, and traces your movements back to us, it'd endanger everything we've built here."

Nysska's glare increased its intensity. "Is there a third?"

Bronna shook her head. "I'd say you've got enough motivation now. One thing at a time, though. You've got to build up your strength, first and foremost, so you don't lose control of the runes."

Nysska's eyebrows almost bumped into her horns. "That could happen?"

"The Empire's real careful with its new implantees. We're not set up to go to those same lengths here."

Bronna Smith went to the door, opened it, and called out to someone. Another Gemini, this one male and visibly terrified of Nysska, came in and set down a small but complete meal on a wooden tray on the little table beside her bed before scurrying out.

"Eat," Bronna said. "Nobody ever got anything important done on an empty belly."

At that, Nysska's stomach growled like a grizzly coming out of hibernation, and Bronna Smith left the room.

10

Nysska's eyes had only been open for a few moments when Hix knocked at the door. "May I enter?" he asked, and when she didn't respond, he opened it a crack and peered through timidly, as though afraid of what he might see. "Are you decent?"

She stretched beneath the blanket, carefully, feeling her way so as not to put any undue strain on her mending bones. The motion made her feet pop out from the far edge. "I'd be more so if you had supplied me with an adequate blanket."

Hix pushed the door open the rest of the way—showing Nysska a glimpse of trees and green grass right outside—and stepped into the room, his hands full with another tray of food. Moving with more confidence, Nysska pushed the blanket aside, swung her legs over the edge of the bed, and sat up.

"Hey now," Hix said, approaching with the tray. "Let's not put the cart before the horse here."

Nysska looked down at the camisole-like night garment she'd been given. It came to her knees but left the rest of her legs and all of her arms exposed. She raised one leg, gazing down its length at the sutures and the randomly shimmering metal under the skin. Hix set the tray down across the arms of the room's single chair. "How are you feeling?"

Nysska picked up the cup of steaming coffee from the tray with a graceful motion, no shaking in her arm or hand at all. After a sip, she said, "Like a prisoner."

Hix shook his head. "You'll be able to leave just as soon as you've healed enough."

She didn't look at him. "Not what I meant, as you're well aware. How many days have I been here?"

"You were unconscious for four. It's been three since you woke up, so…one week, give or take."

"And how long will it be before I'm 'healed enough'?"

"Impossible to say." He rubbed the back of his neck. "Bronna keeps track of the political situations in the Empire. Things are not so dire that we need to send you off before you're ready, I don't think."

Nysska picked up the plate of bacon and ate a strip, chewing slowly. "You say 'we.' And yet you're human. Have you taken up the Gemini's cause as your own?"

Hix set the tray of food on the bed beside her, pulled the chair back a respectful distance and sat down. "I didn't, at first. My master does, and he took me along with him, so I suppose you could say that I had as little choice as you have. But the more I talk to Bronna and the others, the more I think about how they were treated and the options open to them, the more I sympathize, yes. I am not a prisoner here. I'm staying because I want to."

One of the other small dishes on the tray held a few fresh strawberries, the tiny green crowns already plucked off. Nysska took a bite of one, examined its interior, and popped the rest of it into her mouth. After she'd chewed and swallowed, she said, "I've been trying to find some way to make peace with this. Trying to summon what little wisdom Atiina ever taught me."

"Atiina. That's one of the sethyd gods, isn't it?"

A long, raspy sigh escaped her. "We do not have gods. Atiina is a role model. A somewhat idealized role model, with a certain amount of ritual surrounding her, but that's all she is. A sethyd I try to emulate when I can."

Hix seemed genuinely interested. "So Atiina is a real person? A living sethyd, I mean?"

Nysska faltered. "It…is not clear whether Atiina truly lived, or whether she is simply a collection of ideals. She is our Exemplar of Wisdom. Ultimately it doesn't matter whether she was ever a living woman. According to her, faced with the situation in which I find myself, I should accept it and learn to function within it."

Hix's face brightened. "So you'll help us?"

"I'm still thinking it over. But at this point it seems inevitable that I shall do as Bronna Smith has asked me to, yes. As you humans would say, she has me over a barrel." Nysska took another sip of the coffee. "Though I fear Bronna overestimates the influence I have among my people."

"But they've *got* to listen to you, don't they? Aren't you—that is to say —you must be *famous* among them, yes? The first sethyd in the Cathedral's employ, and in the Thaumetallicon, no less! Instrumental in saving Governor Vachs's life and keeping the Green Needles Territory from falling under enemy control. Defeating Lockridge. Surely your name is on the lips of *every* sethyd, isn't it?"

"We are not an easily impressed people, I'm afraid."

Hix took a breath. Paused. Glanced at the floor, then at the ceiling. "I, ah—I was there."

"Excuse me?"

"I was in Tember. The day you fought Lockridge. Master Seeley and I had come from Taurus Hill on College business, and I was there, at the edge of the city center. I saw the whole battle." His eyes darted up to her horns. "I'm glad the runes are helping you grow that one back."

Nysska had not given her horns a second thought since she'd first awakened in this bed, and the room had no mirrors in it. Her hand flew up to her left horn—and she gasped as her fingertips touched its ridged edges, almost back to its proper length.

Hix leaned forward. Only a couple of centims. His voice took on a subtle but noticeable difference in quality. "Nysska, no matter what Bronna has said to you—what she's forcing you to do or not do—I want you to know, I'm on your side. If it were up to me, as soon as your body heals, I would ask Master Seeley to remove the runes. Unless you want to keep them. I—I would only do what *you* wanted."

The coffee cup came to a halt halfway to Nysska's lips. She'd been getting better at discerning human moods and emotions, but Hix's dilated pupils and heavier breathing might as well have been a sign around his neck. She wondered if he thought he was being subtle.

Nysska set the coffee cup back down, pulled the blanket up around her, and said, "Look, Mr. Hix, I—"

Bronna Smith banged into the room, cutting off whatever Nysska might have been about to say. "Can you walk?" she asked, ignoring Hix entirely.

"I don't know," Nysska replied, happy to shift her focus somewhere else. "If you give me some real clothes I'll have a go at it."

"Good," Smith said. "I want to show you around."

"We call this place Glenmarsh."

Bronna Smith led Nysska down what could have been called a street if one were feeling generous. If so, it was the village's only street, as Glenmarsh seemed to consist of little more than a dozen cabins and some gardens scattered around.

"Why?" Nysska asked. "It appears to contain neither a glen nor a marsh."

"We named it after one of our founders. A man who helped bring us here, get us settled. Provided for us. He paid for that with his life."

It was mid-day, and none of the residents of Glenmarsh were inclined to stop and talk. Nysska knew exactly how labor-intensive it was to scratch out a survival when it was just one person and the land around them. Every garden patch had one or more Gemini tending to it. She picked out corn, potatoes, okra, and tomatoes growing, and spotted a few fruit trees—pear and apple, if she wasn't mistaken—behind one of the cabins.

Bronna Smith stopped by a blueberry bush and picked off a few berries to eat. "We're lucky to have the stream." She gestured toward the wide creek that made its way through the village. "That gives us fresh water. Over there..." Smith pointed toward the far end of Glenmarsh. "That cabin we built around a hot spring. There are no fires in Glenmarsh. Ever. Know why?"

"I'm guessing because there's not much easier way to spot a settlement than watching the sky for smoke?"

"Exactly. Everything cooked is thanks to the hot spring. Until we get some sethyd protection, Glenmarsh's secrecy is the only thing keeping us breathing."

Nysska picked off a blueberry. She tried to hold the flavor of it on her tongue after she'd chewed and swallowed it. "You act as if you're helpless little kittens."

"I'd hate to put it that way. But it's not far from the truth."

"Bearshit. I fought Lockridge myself. And let's not forget about that— that *device* made of chervoxite that caused the Argonium Infantry's runes to burst into flame. I know that was a Gemini creation. Lob a few of those into Caulspring and the Empire would be yours for the taking."

Smith guided Nysska back toward her cabin. "That's simplistic. And reductive. And moot, as it turns out, since building one of those rune destroyers requires a massive amount of chervoxite. No Gemini has the resources to make any more of them now, since somebody decided to tip a whole shipment into a magma stream."

"You call them 'rune destroyers'?"

"What would you call them?"

Nysska didn't answer. She'd never been able to think of a label she liked for the vicious little bauble. Besides, just thinking about the horrifying destruction the thing had caused to the three Argonium Infantrymen right in front of her eyes—especially now that she had runes beneath her own skin—made her want to forget such a thing had ever existed.

"So, are you saying there are no more rune destroyers?"

"I don't know of any. And we sure don't have any of them here. I'd give my left hand for a couple, though. Which goes right back to what I've been saying this whole time, Miss Stonegate. If we're discovered here, we're all dead. Glenmarsh is way, way off the beaten path for the Empire, but all it'd take would be one Imperial citizen getting off-his-ass lost and stumbling across us." Bronna Smith stopped and faced Nysska. "We need your help. We *have* to have it. If we're going to live, you've got to help us."

They walked the rest of the way back to Nysska's cabin in silence.

11

Over the course of the next seven days Nysska grew stronger. Physically stronger, anyway. Her longing to go searching for Cam weighed on Nysska like the proverbial millstone around her neck.

Every day Ruth brought her food and attended to what little housekeeping the cabin required. Every day Bronna showed up to monitor her progress. And every day there was Hix, helping her, encouraging her. He brought her a set of comfortable crutches to begin with. Then fashioned a series of walking rails to help her get from the cabin to the latrine and back. Finally he set out a series of exercises for her to do—*gently*, as he frequently reminded her—that made her think of the physical activity classes she had taken with Gerrit and Tylar and Randolf when they were small together back in Fajrosxtono.

Each day the battling, roaring tides of the ants beneath her skin receded, bit by bit. In correspondence with that recession, the random, flickering glow of the runes grew less and less pronounced. By the end of the week the runes only shimmered every now and then.

Following an afternoon exercise session, she sat down with Hix outside her cabin and drained half a pitcher of water. "What aren't you telling me about these runes?"

Hix thanked her when she handed him the pitcher. After a long swig, he said, "I'm not sure I understand the question."

"I've seen the way you watch my arms and legs when I'm doing your little exercises. I've seen the way you watch my breathing. You're looking for something."

Hix took quite a lengthy pause before he answered her. "You are one of a kind. That's, uh, that's a factual statement, not personal sentiment. The first of your kind, at least to our knowledge. The study of argonium runes is why the Imperial Colleges were built in the first place. We know their effects on humans. We do not know their effects on sethyds."

She looked down at one arm. As if on cue, the runes glimmered magenta from her elbow in a wave down to her wrist. "These are not pure argonium."

"Well. No."

"These are like the ones Lockridge had."

"Correct."

She turned her head and fixed him with her gaze. The color rose in his pale cheeks. "Lockridge and the other insurrectionists used these red runes to animate corpses. And Lockridge gained all the strength and speed of a tarn with no loss of intellect or control. The argument could be made that these are superior to pure argonium."

Hix shook his head a little. "Not really superior. Just different. It's a whole different branch of thaumaturgy, alloying argonium with chervoxite."

"And by implanting them in me—yes, yes, I know, this was the only way to save my life. I remember. But I am also the subject of an experiment."

"I suppose that's one way to look at it, yes."

"So what do you call it?"

"Excuse me?"

"What do you call this new metal? The argonium-chervoxite alloy?"

"We...haven't yet settled on a name. There have been a few contenders thrown around. Or there were, before Master Seeley and I left Taurus Hill."

"Contenders such as...?"

"*Ugh.* None that I liked. None that were any good."

"What was the least objectionable?"

He made a sour face. "Quite a few people wanted to call it 'valconium.'"

"Oh. Wow. That is *terrible.*"

"Isn't it, though?"

"*Valconium runes.* Ugh. No. I can't."

"No one should."

A silence fell. After roughly a minute, Hix said, "Can I get you anything?"

"No. Until Ruth brings my dinner, I just want to wash off and stretch out for a while."

His cheeks turning an abrupt scarlet, he said, "And could I help with that?"

It startled Nysska so much that she barked a short laugh, and Hix threw both his hands up. "I'm sorry, I'm sorry, that was completely inappropriate, please forgive me."

Nysska watched him for a few moments, trying to keep from grinning. "Shooting for high-value targets, are we?"

He buried his face in his hands. "I don't know where that came from. I never say things like that. I shouldn't have said that to you." After a pause, he raised his head. "Am I blushing? I feel like I'm blushing."

"I've seen cherries less red than your cheeks."

Hix dropped his face back into his hands. "I think I'm going to walk off into the woods now and, I don't know. Starve to death. Or let a bear eat me."

Nysska nudged him with an elbow. "Hey."

He tilted his head to look at her with one eye. "...Yes?"

"It wasn't *that* inappropriate."

He brought his head up the rest of the way. "It wasn't?"

"If circumstances were different...I might be open to a bit of...mutual exploration."

Hix made a tiny, choking sound.

Nysska continued. "But circumstances are *not* different. My heart belongs to someone else."

He put an elbow on one knee and propped his head up on the heel of his hand. "Of course. Of course it does. As if I could compete with a sethyd."

Nysska tried for a gentle smile. "We are not...how did Bronna put it? We are not a monolithic people. Not all of us require violet skin and horns of our lovers. And I'm serious—you have been kind to me, and helped me a great deal when you didn't have to. I think of you with great fondness."

He groaned, but smiled while he did it. "Please don't tell me there's some nice sethyd girl out there for me somewhere."

Nysska laughed. "All right, I won't tell you that. Whether or not it's the truth. Now. I really would like to go inside and get cleaned up."

Hix sprang to his feet and offered her a hand. "Of course. Here."

Nysska took his outstretched hand, and both she and Hix yelped and jerked their heads away from the blinding flash of pure ruby-red light that blazed out of every one of Nysska's runes.

Hix lost his grip on her hand as Nysska sagged against the cabin door. Her eyes rolled in her head. Her arms and legs spasmed.

She flopped sideways, hitched onto her back, heels drumming the earth. Something like a bronze vise squeezed her heart and her lungs as her arms drew up tight, fists clenched, fingernails gouging flesh out of her palms. The back of her head slammed into the ground, again and again, until someone put something soft behind it, and she heard screaming voices but all she could see was the brilliant ruby red of the valconium runes.

Valconium runes.

The sheer idiocy of the name sliced through whatever thick fog had enveloped her mind. Her fists began to unclench.

Emperor Valco.

Nysska fought to picture his elderly, smug face, and the clearer it got, the slower the tattoo her heels beat into the dirt.

Still befouled by the fog, the wheels inside her mind turned, slowly, slowly. A thought came to her. *If concentrating on something I hate will bring me out of this...*

Gerrit.

Nysska envisioned her brother's face. It came to her as clear as window glass. Every hate-filled line of it. Every smirk as he held their mother's life over her head. The snarl of rage as she sent him plummeting into the lava-stream at the bottom of Solace Canyon.

Nysska lay still. Panting. Her eyes found their way back down out of her skull and focused—first on the blue of the sky directly overhead, then on Hix's tear-stained face as he knelt beside her. He reached out hands to help her, but she waved them away. *Barely.* She couldn't recall the last time she'd felt so thoroughly, utterly *drained.*

"Don't touch me," she said, to make sure he understood. "I'm fine."

"You are clearly *not* fine," he shot back, as Nysska struggled up to her elbows.

A small crowd of curious Gemini villagers had gathered, staring at her from a short distance. First and foremost among them was Bronna, eyes narrowed.

By the time Nysska struggled up to her feet, Bronna had turned and disappeared into the crowd.

"It's a question of accepting the runes, I suppose you could say." Hix gnawed at a fingernail. Nysska had spent enough time with him to know that meant he was worried. "Or of the runes accepting you. It's a process. One with which none of us are familiar."

From her bed, Nysska said, "Yes, yes, you've made it abundantly clear. We are in uncharted waters." She flexed her arms, then her legs, probing, testing. "What happens if the runes reject me outright? Or I reject them?"

Hix frowned. "I don't see that happening, honestly. You're ready to have your sutures out—let me express just a bit of envy that sethyds truly don't scar—and there's been no sign of inflammation or shifting."

"Does that happen when the runes reject a human?"

"Human rejection is exceptionally rare. The vetting process is thorough, and the runemasters design every set for a specific recipient. I've never actually seen a human's runes go bad. Only read about it in textbooks. But I think you're in good shape. When's the last time you even saw one glow?"

They were thirty-six hours on from Nysska's seizure. "Not since before the, ah, the incident."

Hix seemed satisfied at that. He tilted his head to one side. "So assuming Master Seeley deems you fit to go...*are* you going to do what Bronna asked? Or are you going to say 'fuck it' and go straight back to the human you're in love with?"

"That question represents an impressive blend of duty and personal interest."

Hix's cheeks only turned a little pink. "Sorry."

"To answer your question...I've been giving it a great deal of thought. And I think it would be best for all the humans I know to continue believing me dead. For now. There's already more than enough ill will pointed in my direction. I don't want them affected by it any more than they have to be."

Hix had been standing next to the door, leaned against the wall with his arms folded. Now he came over and sat in the straight-backed chair next to her bed. "There is another matter to discuss. Regarding your seizure."

Nysska watched him through half-lidded eyes. "You came to the same conclusion I did, then."

"You were doing fine. Better than fine. Your progress was exceptional."

"Until I touched you."

Hix's mouth twitched. "So the question is—what does that mean?"

"Exactly. Was it coincidence? Did it happen because I was tired from your exercises?"

Quietly, he said, "Was it triggered by an emotional response?"

Nysska let that question hang in the air. She didn't have a good answer for it. Not one that satisfied her, in any case. "I don't want you to take what I'm about to say in a manner not intended..."

He cocked one eyebrow up. "All right. In what manner do you intend it?"

"How I feel hasn't changed. I hold you in high regard, Mr. Hix, and I am truly grateful for all you have done for me. You do not, however, inspire fluttering in my belly."

"Ouch."

"I'm only trying to say that if an overwhelming emotion is what caused the seizure, I don't think it came from me." She paused. "And I'm not saying you should blame yourself, either. It was not your fault."

Hix frowned, staring at the floor. "So you think it could've been because *I* was feeling a strong emotion? That the...the runes responded to someone they weren't bonded to?"

"You think that's a stupid idea?"

"No, no, it's just one I hadn't considered. But, as you know..." He waved a hand in the air, and in unison he and Nysska said, *"Uncharted waters."*

A short rap at the door led to Ruth coming in with another tray of food. Nysska pulled her legs up underneath her to sit cross-legged on the bed, and thanked Ruth as she set the tray down.

"Enjoy your meal," Ruth said perfunctorily and left as quickly as she could.

Nysska spoke around a mouthful of bread. "I scare her."

"You scare a lot of the Gemini, I would say."

"Needlessly so. Especially in my current condition." She nudged the tray closer to him. "Do you want some? I rarely finish the entire meal."

"No thank you. I'm meant to dine with Master Seeley this evening."

Hix stood and took a step toward the door but stopped and turned to face her again. It took him a while to get his words out. Nysska calmly ate and waited. "I...have heard...as well as read...*ahem*. Please correct me if I've been given bad information. I have heard that romantic, uh, coupling among sethyds lacks the traditional structure present in human society."

Nysska took a sip of water and swallowed the bite of bread. "Have you, now?"

Hix wouldn't look at her. An outside observer might have thought he found the bedspread fascinating. "I have heard that marriage, as we know it, does not exist among the sethyds. And that the lover—or lovers—a sethyd woman takes is entirely a matter of her choice."

"Mm-hmm?"

"And that it is not entirely unheard-of for a sethyd woman to have multiple lovers. If she so chooses."

Nysska let out a long, slow breath. "Now you can correct *me* if I have received a faulty impression of *you*."

Brown eyes met yellow. "Yes?"

"You're not the kind of human who wants to share. Are you? Anyone you care for enough to take to bed, you want that someone all to yourself. Isn't that true?"

Hix murmured something. So quiet that not even her ears could pick it out.

"What was that?"

He put more force into it. "My name is Rowan. Rowan Hix."

Slowly, carefully, Nysska unfolded her legs and moved past the tray of food, feet touching the cold wooden floor. She stood and approached him, towering over him by a full head, not even counting her horns. Stood and watched him tremble. "It's a pleasure to meet you, Rowan Hix."

It took him several seconds to realize she was holding her hand out, and when he did it made him take a step backward. "Are you—are you sure?"

Nysska didn't move. Neither did her hand, held out in the universal greeting.

Hix put his hand in hers, and she squeezed and shook it politely.

She said, "See? No seizure."

The corners of his mouth turned down for a heartbeat. "But no fluttering in the belly, either."

"I'm afraid not."

Hix took his hand back and this time made it all the way to the door before he paused. "Maybe meeting you hasn't affected my life in quite the way I'd hoped it would. But it has affected my life in a way I wouldn't give up."

Nysska dipped her head and smiled. "Good night, Rowan Hix."

"Good night." The door latched softly behind him as he left.

Five more days passed, faster than Nysska expected them to. Hix continued working with her, bolstering her coordination and speed, and to her immense relief any tension that might have lingered between them didn't interfere.

By the afternoon of the fifth day Nysska's runes had stopped glowing altogether, and she hadn't felt the warring-ants vibration under her skin in...she wasn't sure how long.

Nysska and Hix stood in a small clearing at the edge of the village, where Hix had laid out a series of rocks and asked her to leap around them in a complex pattern. Once she'd done it flawlessly three times, he grinned and signaled to someone in the village proper. A young man came out to them, holding a plain longsword in one hand and—Nysska's eyebrows raised—a sethyd khopesh in the other. The young man handed both swords to Hix and retreated without ever looking directly at Nysska.

"Where and *how* did you get that?" she asked as Hix handed her the long, sickle-like weapon.

"Oh, the Imperial College has its influences. I thought we might do a little sparring."

Nysska hefted the khopesh in her right hand. She figured it at ninety-two centims from the pommel disk to the curved tip. Hix's face lit up as she twirled it and went through the first four movements of her favorite sword form.

"So that *is* a sethyd weapon! And look at you go with it! I didn't know you were a sword master."

"Believe me, I'm not," she said, admiring the bronze blade. "No more than any other sethyd schoolchild. And did I hear you say you wanted to *spar*? Since when did apprentice runemasters have time to practice swordsmanship?"

"We don't," he shot back with a laugh. "I really just wanted to see a sethyd sword in action. What do you call it?"

"The proper name is *khopesh*. Don't ask me where that came from, I have no idea. More commonly it's known as a *senarmiga glavo*. A 'dis-arming sword.'"

"Care to demonstrate?"

Nysska shrugged. "Try to cut me."

Hix drew the longsword back and swung at her, the blade arcing around in a wide slashing cut, but at no more than half-speed. Nysska's khopesh darted out and hooked around the longsword, turning the blades flat-to-flat, and with a pop of her wrist she took Hix's weapon out of his hand and slammed it into the ground at his feet.

Hix danced backward, laughing harder now. "That was *amazing*! What else can you do with it?"

She used the khopesh to gesture at the longsword. "Try to stab me now."

Hix came closer and retrieved the sword, and as he was straightening back up he shoved the point at her mid-section—again at no faster than half-speed. Nysska turned, the longsword's blade ringing as it slid along the khopesh's arc several centims from her face, and with a move so beaten into her muscles that she gave it no thought at all she sprang the longsword's pommel from Hix's hand, caught it with her free hand and slid behind him, his own blade pressed lightly against his larynx.

"Stop laughing," she said, close to giggling herself. "You'll cut your own throat."

"If you two are done flirting," Bronna Smith said from the edge of the clearing. Hix all but jumped a meter away from Nysska, coming to attention as he landed.

"We weren't flirting. Nysska was just showing me some sethyd combat techniques."

Bronna waved a dismissive hand. "I don't care. Nysska, you're leaving tomorrow. I've got a ferryman in place at the Chang River crossing. That's ten kliks through the woods due west of here. Be there at high noon tomorrow and he'll take you across."

Nysska considered that, frowning. "Do you have a horse for me?"

"No. We can't spare one, and as far as I'm concerned, a horse would only get you noticed faster. You *can't get caught*. Do you understand? If anyone finds out where you're going or why, our deal's off."

Her lips tight, Nysska said, "I'll leave at first light, then."

"Good. Things're happening in the Crags, and we can't afford to wait. Besides, according to Mr. Hix here, you're all healed up."

Nysska nodded slowly. "I do feel recovered. More or less."

"Great." Bronna Smith cast a glance at Hix. "Take tonight to say your goodbyes, or whatever you're going to do."

Nysska spent the evening altering a set of traveling clothes the Gemini had given her so that they at least sort of fit properly. She was expecting Rowan Hix to come by her cabin, but the only person she saw was Ruth, who said not a word as she came in, set down the dinner tray, and left quickly.

When she'd finished the clothing she spent an hour or so honing the razor-sharp outer curve of the khopesh.

Lying in bed that night, the lantern extinguished and only the occasional distant voice from the Gemini village reaching her ears, she thought of Cam. Her flawless, deep brown skin, the lines and curves of her legs and waist and breasts, the feel of her arms wrapped tight around her.

On the verge of sleep, the image of Cam flickered and slid to one side.

Making room for Rowan Hix.

"Perhaps in another life," she whispered before dropping into a profound sleep.

A knock at the door woke her the following morning. She heaved herself out of bed and got dressed, picked up the stocked pack Ruth had brought to her the night before, and slid the khopesh into the clever sheath she was sure some Gemini had designed, as the craftsmanship was like nothing she'd ever seen in her homeland.

Outside the cabin, Rowan Hix and Bronna Smith waited for her. No other Gemini had come to bid her farewell. That suited her just fine.

"If you leave now you'll have plenty of time to make it to the ferry," Bronna said without preamble.

Nysska loomed over the small woman like a bear staring down a raccoon. "I am grateful to you for saving my life. And I understand what you're trying to do and why. But you need to understand this: if I succeed in this mission, and then you try to go back on your word to take these fucking runes out of me, I'll crush your head like a ripe tomato."

If even a single one of those words caused Bronna Smith any distress she didn't show it. "What's the most sacred oath a sethyd can take?"

Nysska blinked. "What?"

"I don't think I stuttered. What's the most sacred, unbreakable oath a sethyd can take?"

Nysska glanced at Hix, but he hadn't expected this. She said, "We don't often take oaths. There...is a means of binding a sethyd's word to their favored Exemplar."

Smith nodded. "The most sacred oath the Gemini can take is this: *I swear on the lives of all Gemini that should I break this vow, I will be forever cast into the outer darkness.* I'll make you a deal. You bind your word to your favored Exemplar that you'll carry out this mission *and keep it secret,* and I'll swear on the lives of all Gemini that we'll safely remove your runes once you're back. Agreed?"

Nysska took a long moment. Shifted her stare from Smith to Hix and back. Finally she narrowed her eyes and said, "You first, then."

Bronna Smith nodded. She took a step back and inhaled, fully and deeply, twice. Then she rested the fingertips of both hands against her forehead. "Nysska Stonegate, I make this vow to you. Keep your mission secret, and secure us safety among your people, and we'll take out your runes when you get back. I swear on the lives of all Gemini that should I break this vow, I will be forever cast into the outer darkness."

Nysska let out a long, slow exhale. "You really meant that, didn't you?"

Smith dabbed away a tear from one eye. "This is the first time I've ever made that vow. And yeah. I fucking meant it. I know none of this is fair to you, but our lives depend on you succeeding. So this is the best I can do."

"All right. ...All right." Nysska squared her shoulders and placed a hand over her heart. "I take this oath, armed and armored by the wisdom of Atiina. I will keep the secret of my purpose, and do everything within my power to find safe harbor for you and yours among the sethyds of Slocum. My life and my word so bound."

Bronna Smith gave Nysska a short, crisp bow. "It's official, then."

Nysska turned to Hix. "And you. As truly, purely fucked up as this entire situation has been, I am glad I met you." She held out her hand for him to shake.

Hix surprised her by taking her hand in his, turning it knuckle-side up, and bringing it to his lips.

As soon as the kiss made contact Nysska screamed and the runes in her arm and chest flared like the light of a red sun. Her arm shot forward like a battering ram and her knuckles caught Rowan Hix just below the notch of his collarbones. The impact slammed him backward into the wall of the cabin with a horrible wet crunch.

Hix slid down out of the crater the impact had made in the cabin's wall. Nysska stood, frozen, staring down in horror at the red light fading inside her—and then at the wreckage that had been Rowan Hix only a heartbeat ago.

At how the top half of his ribcage had caved in.

At how the back of his skull had ruptured, leaving gray matter on the cabin's wall.

At how Bronna Smith stared at her, mouth locked tight in a white-lipped straight line.

From behind her, voices called out. The sounds of doors opening.

"I didn't—"

Smith said, "I know."

Nysska's vision blurred. She couldn't breathe. "I didn't—I didn't mean to—that wasn't, it wasn't *me*, I didn't, it just *happened*, I—"

"I *know* that. I saw. Now you need to go."

Nysska's jaw fell open. "What? I can't *leave*! I'm not in control of the runes! Hix—he—Atiina guide me, I—"

Bronna Smith rose up on her toes to put herself as close as she could get to Nysska's face. "I saw what happened. I understand. But we *can't* wait. You need to get to the Crags and secure us some allies *now*."

"But—"

"Go," Smith said, and then screamed it, "*Go!* And just—for the sake of Rowan Hix, don't fucking *touch* anybody! And don't let anybody touch you!"

As the crowd of Gemini drew closer, Nysska grabbed up her pack and sprinted away into the woods, headed west, almost blinded by tears.

12

Nysska ran and ran. The tears burned in her eyes, welling up faster than she could swipe them away with the back of one gloved fist, and beneath the forest's canopy the trunks of the trees blurred into the legs of great titans, towering above her, raining scorn down onto her heart.

Her thoughts spun and yawed in a figure-eight of desperation, self-hatred, fury, and a sadness that clawed and hooked its way into every corner and nook and shadow of her soul and dug inside her. Weakened her. *I could just keep running. Run deep into the forest, away from Bronna Smith's ferry, far into the wilderness and stay there alone. So I can never hurt anyone ever again.* That swayed and shifted into *This is the Gemini's fault, fuck them and their stupid longing for peace in the Empire, I could slaughter that whole village, no one there could stop me,* which led to *Someone's got to take these runes out of me, sooner or later someone will touch me and I'll kill them, I won't be able to help it, I've got to find a runemaster and force him to take these fucking things out of me.*

All of those funneled into a desire simply to sit down beneath one of the great trees flashing past her. Sit down and stop moving. Expend no energy on finding food, or shelter, just...maybe just go to sleep. Sleep and hope that everyone who'd ever met her would forget her name and go on with their lives as if she'd never existed.

Nysska whispered, "Rowan," and the ram of pain and guilt struck her anew, a devastating blow right below her ribs, and a sob vanished amid the pine needles.

The question appeared in the forefront of her mind for the hundredth time since she'd bolted away from Glenmarsh. From what she'd done to Hix.

What if that had been Cam?

Nysska stood on the edge of that thought and peered down into its abyssal depths even as her feet kept moving. It would be easier to concentrate on running—put every bit of her focus on the forest floor directly in her path. Make sure her shadow stretched out long and straight in front of her as the rising sun shot needles of light through the trees and into her back.

What if that had been Cam? What if I tried to hold her, and my arms snapped her spine? What if I tried to caress her and my hand pierced her heart? What if I tried to give the woman I love a tender kiss, and before I knew what was happening I was covered in her blood?

Nysska stumbled in her mind and plummeted into the abyss even as her feet maintained a quick, steady pace.

What if I had to cradle her in my lap and watch the life drain out of her?

What if she held onto some scrap of consciousness, and stared up at me with silver eyes turning to glass—eyes filled with hurt, and confusion, and the need to know why?

Nysska heard the river first. Or rather, she heard the cries of waterfowl, then saw the thinning of the trees ahead. When she came out of the tree line, only one human stood there at the ferry—little more than a floating platform with two large bronze rings mounted on either end, through which ran a thick cable strung across the river. The kind of vessel propelled by a single man with a pole. The human waved her to him, almost frantically.

"You're from Bronna Smith, right?" He looked her up and down. "She said she was sending me a demon, but I had to see it to believe it."

She didn't even blink at the word *demon*. "Do I need to give you money?"

The ferryman shook his head and pulled a tarp aside from a stack of crates. A small, narrow space had been left between them. "Just crawl in there. I don't know if I'll have any other passengers, but Bronna made it clear that your passage has to be secret."

Nysska wriggled into the space. She had to take off her pack and keep it in front of her. It would have been more comfortable to take off the khopesh as well, but she kept the leather sword belt in place. The crossing couldn't last longer than she could bear a bit of discomfort.

It's discomfort you deserve.

The thought came to her unbidden, arising from nowhere.

That's not true. You know exactly where it came from. You deserve the pain. You deserve punishment.

Nysska remained silent as the ferryman covered her hiding place with the tarp. After a few more minutes the ferryman shoved off.

The sunset that night found Nysska deep in the forest again. Before the dark settled around her, but after she'd constructed a hasty but effective lean-to, she dug through the pack Bronna Smith had given her. There had been no time for Smith to explain anything about it—

Nysska froze, her eyes sliding shut.

Because of what you did to Hix.

Somewhere in the tens of kliks she'd traveled that day she had decided to tell herself that Hix's death was not her fault. It was the Gemini's. They were the ones who fished her shattered body out of the sea. They were the ones who shoved the unwelcome metal under her skin. They were the ones who'd insisted that Hix watch over her. Nysska had asked for none of it.

She wondered how many times she'd have to repeat all of that in her head before she came close to believing it.

In the pack was a decent supply of dried meat, a few pouches of dried fruit, a small bit of what smelled like dried fish, and several loaves of extremely hard bread, each wrapped in a bit of rough white cloth. Nysska also found a map. It did not display Glenmarsh's location, but it did have all the Imperial highways and byways marked on it, with a few fairly detailed landmarks to aid her navigation.

To the northwest—a good bit farther north than west—lay the Crags, and in their center the town of Slocum. Her destination.

Nysska sat inside her lean-to and tried to ration the water in her canteen while still sipping enough to make the dried meat and bread edible. Once the first moon had risen she spread out the meager bedroll the Gemini had given her and warily approached the idea of sleep.

The next several days took on an agonizing sort of uniformity.

Following the most likely route on Bronna Smith's map—the route that would keep her away from any towns, skirt the larger farms, and only cross Imperial roads in little-traveled places—it would take her a solid two weeks to make it to Slocum. Parts of the journey would be far easier on horseback, but ultimately she had to agree that Smith's reasoning was sound. She'd attract the least amount of attention on foot.

Each day Nysska climbed hills, slid down into ravines, navigated rock-slides, and grew hungrier and hungrier as her food rationing grew more stringent. She could have taken the time to set some traps. Wait for whatever game to come along and offer themselves up for dinner. Just the thought of a plump hare slowly rotating over a bed of red coals made her mouth water. But if Smith's dire warning was to be believed, and whatever political turmoil among her people was indeed coming to a head, Nysska couldn't spend the extra hours. She did take the time to construct a quick lean-to for shelter each night, as well as to destroy it the next morning, leaving no trace of her presence.

On the eighth day she spotted a couple of thin plumes of smoke above the trees. They looked to be at least a couple of kliks away, so she kept moving, and soon they faded out of sight behind her. Hunters? Other travelers? Imperial military encampments? She'd never know.

That night, stretched out on her bedroll, she found herself missing Flax and Jax to a degree that surprised her. The two of them, or even just one of them, would have been the perfect traveling companions for a journey like this. As good as Nysska was at traversing the woodlands unnoticed, the two blood lynxes made her look like a bumbling, clanging idiot. She wished she could hold Flax against her chest and feel the rumble of her purr.

The thought shredded and fled as Nysska's eyes popped open.

What was that?

A sound. Nothing so obvious as a snapping twig. She had heard a sliding—a sort of rasping.

The kind of sound metal made when passing across leather.

Nysska silently pulled the khopesh free of its sheath with her right hand. With her left she drew the long, slim dagger she liked to wear strapped to her thigh. Keeping the weapon on her all night made it impossible to sleep on her left side, but that was another discomfort she'd been willing to endure. Nysska slowly got her feet under her, eyes and ears straining in the darkness as she put her back to the broad tree trunk against which she'd built her lean-to.

The blood lynxes would have alerted her before the danger reached this level. Just as much as the guilt and grief over Hix's accidental death had pummeled her ever since she'd left the Gemini village, now she felt an immense wave of *loneliness*. Isolation.

Abandonment.

She almost cried out when a man's voice spoke from behind a tree ten meters away. "There's no need to get testy."

A dark shape moved out from the tree, slivers of him revealed in the light of the second moon. Human. Her nostrils twitched as she picked up the mingled scent of ground-in dirt and body odor.

The smell took her back instantly to the night she'd met Wendell Anwar, the human who had invited her to take a position in the Thaumetallicon. She had saved Anwar from a band of brigands who'd called themselves the Rock Knives. Between the stench of blood and shit that had come pouring off their bodies as she killed them, each and every one of them had smelled just like this stranger.

"Aren't you gonna say somethin'?" the man asked. He took a couple of steps toward her, holding up empty hands. "No need to be all mysterious-like. If you don't say nothin', I'm liable to get spooked."

Nysska darted around the tree, putting it between her and the stranger, and both felt and heard the impact of the arrow that thudded into the wood just where her head had been.

"Get 'er, boys!" the foul-smelling man shouted, and Nysska had time to take a single running step before humans poured out from behind the surrounding trees.

Secrecy. The mission requires secrecy.

That kept her from unleashing a battle roar on the spot. Even though it would have incapacitated half a dozen of the men directly in front of her, it would also have alerted every human in a klik's radius that a sethyd was there in the woods, fighting for her life.

"No need for all the muss and fuss," the stranger said from behind her. "Just come quietly, and your head can stay attached to your shoulders."

Nysska's khopesh swung out in a flat, brutal arc, and the razor-sharp convex edge split the nearest man's head in half horizontally, leaving only a spurting red mush from the bridge of his nose up. She had intended the wound to be as horrific as possible, but while the two men nearest the dead one yelped and flinched, the crowd advancing on her did not part.

Reversing the motion of the blade, Nysska sank the prow hook into the back of the next man's neck and yanked him to her, where her waiting dagger slid straight between his ribs and into his heart. The killing of the two men had taken just north of three seconds, and under better circumstances would have cowed her attackers into a few crucial heartbeats of indecision. Tonight, though, the darkness worked against her, as not all of the brigands—if that's what they were—had even seen what she'd done.

As the half-decapitated body fell, Nysska shoved the heart-stabbed man into the one straight to her left, knocking him off-balance, then leaped through the gap and ran.

Something whirred out of the darkness and wrapped tight around her legs. She almost lost her grip on her weapons as she slammed chin-first into the ground, but not quite, and she used the dagger to slice through the leather-and-bronze tangler that had brought her down. The humans rushed in, a barrage of grunts and shouts and stench, and the swords and axes that swung for her out of the darkness would have taken off chunks of her flesh if she hadn't rolled over backward, sprung to her feet, and resumed her sprint—

She ran, but her fall to the earth, however momentary, had given the brigands enough time to surround her. Something cracked against the back of her skull with enough force to send her sprawling again.

A voice cried, "Now!" and a heavy net dropped on top of her.

The ropes snarled up the khopesh and wrenched it out of her grip, and she tried to stand, but more and more of the men came scrambling out of the dark and pinned the edges of the net to the ground, forcing her prone. They were silhouettes in the darkness beneath the trees, man-shaped holes in the night, more and more of them bearing down on her, crushing her. Splayed out flat, barely able to move at all, Nysska drew a great breath for a battle roar, consequences be damned—

When one of the silhouettes yelped and dropped to the ground with a thud.

The first man who'd spoken barked, "What the fuck was that?"

A terrible, ragged sound came from the outer edge of the crowd, and another man tried to scream but got cut short.

Something else had arrived seconds after the brigands. She watched the humans dissolve into panic at the mysterious new presence.

One man trod on her back as he tried to get to safety, but something Nysska couldn't see intercepted him just as he passed beyond her field of vision. A spray of hot blood fell across her face.

Nysska twisted under the net's weight, wriggling over onto her back.

The men screamed then, screamed in earnest, the kind of terror-filled sound that Nysska had always thought of as humans' natural alarm system. These were not battle cries, nor even threats, but the sound that clawed its way out of human throats when they faced bloody, horrible death.

One by one the screams cut off.

Is this what Wendell Anwar felt like? When I killed the Rock Knives there on the dock, out of his sight, and he could only listen? Her heart thundered against her breastbone. *Was he this terrified?*

At last the forest fell silent. Above her head, heavy footfalls crushed the dead leaves and dry grass, and Nysska tried to crank her neck to see who or what was making them, but her horns had tangled in the net and prevented her.

In one motion the net lifted off of her, as easily as a house servant stripped the sheet off a bed, and Nysska bounded up to her feet. The khopesh still lay there, knotted into the tangled ropes, but she'd kept hold of her dagger and held it at the ready, poised to tear into whatever fearsome being had just slaughtered at least two dozen men.

The light of the third moon came in at a new angle as it rose, revealing a massive shape covered in black fur, standing upright on two legs. A pair of luminous silver eyes gleamed from the elongated skull of a huge timber wolf.

"Are you hurt?"

The wolf-man said the words in the Tongue of Truth—the native language of the sethyds, which Princess Aschling of Borealis had called *Esperanto*—just as a slender girl with brown skin, curly black hair, and brown eyes stepped out from behind him.

Nysska gasped. She said, "Kagan?" and then *"Singer?"* and sheathed her dagger, about to fling herself around the giant wolf-man's neck—but stopped in mid-stride. The image of Hix's shattered body splayed across her mind in gory, vivid detail. The delight in Nysska's voice cracked and died as she stifled a sob, and she staggered back, away from them, until her shoulders thumped against a tree trunk.

"We better check her," Singer said, her Esperanto more confident than Kagan's. "She acts like maybe she take a blow to the head."

13

"irst things first," Nysska said, trying her best to stare through the darkness, "we'd better get away from here. There's no telling how many more of these assholes are creeping around, waiting to catch us off-guard."

"No, I think this is all of them," Singer said. She nudged one with the toe of her boot. "Their camp—their *secret* camp, I think is what idea is supposed to be—it is right over that hill."

Nysska blinked. "So I just stumbled into a—a nest?"

"Kick anthill," Kagan rumbled.

"Kick *an* anthill," Singer said. "Not just 'anthill.' An anthill. Remember?"

Kagan growled—

And Nysska's stomach growled in sympathy. She hoped it hadn't been loud enough for Kagan or Singer to hear it, but then remembered they were both God-Touched. Of course they'd heard. "Is there, by chance, food in this secret camp?"

"Don't know." Singer shrugged. "Worth looking."

Kagan pointed. "That way."

The three of them left the mangled bodies of the brigands behind as soon as Nysska had recovered her khopesh. She followed Kagan over a gentle rise, with Singer bringing up the rear, and together they soon saw the entrance to a cave concealed by an interwoven screen of leafy branches. It reminded Nysska a little of the camouflage that had hidden the entrance to the box canyon at Altamar. The memory put her on edge.

Inside the cave, which opened up into a spacious, smooth-floored cavern, they found dozens of bedrolls, a number of places where cook-fires had been built, used, and extinguished, and a stack of barrels which contained, to Nysska's delight, fresh drinking water. Kagan sniffed a couple of times, crossed the cavern floor, and pulled a tarp away from a series of low crates filled with vegetables, dried meat, and a brown, seedy variety of the trail-hardened bread the Gemini had sent with her.

"So we really cleared them all out," Nysska said, turning in a circle as she took the place in. "I was afraid they'd been tracking me somehow. Which, I don't mind saying, would have upset me a lot more than tripping and falling into their laps." She might have gone on, but Singer moved close to her, and Nysska took a hurried step to one side to avoid contact.

Singer shot a look at Kagan, and both of the God-Touched squared up on Nysska.

"You talk," Kagan said to Singer.

Singer sighed. "He wants me to talk because I learn Esperanto better than he does, but believe me, Nysska, both of us have questions—" She made a theatrical gesture over her head. "Up to our scalps! The first one I say is, 'Where the fuck do you go?' But not until you tell us why you are acting like..." Singer had to stop and think. "Nervous...squirrel."

Nysska folded her arms across her chest, realized how defensive that made her look, and dropped them to her sides. "I can't."

Kagan's silver eyes glittered. "Why not?"

Nysska sighed. "Where you two come from—Borealis. Do you have oaths?"

Kagan's expression didn't change, or at least Nysska didn't think it changed. She found it difficult to read the mood of a gigantic half-human half-wolf. On the other hand, Nysska had never seen Singer try to hide her emotions in any way. As if Nysska had just asked her if she knew where her own nose was, Singer said, "Of *course* we do. What kind of a question is that?"

"I've been given...no. More like entrusted. Wait, no, that's not right either. I have been *charged* with a mission. And I took an oath that I would keep it secret." She thought about how she'd almost embraced them both when they'd rescued her. "Part of that oath is that I can't touch anyone. Or let anyone touch me."

Now it was Singer's turn for her face to go unreadable. Her lips pursed a little and scrunched to one side as she stared at Nysska.

Kagan blew out a heavy breath. "Fine. You swear oath. We do not touch you."

Singer glanced up at him in visible surprise, but her voice stayed even. "We don't?"

Kagan shook his head as he reached one long, black-furred arm into a crate and pulled out a slab of salt-cured ham the size of Nysska's forearm. "We owe Nysska and her friends our lives. Remember?"

Singer's mouth stayed scrunched for a moment before smoothing out. She shrugged again. "Yes. All right, fine."

Nysska had been waiting for much worse. "That's it?"

Kagan tossed the entire slab of ham into his elongated, toothy mouth, chewed a couple of times and swallowed. He shrugged. "That is it."

"Which brings us to the other question," Singer said.

Nysska couldn't help smiling a little. "And what question was that, again?"

Singer raised her voice a notch, as if repeating something to a dim child. *"Where in fuck do you go for three months?"*

Over the course of the next twenty minutes, in between bites of food, Nysska gave Kagan and Singer a halting, heavily edited version of the truth that, even to her own ears, sounded like bearshit. When she finished, Singer said, "So...some people rescue you. But you are almost dead. And they nurse you back to health. But now you have to do something for them. And you cannot tell us who they are or what you do for them, plus you cannot have any touch of any other person?"

Nysska spread her hands. "I know. I *know*. It's ridiculous. And I owe you both an explanation, but I can't give you one. In fact...especially, *especially* since you saved my life, I have no right to ask anything of you, but—"

"Ask," Kagan said. He didn't sound upset. He didn't sound any particular way that Nysska could tell.

"All right. Thank you. First—how is everyone else? How is Cam?"

Kagan looked over at Singer as he chewed another bite. "Yes, yes," she said, "Leave it to me." She counted on the fingers of one hand. "Everyone in the Ninth is fine. General Cullen is fine. Morrin James takes her dog and goes back to her..." She groped for the word. "Her thaumaturgy... smell...house, so I think they are fine too." She paused. "I *say* they are all fine. They are fine in body." She thumped her chest over her heart. "How do they feel? Not good. Cam goes out on a boat every day the first week, hangs over the edge, shines eyes down into the water."

"Looking for my corpse," Nysska murmured.

"General Cullen gets word from—one in charge of Thaumetallicon. What is his name? Brinn?"

Kagan nodded. "Overmaster Brinn."

Singer went on. "They believe you are dead, so Brinn assigns a new Enforcer for the Ninth, and they leave Cliffside and go do things Crucibles do."

Nysska exhaled. "All right. All right. What about the two of you, and Princess Aschling?"

Singer gave Nysska a wide, sardonic grin that showed off her fangs. "Have to check on the important people first, eh? Get to the rest of us later?"

Nysska's eyes grew very round, and she spluttered, "*No*, that's not—I wasn't trying—I didn't mean—" before she realized Singer was teasing her. Kagan shook his head and growled deep in his chest.

"Relax," Singer said. "I just fuck with you. The look on your face! The three of us are fine. Asch stays at Cliffside—General Cullen turns a barn there into place where she builds things. She barely ever comes out since you fall off the cliff."

In an unmistakably weary tone, Kagan said, "Singer, *please*."

With an impish gleam in her eyes Singer said, "I do all the heavy lifting here. Why don't you practice and tell Nysska how we found her?"

"Wait," Nysska said. "I *do* want to know that, but first—Singer, it just hit me! Your eyes are *brown*! How? How do you have brown eyes?"

Singer's hand flew to her face. "Oh! Right! Shit, I forget I wear them." She leaned closer, eyes wide, letting Nysska get a good look. "Nice, yes? Aschling tells General Cullen to bring her glass-maker. 'Find me best glass-maker.' So little old woman comes to Cliffside, Aschling tells her what to make, and week later she gives me these. Aschling calls them 'disguise lenses.' Little old woman thinks Aschling is not proper in her brain." Singer chuckled. "Woman almost pisses herself, she is so scared when she sees me. We never even let her see Kagan."

Nysska had been frowning, listening, trying to understand. "You've got *glass* in your eyes?"

"Very very *very* thin glass, yes," Singer said. "Curved. Like my eyeballs. Takes some time before you do not notice them so much. Hurts at first. But now I go out in public and no one screams and faints!"

"Lucky you," Kagan said, in such a dry fashion that Nysska almost laughed. Kagan had spoken around another mouthful of food, which he finished chewing and swallowed. "No glass on my eyes lets me move among humans. General Cullen does not want me to be like caged animal. He owns land farther north. He says he goes there to hunt. He asks if I want to go there. Go where no one bothers me."

"See?" Singer said, and nudged Kagan with her elbow. "You *can* tell a story."

Kagan grumbled and reached out one enormous, black-furred, claw-tipped hand and enveloped Singer's entire head, in the most decisive *be quiet* gesture Nysska had ever seen. In fact it was almost identical to a gesture she'd seen Percy use on the blood lynxes when one of them had been acting particularly obnoxious.

Singer laughed and batted Kagan's hand away. As if Singer had not spoken, Kagan continued. "I roam General's hunting grounds. They are good. But soon I get restless. I decide to go farther. I think about how no one ever finds your body. So I creep along shore near Cliffside. I think I find a trail. And one day Singer gets bored and comes to visit me." He glanced over at the girl. "Singer gets bored a lot."

"I am not listening to you," Singer said, gnawing on a piece of bread.

"I tell her that maybe I imagine things. Maybe I think I get trace of you because I *want* to. Want you to be alive. But I show her. And Singer says she smells same thing. So together we start tracking. Except by then you are moving. We follow. We catch up to you. Men with foul odor have you in big net."

Nysska had been twining a lock of her hair around a finger as she listened to Kagan, and realized she was in danger of pulling it out. "And that brings us to right now? I—I truly cannot tell you how grateful I am. I'd be dead if not for you two." Singer shrugged—her favorite gesture—and Kagan nodded his great, shaggy head sagely. Nysska continued. "But...this is really difficult for me to ask of you, but when you go back to General Cullen's property, you can't tell anyone that you saw me. I wasn't supposed to talk to anyone about what I was doing. So I need you to maintain my secret."

Singer frowned. "Go back?"

Ah. Too fast. "Now that you have found me," she said, a little slower and with careful enunciation, "you cannot tell anyone that I'm alive. Or even that you have seen me. What I am doing has to stay a secret until I am done with it. So when you go back, you must not tell anyone that you saw me, or that you know I am alive."

Singer laughed and mimicked Nysska, speaking painfully slowly. *"You...must...not...tell...anyone..."*

Kagan nudged Singer, but spoke to Nysska. "We understand you," he said. *"You* misunderstand *us.* We are coming with you."

Singer nodded. "Right."

Nysska stared at the two of them for longer than she should have. "No, I think we still have a gap in our communication here."

Singer leaned forward. "There is no gap. Do we want to know what you are doing? How you survived? *Tahk.* Yes. But we are also both very much—" She looked at Kagan. "What is the word?"

"Bored," Kagan said without hesitation. "I just say that in last two minutes."

Singer nodded emphatically. "Bored. Yes. We go out of our heads. I am bodyguard to Princess Aschling. How do I guard her when she sits all day in workshop, in a place owned by a giant military man? And Kagan—he has to live like an animal, out in the wilderness. He is *not* an animal." She peered up at him. "Are you an animal?"

Kagan growled. "In my home...I am a leader. Like General Cullen. Thousands of soldiers do as I say." He ran his long black tongue out and licked the tip of his nose. "No. I am no animal."

"I'm—I'm going to—" Nysska fought herself over how much she could say. "I'm going to the Crags. To the sethyds' new home. It's even more important for the sethyds not to see you than it is for the humans not to see you." When neither Kagan nor Singer responded, she said, "You will have to stay hidden, Kagan. The same way you are on the General's hunting property. No one will be able to know you are there."

Kagan picked a shred of food out from between two sharp teeth with the claw on his smallest finger. "I understand that."

"Well, then—how would you be able to help me?"

Kagan scoffed, and Singer said, "How do we help you tonight?" She made a show of looking around. "Do any humans know we are here? And do you go on breathing because of us?"

"We can't just slaughter every group of humans we encounter, though!"

Kagan cocked his head to one side, his ears moving independently of each other. "You say mission is secret. You avoid other people. Fight tonight is mistake?"

Nysska shrugged with her eyebrows. "Well, yes."

"Then we help you. Until you get to Crags." Kagan made a raspy huffing sound. "Until you get to *the* Crags." He extended his index finger and gestured around her face. "Your nose and eyes and ears—they are better than human. Yes? Yes. Singer's are better than yours. Mine are better than Singer's."

Singer said, "Gloating is not nice."

Kagan continued as if Singer hadn't spoken. "We move through...*the* wilderness. Together. Three of us. Until you reach the place. Do thing you have to do. You do the thing. After that...we take you back out of the place. Make sure you stay safe."

Singer reached out and tried to chuck Nysska on the shoulder, but Nysska recoiled from the touch, and Singer jerked her hand back. "Sorry. Sorry. I forget." The girl offered a smile. "Tonight is first night we have fun in a long while. Just accept that we help you, yes?"

A wave of fatigue swept over Nysska, and she stretched hugely. "It would be *immensely* helpful if one of you could take the first watch, then."

Singer laughed, a low, unself-conscious bit of music, and Kagan let his jaw drop open enough for his long tongue to loll out one side. He said, "Good choice."

14

Seven days later, Nysska, Kagan, and Singer stood at the top of a heavily wooded crest, gazing out and down at a wide valley below. The valley was enclosed on three sides by mountains that looked as if the spear-tips of weapons wielded by world-sized deities had erupted from the ground—towering, spike-tipped monoliths.

The floor of the valley had cracked along multiple perpendicular fault lines, and the sections had settled unevenly, giving the whole area a bizarre, squared-off appearance. As if the child of one of those world-sized deities had spilled their toy blocks all over the ground, each block easily the size of a village all on its own.

That naturally occurring variation in elevation had led to the city of Slocum getting divided into distinct neighborhoods and districts, with adjacent ones connected by long, road-width steps carved into the blocks' exposed sides. Here and there, if two districts rose up on either side of a third in the middle, the residents of the higher ones had strung suspension bridges between them.

Low stone buildings covered most of the great stone blocks—a hodgepodge of architecture, most of traditional human design, others a hurried, less sophisticated version of recognizable sethyd structures.

"So that is Slocum," Singer said quietly. They were still about a klik from the town, but Nysska wasn't sure how heavily patrolled its perimeter might be, so they stayed amid the shadows cast by the trees and kept their voices low. "It is like a city sent out away from other cities as punishment for something."

Nysska stared, trying to pick out bits of activity, but they were too far away to see individuals. "From what I'm told, it started as a fur-trading outpost, then someone discovered a big silver deposit and the miners moved in. But when the silver ran out, the humans abandoned it, more or less. I once heard Cam call it a 'ghost town.'"

"No ghosts now," Kagan said, also staring. He lifted his head. "Living beings. Like you, Nysska. A lot of them."

Singer said, "Don't tell me you can hear them from this distance?"

Kagan grunted. "No. Smell."

Nysska said, "You wouldn't hear them. Going about our days, sethyds don't actually talk to each other. Unless they absolutely have to."

Frowning, Singer asked, "Why?"

Nysska made a noncommittal sound. "We prefer silence in public. Loud noises, especially loud voices, are considered rude." She paused. "Unless we're drunk. Then all bets are off."

"Hmph," Singer said. "Sounds boring. Sorry."

Kagan said, "Silent city," as if musing about it. "Not like home."

Nysska straightened her jacket. "All right, this is where we part ways. It's going to be dangerous enough for me to go down there. I don't want to see the two of you strung up just for helping me."

Singer pointed at the ground beneath her feet. "We come here, every morning at sunrise, and every night at sunset. We wait for you. When you are finished, you come here, and we all leave together. Yes?"

"Yes. And thank you again."

Kagan swung his shaggy head around until his muzzle almost touched Nysska's face. "You be careful," he said. "We do not want to go into sethyd town and make trouble. But we do it if you need us to."

Nysska gave him a tiny smile. "I'd hug you both if I could."

She left them there, silent, watching her, as she descended into the valley.

It had been a solid three years since Nysska had set foot in the Crags. Three years since the Mountain Bulls had run her and her mother Simana out, sentencing them to exile—which meant, considering how most humans felt about the sethyds, a solitary existence in the middle of nowhere. Nysska had spent the first two of those years taking care of Simana, who had been damaged cruelly by the *Krizo*. Then, shortly after

Nysska's chance encounter with Wendell Anwar, she'd gone straight into the Thaumetallicon.

While Nysska's brother, Gerrit, had taken Simana hostage, and demanded that Nysska report her Crucible's activities to him upon pain of their mother's death.

Now, creeping down a wooded slope and keeping away from the trails and roads, Nysska felt as if she were invading enemy territory. She had a destination in mind, but skirting all the more heavily populated areas meant it would take her all day if she wanted to remain undetected. She passed by one heavily terraced farm, where a crop of soybeans would grow in stair-stepped rows hacked out of the side of the mountain once the weather warmed in the spring. Then by a big, sturdy water wheel, turning thanks to the force of a narrow falls. A few of the goats and sheep in a field raised their heads and blinked in her direction, but none of the farmers saw her. Or at least, if any of them did, they raised no alarm.

As the sun threatened to dip below the horizon Nysska came to a stop in a copse of trees across from the entrance to the Canyon of the Word.

She had long lost track of the proper Devotion Days, but judging by the lack of foot traffic, she didn't think this was one of them. Darting from one clump of bushes to another, she crossed one of Slocum's hard-packed dirt roads and slipped through the entrance. Her breath came close to catching in her throat.

Her job as a priest-singer had been to perform all of the Devotion Songs dedicated to Atiina, the Exemplar of Wisdom, on the three days leading up to a Devotion Day, at regular intervals on the Day itself, and then for the three days afterward. Devotion took place every nineteen days, so Nysska and the other priest-singers spent the time between prac-ticing and, occasionally, learning new songs.

Nothing like the Canyon of the Word had existed back in Patri-nomonto.

Each Exemplar had their House of Devotion, and some care was taken to maximize and refine the acoustics inside so that the Devotion Songs sounded their best and reached as many ears as clearly as possible. But structures of stone could only go so far, Nysska had learned.

The Canyon of the Word was already there in Slocum when the sethyd refugees arrived. Waiting for them. A massive, miraculous, natural amphitheater, a chasm defined by ancient earthquakes and the flow of water over...how many tens of millions of years? Nysska had no idea. The humans hadn't even been using it, but as soon as the priest-singers saw it

—the priest-singers from every Exemplar—they recognized the magnitude of the gift they'd been given.

A series of caves ran around the Canyon's top edge, making it even more perfect. *As if by design*, Nysska had heard a few sethyds say. Those caves, following a bit of shaping and refining, quickly became the quarters of the senior priest-singers. Now, standing at the Canyon's entrance, Nysska lifted her eyes to the northwest quadrant of the lip and counted, three from the left. *There.* That tiny entrance, innocuous and plain. That had been her home. Her home and Simana's, as well...for seven months. Until Simana's political stance and refusal to be silent got them exiled.

The Canyon of the Word allowed a single priest-singer to deliver the Devotion Songs more perfectly than ever before, amplifying one voice so that it rang like a choir of hundreds. The Exemplars took turns, so to speak, with each Devotion Day seeing the senior priest-singer of one Exemplar taking the favored spot. Nysska had never been the senior priest-singer. She'd always hoped to be. Once she saw the Canyon of the Word, and heard what it could do, she even dreamed of it.

Until her brother Gerrit and the rest of the Mountain Bulls decided that the words of an old, crippled woman were too dangerous to be allowed to stay in the Crags.

Nysska left the Canyon and stole up a narrow, steep trail to a neighborhood known as Granite Village. She didn't know why it was called that. It was little more than a meadow, filled with sawgrass in the places where small, modest houses had not been built. Dusk had come fully upon Slocum, and as she watched, one lantern after another lit from inside the homes. Nysska padded around the edges of the village until one particular house came into view. Hoping with all her might that its occupants had not changed while she'd been gone, Nysska crossed to the back door, found it unlocked, and slipped inside.

She stood in the kitchen. Directly in front of her, on the far side of a small table—a plate of food before her, a carving knife in one hand, and a look of perfect shock on her face—sat a young sethyd woman.

Her face was a little fuller than Nysska's, her horns smooth and curved, and a handful of ruby-red streaks lit up her shoulder-length, straight black hair. Her candleflame-yellow eyes had opened painfully wide.

"Nysska," the woman whispered. She shot a quick, worried glance at the front door.

"No one saw me come here," Nysska said very quietly, and moved closer to the table. "Hello, Tarca. You're looking well." Tarca slowly pushed her chair back and stood, and Nysska suppressed a gasp. "You're looking *very* well."

Tarca's swollen belly meant that she was at least halfway through her pregnancy. Remembering Tarca's fearful look at the door, Nysska said, "Where is Jedaiah?"

Tarca's lovely face clouded, which Nysska had been expecting, and her tone turned sharp. "Hunting. He won't be back for days. For which you should be grateful."

Nysska sighed. "I need to talk to you. May I sit?" Tarca's expression grew darker, but she waved a hand at one of the other chairs around the table. Nysska sank into it. "He's still upset with me?"

Tarca rolled her eyes. "They talk about you." She sat back down, picked up a fork, and began carving what appeared to be half a roast chicken. "I'm sorry, my appetite is insane these days." She ate a bite, just as delicately as Nysska remembered. "They say you've sold yourself to the humans, that you're their puppet. Every time Jedaiah hears your name it rips the wound open again." She paused to look Nysska up and down. "You're the *same*. You haven't changed a bit!"

Nysska groaned softly. "If only that were true."

Tarca appeared to grow impatient with the fork and carving knife in her hands, and simply picked the half-chicken up and tore off a chunk with her teeth. "What are you doing here?" she asked around the food. "You and Simana were *banished*. Exiled. That's..." Her eyes darted at the front door again. "It's not the kind of sentence you can serve and then come back from. They threw you out *permanently*."

As Nysska tried to put together the proper words in the proper order, Tarca pulled off a chunk of breast meat and handed it to her.

"Here. I can only take you eyeballing my meal for so long."

Nysska accepted the chicken with her best gracious grin. "You were always good to me." She took a bite, and the taste—the blend of spices she'd never encountered among the humans—unleashed a flood of memories.

Nysska and Tarca, the best of friends, attending their first singing lessons.

Playing hide-and-seek with Tarca's brother Jedaiah...and Gerrit. And Tylar and Randolf.

The kiss Jedaiah had stolen from Nysska, just as Tarca walked in on them.

Nysska's first Devotion with Tarca together, voices praising the wisdom of Atiina in unison.

The night Jedaiah had told Nysska he loved her. The look of devastation on his face when she told him she didn't feel the same way.

Tarca and Nysska arguing, a fight that escalated to screaming and nearly to blows, the same night the *Krizo* happened...rushing to evacuate their families...panting, lungs burning, trying to outrun the glowing, scalding clouds.

Tarca helping carry Simana to the boat, Nysska pulling the little cart loaded with what worldly possessions they could carry.

Tarca holding Nysska's hand as they bid Patrinomonto goodbye.

"I never meant to hurt your brother. I hope you know that. I hope *he* knows that."

Tarca made a sour face. "You were his first love, you know. His *only* love. Since we were children. He wanted to be with you forever."

In the past, Nysska might have said, *Who wants to be with just one person forever?* But that was before she'd met Cam.

"I would've made peace with him. Or tried to. Eventually."

"You avoided him once we got here!"

"My mother was sick! You of all people should know how sick! You were on the boat with us!" Nysska softened her tone. "Then we got exiled, and it didn't matter anymore."

Tarca finished her meal in silence. Nysska waited.

Finally Tarca said, "I'll ask again. What are you doing here?"

"I need to know the lay of the land. Who's in charge? Who wields the power? Is it still the Mountain Bulls?"

Tarca blew out a long, laborious breath. "How much time do you have?"

"A lot less than I'd like."

"All right. ...All right. Let me try to be concise. You and Simana got driven out, and the Mountain Bulls took over. They'd been influential up to that point, but with Simana gone, she was like the last obstacle in their path, and they started gathering followers left and right. But then..."

"Yes?" Nysska leaned forward, her elbows on the table. "Then what?"

"I...couldn't even tell you how it happened, honestly. One day the Mountain Bulls were calling shots, and the next—well, they weren't in charge anymore. Technically."

Trying not to sound impatient, Nysska said, "Who was? Who was in charge?"

"There's a new—shit, I don't know that I've said these words out loud myself before. I—Nysska, this is difficult." Tarca took a deep breath, her eyes glimmering. "There's a new Exemplar."

Nysska blinked. Sat back in her chair. "There's a what?"

"I know. Believe me, I know. There's a new Exemplar. Her name is Yshtarra."

Nysska rubbed her scowling face. "But they—they can't *do* that."

Tarca spread her hands on the tabletop. "I felt it. Everything you're feeling right now. I felt it, too."

"You can't just *create* a new Exemplar! The Exemplars are set! They've been set for—for forever!"

Tarca squinched up half her face. "Well, if you want to get semantic about it, the original Exemplars *were* created. By us. At some point. That's their whole purpose, isn't it? Us, showing ourselves what to aspire to?"

Nysska stood and paced back and forth across the cabin's wooden floor. "Yes, yes, they're role models. But the system is—is *set*. It's *locked*. How can there be a new one? What is this Yshtarra supposed to be the Exemplar *of*?"

"Please sit back down. You're making me uncomfortable."

Nysska cast a fiery glance at her. "Handing out bad news is too much for you?"

"No. But you going back and forth is making me queasy. If you're really lucky I won't vomit on you while you're here."

For a moment, the easy smile they used to share every day passed between them, and Nysska returned to her chair. "Sorry. Sorry. I know your condition presents certain challenges."

"You're still without children?"

"With Atiina's grace, I shall remain so."

"As you wish. Nysska—I'll tell you what Yshtarra exemplifies. But there's something else about her, and if the news of her mere existence caused you distress, you need to brace yourself for this."

Nysska gripped the edge of the table. "Give it to me."

"She's real."

Nysska narrowed her eyes. When Tarca didn't elaborate, she said, "What do you mean, 'she's real'?"

Tarca chose her words carefully. "Yshtarra is a real, breathing, living sethyd. She's not just an idea. Not just something represented by statues and motivating words and songs on Devotion Day. I've seen her. She's beautiful, and…her horns are golden."

Nysska's lips wanted to curl into a snarl. She had no words in the Tongue of Truth to describe this…unacceptable turn of events, but the humans had a word for it. She'd heard Raoul use it more than once when discussing something related to the Great Silver Dragon. Nysska whispered the word to herself.

"*Sacrilege.*"

"What was that?"

"Nothing. All right, now I have to know."

"Know what?"

"I have to know what this Yshtarra exemplifies."

Tarca winced. "She's the Exemplar of Conquest."

Nysska's jaw fell open. She stood again, but stopped herself from pacing, and instead dug her fingers into the chair's backrest until the wood cracked. "*Conquest?* There's a fucking Exemplar of fucking *conquest?* What are her Devotion Days like? Do her officiants encourage her followers to raid and pillage? Are they raping women and stealing children and burning down libraries?"

Tarca had brought one fist to her mouth, partially hiding her lips. "Nnnn…not yet."

Nysska spun the chair around backward and straddled it, staring over the backrest she'd almost reduced to splinters. "How? How are people following this—this thing? No, wait, forget I asked that. I'd wager every single Mountain Bull is a devotee of Yshtarra now."

"Down to the last one."

"But she's picking up more?"

"More every day, yes. Her people are already the majority."

"Fucking hell. *Fucking hell.*"

"There's, um. I'm not really doing a very good job of summing all this up. I'm sorry. There's more."

Nysska calmed her breathing. Or tried to, in any case. "Yes?"

"Well, see, I don't think Yshtarra would have gotten this popular this fast if it weren't for the plague."

Nysska's attempts at calming her breathing failed spectacularly, and she had to fight off full-blown hyperventilation. She opened her mouth, realized she was about to scream, and fought it back to a whisper. "*There's a fucking plague?*"

"Well. It's a sickness. Nobody's been able to figure out how it's spreading yet."

"And you didn't think to mention this *right from the start?*"

"I'm sorry! You've been gone, and—and there are rumors about you all over place, and—and I got flustered. I'm just a sethyd, all right? Maybe give me a little understanding here?"

Nysska drummed the fingers of both hands on the table. "What does this plague do, exactly?"

"They're calling it the 'sapping sickness.' If you get it, it makes you completely exhausted, and it's hard to keep food down, so you're left bedridden. Except Yshtarra has a treatment."

Nysska frowned. "There's a cure."

"Not a cure. A treatment. You go to her Devotion House—that's up in the Northwest Heights—every two or three days, when you feel the sickness taking hold, and she's got a treatment you drink. It fights the sickness off."

Nysska folded her arms over the top of the chair's backrest and settled her chin onto her forearm. "Well. I have to say. That is awfully fucking convenient."

Tarca's face grew a shade lighter. "What do you mean?"

"Is it not obvious? Not *blatantly* fucking obvious, Tarca? A new Exemplar shows up out of nowhere, and right after that this *sapping sickness* starts affecting people, but Yshtarra has the answer? Let me guess—she's the only source of it. The treatment, I mean."

"Well...yes..."

Nysska scoffed. "And how did she justify all this? What did she tell the people to convince them she was the one they should trust to fix their new problem?"

"She said the sickness came from settling in human lands. That one of their—their 'vermin diseases'—finally caught up with us." Tarca paused. "Are you saying she's *lying*?"

Nysska squeezed her eyes shut. Either the sapping sickness affected how well its victims' brains worked, or she had spent the last three years massively overestimating her own people. "And you heard this directly from her. From this new Exemplar."

"Well..." Tarca began. She sounded defensive. "She, uh—she doesn't actually—Yshtarra doesn't address the devotees herself." She put a hand up as if to stave off Nysska's as-yet-unspoken objection. "She's there! She's there with her officiants. But they're the ones who relay her, her, her message. Yshtarra never speaks."

Nysska wanted to groan but kept herself from it. Barely. "And who are these officiants? Are there a lot of them?"

Tarca shook her head. "No, no, only two—Nysska, you *know* them! We both do! That's why it's all right!"

"Who? Who are they?"

"It's Tylar and Randolf!"

Nysska's face drained of blood.

From outside, the sound of opening and closing doors reached them, along with several voices. Nysska said, "What's happening?"

Tarca got to her feet. "No need to be alarmed. You said no one knows you're here, yes?" She went to a shutter-covered window and beckoned. When Nysska joined her, Tarca lowered one of the slats so they could peer through. "Granite Village is still home to almost all of the junior priest-singers. They go up to Yshtarra's House together to receive their treatment."

Nysska peered out at the two dozen sethyds gathering in the center of the village—and her heart stood still inside her ribcage.

It wasn't just Tarca.

Every single sethyd woman there was heavily pregnant.

Nysska backed away from the window, mind bucking and whirling. "Do you need to join them?" she asked, with more ice in her tone than she'd intended.

Tarca dipped her head. "I went for mine last night. Won't need it again for a couple of days."

"And the—all the—" Nysska made a curved motion over her belly.

Tarca nodded. Maybe a little ruefully. "Yshtarra says we need to make as many new fighters as we can. She says it's our noble duty. This way it won't be that long until we have enough soldiers to overrun the human lands." At the look on Nysska's face, she hastened to add, "It wasn't my idea, Nysska, I hadn't planned on having children at all this year! But—Yshtarra's people—there's a lot of pressure. Too much."

Nysska had no response to that.

She waited until the brilliant second moon had set before she slipped out the back door the way she'd come and headed east.

15

Nysska didn't have to wonder if Franklun still lived in the same house, as she had with Tarca. She could simply follow her nose. Franklun Simeon had established a nation-wide reputation as the best sausage maker the sethyds had to offer, and Nysska felt a silent delight that he'd been able to keep it up in as inhospitable a location as the Crags. His house was located most of the way up a slope on Slocum's eastern edge, so as to bother the fewest people as possible with the scents involved in the sausage's preparation. Nysska had never minded the mélange of aromas growing up in Fajrosxtono. After spending two years in the wilderness, catching game and tanning hides, now it struck her like the finest perfume.

Darting from tree to tree, avoiding what little light the third moon provided, Nysska arrived at Franklun's back gate without raising any alarms. She scanned the city spreading out below her—the modest houses. The craftsman's district below that, with shops and tanneries and farriers, giving way to the central governmental district. Of course that was only one small chunk of the sprawl that made up Slocum.

With its cracked, uneven valley floor, the great blocks of earth that dipped or raised at random, the city felt to Nysska like a place designed to separate its inhabitants. To let some of the citizens loom over others. To force sethyds who'd been equals back in Patrinomonto to feel as if they mattered less than others, based purely on where they lay down to sleep at night.

She hated this place. The Canyon of the Word was not enough. Nysska wished Emperor Valco had given them someplace else to call theirs. Almost any place else.

Smoothing down her trouser fronts and straightening her jacket, Nysska crossed Franklun's backyard and knocked at the house's rear door.

"Who's there?" came Franklun's voice a few moments later. Still rumbling up from the bottom of his ribcage, but with extra gravel in it now.

Nysska glanced left and right, wishing Franklun's neighbors were situated farther away. "It's Nysska. Nysska St—Nysska Kaur."

The door wrenched open, and standing there was a sethyd boy of maybe thirteen years. He had already reached his full height, but his shoulders and chest hadn't yet filled out, and when he spoke his voice cracked. "Atiina spank my ass," he said. "It really is you!"

"Move aside," came Franklun's voice from behind the boy, and Franklun Simeon rolled himself into the house's small kitchen, operating his wheelchair as skillfully as ever. The boy did as he was told, though he didn't for a second stop staring at Nysska with wide orange eyes. Nysska quickly stepped inside.

Franklun's hair had been granite gray for as long as she'd known him, which was all her life. He'd always been one of the elders in the governing council of her hometown. Dispensing wisdom and deciding the outcomes of disputes when he wasn't making his famous sausages, all from the wheelchair he'd built himself. Now his hair had gone snow-white, his weathered, deeply lined and wrinkled violet skin had faded to a patchy lavender, and his heavy, spiraling horns had grown brittle, cracked and chipped. For all that, his brilliant yellow eyes shone with every bit of the ferocity she'd been expecting, and she allowed herself a smile as she faced him.

"Fucking hell, Nysska," Franklun said, using the distinctive human curse in Plainish before he switched to the Tongue of Truth. "What do you think you're doing here?"

Franklun didn't seem to be angry with her. Just genuinely perplexed and, to her relief, concerned. She said, "So Tarca was right? I'm not welcome in Slocum? Is that an official position, or am I simply unpopular?"

"It's hard to say these days." Franklun cut his eyes to the boy and gestured with a small movement of his head, and the boy sprang behind the chair, gripping its handles. "Let's go to the den," Franklun said. "Then make sure all the doors and windows are locked." He reached back behind him and gripped one of the boy's wrists. "Nysska was never here. No matter what we talk about tonight, this visit never happened. Do you understand?"

"Yes, Grandfather," the boy said. "Of course."

Franklun spoke to Nysska as the boy turned his chair around. "This is my youngest daughter's youngest son. Introduce yourself, lad."

The boy stopped pushing the chair and spun toward Nysska. His eyes were still huge, and for a few moments he appeared to have forgotten how to talk. "My name—everyone—is called—I'm Axel." He stuck out a hand. "My name is Axel."

Nysska backed away a step. "It's a pleasure to meet you, Axel, and I beg you not to take offense, but I cannot shake your hand."

"Oh! Oh—no, I—of course, of course not." Axel pivoted back to his grandfather and pushed the chair out of the kitchen.

"You'll have to forgive him," Franklun grunted. "You might not be very popular among the government set, Nysska, but the younger generation around here wants to make you their new Exemplar."

"Yes, speaking of that," Nysska said. "We need to talk."

Several long minutes later, after Franklun had finally told Axel to leave the room since that was the only way to keep him from staring at Nysska, Franklun tapped one knee with the knuckles of his right hand.

"Yes," he said. "I fear I can confirm everything Tarca told you."

"Are you affected? Do you—the two of you—have the sapping sickness?"

"No. Neither of us. His family's got it, though."

"They're all right," Axel piped up from just around a corner. "They've been taking the, uh, the treatment, like your friend mentioned."

Franklun stared into the flames in his fireplace. "Can't for the life of me figure out how it's spread. Makes no sense." He chewed on his lower lip. "There's no *pattern* to it." He leaned toward her. "Well. Now that we've established how Slocum has turned into a giant steaming shit cauldron, why don't you finally tell me why *you're* here?"

She sighed. "I've sworn an oath to keep this a secret. Until it needs to *not* be a secret."

The skin between Franklun's horns wrinkled up. "Are you doubting my discretion?"

"Not at all. But I've known you since I was old enough to recognize faces." She gestured toward Axel. "Your grandson, with all due respect and no offense intended, is another story."

"Axel." When the boy popped out from around the corner, Franklun fixed a baleful eye on him. "Boy, if you breathe a single, solitary *word* of any of this, to *anyone*, I'll break both your horns off with a hammer." Axel stammered, and Franklun said, "*Look at me*, boy. Do you think I'm telling the truth?"

Nysska thought for a moment that he might salute his grandfather. Instead he put a hand over his heart. "I swear to you by my mother's life and the wisdom of Atiina, I won't say a word."

Franklun huffed. "Dramatic." To Nysska, he said, "Does that satisfy you?"

Nysska hesitated...but decided she could use every ally available. "Yes."

"All right. Axel, you can stay, but quit staring at her."

Axel sat back down and kept his eyes on his feet. Franklun turned all his attention back to Nysska. "All right. Out with it."

Nysska had practiced this conversation in her head several hundred times, and as soon as she opened her mouth all the carefully ordered words and neatly arranged thoughts left her like seeds blown from a dandelion.

"You—um. You know about the Gemini. The, ah, the ones that we'd been calling 'skin-shifters.'"

Franklun's eyes narrowed at her. "If you're going to be this halting the whole way through, we'll be here all night."

Nysska sighed. "All right. As Tarca said earlier, I'll try to be concise. The Gemini want the Emperor dead, and they wouldn't lose any sleep if the whole Empire crumbled, yes?"

"That's what I've heard, anyway."

"Well, it's not entirely true. Some of them just want to be left in peace."

"We're talking about the same people that the Church of the Great Silver Dragon conspired with to slaughter an entire settlement of sethyds, are we not?"

"We are. But not all of them were involved in that, and not all of them would have been if given the chance."

Trying her best to speak fluidly, Nysska told Franklun about her plummet from the balcony at Cliffside, her awakening in the Gemini village, how they nursed her back to health, and how they enlisted her to come to Slocum to campaign on their behalf in an attempt to secure allies.

Franklun's expression had grown more and more incredulous the longer Nysska spoke. When she stopped, he said, "All right, allow *me* to sum up. These people who—correct me if I'm wrong here—were all in some sort of bizarre *sleep* until five years ago, and who can change their faces to look like practically anyone—people who, I'm sorry, may as well have been *designed* for deception—some of them want to be good little citizens of the Empire, and they want to cozy up to *us* for protection?"

Nysska sat back in her seat. Lifted a hand, let it drop in her lap. "I know. Franklun, I know how this sounds. But for what it's worth, I believe them. Their leader, a woman named Bronna Smith—I really do think she means what she says. There aren't many of them. It wouldn't be like when we washed up on Imperial shores by the hundreds of thousands."

"How many is not many?"

"Maybe seventy-five. Total."

"So they want to...what? Come and live here in Slocum?"

"Potentially? Yes? I think so."

"Why come to us? Why not petition the Emperor directly?"

"Come on. You know the answer to that. Valco had most of them killed. No one has more reason not to trust him."

Franklun leaned to one side, propping an elbow on an armrest and his chin on his fist. "Valco does want to stay in our good graces, from what I understand. So this Bronna Smith thinks if some sethyds go to the Emperor and tell him what great people your Gemini friends are, he'll make an exception for them."

"They just want to live in peace. Not be hunted. Maybe feel as if they've got a home somewhere."

"And you came to *me* because..."

"Because you've always had a lot of pull. People listen to you. *I* listened to you talking with my mother on quite a few occasions. I know you're no friend of the Mountain Bulls."

Franklun's face clouded over. "Never in a million years would I have considered them the lesser of two evils. But now..."

"Yshtarra?"

"I wasn't sure how much the word had spread outside of the Crags."

"It hasn't. Tarca told me."

He groaned softly. "Yshtarra has commanded every sethyd woman to bear as many children as possible."

"I saw. I...have to admit, I'm surprised word of *that* hasn't gotten out."

Franklun shook his head. "I don't think the humans realize what it means. They're accustomed to their own nine-month birth cycle." He peered at her. "I also don't think the humans don't know what a three-year-old sethyd is capable of."

Once that sank in, Nysska's voice almost rose to a shout. She strangled it into a hoarse whisper. "*Child soldiers?*"

"Her devotees consider it the highest honor. Producing fighters for her. And every other sethyd is too cowed to tell her no." Franklun wheeled his chair half a meter closer. "You haven't told me everything."

"What? What have I not told you?"

Franklun's body may have been old and worn, but the same keen intellect gleamed in his eyes that she'd seen as a tiny girl. "That's what I'm asking you. I know there's something. I can see it in every line of your face."

Knowing it would only reinforce his suspicion, she lowered her eyes and dipped her head. "I've come to deliver a message. To recruit allies. Is that not what I'm doing?"

"It is. But you haven't told me *why*."

"I have! Oh yes I have, don't look at me like that. They saved my life."

"People you have no reason to trust otherwise. People who killed your brothers and sisters. People who could be manipulating you. You are not one to be manipulated, Nysska."

She almost choked, thinking of how long and thoroughly her own brother had done exactly that.

"Look. Franklun. If anyone in the Crags can help these people, I know it's you. Don't tell me you don't still have plenty of influence."

He sat back, still gazing at her more intently than she would've liked. "I am still a part of a circle of like-minded sethyds, yes. Those who share the ideals that I shared with your mother, may her memory never fade. If you brought some of these peaceful Gemini here—and if I were to decide to believe them—then yes, I believe we could give them shelter." He paused. "But that'll never happen."

"What? ...Why not?"

"*Because of Yshtarra.* Have you not been paying attention? Yshtarra and her disciples have a hold on this valley that I don't see breaking any time soon."

Nysska fell silent for a few moments. "You know...we spend a lot of time telling ourselves we're better than the humans. Superior to them in every way."

Sounding surprised, Axel said, "Aren't we?"

She waved a hand in the air. "We're stronger than they are. Faster. In general, I would say, smarter. Yes, we are their superiors in many ways, and yet almost the entire surviving sethyd population has fallen under the thumb of *Yshtarra*." Nysska didn't bother trying to keep the contempt out of that last word.

"Be that as it may," Franklun said. "The sapping sickness sealed the deal completely, yes, but she was already gathering followers by the hundreds before the sickness broke out. She's got all the Mountain Bulls and the Spiders in her fold now. There's no resisting them. Not for the rest of us."

Nysska chewed on her lower lip. "So I need to get rid of Yshtarra."

Franklun stared at her for a few seconds before letting loose a deep belly laugh. "Why don't you snap your fingers and grow wings while you're at it? That's not the point, Nysska, listen to me. Even if you could do it, getting rid of Yshtarra *wouldn't solve the problem*."

She frowned. "Why wouldn't it?"

"Because she's not the real problem! It's all the sethyds who were *instantly* ready to follow her! You take her down and her devotees will just create another 'new Exemplar.' If you're going to get rid of her, you've got to get rid of what she represents, and that's going to mean changing the way those sethyds *think*."

"All right. ...All right. How do I do that?"

"I have no fucking idea."

Nysska turned and gazed into the fire. "Franklun...going back to something you said a minute ago."

"Yes?"

"You mentioned my mother, and said, 'may her memory never fade.' I had *assumed* she was dead. Were you aware of Gerrit abducting her?"

"Word came to me of what he'd done, yes."

"Then I saw that he was wearing her favorite horn ring. And I confronted him, accused him of killing her, and he did nothing to change my mind about it."

"Gerrit held Simana's funeral last spring. I...was there. When he lit the pyre."

Nysska's stomach had become a tiny, icy tempest. She had thought she'd be sufficiently prepared when she finally received confirmation of her mother's death. She wasn't, and the tears she hated so much burned her eyes.

"Are you all right?"

She nodded. "I'm all right enough." After a sniffle, which only irritated her further, she said, "So you're saying that if I can get the Gemini here, you'll take them in. And speak to Emperor Valco on their behalf."

"Yes. I'm also saying I'm about to get up out of this chair and dance a jig."

"I'm serious, Franklun."

He made a sound like *pfff*. "If you try to oust Yshtarra and her followers, you're going to end up dead. I don't want to see you dead. Neither do a lot of other sethyds. None of them will admit it, except maybe Axel and his little idiot friends, but you're a kind of hero among them. You're the sethyd who joined the Empire and beat them at their own game, and on *your terms*. Use *that*, Nysska. Use your reputation. Go back and make something meaningful happen as the Thaumetallicon Enforcer. Don't go pulling any stupid shit up here, because it won't end well."

Nysska stood. "Your confidence overwhelms me."

"I haven't gotten this old by being impractical."

"Thank you, Franklun. You will...probably be aware when I make something happen."

As he shook his head, Nysska went to the house's rear door and turned the latch. Franklun called out after her, "I don't want to see your pyre lit," but instead of responding she slipped outside into the darkness.

Nysska had made it about three quarters of the way back to the goat trail that would lead her up to the rendezvous point with Kagan and Singer when a number of raised voices stopped her. She ducked into the shadow of a house's chimney. The voices grew louder and closer, so Nysska scaled the stone of the chimney and took refuge on the side of the house's steeply tilted roof.

A group of sethyds came into view below her, making their way slowly along the stone street, half of them laughing and the other half engaged in at least semi-drunken conversation. That was the only circumstance, as she'd mentioned to Kagan and Singer, in which a group of her brothers and sisters might relax enough to act this boisterous: when intoxicants were involved. As far as she knew, none of the sethyds' liquid fire had made it out of the Crags and into the Empire's populace. That was for the best. As fragile as most humans were, she doubted they could handle what her people knocked back on a regular basis.

Nysska lay down on the rooftop, making sure her horns weren't protruding in obvious silhouette, and watched the group. She'd been away from Slocum for three years, yes, but truth be told, she hadn't had all that many friends even back in Patrinomonto. None as close as she'd grown to Cam and Percy and Raoul. She couldn't decide whether or not to be jealous of the friendly crowd...and couldn't help marveling at the sheer variety of them.

Not physical variety, of course. Every one of them—man, woman, or otherwise—rose to the same height, shared the same kind of physique, wore the same violet skin. The only real ways a sethyd had to differentiate themselves at a glance lay in the way they wore their hair, the shape and decoration of their horns, and their clothing. A wild array of colors and shimmers and moonlit sparkles passed beneath her. A man dressed head to toe in royal blue and purple. A woman who had threaded long gold strands through her straight black hair. A *neengagxita* who sported a shiny black leather jacket, scarlet trousers, and flashing silver chains wound around their horns.

She had no doubt that in the morning they would all exchange their attire for something more muted. Something to match their no-longer-inebriated, taciturn personalities, determined not to speak to anyone unless they had good reason to. But the variety would remain, simply expressed in less flashy fashion.

Nysska sighed to herself. Did she truly miss the company of other sethyds? Or was she imagining the possibility of shelter here, away from the Gemini and Emperor Valco and Argonium Infantry snipers?

The conversation between two of the sethyds making their way slowly along the street below her—a fellow with spiraling horns that stood straight up from his forehead, and the woman with the gold strands in her hair—increased in volume and lost its playful tone. Nysska hadn't been paying attention to what they were saying, but the woman's voice reached her with perfect clarity.

"That was fucked up, Charl."

Charl—the spiral-horned man—stuck his chin out in obvious defiance. "Maybe. But it's the fucking truth."

The rest of the group spread out around the pair, forming a ring. Nysska heard various voices offering things such as *She'll break your neck, Charl* and *He's not wrong, regardless* and *I wouldn't have said that out loud.*

Gold Threads sneered and launched a punch at Charl's nose that would have smashed rocks if it had connected. Charl grunted and slipped it, to Gold Threads' annoyance, and when he pivoted around behind her a knife had appeared in his right hand. He stepped in fast, but Gold Threads ducked and in the same motion drove an elbow straight up behind her. It slammed into his chin with a sound like a tree trunk breaking, and while Charl staggered backward Gold Threads spun and took the knife out of his hand and flung it away. Nysska held her breath as the knife buried itself point-first in a crack of the chimney she'd climbed moments before.

Gold Threads wasn't finished with Charl. Before he could regain his balance she swept one of his legs, sending him to his opposite knee, then took great handfuls of his collar and his belt and—as the rest of the crowd gasped and laughed—picked him up and held him over her head.

"You going to apologize now?" she bellowed.

"I'm sorry!" Charl squirmed in mid-air. "Put me down!"

Slowly, carefully, Gold Threads placed Charl back on his feet and turned him to face her. "A knife? Really?"

Charl shrugged. "It was dull."

Gold Threads grinned and slapped him on the chest before pointing a finger at his nose. "You can be a real asshole sometimes, you know that?"

Charl grinned back. "You love me anyway."

"I *tolerate* you."

The group came back together amid much teasing at Charl's expense, which he laughed off, and they continued on their way along the stone street. Nysska waited till they were gone before dropping back to the ground again and heading between the houses for the goat trail.

Two hours later, as the third moon had begun to set, Nysska moved silently under the trees and strained to see either of her friends. She opened her mouth and drew breath to call out, and from right behind her Kagan whispered, "Do not raise your voice."

Nysska spun, moving back out of his reach thanks to the habit she'd cultivated and hated at the same time. Kagan pointed to a cluster of maple trees and led the way. Within the cluster Singer waited. Pitching her voice low, Singer said, "Is your work done?"

"Not yet. I need to find out a lot more about this..." She trailed off, wondering how to explain the appearance of a new Exemplar to two people who knew nothing about sethyd culture and didn't have time to learn. "This sethyd called Yshtarra. She stays in a Devotion House in the Northwest Heights, and probably has a huge security force around her at all times."

"So how do you do this?" Kagan rumbled. "Sneak in? Like you sneak into place with..." He closed his eyes, and after a moment said, "Archives?"

"Partially, yes. But all the guards she'll have around her—dangerous soldiers, much more dangerous than I am—I can't get past all of them. Which is why I need your help. Both of you."

Singer's lips peeled back, revealing the fearsome set of fangs she ordinarily kept hidden. Kagan's tongue lolled out, and his breathing grew faster. "Yes," he said. "Three of us break through soldiers."

Nysska put her hands up and shook her head. "No, no, no. There are too many of them. Even for the three of us. I'm not asking you to charge the place with me. The trouble is...what I *am* asking you to do will be almost as dangerous."

Singer tilted her head to one side. "And what is that?"

"I need you to create a distraction. A big one. I'm sure even if a volcano erupted in the middle of Slocum, Yshtarra still wouldn't be left completely alone, but if you can pull *most* of the soldiers away, I'm pretty sure I can do the rest." She paused, pain in her expression. "But these are highly trained sethyd warriors. They're all as strong and fast as I am, and they've been trained to fight much better than I do. And it's not just fighting—they're good trackers, too. The ones who come to investigate the distraction—you can't let them catch you. If they catch you, they'll kill you."

Singer scoffed. "*If.*"

Kagan reached up and scratched his ear. "I do not think I will see my home again. If I die helping you do something important..."

Singer said, "That will be enough."

Kagan nodded. "Enough."

Nysska's heart became a massive stone in her chest. "I can't begin to thank you for this. Just—just don't get caught, all right? I'll never forgive myself if anything happens to either of you."

Kagan waved her words away. "Tell us where you want distraction."

Singer grinned. "And how big."

16

Nysska re-entered Slocum as soon as the sun went down. In the darkness before even the first moon had risen she broke the lock on a tailor's shop and stole a set of clothing. She couldn't do anything about her horns, of course, but she found a dark blue knit cap that let her hide her loosely braided mane. Ever since she was a tiny girl, she'd always been pleased by and a little proud of the cobalt blue streak that ran from her scalp down to the tips. Tonight it would be a liability. The shape and size of her horns was common enough to be unremarkable. Between that, the knit cap, and the plain tunic and trousers she'd taken, both in a bland sort of brownish gray, she ought to be able to pass for a low-level physical laborer either trudging home or headed for a night job.

Moving at a pace she meant to be seen as purposeful, yet not hurrying, Nysska joined the throngs of sethyds heading to their houses and flats.

The Northwest Heights district of Slocum lived up to its name, resting higher on the valley floor than most of the other blocks. Nysska made her way out of the garment district, past a series of butcher shops, and skirted a massive pig yard that gave off wave after wave of airborne manure stench. Soon the first of the stairways up to the Heights came into view.

Nysska had taken the day, hiding on a high, disused rooftop, to map out her path. Yshtarra's House of Devotion stood on the far western edge of the Heights, backed up against a steep, almost sheer mountainside.

That made a lot of sense if she thought of the place as a fortress to be invaded rather than a place for people to center themselves and realign their moral compasses.

She shook her head, and almost said the words out loud: *What am I thinking?*

Yshtarra was the Exemplar of Conquest. There was no re-centering. No re-alignment of morality. Her Devotion House was a place of obscenity and perversion.

Nysska's jaw clenched. She had to stop her teeth from grinding through an effort of will. The longer she'd spent thinking about it, the angrier she'd grown.

Nysska joined a group of sethyds mounting one of the staircases. Most of these would be people who made their homes in the Northwest Heights, rather than just working there, which meant they were better off financially than the rest of the city. Their clothing certainly bore that out. A couple of them glanced at her but paid her no mind. They probably took her for a servant. None of them spoke to her, of course, for which she was grateful. If this had been a human city, some stranger might well have tried to strike up a conversation, ask where she was headed, what she was going to do there, a gesture of benevolent curiosity.

None of the sethyds made even the first move to speak to her. Nysska climbed alongside them in the shared silence.

Once she'd made it up to street level she looked for a new place to hide. She and Kagan and Singer had agreed on the time for the diversion to take place, but aside from promising her that no one would get hurt, they had been stingy with details to the point of frustration.

Nysska spotted a merchant's office. As she lingered at a street corner, she watched the lantern light go out inside each window, one by one, followed by several finely-dressed sethyds exiting the building. Once they were gone, she moved around to the building's rear, climbed a short flight of stone steps to its back door, and tucked into a thick nest of shadows. No one would have any reason to come here—unless the merchant had arranged for a crew to clean after business hours. If that were the case, she'd deal with it when she had to. Nysska couldn't see the actual moon at first rise because of the bulk of the office building, but she could see the light on the face of the building across from her. All she had to do was wait.

Voices reached her from the street. None of them got any closer. She relaxed a bit. Slowly Nysska raised her right hand and flexed her fist, running the fingertips of her left along her forearm. Was she imagining the aches and pains she'd been feeling the last several days? Were they normal symptoms of someone perhaps still not fully recovered from a devastating fall? ...Or was she feeling the effects of the toxic argonium poisoning her skin and muscles and bones?

Crouched there, alone in the dark, the image of Hix's shattered body came back to her as vividly as if she had killed him only seconds ago. *No one has ever implanted runes in a sethyd before.* She could hear his voice saying the words. To her horror and shame, she could even smell his scent. The unique signature of his skin and hair, of his breath against her cheek when he'd leaned over to give her a drink of water as she lay in bed.

The controlled insistence of his lust.

He hadn't asked for anything that happened to him. He only wanted to help the Gemini. Hix had never signed up for assisting his master to implant runes in a sethyd, or getting to know the subject of his experiment. Or...maybe...falling in love with her.

Nysska almost jumped out of her horns when something brushed against her calf—a lean, tabby-striped cat, almost surely a stray, nuzzling against her. She reached out a hand—but snatched it back.

Every time her runes had gone berserk, it had been when she'd either touched someone or been touched. *Well...it happened when Hix touched me.* Still, Nysska could think of no reason for it to have been triggered by him and him alone. That made even less sense than the runes responding to strong emotions.

"I'm sorry," she whispered to the cat. "I can't help you. You need to go away."

The stray pushed itself into the space between her calves and thighs, nuzzling and purring, and wound around her shins and ankles, utterly unconcerned with what she wanted it to do.

She tried waving it away. Making the kind of *shoo!* gesture she'd seen Simana make at the occasional stray dog that had come sniffing around their house looking for scraps. "Go," she murmured, unwilling to raise her voice for fear of being heard. "Go on. Be on your way."

The cat jumped up and perched on Nysska's left knee. Before she could decide what to do, it stretched out both front paws, planted them on her collarbones, and nuzzled her firmly on the nose, purring ferociously.

Nysska squirmed, but the cat wouldn't be dislodged. "I don't want to touch you," she whispered, more urgently now. "Don't make me touch you. It could go horribly wrong."

The cat dropped down into the V formed by her thighs and abdomen. It yawned, purring all the while, and kneaded her belly with both front paws.

The light of the first moon came out from behind a cloud and washed over the building across from her, painting the stone blocks in dim silvery radiance. Nowhere near as bright as the second moon, but still enough to push away a bit of the darkness.

"Something's about to happen," Nysska whispered to the unconcerned cat. "And when it does, I'm going to have to leave you." The cat gazed up at her with clear green eyes. Nysska went on. "I'd take you with me if I could. You make me miss my other cat friends. But where I'm going, you would only be confused and frightened and in terrible danger." She reached into a pouch on her belt and pulled out a morsel of salted ham. The cat instantly jumped up, eyes fixed on the meat, and Nysska held it out to her side, luring the animal. "Is this why you were so friendly in the first place? Could you smell this? You smelled this, didn't you? I should have thought of that earlier." She set the ham down near the merchant's back door. The cat hopped off her lap, picked up the morsel in its teeth, and without even a backward glance stole off down the stairs.

As if the cat's departure were some kind of signal, a thunderous, cracking, rumbling wave of sound and pressure washed over her, and the whole of Slocum erupted into screams.

Nysska risked a look around the corner of the alcove where she'd been hiding and felt a fleeting urge to scream herself.

Across the valley, halfway up the eastern mountainside, the light of the first moon revealed the biggest landslide she'd ever seen. A massive shelf of rock had split off from the face of the mountain and now came roaring down into the valley like the wrath of some vengeful human god. There was nothing over there but a few pastures. Nysska hoped any livestock that hadn't been brought in for the night had the sense to get out of the way.

As the grinding, crashing mass slammed into the valley floor, Nysska caught a flash of movement from the mountain above where the slide had originated. Her breath and her heartbeat both took momentary leaves of absence as a volley of fire arrows arced out into the night sky, one after another in rapid succession, descending to plant themselves at the outer edge of the rubble field the landslide had created.

"Well, that's one way to make sure no one thinks it was just a natural disaster," Nysska murmured, but Kagan and Singer weren't done. Even as the flames of the fire arrows illuminated the billowing dust from the rockslide in shifting, abstract patterns, a *howl* arose. Faint with distance at first, but then gaining in volume and power and...sheer *menace*. Every centim of Nysska's skin puckered in gooseflesh as the sound—a sound never heard on this side of the Salt Ocean, she felt very sure—echoed around the valley, a rasping, eardrum-bursting, ice-cold shriek of malice and hunger.

Soldiers in midnight blue leather sprinted past her on the street, heading for the landslide. Shouts and barked orders filled the space left as Kagan's howl faded away. Every available sethyd had just been ordered to identify and deal with this otherworldly threat.

Keeping to the back alleys and doing her best to remain silent, Nysska hurried toward Yshtarra's Devotion House.

The three-level house looked to be one of the most solidly-constructed buildings in all of Slocum. One of the largest, as well, at least as far as something meant to be a private residence. Nysska spotted signs of recent construction. Following them toward the back, she realized the house didn't simply crouch against the near-sheer face of the western mountain. It had been built into it. Her knowledge of how proficient sethyds were at mining led a low, soft groan to escape her lips. After her experiences in Altamar, Solace Canyon, the thieves' den outside Taurus Hill, and the nameless mine where the Ninth Crucible had discovered and rescued Kagan, Singer, and Aschling, the last thing Nysska wanted to do was explore more subterranean rabbit warrens.

To her mild surprise and greater distress, she found herself hesitant to approach the house.

What exactly was the purpose of creating such an elaborate diversion and sneaking into what might as well be a nest of vipers? She wanted to find out as much as she could about Yshtarra as possible. But did that mean *get rid* of Yshtarra if the opportunity arose?

Nysska had killed before. More times than she wanted to contemplate. But she'd never taken pleasure in it, and she'd never done it when she thought another path was possible. Had she really become an assassin?

The line of cause and effect presented itself to her clearly enough. She needed the chaotic, deadly runes out of her body. To make that happen, she had to secure safety and allies for the Gemini among the sethyds. And to make *that* happen, Yshtarra had to go.

Nysska touched the twin daggers she'd hidden in sheaths strapped to her thighs, accessible through slits she'd made in the pockets of her trousers. She'd had to leave the khopesh behind. Not much chance of going unnoticed with a meter-long sword at her hip. Nysska took a deep breath, crossed the empty yard at the back of the house, and ducked through a servants' entrance.

No sooner had she closed the door than an elderly sethyd man with patchy white hair and a long white beard hurried around a corner and fixed his eyes on her. "What is happening?" he all but shouted. "Are we under attack? What do we do?"

Abruptly inspired, Nysska filled her words with urgency. "The soldiers are saying it's gas. Maybe poison."

The old man's face grew a shade lighter. "Yshtarra help us."

It would've been more effective if she could've grabbed his shoulder, but she stopped herself just in time. "They're sending people house to house with the message: go to your quarters. Lock your doors and windows, and put towels around the cracks. Stay there and don't come out until you get the official message."

His pale yellow eyes had grown wider and wider. "Ah-all right, yes, we can do that."

"Tell the rest of the staff! Everyone needs to go to their quarters! *Right now!*"

The man gave out a tiny yelp, spun on one heel and hurried away. Nysska stayed where she was, listening to frantic, muffled voices and, within half a minute, a series of slamming doors.

The house grew quiet. She didn't even hear voices from outside anymore. All the soldiers who'd been sent to the site of the landslide were already well on their way, far from here. Nysska silently climbed a set of stone steps, just enough to take a peek at the floor above, which consisted of a hallway lined with doors—several of which, as she watched, had the lantern light shining around their edges blocked out from within. She couldn't imagine any business of import being conducted on the floor *above* the servants' quarters. Especially when she suspected the part of the house visible from the street was more than likely the tip of the proverbial iceberg.

Nysska padded from room to room on the ground floor. She found a couple of receiving rooms—no doubt places where Yshtarra's mouth-pieces, Tylar and Randolf, could talk to devotees—as well as a large chamber at the front that looked like the sort of grand hall where victims of the sapping sickness could come and receive their Exemplar's treatment.

The very thought of it made Nysska's gorge rise. A living, breathing Exemplar. She wanted to hawk up a venom-filled glob and spit it in the center of the floor, but fought the urge down.

At the back of the first floor, around a crook in a hallway she hadn't noticed to begin with, Nysska found a door that looked sturdier than the others. Thick, dark wood, probably cherry, with heavy bronze hinges and latch. Her hand trembled as she reached for it.

If she encountered anyone beyond this point who challenged her, or threatened to raise an alarm, she'd have to act—which would upend an hourglass and begin marking the seconds she had left. And that was if she even *could* overpower whoever opposed her. She was among her own people now, not the slow, clumsy humans. There were thousands of sethyds who—just like her late brother, Gerrit—had been trained to fight much, much more skillfully than she had. If she ran into one of them or, Atiina forbid, more than one, the chances of her making it out of the house alive were infinitesimally small.

And yet she had zero choice in the matter. Repeating something she had heard her grandmother say more than once—*There's nothing for it but to do it*—Nysska turned the latch, swung the door open, and stepped through.

She stood in a long, rectangular room, chiseled straight into the mountain's bedrock. The floor and ceiling were every bit as smooth and featureless as the walls, with only the occasional tool mark to indicate that the room was sethyd handiwork. She sensed no one else there, for which she gave a quick, silent thanks, and looked around.

Rows of shelves lined one wall, while a long, low work counter stretched along the other one. It was a vegetable cellar, pure and simple. As far north as Slocum was, and as solid as the stone around her must be, she had no doubt that this room would stay cool even on the warmest day of summer.

The room held no vegetables now. It was almost bare, as far as she could tell in the light from the two lanterns hung from the ceiling. Only a few empty bags lay at the far end of the work counter, and the shelves held nothing more than a cluster of squat ceramic jars.

At the far end of the room, another door similar to the one she'd come through had been set into an otherwise featureless wall, with a thick rug covering the floor right in front of it.

Nysska went to the jars first. They'd been cast by a superior craftsman judging by how snugly the lids fit. Only with a surprisingly firm pressure could she dislodge one, revealing a golden brown powder inside. She leaned forward, just close enough to put her nose within scent range, and took a tiny sniff.

Flowers?

Nysska tore a square patch out of the hem of her tunic and, using one of her daggers, scooped a measure of the powder onto the cloth. Carefully folding it up into a relatively neat package, she tucked it inside her boot, then turned to look at the pile of what appeared to be empty, discarded sacks.

She judged each one to hold about a kilgram's worth of...whatever. She still had the dagger in her hand, so she used it to prod through the pile—and as the sacks moved, a scent wafted out from them that made her flinch.

It also caused the runes beneath her skin, which had lain dormant for long enough that she had *almost* forgotten about them, to shiver and buzz.

Gritting her teeth, Nysska forced herself to move closer, centim by centim, ignoring the instincts that told her to get far away from there as fast as possible. She poked the tip of the dagger into the hem of one of the bags and lifted it. The scent—no, the *stench*—slapped her hard in the face again, but aside from giving her feelings of panic and making the foreign metal inside her body tremble, nothing else appeared to be happening. She could still breathe. Her vision wasn't going dark. She felt no trace of paralysis. With an effort of will Nysska looked inside the bag.

It contained traces of a dull gray powder. She wasn't sure if she was imagining it or not, but actually looking at the substance with her naked eyes made her runes vibrate even more disconcertingly, in a twisted, syncopated counter-rhythm to her heartbeat that made her want to vomit.

Nysska spotted something protruding from beneath another sack. She used the dagger to flick the pile aside. This revealed a short list of numbers and letters in columns on a piece of parchment that had been folded into a small square at some point. Nysska got none of the same feelings of panic from the parchment as she had from the sacks, so she gingerly picked it up with the tips of her index finger and thumb. It looked like the sort of thing someone might discard carelessly, artifact of a task already completed and, no longer necessary, put out of mind. The numbers made no sense to her. Nonetheless she folded the parchment back up and tucked it into her boot alongside the little powder envelope.

She approached the second door, but hesitated when the toe of her right boot caught on the edge of the rug in front of it.

No sense in not being thorough. She bent down and pulled the rug to one side.

Nysska had not been expecting to see a heavy, round, bronze hatch set flush with the stone floor, but one stared her in the face. With the rug shoved back, she could hear something below the hatch—some kind of droning, rushing sound—and she didn't hesitate to hook her fingers in the recessed handhold and pull it open.

It swung up on well-oiled hinges to reveal a broad stream of rushing water.

Nysska couldn't tell *how* broad. Judging by the speed and sound of the current, the bronze hatch only showed her a tiny window onto what might have been an actual underground *river.*

Nysska's head jerked up at the faint but distinctive sound of a bell being rung on the other side of the second door. The kind of bell someone confined to a bed might ring when in need of food.

She lowered the hatch into the floor and covered it with the rug. Still no one had come in from outside. And if there had been any able-bodied sethyds on the other side of the door, there would have been no need for anyone to ring that bell.

Correct?

Nysska argued with herself until she heard the bell again.

The heavy door wasn't locked, but the hinges squealed when she pushed it open. Only a single oil lamp lit the room on the other side—a bedroom, it appeared to be, no more than four meters square. It reminded her, in a sad, pathetic sort of way, of the room that had belonged to Naveed Olkoff's prostitute in Taurus Hill. A bed, a dresser, a battered porcelain wash basin, a shit bucket in the corner. The figure covered with blankets in the center of the bed reached one violet-skinned hand out and slowly pushed the covers down.

"Who's there?" a voice called out, weak and shaking. "Tylar? Is that you?"

Nysska saw a pair of horns that had been painted gold, exactly as Tarca had described Yshtarra. But that wasn't why her knees had gone weak. That wasn't why she clutched at the doorframe to keep from pitching forward onto her face, all the nerves in her body rendered limp and unresponsive.

The face came into view, the face that matched the voice she had recognized, and as the fiery orange eyes focused, the woman in the bed said, "Nysska?"

"Mother," Nysska cried, and rushed forward.

17

S imana Kaur pushed herself up in the bed—or tried to. She didn't quite make it to her elbows before she collapsed into her pillow. Nysska rushed to her side, and Simana held her arms out, and Nysska choked on a sob as she pulled back.

"Let me hold you," Simana said. Her voice was so weak. Every word sounded like an act of will just to get it out. "Let me touch you. I need to make sure you're real."

Nysska knelt on the bed just out of her mother's reach. "I can't. I'm sorry."

Simana swallowed with some difficulty, and her brows drew tightly together. "Why not?"

"It's a long story—*Panjo*, I thought you were *dead*. Everyone *told* me you were dead! They said they went to your funeral—they said they saw you burned!" Nysska's eyes roved over her mother's hair and horns. Someone had turned her lustrous black hair a coarse red, probably to make her even less recognizable.

Simana started crying. Nysska's heart frayed and tore at not being able to wipe her mother's tears away. "It was Gerrit. He and Tylar and Randolf took me—that night. You remember. At first they just kept me locked up. It was to force you to do things for them, wasn't it?"

Nysska turned to look at the door. She heard nothing from outside in the cellar, but lowered her voice when she turned back to Simana. "I had to do what you said I should do. I went into service for the Cathedral. They put me in the Thaumetallicon." She let a tiny smile dance on her lips for a moment. "Your daughter's an Enforcer." The creases on Simana's face changed. She reached out a hand, but Nysska shook her head sharply and said, "I can't. I'm sorry. But I can't touch you." Through a black scowl she added, "Which means I can't carry you out of here."

Simana sank back farther into her pillow. Her fire-orange eyes looked so sunken, surrounded by the deepest of dark circles. *They aren't clouded over anymore, though.* Nysska remembered the blindness the *Krizo* had inflicted on her mother.

Simana managed a weak smile. "Yes. I can see again. I've still been healing. Slowly. There is that to be thankful for, at the least."

"What have they done to you, though? How—*why* are you this—this Yshtarra?"

"I'm a puppet, is what I am," Simana said, her hands digging into the bedclothes. "I don't know what they're giving me, but it keeps me here, weak as a fucking kitten. That was all Gerrit did, but then Tylar and Randolf had this idea about 'Yshtarra.' They needed a sethyd, but everyone knew them, so they couldn't do it. Then they realized I'd been gone for long enough that if they changed my appearance—and didn't let me talk—I could be their new Exemplar." Simana's leg moved weakly beneath the sheets and blanket. "They told me...they told me Gerrit was dead. And...that you were the one who killed him."

Nysska said nothing.

Simana sobbed, fresh tears spilling down her cheeks, but within seconds she wiped them away.

"I'm sorry, *Panjo.*"

Simana's mouth twisted. "What did I do wrong? How did I let my son turn so—so rotten?" When Nysska didn't respond to that, Simana said, "What was the breaking point?"

"I'm sorry?"

Her tears had already stopped. Simana radiated pain, but she focused it into something diamond-hard. A process Nysska had seen in her mother many times in the past. "You let him manipulate you for—for months, wasn't it? A year? Because he said he'd hurt me if you didn't comply. What changed?"

"Well...he led me to believe you were dead."

Simana's orange eyes narrowed. "That makes no sense. Why would he get rid of the only bit of leverage he had over you?"

"He didn't *tell* me you were dead. But his demeanor made me believe you were. And...he had your favorite horn ring. I thought it was a trophy."

"You *assumed* I was dead? And that led you to kill your brother?"

"It...wasn't just that. There were other factors. Mother—you were right to call him rotten." She thought about the massive shipment of chervoxite ore she'd destroyed at Solace Canyon, and what Gerrit would have done with it. With the power that ore would have granted him and the rest of the Mountain Bulls. "All the conquest—all the death the Mountain Bulls wanted. The mass murder of the humans. Gerrit would have carried it out if I hadn't taken him down."

Simana closed her eyes and covered her face with her hands. She stayed that way long enough to exacerbate Nysska's anxiety about being discovered. Finally her hands dropped to her chest. "You have always been one of the brightest sethyds I've ever known. If you believed it was necessary..." She looked down at her own drug-weakened body. "Then I believe it was necessary as well."

Nysska scooted slightly closer. "*Panjo*—the reason I'm here—I know about the sapping sickness. I know Tylar and Randolf are using you to secure power. I know they've rekindled the desire to overrun the humans."

Simana winced. "Is there no one like me anymore?"

"There is. I came here from Franklun Simeon's house."

Simana grew more intense. "Franklun! He's still alive..."

"He still has friends, too. Friends who want to pursue peace and wisdom. But to do that, he needs Yshtarra gone and her followers weakened." When the orange of her mother's eyes deepened, her mouth tightening to a thin line, Nysska said, "Obviously I'm not going to get rid of you! Relax! Please!"

Simana's muscles did ease out of their sudden clench a degree or two, but she still looked worried. "So what are you going to do?"

"I need to understand everything about this sapping sickness. Tarca—I talked to her, too, before I came here—she and Franklun called it a plague, but it seems to me that I've found traces of some kind of poison, and an efficient way to put it into the city's water supply. Along with the herbs they're using as a treatment." Nysska's eyes unfocused for a heartbeat. "*That's* why Franklun couldn't figure out how it was spreading—and why he and his grandson were unaffected. Their house gets its water from a falls, not the main system."

Simana reached for Nysska's arm, but pulled her hand back. "All right.

All right. If you can't carry me…then you've got to get the word out about what Tylar and Randolf are doing." Her tone grew stern. "Do not just shout it from the nearest rooftop, either. No one would believe you, and you'd be killed. Quickly."

Nysska nodded. "What I don't understand is what the poison *is*, or where they get it." She pulled out the folded parchment and held it up. "Is this a schedule? Is the poison *delivered* here?"

"I knew *something* important was happening once a month. I just didn't have details." She squinted at the parchment. "What's today's date?"

Nysska ticked off days in her head. "Fifth November."

"All right. That makes sense. Look." She tapped the parchment with one fingernail. "These letters. They stand for human cities."

Nysska's eyes widened as the list's meaning became clear. She thumped the side of her head. "Right. *Right.* It's a delivery route. So that's…uh…"

"Remember your geography classes," Simana said, sounding very much like Nysska's mother now. Everyone had studied human geography back in Patrinomonto. *Know one's enemy as one knows one's self.*

Nysska let her eyes unfocus, imagining a map of the Empire. "The route would start in Klyburn, that's the 'KL'—then Ransom Falls—it goes almost directly southeast to northwest, and ends up in…"

"Mount Stark, I would say," Simana finished the sentence. "The closest human city to Slocum."

Nysska said, "I've traveled across the Empire incognito. It takes a long time, but it's possible. Why would anyone bringing poison to Slocum stop at human cities—oh. To check in. There would need to be some kind of contact in each place."

Simana yawned. "Sorry. I'm fading. Nysska… if you can figure this out. If the sickness goes away…"

Nysska finished the thought. "Yshtarra's hold on Slocum goes with it." She paused. "I promise, *Panjo*. I won't leave you here. We'll get you out, and get you better."

Simana opened her mouth to say something else, but snapped it shut when they both heard the sound of the outer door opening, along with multiple voices.

Nysska rushed to the door, a dagger in each hand. She cracked it just enough to look out with one eye—and threw it the rest of the way open when one of the four sethyd men in the cellar spotted her and pointed, shouting.

All four of them wore the midnight blue leather of the *Araneoj*. The Spiders. The same beyond-elite force that had trained her brother Gerrit. Nysska stepped out into the cellar and pushed the door to her mother's room closed behind her. No sense in Simana getting traumatized by the sight of her daughter's violent death.

"Who are you?" one of the men demanded. "What are you doing in there?"

"She's armed," another of them said. "Emmet—go make sure Yshtarra's all right."

One of the four moved toward Nysska, heading for the door. She had received only cursory training in the use of daggers, but unless she could pry a sword away from one of the Spiders they'd have to do. "You're not going in there." She tightened her grip on the long, slim knives. "In fact, none of you are leaving this room."

The one who'd been heading to check on Simana froze in his tracks, but not out of fear. He had a look on his face that would've been appropriate on someone who'd just heard a puppy speak a full sentence in Plainish.

"Is that so?" he said, and something like the kick of a wild horse struck Nysska in the ribs.

She slammed against the wall beside the door—*I never even saw anyone move*—but kept her feet. Her head and heart both pounded, the fire flooding her veins the way it always did in a crisis. One of the Spiders moved in, reaching for his own sword, and Nysska took a long step inside his reach, dagger driving toward his armpit.

The dagger left her hand and flew across the room, clattering on the smooth stone floor, and pain flooded her shoulder as her arm went limp. The blows were coming in too fast for her even to be aware of them, much less parry or block, and one of the Spiders wrenched her other arm up behind her back and took the second dagger away from her.

Someone else, she couldn't tell which of the four men, pulled the knit cap off her head, revealing her coal-black hair with the cobalt blue stripe running through it.

A voice said, "Fuck my mother, it's Nysska Kaur."

Another one barked an order: "Hold her! *Hold her!* I've got her arm, you get the other one—you two, grab her legs!"

Hands and arms as hard as seasoned wood clamped onto her limbs and pulled her off the floor. She kicked and squirmed, writhing, trying to break their grips, but they had her elbows and knees in the kind of expert locks that could tear ligaments and tendons with little effort.

"Let's get her out to the main hall," one of the men said—the one who'd recognized her. "Tylar's supposed to be back soon. He can decide what to do with h—"

The words broke off as every rune in Nysska's body flared in a volcanic explosion of light that filled the cellar with eye-searing crimson. The fingers of her right hand dug into the chest of the man holding it, piercing skin and muscle and bone until her hand closed around his sternum and crushed it to wet powder.

None of the other three realized what had just happened—it had taken less than a second to kill the fourth—but the one holding her left leg loosened his grip, and without any thought or control from Nysska that leg bent at the knee and drove its heel into the man's chin, which pulverized his jaw and his neck and tore his head most of the way off his body.

One of the men screamed, and Nysska joined him, yanked his head down close to her mouth as a brain-rupturing battle cry tore itself from her throat. She watched as her fingers wrapped around his neck and his windpipe collapsed in a geyser of brilliant red blood, a red that joined with the furious radiance pouring out of her body.

The last sethyd had turned loose her leg, letting Nysska crumple to the floor, and she watched as he bolted for the exit. She screamed, "Stop it, stop it, *stop it*," but control of her body had left her utterly, and her legs took her airborne. Nysska crashed into the fleeing sethyd, sending them both to the floor in a tangle of arms and legs, and her hands dug through his leather armor and his skin and his muscles and locked around his spine and tore it splintering out of his body.

Nysska rolled over onto her back, panting, her vision swimming in and out of focus as the ruby radiance faded.

From the other side of the door, almost too faint to be heard, Simana called, "Nysska? What just happened? Nysska, are you all right?"

"I'm fine," she said, and made her way up to stand on shaky legs. "I'm fine! I'll be back for you as soon as I'm able!" Nysska looked down at the bodies of the men she'd just slaughtered, and at her own body, splattered with their blood, and bolted out of the cellar.

Hurtling up the stairs, she encountered no other soldiers, and the servants appeared to be staying in their quarters. The house was silent enough to make her think she might be able to make a clean escape—

Until she rounded a corner, heading for the back hallway through which she'd entered, and ran face-first into Tylar.

Nysska rebounded, almost falling, and hitched up short against the nearest wall. Tylar stayed where he was, staring at her, his face stony, until Randolf came out of the nearest room, speaking as he moved. "Apparently someone told the servants to stick to their quarters, which, given the magnitude, wasn't a bad idea—"

Randolf broke off when he saw her, standing there motionless next to Tylar. Nysska panted, eyes darting. She wore no armor. Both her daggers had disappeared in the bloody chaos downstairs. Tylar and Randolf faced her in the midnight-blue *Araneoj* armor, khopeshes at their hips, daggers in sheathes strapped to thighs and across chests.

Neither one had changed all that much in appearance since she'd last seen them. Tylar was still ridiculously handsome, with his close-cropped black hair and stunning white eyes. Randolf still had the brutally square jaw and wavy dark blue hair.

The Spider leather was new. They must have followed in Gerrit's footsteps once they got to Slocum.

Nysska surprised herself by reaching for the runes. She had no idea how to do it, but tried nonetheless, like attempting to flex a muscle that had never been used before. The effort brought her nothing. No vibrations beneath her skin, no ruby light. At that moment she was nothing more than an exhausted woman, covered in blood, facing two of the deadliest warriors the sethyds had ever produced.

Tylar said, "I should—"

Randolf cut him off, holding up a hand. "No. Nysska would never hurt her mother."

Tylar frowned. "Then whose blood is that?"

Nysska's mouth had gone dry. Her head spun as she stared at the two living remnants of her past. "Listen—boys—can we talk about this? Can we talk about what you're doing?"

Randolf's brows drew together. "What is there to talk about?"

"I know you!" The words came out sounding more desperate than she meant them to. "We *grew up* together! I don't—I don't understand why you're doing all this!"

Quietly, Tylar said, "We're doing it for the good of sethydkind. So we can take our proper place in the world."

Nysska shook her head. Stalling. "That's the Mountain Bulls talking. Build an army, conquer the humans. I've heard all that. But creating a new

Exemplar? And enslaving someone to do it? Where the fuck did that come from?"

The muscles in Tylar's jaw rippled. "From Gerrit," he said.

Randolf unsheathed his khopesh. "Enough of this bearshit."

Tylar nodded and drew his own sword.

Nysska's breathing grew ragged as pure, freezing terror started in her gut and radiated out to her limbs. They were going to kill her. Nothing she could do would prevent that. It would be easier, faster, maybe even more dignified to throw herself straight onto Randolf's blade and get it over with.

She wasn't sure whether it was the sudden, horrible thought of never seeing Cam again that made her speak, or simply a perverse desire to get the last word in. "Did they tell you how Gerrit died?"

Randolf had shifted his weight to take a step toward her but froze in his tracks.

Nysska said, "I have no doubt that you took at least one of the Dragon worshippers. Made him talk. Made him describe what happened at Solace Canyon."

Tylar said, "Shut your mouth, Nysska."

"Oh, I think Randolf wants to hear what I have to say. Because I'm not some terrified human, relaying what he *thinks* he saw. I was there." Not entirely sure where any of this was coming from, she let her voice rise. "I saw the great gray bear bite his arm off. I saw him stagger away in agony. I saw the Arch-Pastor—a *human*—holding Gerrit helpless, a knife to his throat, standing there on the bridge."

Tears began in Randolf's eyes.

And when Tylar put a hand on Randolf's shoulder, everything became clear.

"Oh. *Oh.* I see. When I used my axe—the axe the humans gave me—the axe Gerrit *forced* me to take. When I used that axe to cut the cables on the bridge, I took him *away from you.* Didn't I, Randolf?"

Randolf's lips skinned back away from his teeth as his jaw clenched. He swiped the tears from his cheeks with the back of his hand. "How *could* you?" Anguish turned his voice into something like the cry of a wounded animal. "He was your brother! He was your *blood!* How could you do that?"

"He was a terror-monger."

Randolf dropped his chin to his chest, his shoulders trembling, and Tylar slipped an arm around him and held him tight. "Shh, shh," Tylar murmured. "We'll make her know how much it hurt to lose Gerrit. We'll make her feel all the pain we've felt."

Nysska's stomach dropped even further. Killing Gerrit had broken *two* hearts.

"Did Gerrit know what you were going to do to our mother?"

Randolf raised his head and blinked tears away. "What?"

Nysska made a broad gesture toward the downstairs. "He took her and threatened her life and kept her prisoner. But what you two have done... Drugging her? Making her pretend to be a *new Exemplar*? Turning her into a marionette." She made herself sneer. "Gerrit would have been horrified."

"Fuck you," Tylar spat. "You never knew a single fucking thing about your brother." He thumped his chest. "*We* were the ones he cared about. *We* were the ones he loved!"

Randolf gently disengaged Tylar's arm from around him. "She's trying to provoke us," he said, visibly regaining his composure. "She either thinks she can irritate us enough to grant her a quick death, or she's trying to distract us in hopes of getting away somehow."

Nysska blinked, and in that tiny fraction of a second Randolf's khopesh hooked around her neck, the needle-sharp backswept spike dimpling the skin.

The move had put Randolf close enough for Nysska to see the fine pores in his skin. Close enough for her to smell him. She said, "You know I had a crush on you when we were children."

Tylar scoffed. Randolf's yellow-orange eyes narrowed. "Really? You're going to try that? Pathetic, Nysska. Even for a priest-singer."

Slowly she lifted a hand. Not knowing if what she was about to try stood a chance of working. "I see now," she said. Not seductively. But not afraid, either. Randolf's khopesh stayed where it was as he watched her. "I see I never had a chance. You had eyes for my brother. You both did. And he was handsome..." She rested her palm lightly on Randolf's chest. "At least until I dropped him in a stream of magma and watched him burn."

The jolt of rage that burst out of Randolf's heart made Nysska's runes go berserk in a way she hadn't felt before, and she had just enough control to twitch sideways, taking her neck out of the curve of the sethyd blade—before her flattened palm slammed Randolf out of his boots and sent him smashing into Tylar like a stone flung from a trebuchet. The crimson light pouring out of Nysska's body left her halfway blind, but it drove her feet and legs to move—away from Tylar and Randolf's screams of agony—to fling her down the hallway and out the Devotion House's back door. Blazing like a miniature red sun, she shrieked and flailed her way up the mountainside and into the dense forest beyond.

———

Several days later, looking and feeling a lot like a drowned rat, Nysska emerged from a dense line of trees and climbed to the top of a ridge. She had retrieved her khopesh from the rendezvous site where she'd hoped to meet Kagan and Singer. There'd been no sign of them. She tried not to let that worry her, since they'd agreed on what to do if they got separated, and the sethyd search party she'd almost stumbled across had been complaining bitterly about not apprehending their quarry.

Nysska had to get to Mount Stark. That was where the courier trans-porting the poison was supposed to check in next, if the list she and Simana had deciphered was still accurate. The problem was that Nysska no longer had a map of any kind, wasn't all that familiar with the terri-tory, and had no solid idea of where she even was. All she had to go on was the knowledge that Mount Stark lay to the south and slightly east of Slocum. Kainos was a large continent. Her belly growled, her worker's clothes hung on her in tatters after the multiple frigid plunges she'd taken in stream after stream, and she still didn't feel confident she'd scrubbed all the blood away.

Nothing in the landscape that sprawled out before her gave any indi-cation that a city might lie ahead. There were trees and ridges and more trees and—

She froze. Throat abruptly locked up.

A single slender column of smoke drifted up from beyond the next ridge.

Wondering what bit of food or protective clothing she might steal from whomever had built the fire, Nysska heeded the rumbling in her stomach and headed that way. The simple cloth-and-hemp shoes she wore did next to nothing to protect her feet from the jagged rocks over which she trod.

Half an hour later Nysska crawled like a snake to the crest of the next ridge, peered over—and had to stifle a sound. It might have been a yelp of surprise or a whoop of joy.

A Cathedral encampment lay in the narrow valley below. Though she had never seen the flag flying above the largest tent herself, she'd listened to both Percy and Raoul describing it in great detail. A white and gray background with two black bars and a right hand, palm out and divided in half vertically, one side red and one side green.

She rolled onto her back and gazed up at the vault of blue overhead, weighing her options. Eventually she crept into the trees and waited until night fell.

Before the second moon had a chance to rise Nysska left her khopesh in the crook of an oak and crept down the ridge slope. She avoided the two soldiers patrolling the camp's perimeter as well as a little knot of men listening to another one play a stringed instrument, and before anyone even knew she'd entered the camp she slipped under the back wall of the largest tent.

No sooner had she gotten her bearings—taking in the utilitarian bedroll, the folding table and chairs spread with maps, the weapon and armor rack—than she heard a familiar voice outside the tent's entrance flap. General Boris Cullen bid goodnight to whomever he'd been talking to and stepped inside, and Nysska held up her hands in as non-threatening a manner as she could. Cullen froze, eyes widening, and she laid a finger across her lips and made a tamping gesture with her other hand that she hoped conveyed a clear message: *Please don't make a sound.*

The General let the tent flap fall closed and frowned at her. Nysska whispered, "Don't be alarmed, General. You're in no danger."

His frown deepened, but he spoke softly. "I have to admit, Enforcer, I'm impressed with your resilience." As he laced the tent flap shut, he said, "Care to fill me in as to how you're still drawing breath?"

"I'd be happy to, sir. But I'm afraid I'm going to have to ask you to take a *lot* of what I'm about to say on faith."

***

General Cullen sighed. "So you're looking for someone—probably a sethyd—who's either in Mount Stark right now, or will be showing up there soon. But you can't tell me who this person is or why you're looking for them."

The General sat cross-legged on his bed, elbows on his knees and his chin resting on his folded hands. He'd taken off his armor and now wore only his plain Cathedral field uniform. Nysska perched on the edge of a folding chair. She said, "I'm afraid that's the case, sir, yes."

"But finding this person is of utmost importance."

"Lives depend on it. Many, many lives."

"But no one can know about it."

"The fewer people know, the better, sir, absolutely."

General Cullen stretched. "If it were anyone else telling me this—and I mean anyone, my son included—I'd demand to see at least a little proof. But coming from you…I'm inclined to take you at your word."

A tiny bit of weight lifted from her shoulders. "Thank you, sir. I can't tell you how much I appreciate this."

"Oh, don't thank me yet. I was already on my way to Mount Stark. For a completely different reason."

Nysska paused. "Oh?"

"Yes. And that whole fewer-people-know-the-better thing of yours might end up getting put to the test. The Ninth Crucible are set to arrive in Mount Stark tomorrow morning."

Nysska's stomach sank. "I—that's—I would prefer them not to be involved, sir, I—I should be dealing with this alone—"

General Cullen looked at her sidelong. "Except you're *not* dealing with it alone, or you wouldn't be sitting in my tent. Now. Let's get you some food and some clothes that don't look as if they've been gnawed on by weasels." His eyes roved over her face and hair. "Also, you're still wanted by the Emperor for questioning. If I were truly doing my job, I'd have you in shackles. So let's make you a little less recognizable. Are you married to having your hair that length? Also, how do you feel about dye?"

Nysska buried her face in her hands. "I'm partial to red," she said, voice muffled. "We'll need to do something about my horns, too."

The General nodded. "I'll ask one of our farriers for a hoof file."

PART III

THE CONQUEROR

18

Wind howled and shrieked outside Mayor Ragwild's house, driving the rain against the windows like a barrage of stones. The sound barely registered on Nysska. She sat in a corner, next to the fireplace, slumped in a straight-backed wooden chair with her face in her hands.

The members of the Ninth Crucible—minus Wallace Embry, who was with the Mayor's personal physician, getting his bones set—sat with Nysska in one of Ragwild's guest rooms, a place designed more for comfort than appearance. It was heaped high with bear skins, which would no doubt keep any human warm in even the coldest of winters. Nysska couldn't stand the thought of touching any of them. Not that she felt much of the cold anyway.

"Raoul?" Cam sounded nervous and sympathetic at the same time. "Is there…is there anything any of us can do?"

Nysska sat up and let her hands settle in her lap, but still stared at the floor. In her peripheral vision Raoul stood at one of the windows, gazing out at the winter night. That seemed to be his default position when anything upset him. Pick a place where he didn't have to look at any people and give it a good, long stare.

Without turning from the window, Raoul said, "Where are Kagan and Singer now?"

Nysska realized the question was directed at her. "Cliffside. Or on their way. They agreed to head back there if we got separated, which we did. I eavesdropped on one of the sethyd search parties long enough to confirm that they hadn't found anyone."

Still unmoving, Raoul said, "So the sethyds worshiping their new Goddess of Conquest *probably* won't invade my family's estate."

"She's not a goddess," Nysska said, too quietly for anyone but the blood lynxes to hear her. Both of the big cats sat in front of the fire, staring at her. They had sat like that the whole time she'd spent explaining everything that had happened to her since the Gemini pulled her out of the water. Nysska wished she could even guess what the lynxes were thinking.

Raoul wasn't finished. He turned to face her, and she wished he hadn't. "This is a real pattern with you, isn't it?" As her stomach sank, he said, "You keep secrets from us, and when we find out what the secret is— because we *always do*—it turns out to be something fucking horrifying. But then we forgive you, because as horrifying as whatever bearshit it is, you always manage to come up with something that justifies it."

"I swore an oath," Nysska said, now just loudly enough for everyone to hear her. She sneaked a look at Cam. The woman she loved more than anything else on the planet sat turned ninety degrees from her, arms folded, silver eyes half-lidded and focused on nothing. *Come to my side. Come to me and defend me. Come to me and say you understand. Come to me and say* something.

Percy swung one of the other chairs across the floor and planted it across from Nysska, sinking into it with his eyes on hers. "Dragon fucking *damn it*, Nysska, we're your fucking *family*. How long are you going to keep *lying* to us?"

"I never lied to you." That came out much more defensive than she'd meant it to.

"Like fuck you didn't. We could've helped you! We *would've* helped you. Family are the ones you don't keep secrets from, because you don't *have* to. Your secrets are our secrets! It's as simple as that, and I'm fucking furious with you that you don't seem to understand it!"

Before Nysska could think of a response to any of that, Raoul said, "If you hadn't come here, my father would still be alive."

"No." Cam turned to face the group. "No, Raoul, that's not true. Your father was coming here anyway. He was coming here to see *you*. He would've been here, and we would've been investigating, whether Nysska had been here or not." Raoul's face clouded, and he opened his mouth to say something, but Cam cut him off. "If Nysska *hadn't* been here, that monster would still have killed him. And then she would've killed all of us. Nysska saved our lives. Again."

Silence filled the room.

Jax yawned, moved closer to the fire, and curled up in a great tawny ball. Flax sniffed once, padded across to Nysska and, after staring at her for several more long seconds, jumped up into her lap and flopped down. Nysska scratched her between the ears and under the chin. Flax's purrs rivaled the crackle of the flames for volume.

Percy looked as if he'd just bitten into a particularly sour lemon. He said, "You told us there wouldn't be any more secrets. I remember it really fucking vividly. We were riding away from that broken down, Dragon-forsaken mill, after we found out what your fuckhead brother had been doing, and you told us there wouldn't be any more fucking secrets."

Nysska let out a raspy, tired sigh. "You're right. You're right, I said that, and I absolutely meant it. Percy, the Gemini—Bronna Smith—she made me swear on Atiina's wisdom. That's—that's the highest. The most binding oath I could possibly take. That's one thing. But she also told me, and I *believed* her, that if anyone found out what I was doing—or that I was a sethyd bearing runes—that she would make sure the runemaster who implanted them would *never* take them out again."

"Not to mention the debt you owed them for saving your life," Cam said neutrally.

Nysska wasn't sure how to interpret that. "Yes. Not to mention."

Raoul frowned and folded his arms across his chest. "I notice you didn't dump Flax off your lap."

Percy's eyes widened in sudden realization, but Nysska showed him her palms and spoke quickly. "It's all right! It's all right. The, ah—all the random, horrible things that happened with the runes before—that won't be a problem now. Hix and Master Seeley weren't sure when it was going to happen, or even *if* it was going to happen, because no sethyd had ever been implanted with runes before. But I *have* bonded with them. It happened when I fell off the tower with Jinna Marsdown." She rolled up her right sleeve. "Watch." The runes along her forearm lit up, shining crimson through her skin, then dimmed and went out. "They're doing what I tell them to now." Nysska risked a direct look and found Cam watching her, silver eyes reflecting the firelight like mirrors. "Just like yours."

"Just like mine," Cam repeated softly.

Sounding utterly unconvinced yet still icy calm, Raoul said, "So what does this mean for your oath? For the promise that Bronna Smith made to you? Are you just abandoning that now?"

Nysska took a slow, deep breath, in and out. "I told Smith that the oath I took for her was the most sacred one a sethyd can swear, and I wasn't lying. On top of everything else, believe me, I feel like a hundred kilgrams of shit that I broke it. But it was either that or let Jinna Marsdown kill Cam." She rubbed her face with both hands. "I can still fulfill part of it. We can still keep it secret that I'm bearing runes. The whole Empire knows about my fight with Lockridge. They know red runes equal *bad*. Equal *enemy*. Which means they'd be coming for *my* head, first and foremost, but if word gets out that sethyds can be runebearers, I think the Empire would turn against them in a hurry." She glanced around at their somber faces. "I don't want a war. I don't want a genocide."

Percy snorted. "Would that be humans wiping out sethyds? Or the other way around?"

Nysska shook her head. "Either way. I don't want it happening. And we can keep the peaceful Gemini's location a secret, too." Quietly she added, "Atiina help me, I cannot call them 'the Parakeets' with a straight face."

Cam slowly moved closer to Nysska. She sat down on the armrest of a couch a meter away, eyes moving from the fire to Nysska and back. "So what needs to happen?"

Nysska looked to Raoul. "I'm in no position to be setting a course here."

Raoul's mouth tightened. "Like fuck you're not. You've been in charge of this Crucible since you joined it, Nysska. There's no reason to pretend otherwise."

He didn't sound angry. Not even indignant. Just resigned. *Tired.* She said, "Raoul...you shouldn't even be worrying about any of this. Not with what just happened."

Raoul's ink-black eyes flashed, the deep brown skin of his jaw rippling in the firelight. "What, you want me to step aside? You think I'm too crippled with grief to be of use?"

"I fucking would be," Percy said flatly. "My parents bit the dirt when I was only a little older than you are, and I was a fucking *wreck*." He stood and faced Raoul. "Nobody's saying you're useless. We're just trying to get you what you need."

Raoul glared at Percy, then at Nysska, then turned to stare out the window again. "What I need is to *work*. What I need is to solve this Dragon-damned shitstorm we're in." He paused. "What I need, Nysska, is for you to answer Cam's question."

Nysska stood, and carefully stretched. "We've got to finish taking apart this whole Yshtarra nonsense. Expose Tylar and Randolf for what they are—assuming they survived what I did to them, which would surprise me not at all—and get my mother out of there. But to do that, we need to understand all of what's involved." She pointed at the far corner, where the heavy cloth sack they took off Jinna Marsdown's body sat on a small table. "Which means figuring out exactly what *that* is, what's going on in Klyburn to produce the stuff, and who's sending it to Slocum. Cut off the source."

Raoul rubbed his chin. "Assuming this rain keeps up and it doesn't get too cold, the roads'll be clear soon. It's on the way, and someone would've needed to go and tell her in any case."

Nysska blinked. "Someone—I'm sorry, I'm lost. Who are you talking about?"

"Morrin James," Raoul said. "We need to go to Coalgarden. And tell her that my father's dead."

Nysska stood at the window of her room, staring out at the rain, in a conscious imitation of the posture Raoul had taken earlier. She wasn't surprised when she found that it didn't help her think any more clearly.

A soft knock at her door almost made her jump. "Yes?"

From outside, Cam's lowered voice barely made it through the wood. "May I come in?"

Nysska crossed to the door and opened it. Cam stood there, looking delicious as usual, but hesitated to cross the threshold. Sounding more tentative than she meant to, Nysska said, "You did want to come in...?"

Cam nodded and moved past her. Nysska paused in the middle of closing the door. "Or did you want me to leave this open?"

Cam hesitated again. It made Nysska's heart sink. "No, no, you can close it."

The room Mayor Ragwild had assigned her held a bed, a fireplace, one of the much-too-common bear skin rugs, and a couple of leather-bound chairs. Nysska gestured to one of them, careful not even to look at the bed, and when Cam took a seat in one she settled into the other. "I would offer you refreshment if I had any."

Cam glanced around the room. Nysska got the impression it was just as much so she wouldn't have to make eye contact as to take in the décor. Letting her line of sight settle on the fireplace, Cam said, "I thought I knew what I was going to say when I came in here."

"I was wondering if you'd come to talk. Just the two of us, I mean."

"You were really surprised that I'd want to see you?"

Nysska couldn't tell what was loaded into that question. Only that *something* was. Instead of answering, she said, "This makes me think a little of the first time you came and knocked on my door. Back in Tember, at Wendell Anwar's house. Remember that?"

"Of course I remember that."

Cam still stared at the fire. Nysska wanted to follow up with, *That was the first night we made love,* but in the moment it felt inappropriate, so she kept her mouth shut. After a few more seconds, she settled on, "I hate how awkward this is."

Those silver eyes that Nysska simultaneously hated and loved so much snapped up and fixed on her own. "I thought you were *dead.*"

Nysska drew a deep breath. "I know."

"I watched that arrow punch through you. I tried to hold you, when you tipped over the railing, do you remember *that?* I tried to hold you, but you were too heavy. And I was too weak. And if I'd kept holding on, you would've dragged me over the edge with you. We both would have fallen." Cam's voice caught in a hitch as tears shimmered silver in her eyes. "So I let you *go.*"

"Of course. That's exactly what you should have done."

Cam sobbed, once, a sound and a tremor in her chest that seemed to catch her off-guard, and she stood up from the chair and faced the fire. "I don't think you understand what I'm saying. I don't think I'm making myself clear."

Nysska stood as well, arms aching to encircle her, to press Cam's back against her chest, to rest her chin on the top of Cam's head and hold her and tell her that everything was going to be fine. Nysska didn't move as she spoke. "Whatever you have to say to me, I want to hear it."

Cam didn't move either. "I let you go."

"Yes."

Now Cam turned, head tilted back to look Nysska in the face. "*No. I* mean *I let you go.* I *mourned* you, Nysska. I accepted that you were dead." She hugged herself. "And I said goodbye."

"Oh." The implications of that grew larger the more she considered them. "Oh." Then, "So…you…were not pleased to see me?"

Cam scoffed and took a few aimless steps away. "Of course, I was pleased to see you."

"Because you seemed genuinely upset when I said I couldn't touch you."

"Are you really going to make this difficult?"

Nysska almost made a sound in response to that mule kick to the gut. "Am I—am I making *what* difficult?" She closed the distance between them. "Are you ending things with me?"

"Am I—? Fuck *no*! I came here to apologize!"

Nysska let her brows draw together. "Really?"

Cam put her hands on either side of her forehead. It looked a bit as if she were trying to keep her brain from blowing out of her skull. "And I'm doing a truly shit job of it." Her hands fell to her side. "I say this with all the love in my heart, Nysska, but you are a *lot* to deal with."

"Let us come back to that part. You are *not* ending things with me?"

"I…" Cam clenched her jaw. "I—fuck. Can I touch you or not? That wasn't part of your oath, was it?"

"Yes, you can touch me, that was just because I didn't have control of the runes yet, I told you all before that it's safe n—"

Nysska's words cut off as Cam threw herself into her arms and found Nysska's lips with her own.

Nysska felt a little dizzy when she finally set Cam down, and Cam herself panted a little. As she tugged Cam's shirt free of her trousers, Cam's hands grasped both of hers. "Wait. Stop. Wait."

Nysska did as she was asked, pausing in mid-motion. "Yes?"

"I love you. You know that."

"I do."

"I—I meant it. Nysska. When I said I let you go. I *had* to. If I hadn't, I would have died. The loss would have killed me. I said goodbye to you. And I—I *moved on*."

Nysska took a step backward. "You've found someone else?"

"No! That's not what I mean. I mean I—I accepted your death. But now you're back."

"I am. Yes. I'm right here." Nysska swallowed and softly cleared her

throat. "So…what does this mean? For—for us?" When Cam didn't immediately answer, she added, "What can I do?"

Cam took Nysska's hands in hers again and brought them up to her
lips, kissing the knuckles. "I don't know exactly what it means. I'm still
recovering from seeing you walk through the door, back from the dead. I
just know…going forward…whatever we have. It's going to be different.
It's different now."

Nysska kissed Cam's knuckles in turn. "Different good? Or different
bad?"

"I don't know. I only know it's not the same as it was before. I don't
see how it *could* be."

"But this new thing…it could be good? Yes? We could make it good?"

A tear spilled out of Cam's right eye. Nysska watched it reflect the
firelight as it tracked down her perfect cheek. "I want it to be."

Nysska pushed the tear away with the back of one finger. "Would it be
disrespectful to tell you how much I want to make love to you right now?"

Cam's fingers darted forward, suddenly busy with the buttons of
Nysska's trousers. "No. It's healthy. It's taking hold of life. Proving to
ourselves that we're still here." Nysska pulled Cam's shirt up and off of
her, and Cam twined her arms around Nysska's torso and squeezed.
"Great Dragon, Nysska, I thought I'd lost you. I thought I'd held you for
the last time." She pulled her face away from Nysska's breasts just far
enough to look up at her. "I thought you were dead *because of my
weakness.*"

Nysska led Cam to the edge of the bed, but kept her standing as she
undid the fastens of Cam's trousers. As the leather slid to the floor,
Nysska slipped her hands under the camisole and raised it slowly over
Cam's head. She tossed the garment aside, bent down and turned her
head to accommodate for her horns, and kissed her way from Cam's forehead down to the tip of her nose and then her lips. "What happened to me
was not your fault."

Cam's body shuddered, and more tears came to her eyes, but she
wound her fingers into Nysska's hair.

Nysska pushed Cam down so that she sat on the edge of the bed, knelt,
and left a trail of kisses down Cam's neck and across her collarbone and
dropping to her left breast. Nysska kissed one nipple, then the other, and
repeated the words. "What happened to me was not your fault."

"But…"

"Sshhh."

At the urging of Nysska's fingers, Cam raised her hips enough to let her underpants slide down. Nysska pulled them and Cam's trousers free and tossed them on top of her shirt and camisole, and nudged Cam's knees apart. She kissed the inside of one knee, making her way up the inner thigh.

"I've dreamed about this," Cam whispered, and Nysska felt a teardrop land on the back of her hand. She reached up and gently guided Cam to lie back.

"What happened to me," she said between more kisses, "was *not your fault.*"

As she made the woman she loved writhe and whimper and moan, Nysska hoped Cam might someday believe those words.

19

The Keeper in Nysska's original Crucible, a man named Staige, had often waxed poetic about the history of the Empire once he'd gotten good and soused. Since he got good and soused every single day, Nysska had spent many a long ride between villages listening to him regale her with tales of the amazing things humans had accomplished. She'd listened politely as long as he stayed downwind.

As Staige had explained it, Coalgarden straddled the line between "large town" and "small city." It took its name from a long-defunct coal mine that left in its wake a sprawling boom town of hastily-constructed homes and businesses. Upon surveying the almost-completely-abandoned region, the Cathedral's engineers decided its underlying infrastructure, particularly as applied to the running water threaded throughout the town from the nearby Chang River, meant that it was worth repurposing. For the last seventy-five years Coalgarden had been the Cathedral's administrative hub. Only recently had Nysska learned that it also served as General Boris Cullen's second home.

Raoul sat in a coach with Cam and Nysska as the horses made their way through one of the narrow mountain passes that allowed access from the west. Percy had chosen to drive, much preferring to stay out in the wind. The blood lynxes took turns, one riding on the bench next to him while the other prowled along the side of the road, occasionally pouncing on some small critter moving in the tall grass.

Nysska said, "It doesn't feel good. Asking Morrin to help us right after we tell her about the General."

Cam let her knee touch Nysska's. "It's what she does, though. Identifying poisons and such? That's her whole vocation now. None of us have been there, but we hear she's got quite the setup for it. And she'll *want* to help." When Raoul pushed the curtain aside and peered out the window, Cam said, "How long has it been since you've been back here?"

He shrugged. "I came here a lot when I was a kid. That was one of the few ways I could reliably see him. But then I got old enough to join and the visits stopped."

Nysska leaned over beside Raoul and peered out. Seeing the city from a height as they were, coming down the mountain road, Nysska could easily work out the location of the original coal mine. The streets radiated out from it like spokes on a wheel. Unlike towns such as Tember or Caulspring or even Taurus Hill, there seemed to be no unifying flow to its architecture. The structures varied wildly in size and style, as if ten or eleven different towns had been dumped into a bag, shaken up, and poured out onto the ground, the pieces falling where they pleased.

Raoul pointed. "See that quarry? That's where we're headed." He sounded perfectly calm. A little unsettlingly calm.

After they stopped for the midday meal, Nysska and Cam walked a short distance away from the group. "Does Raoul seem all right to you?" Nysska asked quietly. "I'm not sure how I would react in his position, but I don't think it would be like this."

Cam glanced back at Raoul and Percy. Raoul, at the moment, was holding Jax up so that Percy could look more closely at a spot on the big cat's belly. Nysska heard Percy say, "Hold still, you big crybaby."

Cam said, "He's still stunned. He's got to be. The impact hasn't fully struck him yet."

Nysska moved so that her body blocked Raoul and Percy's view and took Cam's hand in her own. "I feel bad for him. You and I have each other for comfort, and Percy has the kitties. Raoul's got no one." She paused. "Now more than ever."

Cam brought Nysska's hand up to her lips. "Do you ever stop to think how far you've come?"

"Excuse me?"

She let Nysska's hand go. "From when you first met us, I mean. That day when you walked into the ballroom in Tember with Governor Anwar.

It was *so obvious* that you didn't want to be there. I mean, you didn't sneer at us, but I got the impression you wanted to."

"Well—I—"

Cam smiled and shook her head. "No, no, I understand why you felt that way, I really do. It's just—you care about Raoul. Really, truly care about him. That's a big change, is all I was trying to say."

Nysska looked back again. Percy had concluded whatever business he'd had with Jax's belly fur, and now Jax had climbed up onto Raoul's shoulders and clung there, mashing the side of his face into Raoul's ear. Raoul reached up and scratched Jax's head between the ears. "He's like a brother to me. He and Percy both are. It means even more now that my own brother is gone."

Still carrying the blood lynx on his shoulders, Raoul waved to them. "We need to get moving!" he called out.

As they walked back to the horses, Nysska said, "I think we should be ready for when the impact *does* hit him."

"Agreed."

The quarry at Coalgarden reminded Nysska of the Canyon of the Word in Slocum. Not acoustically—near as she could tell, the quarry was a place where sound went to die—but in the way its walls had been worked, making it into something that resembled a sort of hive. A long, wide terrace started at the top and spiraled down to the floor, the spiral getting tighter as it went, with both wooden and stone structures built at the entrances of the chambers drilled and chiseled into the rock. It would probably have taken them a solid hour to make their way around and around the quarry's perimeter until they reached the bottom, but that turned out not to be necessary, as multiple staircases had also been built into the design.

"We're headed to the bottom, I take it?" Percy asked.

"Yes," Raoul said. "How did you know?"

"Oh, I just figured that'd be my fucking luck. Down is fine. It's the coming back up that's already making my knees hurt."

Raoul surprised Nysska by showing Percy a smile. "We can borrow some horses for the return trip if you'd like." The smile dimmed. "Depending on what Morrin has to say."

The Ninth left their horses at a stable next to the beginning of the spiral terrace, taken by men in Cathedral-issue armor. Every person she saw, in fact, wore either military armor or a military uniform. The only exception was a pair of women wearing long black coats embroidered with dazzling, swirling golden patterns: high-ranking runemasters from one of the Imperial Colleges.

Raoul led them down one of the long series of stairs. As they descended, Nysska peered around at all the structures dug into the walls. "These look like neither homes nor businesses."

"Because they're not," Raoul said. "These are all offices. I said Coalgarden was the Cathedral's administrative capital, right? Well, this is where all the administrating gets done."

"And Morrin chose this place to work?" Cam asked.

Raoul made a soft sound like *hmph*. "My father chose it, not Morrin. I imagine the Cathedral wanted to keep a close eye on what she was doing." He gestured around them. "Can't get much closer to the Cathedral than right here."

At the bottom of the stairs, after a pair of soldiers had met and vetted them, they were directed to a nondescript door in the quarry's northern wall. As the group moved, Nysska said, "This is a bit bizarre. Everyone looking at the sethyd. None of them realizing who I am."

Raoul glanced at her. "My father had you registered as a consultant. I think probably everyone's wondering what you're consulting on."

Nysska cleared her throat softly. "We'll need to talk about that at some point."

"Talk about what?"

"About my place in the unit. You have an Enforcer now. We left him back in Mount Stark, but he's still a member of the Ninth."

They reached the door, a broad, solid bronze affair under a broad oilcloth awning, with huge hinges driven deep into the surrounding stone. Raoul said, "At some point, yes, we'll talk about it." Without any further words he clacked open the door's latch and swung it wide.

A tall, broad tunnel greeted them, lit by a string of lanterns hung from the ceiling, and Nysska's stomach tightened painfully. *Another fucking rabbit warren.* She'd been in too many life-or-death fights in such places, seen too many atrocities.

The feeling abated somewhat when a rich, complex scent wafted up from out of the tunnel. Beside her, Cam sniffed. "What *is* that?"

Percy sniffed as well, and both blood lynxes' jaws dropped open as they took in the scent. Percy's mouth stretched wide in an unselfconscious grin. "Smells like...everything," he said, and he and the two big cats pushed right past Raoul and made their way down the tunnel.

"I guess we're following...?" Cam ventured. Raoul made a guttural sound of annoyance, and the three of them hurried after Percy as a soldier swung the big bronze door shut behind them.

At the end of the ten-meter-long tunnel, Nysska came out into...

Words initially failed her.

It was a *warehouse*—a vast, cavernous space, not unlike the bizarre chamber where they'd discovered the cocoons from which the Gemini had emerged at Solace Canyon. She remembered Singer's description of it: *Morrin's thaumaturgical...smell...house.* Nysska decided she liked that description.

Row upon row of racks filled this massive room, just as it had in the Gemini cavern. And yet it was *nothing* like that space. For one thing, everywhere she looked, the place was brightly lit, with no dark corners or pools of shadow. For another, the racks and the walls had been painted. Mostly a cheerful, sunny yellow, but here and there along the walls the stone was decorated with murals. Huge, brightly colored paintings depicting summery meadows, or windswept beaches, or revelers around a festive bonfire. To the left of the door, a long table stood against the wall, covered in silver trays heaped with—Nysska stared—*pastries*. As she watched, a man dressed in a long gray coat, intently studying a thick sheaf of parchments, wandered past the table, picked up a custard tart, and ate it as he wandered away again.

"Is it just me," Cam murmured at Nysska's side, "or does this place seem...welcoming?"

It wasn't just the colors, Nysska acknowledged to herself while trying to think of a response to Cam. It was the array, the vast mélange, of aromas. From one second to the next, Nysska detected the scent of pine needles, then baking bread, then ocean water. The air felt thick, but not in an oppressive or unpleasant way. More like—a *caress*. As if the atmosphere were enfolding her in a soothing embrace.

A familiar voice reached them, coming from the other side of the nearest row of racks. "It's really more like a catalogue," Morrin James said, moving closer.

Nysska's overwhelmed eyes focused on the closest section of the nearest rack. The shelf there appeared to contain samples of...things, she couldn't be sure what they were exactly. Dozens upon dozens of small boxes or vials, each nestled into a soft cloth pad, each covered by a clear glass dome with a small bronze handle on top. Nysska squinted. Each of the samples was labeled, though the writing was too small to read unless she got closer.

Cam and Nysska exchanged glances, both quietly smiling. "You think *I've* come a long way," Nysska whispered.

Both blood lynxes, who had been staring around them with great round eyes, recognized Morrin's voice and moved to the front of the group, sitting and staring as they waited.

Morrin drew closer still. "The idea was to take samples of—well, samples of *everything*. Or at least, as many things as we could find. Plant matter, snippets of the coats of different animals, soil samples from different regions. Basically a representation of everything, all across the Empire, stored here so that the Scent Sensors on whatever case—if they didn't recognize something already—could come here and have something by which to compare evidence."

Nysska heard the soft panting of a dog. At the same time, Flax and Jax's tails swished back and forth.

"The plan was to have places like this in key strategic areas around the Empire, so that no Sensor would have too long to travel if they needed to make such a comparison, but we've found there are still plenty of kinks to work out here first."

A male voice Nysska didn't recognize said, "Such as?"

"Well, I said that it was really like a catalogue, and that's the heart of it —the question of how to catalogue things. There might be a plant that grows in seven different regions, and it's known by seven different names. If a poison is used in the Flat Rocks Territory, and one of the ingredients is catsbane, but it's catsbane specifically from the Green Needles Territory, and out there they call it yellowroot, well—which one do *we* call it? And how do we store it and display it, so that any Sensor can find it? The list goes on, but that's really what we're dealing with. A question of standardization."

Morrin came around the end of the rack, followed by her dog, Rosie, and a tall, somber man in a Cathedral uniform. She looked remarkably similar to when Nysska had first met her, a lifetime ago when they both served in the Forty-Seventh Crucible. Short. Milk-pale skin. Not much meat on her bones. Bland brown hair and watery blue eyes and a generous nose, on either side of which the silvery Scent Runes glimmered. And yet at the same time she looked *nothing* like the old Morrin, with her shoulders back and confidence ringing out of her voice, a modified gray Cathedral uniform fitting her with tailored precision. Morrin said, "I've actually begun work on a book that will standardize everything across the Empire—" but broke off when she recognized the Ninth Crucible standing there.

Rosie, a rangy hound with a speckled coat, barked once and charged forward, and Nysska knelt and braced herself just in time for Rosie to spring into her arms and cover her face with dog kisses. No sooner had Nysska laughed and tried to pet her, though, but Rosie jumped out of her reach and barreled straight into Flax and Jax, so that the three of them tumbled across the stone floor. Flax was the first to right herself, and she leapt at the dog, landing squarely on her head. Jax followed suit, and after a few moments of joyous wrestling the three animals streaked away around the warehouse's perimeter.

No such joy could be seen on Morrin's face. She squinted, her weak eyes darting from face to face, and before anyone could speak, she said, "Something's happened to Boris, hasn't it?"

"I believe I have enough to finish my report, ma'am," the Cathedral officer said, and walked swiftly away, casting worried, sympathetic glances over his shoulder, as if he knew bad news was coming and that it would be inappropriate for him to witness it.

Raoul went to Morrin. "I don't think there's any good way to say this," he said, his voice trembling. "My father has been killed."

Morrin took a faltering step backward on shaky knees and bumped hard into one of the racks. She made a sound like, "Nnnnnnn."

Raoul moved closer, steadying her. "I'm so sorry," he said. "I know the two of you had grown close."

As Nysska watched, waves of pain so palpable and clear that they brought tears to her own eyes crashed across Morrin's face. The young woman pitched forward as if she were about to vomit, but though her mouth stretched wide, nothing more than a strangled breath emerged. Her hands groped, nerveless, until they caught hold of Raoul's jacket, and she tugged on it, her limbs spasming.

Morrin's face turned up, her pale blue eyes searching Raoul's face, and one of those malfunctioning hands pressed against his cheek. "You're sure?" Her words came out like the squeal of a corroded hinge. "You're sure he's gone? There's been no mistake?"

"No mistake, Morrin. I'm sorry. He's gone."

Her knees gave way completely then, and Raoul lowered her to the floor as the tears and the wails came in earnest. Other people in gray coats—Morrin's employees—gathered at a distance, hesitant, watching. Morrin clung to Raoul's neck, sobbing, her body hitching—

Nysska witnessed the moment that the raw, ragged agony bursting out of Morrin like flames from a raging fire melted the shell of Raoul's self-control. His back, always held so ramrod-straight, bent as if it had broken, and his arms wrapped around Morrin and held her to him, and his black, steely eyes and determined jaw collapsed into the abyss of pain that Boris Cullen's death had opened beneath the two of them.

A razor-sharp keening rose from Raoul Cullen as he lowered his head and buried his face in Morrin's hair, and the two of them wept in excruciating unity.

20

C am beckoned to a young man in a long gray coat. He approached them at once, but cast concerned glances at Morrin and Raoul, reluctant to speak when he got there.

"Where are Morrin's living quarters?" Cam asked. "Does she live up in the city proper?"

Now that he was right in front of them, Nysska saw the faint silver runes beneath the skin of his face, alongside his nose, just as they were on Morrin. *They're all Scent Sensors. Everyone in a gray coat. She's got a whole fleet of Scent Sensors working for her. And that's all thanks to General Cullen.*

"N-no," the young man said. He had golden skin and the same kind of eyelids that Princess Aschling had, that made her eyes look slightly tilted. "She had quarters built here." He lifted a hesitant hand and pointed across the warehouse floor, to a door decorated with a field of daffodils.

"Thanks," Percy told the young man, as Nysska and Cam approached Morrin and Raoul. "That'll be all." Glancing around, Percy followed that with, "No, not quite all. Who's in charge here after Sensor James?"

"Uh." The young man hesitated again. "That'd be me, I guess."

"And your name is?"

"Nishioka."

"Well, then, Nishioka, you let everyone know that Sensor James is going to be indisposed for a short while, and whatever it is she has you working on, get back to fucking work. Yeah?"

Nishioka nodded and hurried off, approaching the nearest cluster of gray-coats.

While Cam spoke to Raoul, Nysska knelt beside Morrin and gently pulled her out of the sobbing embrace. Morrin's eyes swam in tears still, but focused on Nysska's face quickly enough, though the hurt they contained drilled into Nysska's heart as well. "Nysska," she said thickly. "You're alive. You're alive!" Morrin surprised her by throwing her arms around Nysska's neck. They stood together, slowly, Nysska supporting her as they came up to their feet. "Your hair—and your horns!"

"I'm in disguise," Nysska said gently.

Morrin sniffled. "I don't know what I'm going to do," she said, her words muted against Nysska's chest. "Boris did all this for me. He's the one who made sure it all ran the way it's supposed to. I don't know if I can do this without him." She jerked her head up and pulled away, horror etched onto her features. "Oh, Dragon damn me, that's *awful* of me—he's gone, and I'm thinking of *myself*—"

Cam had helped Raoul to his feet as well. He furiously wiped at his face, slamming the tears away, and stepped in between Nysska and Morrin and took Morrin's shoulders in his hands. "Don't do that. Don't blame yourself, don't be cruel to yourself. This is a shock, I know it's a shock, we all do. But my father held you in the *highest* regard. He would not want you to heap abuse on your own head now."

"What would he want me to do, then?"

"He'd want you to help us out of the shithole we're in," Percy said, eyeing the gray-coats, who had begun to wander slowly away, casting looks over their shoulders. "Maybe we can get inside? That's your living quarters over there, yeah?"

Morrin nodded, wiped her nose on the sleeve of her own gray coat, and led the way to the daffodil door.

At the rear of the group, Cam whispered to Nysska, "I guess we know when it's going to hit Raoul."

Nysska nodded solemnly. "That was the first. Or, at least, the first that we've seen. There will probably be more times like that."

"Then we'll be prepared for those, too."

Morrin produced a bronze key and unlocked the daffodil door, which squeaked a little as it swung open. She led them into a broad, open space that had been divided into different areas based on the clusters of furniture in each one. An enormous map of the Empire dominated one wall. Morrin's quarters reminded Nysska a little bit of the "party room" they'd seen at Sergei Benitoff's home outside Tember, except not tacky and sleazy.

Much like the style of the larger warehouse, Morrin James had decorated her living space in bright, sunny, cheerful colors, and in the far corner sat a huge birdcage holding at least a dozen vividly-hued songbirds. Brilliant lanterns kept the room as well-lit as the warehouse. Rosie, unimpressed by anything in the room, made her way to a plush dog bed near the door and flopped down into it. Nysska watched as Flax and Jax padded across the floor, making their way between leatherbound chairs and around the comfortable-looking bed, straight toward the birdcage.

"Oi, you two," Percy called, and the lynxes paused. "Look, but do not touch, understand?"

Neither cat gave any indication that they'd heard his directive, but when they reached the spacious cage they both sat, perfectly still, and simply watched the birds inside. For their part, the birds didn't seem to care that they were being watched, and continued flitting about the cage, nibbling from small bowls, twittering and cheeping.

Morrin sounded hollowed out. "Please. Sit wherever you'd like. Make yourselves at home." In contrast with her words, she didn't move except to waver on her feet a bit. Raoul had just sat down, but he rose again and steered Morrin to a seat on a couch beside him. When Percy, Cam, and Nysska had likewise found seats—Nysska swung another couch around to face the one where Raoul and Morrin sat—Morrin slumped forward and hugged herself. "How?" she asked, tears not far away. "How did it happen?"

Raoul had regained his usual stony demeanor, but Nysska wondered how deep that really went. He looked over at Nysska. "Does she get to know, too?"

Nysska kept her voice as colorless as she could. "I've already broken my oath. And I trust her. I don't see the harm in telling Morrin everything I've told all of you."

Nysska started first. Much as she had with the rest of the Ninth, she began with being pulled from the water, and went all the way through her journey to Slocum and her arrival at Mount Stark.

Raoul picked up the thread and told Morrin about how they'd been sent to Mount Stark to apprehend a multiple-murderer, and everything that followed. He finished with, "Which is why we came to see you."

Nysska added, "We're fairly certain the poison came from Klyburn. Now we're hoping you can tell us what it is, and maybe something about the treatment for it, if that *is* the treatment that I found in the jars."

Morrin sniffled again. She rose and went to a wash basin resting on a stone shelf carved out of the wall and splashed some water on her face. The towel still in her hands, she said, "Of course. Of course I'll help." Nysska watched as the tears returned—almost overwhelmed her—but suffered a defeat as Morrin fought them off.

Nysska slipped off the slim leather pack she'd been wearing since they left Mount Stark. Inside was another leather bag, sealed tightly with a sturdy drawstring. When she hesitated to open it, Raoul held his hand out. "Here. Let me do that."

Nysska paused but handed it over. Raoul gestured at a small table on the other side of the living area from Morrin's bed. "Mind if I use that?"

Morrin shook her head, watching him—and the bag—with clear interest.

Raoul went to the table, loosened the drawstring, and pulled out a large makeshift envelope created by folding an oilcloth and tying it with another length of the same drawstring. He untied the envelope, set it on the table, and carefully unfolded it to reveal the cargo inside.

"It's a sack," Morrin said, one dubious eyebrow lifting.

"A sack we took off Jinna Marsdown's body," Nysska said. "Full of something that's been poisoning almost the entire sethyd population in Slocum. I, ah—I don't really want to get close to it. It affects the runes in a weird way."

Morrin slowly moved toward the table. As she approached, the runes on either side of her nose lit up—dimly at first, but steadily growing brighter silver. "Cam? Have you tried to look at this?"

Cam didn't move. She had stood up from her chair, but gone no closer to the table and the poison-filled sack lying on it. "*Tried* is right. It's like nothing I've ever seen before. Wait, no, that's not true. It's got something to do with argonium, I know that much. I just don't know what."

Morrin stopped about halfway to the table. "And you said you had the treatment for this?"

Nysska opened a belt pouch and took out the little packet she'd smuggled from the cellar. "Maybe. I don't get any odd feelings from it. It just smells like flowers to me." She handed it to Morrin.

Morrin went to the other side of the table and opened the little packet. The runes in her face lit up like flames from a tiny silver star. She took a deep breath of the flowery dust inside, then another, then a third. Her expression unreadable, Morrin set the packet down, approached the heavy burlap sack and bent over it, runes still flaring as she inhaled.

Nysska had been secretly hoping that she wasn't about to poison her friend. She remembered when Morrin had identified a poison inside a cadaver at Summergray and almost collapsed from its effects. None of that appeared to be happening now, though. Instead Morrin straightened up and backed away, coming to rest in a half-sitting, half-leaning posture against the back of a couch. Her runes dimmed and went out as she folded her arms, frowning.

"Well?" Raoul said. "Do you recognize anything?"

Instead of answering that question, Morrin asked another one. "You've told me everything?" She peered from one face to another around the group. "No important bits you're leaving out?"

Nysska exchanged glances with Cam, who spread her hands. Nysska said, "I don't think so."

"No," Raoul agreed. "We've given you every last detail."

"Well, then, let me just say, I'm impressed with the Ninth Crucible's knack for wading into shit up to your necks."

"I knew it," Percy grumbled. "It's always the shit with us."

Raoul's voice grew marginally louder. "What are you saying, Morrin?"

The young Sensor shook her head and shrugged. "I don't have anything new to tell you about the poison, or the bag it came in. But that 'flowery powder' you scooped up, Nysska…"

Morrin went to a small desk and dipped a pen in an inkpot. Crossing to the huge map of the Empire, she drew a line heading southeast from Mount Stark, through Ransom Falls and Klyburn—but continued the line to a new location, which she circled. "That powder came straight from Fort Slade."

Raoul's eyes widened.

Cam dropped her face into one hand.

Percy let out a short, barking laugh and said, "Well isn't that just fucking typical?"

A short time later, after Morrin had asked one of the gray-coats to bring in some food and the Ninth had gladly tucked in, Nysska wandered out into the warehouse. She told herself it was to stretch her legs after eating, but she really just wanted some time alone to think. Something like an idea had occurred to her and she wanted to give it a chance to gestate.

She moved slowly down an aisle with racks filled on both sides by various flowers. Nysska had never paid much attention to flowers before. She found it a bit hard to believe that there were so *many*. Foxgloves, peonies, daffodils, tulips, roses—they seemed to go on forever, each single example preserved under glass. She wondered what happened when the flower inevitably wilted and shriveled so much as to be useless. Did Morrin have gray-coats constantly combing the countryside for fresh samples? That struck her as impractical, bordering on non-viable.

As if having read her mind, Morrin appeared by her side and said, "It doesn't really work with flowers, not the way we're doing with things like sand and tree bark. I should've thought of that before—I'm thinking I'll have to have some sort of garden. So I can grow actual examples of everything? But that'll present its own challenges, given the wide range of climate and conditions across the Empire. And Coalgarden isn't really a great place to grow a garden anyway, despite the name. I've begun to wonder if maybe there could be some sort of covering over it, so I could keep the temperature and moisture right, but plants need sun, of course, which means the whole thing would need to be made of glass, I suppose. I was thinking maybe Aschling could help me with it. Except that doesn't take into account variations from specific regions. I'm sure we couldn't identify a rose grown in Caulspring by Scenting one grown here. It's a whole ordeal."

Nysska listened, sort of enthralled. When she served with Morrin in the Forty-Seventh Crucible—back when their Commander, Brux Haller, had horribly abused Morrin every chance he got—getting her to say more than five words in a row had been a challenge. Now the little woman with the mousy hair and the weak eyes had blossomed into something else entirely. Someone with enough confidence in herself to head up what was, Nysska had to admit, an impressive and unprecedented endeavor. That blossoming had apparently extended to a natural loquaciousness. Morrin sounded a little like the chirping songbirds in her quarters.

Nysska said, "Have you been in touch with her? Aschling?"

"Only a little. She's not like Captain Kagan and Singer—of course she's not, you know that—so she doesn't have to hide, but no one can know who she really is, either, so when we write letters we can't talk about anything too specific. And especially not that big huge project thing she's working on."

Nysska's eyebrows lifted a fraction of a centim. "So she's really trying to do it? She thinks she can build a ship that will sail through the sky?"

"All she'll say is things like, 'Project continues.'"

Nysska put a tentative hand on Morrin's shoulder. She meant it to be a simple act of comfort, but Morrin immediately moved in and wrapped Nysska up in another hug. "I'm so glad you're alive," Morrin said. "I was devastated when I heard you'd been lost like that." She stepped back and gave Nysska a lopsided smile. "I should've known it would take more than getting shot through the chest and falling off a cliff to kill you."

"Well, it came awfully close."

Morrin's eyes drifted down to Nysska's arms. "So it's really true? The Gemini saved you by giving you runes?"

Nysska made sure there weren't any gray-coats around and pushed up a shirt sleeve. She made the rune nearest her wrist glow for a moment before shutting it down and letting her sleeve drop back into place.

Morrin whispered, "*Wow...*" and then, "What does it feel like?"

"Until I fell off the tower in Mount Stark—I have really got to stop falling from great heights—it was horrible. I kept trying to figure out how to describe it, and the closest I got was having a whole hill's worth of ants under my skin. But now...now everything fits like an old shoe. They grow bright when I tell them to, go dim when I tell them to. I barely even have to think about it."

"And they enhance your strength?"

"Exponentially."

"So no more chance of—um. Of losing control?"

Nysska grimaced at the memory of the four men she'd torn apart in the cellar. Her lips tightened. "I don't believe so. I only wish I could've gained control sooner. For many days I blamed myself for Hix's death..."

"You shouldn't."

"Well, I do. Still. To an extent. But more than that, I blame the Gemini for making me their experiment subject. I blame them for putting runes in me with *no* idea of what would happen."

Morrin laid a hand on Nysska's arm. "Good. That's good." She paused. "But they also saved your life."

"Yes. Because nothing is ever fucking simple."

Morrin sighed and glanced back toward her living quarters. "If that's not the truth, then truth I've never heard."

Taking advantage of a natural break in the conversation, Nysska said, "So...I could not help noticing that you have been referring to General Cullen as 'Boris.'"

Morrin's pale cheeks turned red. "Is that bad? Too disrespectful?"

"Not as far as I'm concerned, no. I simply did not realize that the two of you had...become close."

The blush deepened in Morrin's face. "I could tell, a lot of people in the Cathedral—and in the Thaumetallicon in particular—*hated* me because he showed me so much special treatment."

Nysska glanced around, and gestured at the warehouse. "But it was for an undeniably good cause."

"Well, *I* think so, and *he* thought so. I suppose there were other parts of the Imperial Colleges that wanted the resources he funneled our way." She leaned closer. "If they only knew how much he was sending to Princess Aschling in secret. That was out of his personal coffers, of course, but she's been receiving enough materiel, she could've built a small town by now."

Nysska couldn't help her own salacious curiosity. "But—you and the General were...happy together?" When Morrin stared at her blankly, she said, "I only ask because, well, there was quite an age difference between the two of you. That's significant among humans, isn't it?"

The blank stare continued for a few more seconds, and then Morrin's entire head turned a disquieting reddish-purple. "Oh, Dragon, no—Dragon help me, Nysska, you've got it all wrong!" She clutched Nysska's wrists. "We weren't *together*! Not as a *couple*! Fuck no!"

Nysska had to suppress a chuckle, mildly annoyed with her own brain that she immediately compared the emphatic disagreement "fuck no" with the abbreviated statement regarding the status of General Cullen and Morrin's relationship: "Fuck? No!"

Inappropriate, Nysska.

Morrin had come close to hyperventilating. She gasped out, "Boris was like a *father* to me! And I know he felt the same way, because he flat-out said so, he said, 'Morrin, you're like the daughter I never had.' I never *ever* thought of him in a, a, a *couples* kind of way!"

Nysska tried for her best look of understanding. "All right. All right, I understand."

Morrin's eyes darted back toward the daffodil-covered door again. Almost too softly for Nysska to hear her, she said, "In fact…"

"What?"

"Nnn-nothing."

"Morrin."

"It's just…"

Nysska had a flash of realization and gasped softly. "Morrin! *Raoul?*" Morrin made a *Not so loud!* gesture with both hands, so Nysska dropped her volume even further. "Since when? Not when you were crying in each other's arms?"

"No, no—it's—it's been months. Since Cliffside, really."

"Does he know?"

"No! No. Well, maybe. I don't know." She peered up at Nysska. "Has he said anything about me?"

Nysska pursed her lips. "Not around me. But you have to understand, that doesn't mean anything. The moons and stars have to align *just so* before Raoul opens up. To anyone."

Nysska happened to be looking at the daffodil door when it opened, revealing Percy with Flax in his arms. He caught sight of the two of them, halfway down the aisle as they were, and beckoned to them. Nysska said, "Looks as though we're being summoned."

"Don't say anything to Raoul," Morrin said, softly but urgently. "I'll talk to him when the time is right."

"My leaps are sealed and locked," Nysska replied. As they walked, she tried to picture Morrin and Raoul as a couple. She couldn't, but decided that didn't mean anything either.

Percy waited in the doorway for them to come back inside, then shut the door behind them and locked it. Raoul gestured for them to take seats —he had further rearranged Morrin's furniture, so that the couches and chairs made a circle—and Nysska settled gratefully onto one of the couches next to Cam, who gave her a quick, warm grin.

"Tell me about Fort Slade again," Raoul said to Morrin.

Morrin demonstrated her recently-acquired ability to surprise Nysska by shooting back, "Why? Was I not clear before?" Nysska had to wonder how much of that cheek came from the feelings Morrin harbored for him, and how much from the also newly-acquired pride she took in her profession.

Raoul frowned, but tempered his voice. "I'm not saying you weren't clear. I'm asking you to go over it again because I want to make sure it's firmly in my head." He cleared his throat. "Especially since we shouldn't be writing *any* of this down. So. If you would. Please."

Morrin crossed her legs primly. "Fine. The ingredients that I can identify definitively in the 'treatment powder' Nysska found are catsbane, ruthio, granite lichen, and djinntongue, all of which are plants common to the area right around Fort Slade. But that's not proof. The proof is in the trace amounts of stone mixed in with the herbs—if I had to guess, I'd say that came from the storeroom where they were kept. The more skillful Scent Sensors can pick out which minerals come from which region." She allowed herself a tiny, self-satisfied smile. "And the stone I Scented comes specifically from inside Fort Slade."

"Forgive me for being indelicate," Percy said, "but how the fuck do you know that? Nobody gets inside Fort Slade except people who get fucking *invited*." Flax had perched in his lap, and at these words she flopped over onto her back, clearly directing him to rub her belly. As he did, he added, "Fort Slade might as well be a children's tale."

Morrin folded her arms under the dainty curve of her bosom. "Boris —General Cullen—convinced a lot of powerful people to give me samples for the...sorry, I haven't settled on a name for this place yet. Not one that doesn't sound ridiculous. Anyway, it was actually *part* of the security for Fort Slade. He went to them and said, 'If there's ever a problem here—say, a theft—you'd want it to be traceable, right?' So they gave him samples of things from inside the mountain, including bits of stone from the floors and walls and ceilings. That's what I Scented. Traces of the rock dust."

Cam said, "So...what we're saying...is that the poison has something to do with argonium. Something in the mining or the smelting of it, something toxic."

Nysska spoke up. "Remember, it was a mining waste product that killed all the sethyds in Summergray."

Cam nodded. "Right. All right. So this is some other kind of mining thing, except instead of killing sethyds, it just makes them really weak."

Nysska frowned. "Weak and susceptible to suggestion, I would say. ... And apparently, in concentrated quantities over long periods of time, homicidally insane." She remembered Jinna Marsdown's eyes turning full blood-red. "I saw it happen with the courier. All that time exposed to it. I'm convinced she wouldn't have been hunting humans for sport in Mount Stark if she hadn't been driven half-insane by the poison."

Cam picked back up. "Well. So the poison comes from the one place where argonium is mined and smelted. And that's Fort Slade. But the *treatment* for the same poison *also* comes from Fort Slade."

"That sums it up," Raoul said, looking morose.

"It makes sense." Nysska cracked her knuckles. "For Tylar and Randolf, I mean. To use my mother as a figurehead, as Yshtarra, they manufactured an illness and then provided the cure, and everyone was more than happy to start listening to her. Which meant listening to *them*."

Percy scoffed. "Yeah, that's all fine and dandy, but it doesn't tell us who the fuck in *Fort Slade* is giving the poison *and* the antidote to the fucking sethyds in the first place. No offense, Nysska."

"None taken."

Raoul stood. He looked as if he might be seeking out the nearest window out of which to stare somberly. Finding no windows, he cleared his throat and said, "It has to be someone with access to raw argonium—the argonium that comes straight out of the mine and goes to the smelters —someone *really fucking high up* in the Thaumetallicon, because that's the only kind of person who'd have access like that. Whoever that someone is, they're providing the means for the sethyds to be taken over by a force that, correct me if I'm wrong, Nysska, *wants to kill every human*."

Nysska sighed. "You're not wrong."

21

Morrin leaned forward and put her elbows on her knees. Rosie, who had awakened from her nap at some point, came to her and put a paw on her thigh and nuzzled her face. Stroking Rosie's head, Morrin said, "So we have at least some idea of what's going on. What I want to know is, what are we going to do about it?" She looked at her dog instead of the group as she spoke. "Boris was our link. Wasn't he? If we needed something from the Cathedral, troops or resources or whatever, he had our backs. How do we accomplish anything without him?"

Nysska said, "General Cullen wasn't our *only* link. Morrin, is there a Conversation Stone anywhere around here?"

Morrin took a moment. "Um. Yes. Yeah, there's one in the—"

Her face crumpled and she doubled over, tears flowing. Nysska recognized the phenomenon. The unexpected strike of grief.

Her grandmother had described grief like an invisible phantom, an unseen, cruel prankster who followed you around and, at random times, slammed a fist into your gut. After you lost someone, she had said, the phantom was at its strongest, which made it that much bolder, so the strikes came more often. As time passed, though, the phantom's strength began to fade. Every once in a while he still got in a lucky shot, and it still hurt terribly, but he wasn't as bold anymore, and the strikes came further and further apart. Eventually the phantom got weak enough that the strikes didn't carry much force at all.

How long until the phantom finally goes away? Nysska had asked, and watched her grandmother slowly shake her head.

It never goes away completely.

The phantom had just landed the kind of blow to take someone out of a fight, and Morrin slumped on the couch, hugging herself while Rosie sat next to her and whined.

Raoul swiftly came and sat down beside her and put his arm around her shoulders and pulled her to him. "Hey, it's all right," he said, in a tone Nysska had never heard him use before. "You miss him. So do I. But it's going to be all right. You're going to be all right."

Morrin leaned against him, her face pressed against his chest, and he stroked her hair and made soothing sounds. Nysska caught Cam looking at her, an expression on her face that might as well have said, *Is what's going on here what I think is going on here?* in spoken Plainish.

Nysska twitched her eyebrows and pursed her lips in a sort of shrugging gesture she'd seen her mother make a thousand times. It meant, *Maybe? Who can say?* Cam nodded subtly and sat back in her seat on the couch, watching the show.

After a couple of minutes Morrin collected herself and, without looking at him, moved a short distance away from Raoul. "Sorry. I'm s-sorry. What I was going to say was that I think there's one in the chief a-administration building. That's where Boris had his o-office. Most of the people there tolerate me. I can take you there."

Percy hopped to his feet and made the kissing sound that beckoned the blood lynxes to him. "Well, then, let's fucking get to it."

Nysska stood. "Wait."

The group paused. After a glance at Morrin, Raoul stood as well. "Yes?"

Nysska shoved her hands into the pockets of her trousers. "This is a song I've sung before, but...whatever it is we're about to do—it's because of me. This is my fight. It's my mother, and my people, and I don't have any right even asking any of you to come with me, much less expecting you to."

Raoul startled her by making a loud, obnoxious fart sound with his tongue and lips. "Wrong! It's *partly* your fight, because it's your mother being held captive, and your people being drugged and recruited. But it's also *very fucking much* our fight, because someone in the Thaumetallicon is about to start a Dragon-damned war." He glanced around at the group as Cam stood and moved to stand by Nysska, discreetly holding her hand. "We *still* can't trust the Emperor. Remember that? Remember how he has white runes that no one's ever seen before and we don't know anything about? And now we find out some kind of suspicious shit's going on at the one place in the Empire where they mine argonium. Suspicious shit that could maybe fuck up the supply of the one thing Valco and his ancestors have *always* used to keep the peace? It very much involves all of us. And *because* we can't trust Emperor Valco, as usual, it's going to be us more or less on our own." He sprouted a humorless grin. "I'm fine with that. Everyone else?"

Cam made a sound of assent, and Percy said, "Fuck, Raoul, if we *weren't* wading into neck-deep shit, I wouldn't even know how to act."

"Right, then," Morrin said, heading for the door with Rosie in step beside her. "Everyone follow me."

Morrin led them across the floor of the warehouse and out the door to the floor of the quarry, where Nysska was mildly surprised to see that the sun was about to set, the quarry already deep in gray shadow. A few of Morrin's Sensors trailed along behind them, and she signaled to one, who readily scampered over. "We're going up to the town," she said to the young woman in a tone that sounded as if she'd copied it from General Cullen. "Bring the big wagon."

The gray-coat dashed away, curving around the edge of the quarry, and disappeared into a good-sized cave opening. To Morrin, Nysska said, "Looks as if you've got them all well-trained."

Morrin shrugged in an embarrassed sort of way. "We'll see how long that lasts. I think all the respect was for Boris."

"You shouldn't do that," Raoul said. He was standing ramrod-straight, as usual, arms folded and face stony, but his words for Morrin once again came across as gentle. "You shouldn't run yourself down. Everyone here respected my father, yes. But they can see that you're the right person for this job."

Cam steered Nysska a short distance from the group, and whispered, "What is going *on* with those two? Are they fucking and doing a bad job of being subtle about it?"

"No, they're not together. Morrin *wants* them to be, but she's not ready to talk to Raoul yet. I'm afraid that when she does, though, she's going to find out he thinks of her as a little sister more than anything else."

"You think Raoul's picked up on it?"

"Hard to say."

"Yeah." Cam watched the rest of the group contemplatively for a moment. "Might be good for him to be on the other side of something like this." She frowned. "Not so good for Morrin, though. Think we should do anything about it?"

"Absolutely, positively not. This is not our tree, not our squirrels."

"Fair enough."

Morrin called out to them. "Wagon's coming."

The gray-coat Morrin had sent running returned, driving a single-horse open wagon with two bench seats just big enough to seat three people on each one. The group piled in, with Rosie taking up the extra seat next to Morrin, and Flax and Jax underfoot on the floorboards.

Percy raised an eyebrow at the blood lynxes. "Since when do the two of you like riding in wagons?"

By way of answer, Jax began vigorously grooming himself, while Flax yawned, propped her chin on Percy's foot, and went to sleep.

The wagon took them up the spiraling terrace and out of the quarry, then along one of the spoke-like streets of Coalgarden. Now that it was getting dark the streets emptied out, which made Nysska wonder if there was a specific district for the public houses and brothels. Or maybe military personnel weren't allowed such indulgences. Maybe they all just retired to their residences and brushed up on the latest protocols. It occurred to Nysska that even though she'd been an official member of the Thaumetallicon, which was an extension of the Cathedral, for almost three years, she knew very little about the daily lives of actual soldiers. She wondered if that might be a thing in which she should take greater interest.

The wagon stopped in front of a nondescript, square, gray stone building, a lot like the dozens of other nondescript, square, gray stone buildings Nysska had seen since their arrival, and Morrin led the way inside with no hesitation.

A pair of soldiers stood at the far end of a short entry hall on either side of the only door, and snapped to attention as soon as they saw Morrin. "Evening, ma'am," one of them said. "You're here a bit late, if you don't mind me saying so."

"I don't mind a bit," Morrin said neutrally. "We just need to use the Conversation Stone."

The soldiers shot each other a glance. The same one who'd spoken before said, "We...usually...have authorization from General Cullen for that, ma'am."

Morrin froze, and Nysska feared she was about to suffer another gut punch from the grief phantom. Instead she said, "Well that's hardly going to happen now, is it?" Turning, she pointed at Raoul. "This is General Cullen's son, Commander Raoul Cullen, and we have Thaumetallicon business to attend to. So if you'll open the door, we'll attend to it."

Neither soldier needed *that* much convincing, Nysska didn't think, but Morrin's tone brooked absolutely no debate. They opened the door and pushed it wide, and the other soldier said, "You know where it is, ma'am —last door on the right."

Morrin passed them by with no further words.

The hallway down which Morrin led the Ninth Crucible reminded Nysska of the rest of the town, and even more so of the hive of offices dug into the walls of the quarry. Utilitarian. Not just function over form, but essentially no form at all. A few of the doors stood open, revealing now-unmanned desks covered in parchment, quills, ink pots, and sealing wax. Tall racks filled with scrolls were a common sight. Morrin paid none of the offices any attention.

She pushed open the last door on the right and led them into a room designed specifically and only for use of a Conversation Stone. The Stone itself sat on a typical polished-wood tripod in the center of the room, while the Ring rested on a black velvet cushion atop a small table near the door. Morrin picked up the ring and moved to put it on, but Nysska stepped forward quickly and caught her wrist.

"No. Morrin. Let me."

Morrin pulled her wrist free of Nysska's grip, but without any animosity. "What? Why?"

"Because if anyone here is going to get drained, it should be me."

Morrin looked unconvinced. "And what happens if the Ring interacts in some horrible way with your runes? What if it makes them go berserk? What if it makes you drop dead?"

Cam said, "That's a fair question. I don't know how we'd move forward with any of this if you weren't with us." She took Nysska's hand and gave it a squeeze filled with meaning.

Nysska nodded. "I hear you. But let me at least try it. I'll go slow. At the first sign of trouble I'll drop it, or pull it off."

Percy said, "If any one of us can wear that damn thing without getting fucking cooked, it's going to be Nysska. Might as well let her give it a shot."

Nysska turned to Raoul and found him scowling darkly. She said, "Let me guess. You don't like it. It's against regulations."

Raoul made a sour face. "I agree with Cam. If you're out of commission, I'm pretty sure we're all fucked." His features grew even more sour. "But we should also know what happens if you put it on. So go ahead."

Cam grunted, but got out of the way. Morrin handed the Ring to Nysska, who turned it over a couple of times in her palm. "I hope it doesn't matter which finger," she said, "because I think it'll only fit on my pinky." Before anyone could say anything in response to that, Nysska slipped the Ring on.

Nothing happened.

Raoul said, "How does it feel? Does it hurt? It hurt immediately when I wore it."

Nysska raised her hand and looked at it. As she did so, a dull ache spread out from the ring into her hand. "It hurts a little, yeah, but I don't think I'm about to lose control or burst into flames or anything, so let's do this." She stepped forward and used the Ring to tap the Conversation Stone.

The familiar yet bizarre display immediately formed in the air above the Stone, composed entirely of glimmering green light—the planet, revolving slowly, the three moons far above its surface, and the single great continent shining out of the world-enveloping ocean.

Except now they knew the map was wrong. Kainos wasn't the only continent. Aschling and Kagan and Singer had come across the Salt Ocean from a completely unknown land mass called Borealis. Nysska wondered if the Imperial cartographers would ever get the chance to map its shores.

"There," Cam said, pointing out the shining dot on the map in Tember. Her voice strained, she said, "Please hurry."

Nysska reached out with the hand bearing the Ring and touched the glowing dot. A few seconds passed, and then the image of the planet faded, replaced by a stodgy-looking, pale-skinned man in servants' livery. He recognized Nysska at once—that much was obvious from the look on his face—but still he said, "Whom shall I say is calling?"

"Please tell Governor Vachs that Nysska Stonegate of the Ninth Crucible needs to speak to her. Urgently."

As the pale-skinned man stepped away from the Conversation Stone in Governor Galena Vachs's home in Tember, Nysska glanced toward the door. Raoul had taken up a lookout post there. He gave her a thumbs-up signal: no one was outside listening.

The ache from the ring had taken over Nysska's hand by that point, reducing it to a painful brick attached to the end of her arm. The pain crept up her wrist—but stopped at the bottom edge of the lower rune in her forearm.

Galena Vachs appeared in the luminous green image. Her hair was longer than when Nysska had seen her last, but other than that she looked much the same: still the single most beautiful human Nysska had ever laid eyes on. Galena's mouth curled upward in a lopsided smile. "Nysska—hello, everyone. I would say that this is a pleasant surprise, but I can already tell from your faces that I'd be lying. What's going on?"

The ache sharpened, becoming something more like a knife blade being wedged into each of Nysska's finger joints. She spared a look down at her hand and watched the skin wrinkling. "I'm afraid I can't spare much time on explanations."

Galena nodded. "Of course. Dragon only knows what that ring is doing to you."

"So the pertinent question is this: how fast can you get to Coalgarden?"

Nysska flexed her hand. Cam said, "How is it?"

They sat in Morrin's living quarters again, along with Percy and Raoul and the blood lynxes, where Morrin had encouraged them to get a bit of rest while she continued with her duties. Galena Vachs had assured them she could be there by sundown the following day—which, now that they'd passed hour after excruciating hour staring at Morrin's super-cheerful walls, wasn't very far off—and while it irked Nysska beyond measure to have to sit and wait, trying to do anything at all about the Fort Slade situation without help from someone with actual power would be the sheerest folly.

"It's all right. The Ring didn't sap me the way it did Raoul—everything seems to be confined right here." She waggled her fingers. "The runes stopped the effect, I think. Of course, that might just mean that if I use the Ring for too long my hand will fall off."

Cam took the affected hand and kissed it. "Let's not find out."

"Agreed."

The door opened, and every head in the room turned, including the two big cats. Morrin came in quickly, looking flushed, and held the door. "Right this way, Governor," she said, and Galena Vachs walked into the room.

Galena took a look around, her face lighting up, and said, "Morrin, I absolutely *love* what you've done in here!" As Morrin's face grew pinker, Galena went on. "Not that I know what it looked like before you moved in, but this is the most *cheerful* cave I've ever seen!"

While Morrin sputtered in an attempt to say "thank you," Galena Vachs crossed the floor, grinning and waving. "Hello, everyone! It's so good to see you in person! How long has it been?" She went to Nysska first and embraced her, then hugged Cam and gave Raoul and Percy warm double-handed handshakes. "You all look so good!" Her sapphire-blue eyes twinkled with mischief. "Not at all like a bunch of battle-haggard heroes who've saved the Empire's ass twice now." Galena dropped to one knee and beckoned to Flax and Jax, digging into a pocket as she did so. "Hello, you precious little kitties! Who wants a treat? Hmm? Who wants one?" She pulled out a couple of pieces of bacon and offered them to the lynxes, both of whom readily went to her, took the bacon, and let themselves be thoroughly stroked and scratched. Rosie came to her, tail wagging, and when she'd finished with the lynxes Galena turned and hugged the speckled dog and gave her a treat as well.

Cam whispered to Nysska, "It's like the sun itself just walked in, isn't it?"

More earnestly than she meant to, Nysska whispered back, "She's *dazzling.*"

With a smile, Cam poked her with an elbow in the ribs. "Hey, now."

Galena Vachs stood, brushing her hands off on her thighs, and faced the group as Morrin came to stand beside Raoul. "All right. I had to be harder on a series of horses than I wanted to be to get here this fast. Tell me what you need to tell me."

Nysska said, "We need to break into Fort Slade, and we need you to get us plans for the place so we can do it."

Galena stared at her with those impossibly blue eyes for a long moment before she burst out laughing. "Well, you don't want much, do you?" When Nysska didn't say anything, a vertical crease appeared in Galena's perfect forehead. "But you're serious? You want to break into

Fort Slade. Literally, without exaggeration, the most secure site in the entire Empire. For Dragon's sake, Nysska, *why?*"

Nysska gestured at one of Morrin's chairs. "Please. Take a seat and we'll tell you."

Half an hour later, the Ninth Crucible remained seated, but Galena Vachs paced back and forth across Morrin's floor, as she'd been doing for the last fifteen minutes. She had only requested that Nysska pause a couple of times, and then only to ask intelligent, insightful questions.

Now she finally stopped, right in front of the two blood lynxes. Galena sat down on the floor, pulled Flax into her lap, and petted her as she spoke. "All right, first of all, what you're asking me for is impossible."

"But you're a fucking *governor*," Percy said. "You have access to all that secure shit, don't you? Uh, ma'am?"

Galena shook her head emphatically. "Not to *that* secure shit, no. Do you know what you have to go through to get assigned to Fort Slade? A special office of the Cathedral basically tears your whole life apart to make sure you can be trusted. Then, after you're sent there, the assignment is *permanent*. You and your family go and live there until you die." She chewed on her lower lip. "I'm told the town itself is nice."

Cam rubbed the back of her neck. "So does this mean we're dead in the water? With no way to get inside, we have no way of finding out who's responsible for the poison?"

Galena raised her head and gave them all a clear, even look. "The best I can do—the absolute best—is ask for a tour of the place. And don't misunderstand me, it's not really a tour, it's just them letting you see the parts of it they're all right with you seeing. No eyes on the secret stuff. But I could take a small group of visitors with me. Maybe...hmmm. Maybe two."

Raoul groaned, but Nysska said, "That might work. I might be able to break away from the group—sneak into the secure part. It would involve a lot of improvisation, but it's better than nothing."

Cam's jaw had dropped open. "That is *crazy*. You're huge and purple and you've got horns! How are you going to sneak *anywhere?*"

Nysska said, "I didn't say it was foolproof, all right? I have the runes. They'll give me an even greater advantage over the humans there than I already had. I can make it work."

Morrin cleared her throat. A little too loudly.

Raoul said, "Morrin? Did you want to say something?"

Morrin looked around. The pink rose in her cheeks again, but she straightened her back and took a deep breath. "I have an idea. But I'm going to need to send a message." She turned to Raoul. "And…we're going to need to go back to Cliffside."

22

Three days later the Ninth Crucible arrived at Cliffside, the Cullen family's estate. The protective escort of Cathedral soldiers accompanying Governor Vachs peeled off when they reached the property's border, as the hand-picked officers General Cullen had assigned as security were still in place.

Nysska peered out one of the coach's windows as they made their way along the two-klik smoothly graveled lane that led to the manor house. "Hard to believe we made it here this quickly," she said, maybe a little too loudly.

Cam was the only other passenger. She put a hand on Nysska's knee. "You doing all right?"

Nysska could see, through the trees, the great void that meant they were approaching the sea cliff on which the home had been built. The void that meant the only things past that point were empty air and the cold dark sea.

Not yet ready to talk about how she was actually feeling, Nysska said, "The last time I came here, the Borealans and I had to trek through the wilderness. Avoid all the roads and towns. It took forever."

"I remember." Cam leaned toward her. "So your plan is still to have the red runes removed, once this is all over?"

Nysska sat back in her seat, across from Cam, and chewed on her lower lip. "I'm not sure that's even going to be possible. I don't know what kind of stickler for rules and contracts Bronna Smith is. If—*when*—she finds out that I broke my oath, intentionally or not, she may refuse."

"Yes, but she wasn't the one who did the work, was she? It was a runemaster?"

"A runemaster who never spoke to me directly. I don't know. That's it: I don't know. He may value his loyalty to Bronna Smith above all else and tell me to go fuck myself. He may decide it's worth more to leave the runes in me so he can monitor their effects. Or, yes, perhaps he will agree, and take them out straight away. I don't know."

"Well…" Cam drummed her fingertips on her knee. "Would it be so bad if you left them in?"

"Hmm."

"What?"

"I was wondering if you were going to suggest that."

Cam's eyes flared for a second, and for that second, the same butterflies fluttered in Nysska's stomach as when she first saw Cam use her Sight runes. "It's *not* so bad. Is the thing. Having them."

"I'm a little stunned that you can say that. You were there, in Mount Stark. You talked to Olivette. And yes, yes, I know, you don't want to have the same argument we've had over and over. Neither do I. But seeing Olivette—that was seeing the future."

"Nysska…"

"And that's a whole *other* issue. I don't know how these things are going to affect me. They are not the same as yours, don't forget. The effects of argonium have been well-documented. But chervoxite? No one knows what it does to humans, and they *truly* don't know what it will do to a sethyd. Maybe argonium-chervoxite alloy runes aren't harmful at all. Maybe they're ten times more harmful. Maybe, if they're damaging me, that damage will heal once they're taken out. Maybe the damage cannot be reversed. Who knows? I don't."

"All right. Yes. I can't argue with any of that. But you said yourself, you've—for lack of a better word—you've *bonded* with them. Or them with you. You said you're in control now."

"As far as I can tell, yes."

"So have you tested them? Seen what you can and can't do?"

Nysska allowed herself the ghost of a smile. "Well, since I don't know if they're going to catch fire and turn me into a pile of charcoal, no, I haven't really tried putting them to the test."

"Also a valid point. But—just to shine a light on both sides of the coin

—consider this. You're already *much* stronger and faster than any human. Now you've got these runes, and I saw you pick up a church pew and swing it like it was a Dragon-damned feather pillow. And you said, back in Coalgarden at Morrin's place, that getting into Fort Slade might be possible *because* your runes give you physical advantages. Shouldn't you know what your limits are?"

The coach came to a stop. From the driver's seat, Raoul called out, "We're here."

Nysska leaned forward and kissed Cam, her tongue darting in and caressing Cam's for a brief but exquisite moment. As they parted, Cam said, "I can't decide if I want to say *Quit trying to distract me,* or *Don't start something you can't finish.*"

Nysska grinned. "We shall revisit the subject later."

As they opened the door and climbed out, Cam said, "*Which* subject?"

A second coach pulled up behind them, and Flax and Jax came bounding out from behind a tree, waiting for its door to open. When it did, Rosie the speckled hound leapt out of it as if shot from a ballista, and the three animals tore off across Cliffside's broad lawn—lush and green in the summer, at present covered in low brown grass and dotted with snow —tumbling all over each other.

Morrin and Governor Vachs disembarked a little less enthusiastically and came to join the group as Raoul and Percy climbed down from the driver's bench of the first coach. A stiff, cold wind blew in from the ocean and made all their heavy coats flap about them. Raoul turned and stared up at his childhood home—a massive structure of flawlessly stacked gray stone.

Galena Vachs said, "Is something wrong?"

Raoul spoke to her, but didn't face her. "The last time we had a reunion here, my father was still alive, and we had many more reasons to be joyful." A servant emerged from the house and signaled to Raoul, who said, "Everyone's here. Governor, it's time for you to meet the Borealans in person." His ink-black eyes scraped across the group, one face to another. "Then we have a lot of planning to do."

Percy had been eyeballing the long gravel lane up which they had come. He shaded his eyes with a hand for a moment. "Hey—good timing. It looks like Morrin's guest is here."

Almost as soon as Percy had finished speaking, Nysska heard the crunching hoofbeats of a horse on gravel, and they all turned to see a lone rider approaching them at a steady canter. The bronze-inlaid leather armor of the Thaumetallicon was unmistakable, even at such a distance, as the metal strips gleamed and flashed in the winter sun.

"So this is her, eh?" Nysska said to Morrin.

Raoul's expression had darkened. "For the record, I still object to bringing in someone new. We have the kinds of secrets that *cannot* be leaked."

Morrin shot him a mildly exasperated look. "For the last time, I trust this woman with my life. Which she's *saved*, more than once. I owe her every bit as much as I do Nysska."

The rider arrived, bringing her Imperial mount to a halt right behind the second coach, and dismounted with the kind of grace that only years of experience and natural athleticism could bring. She pulled off her helmet, revealing a thick mane of iron-gray curls, and flashed a dazzling grin full of strong white teeth at Morrin.

"There she is!" the woman cried, and crossed the distance between her and Morrin in three long strides, arms flung open. Morrin giggled with unselfconscious delight and let the newcomer pick her up and squeeze her in the most sincerely joyful bear hug Nysska had ever seen.

When she set Morrin back down, Nysska gave the woman a thorough once-over. She had light brown eyes the same color as her skin, a long, rangy frame, and—Nysska verified Morrin's claims as the woman moved closer—looked Nysska almost dead in the eye.

"I didn't know human women got this tall," Nysska said.

The newcomer pulled her gauntlet off and stuck her hand out for Nysska to shake. "Commander Veronika Brooks of the Thirty-Fourth Crucible. And you are *clearly* Nysska Stonegate. Let me tell you, it's a real fucking pleasure to finally meet you!"

Nysska shook the woman's hand. "Commander Brooks. Likewise, based on what Morrin's been telling us about you." She ended the handshake and gestured to the rest of those assembled nearby. "This is Commander Raoul Cullen, Sensor Camble Delakroy, Keeper Percy Bitters, and Governor of the Green Needles Territory, Galena Vachs."

Brooks gave the group a tidy little bow. "Quite the storied fucking cast you've got here, I must say. Word gets around, you know, about all the exploits—"

She broke off as Rosie, Flax, and Jax all came tearing across the lawn toward them, the blood lynxes in full pursuit of Rosie, who appeared to be having the time of her life. Veronika Brooks said, "Holy *fuck*, what beautiful animals! Here, kitty kitty kitty!" She went down to one knee and made beckoning gestures with both hands.

When the lynxes saw her, both of them came to skidding halts, Rosie instantly forgotten, and stared at Brooks with huge round silver eyes. Then, to Nysska's shock—and Percy's audible gasp—they barreled toward her and launched themselves into her, such that she fell over on her back, there on the gravel, and laughed as the big cats sniffed and licked her face with the enthusiasm of puppies.

To no one in particular, Percy said, "The *fuck* is going on?"

Veronika Brooks somehow managed to sit up while holding both of the blood lynxes in her arms, vigorously scratching their heads between the ears and running her hands down their backs. "Morrin told me about these two, but I could scarcely believe it! *Seraphic* blood lynxes? It's like a dream come true!" Slowly, while gently putting the big cats back on the ground, Brooks got to her feet and turned to Percy. "So you're the talented man in charge of these delightful beasts?"

Percy gazed up at her—Brooks was a full head taller than he was—and, as Nysska watched, his cheeks turned a ragged sort of pink. "I am," he managed. "Well, more like we're in charge of each other."

"I'll fuckin' bet," Brooks said with an easy grin.

Nysska couldn't tell if he did it consciously or not, but Percy reached up and smoothed down his eyebrows.

Brooks picked Jax up and cradled him in her arms, and he settled in and started purring with all his might. "I'd say you and I have a lot to talk about, Keeper Bitters," she said, and nuzzled Jax. "Yes we do! Yes we do!"

Cheeks getting pinker, he said, "You can call me Percy."

Raoul cleared his throat. "Let's all go inside, shall we? I know we're alone out here, but being this exposed still makes me uneasy."

He led the way to the front entrance. Following him, Veronika Brooks fell into step beside Percy, peppering him with questions, while Percy simply stared up at her, the pink maintaining in his cheeks.

At the back of the group, Cam whispered, "First Raoul and Morrin, now these two? Is it something in the water?"

Nysska whispered back, "Let's not get ahead of ourselves," though she couldn't deny that Percy looked as if he'd been struck soundly between the eyes with an axe handle.

Raoul led them through the entry hall, past one of the wide staircases that led to the upper floors, and into the same room where they had met with General Cullen…how long ago? Nysska counted the weeks and days. *Four months?*

As they went, Morrin moved to Veronika Brooks's side. "Commander —I had to be a little cryptic in my message, but—"

"A *little* cryptic? You said, 'If you trust me, you'll do this.' I'd say that was pretty fucking cryptic." Morrin turned even paler than usual, but Brooks clapped a hand on her shoulder. "Relax, would you? I *do* trust you. That's why I'm here." She shot a glance around at the décor. "And I can't fucking *wait* to see exactly what I'm supposed to trust you about."

Nysska spotted Raoul, standing and staring at a framed map of the Empire hung on a wall. She went to him and said, "How are you holding up?"

He answered in a voice so carefully measured she was sure he was fighting back tears. "I see him everywhere." His eyes cut toward her, but then snapped back to the wall map. "I can't get rid of this place. It's been in my family for hundreds of years. But I don't think I'll ever be able to live here again."

"Do you—do you want me to make further introductions?"

He nodded, and gestured toward a door across the room. "They're waiting in there."

Nysska put a gentle hand on his upper arm and turned to the group. "Everyone. There is a tremendous amount of information we need to get through. But before we do that, Governor Vachs, Commander Brooks, we need you to meet some people."

Nysska skirted the group and went to the door to the adjoining room. She opened it a crack, peered inside, then flung it wide. "I'm pleased to introduce Princess Aschling of Borealis, her bodyguard Singer, and Captain Kagan."

Nysska was not disappointed at the reactions from Veronika Brooks and Galena Vachs, though Vachs displayed a bit less shock since she had at least been told what to expect. Singer, now with her true silver eyes on display, and Kagan, wearing a new black leather tunic and wool trousers, moved into the room ahead of Aschling. In heavily accented Plainish, each said, "It is a pleasure to meet you."

The gravity and drama of the situation lessened somewhat when Aschling squealed with delight, ran past the other Borealans, and threw her arms around Nysska. "I knew it!" she said in the Tongue of Truth. "I knew you weren't dead, I didn't believe it for a second, I told everyone that no body meant no death!" Aschling backed away from Nysska for a moment, then threw herself into another embrace as Nysska laughed. "I have studied my tenses while you were gone! I think I have past tense better!" She broke the hug again, now looking abashed. "Oh, I forgot article!" Her eyes widened. "Ahh! That makes it worse! I forgot *the* article!"

"You're doing great," Nysska told her. She looked over at Commander Brooks. "How are *you* coping with all this?"

Veronika Brooks couldn't seem to stop staring at Captain Kagan. She finally shifted her focus to Nysska and said, "I...feel as though...my world just got a lot bigger."

Nysska guided her toward a chair. "You have *no* idea."

Half an hour later Nysska found Singer and Kagan at a table piled with savory, meat-filled pastries. Kagan had a plate and was in the process of building himself a small pyramid. Singer simply kept popping them in her mouth.

Nysska put her arms around both of them and hugged them tight at the same time. Kagan said, "You will make me drop my plate," but he sounded good-natured about it.

"I'm just so happy to see you both! I was worried!"

"No need," Singer said, after she'd finished a pastry. "The men with horns think they are very clever. Not so clever as we are."

Nysska took a step back from the two of them and adopted a theatrically serious face. "I said I wanted a big distraction. But a *landslide*? I wasn't asking you to knock down half the city!"

For the first time since she'd met her, Singer grew visibly embarrassed, a condition made worse by Kagan's low, unmistakably mischievous laughter.

"What *happened* up there?"

"Ask Singer," Kagan said, and ate two pastries at the same time.

Singer held up a single finger. "One boulder!" She threw her hands wide. "That is all it is supposed to be! One boulder, bounce down mountain, make some noise, get some attention. Then we fire off arrows, make sure everyone knows is deliberate thing! I find nice big boulder, I give it a little push, and then..." She imitated the sound of the mountainside collapsing.

Kagan laughed again. "Just one boulder," he said, and laughed a little harder. "One little boulder."

Singer threw her hands straight up in a universal signal of resignation. "Yes. One boulder. I need a drink now."

Nysska escorted Singer to the liquor cabinet, leaving Kagan laughing with the pastries.

Over the next three days Nysska engaged in a compressed, intensive, sometimes frantic course of study with Commander Brooks. She wished she had more time. They all did.

Raoul, never one to pass up the chance to complain or point out the worst possible outcome, said on the first day, "Creating a disguise like this normally takes weeks. And we've got how long?"

From where she was sitting with Cam and Morrin in a far corner of the parlor, Governor Vachs called out, "Three days. And I apologize. That's the only way I can make any of this work."

"No need for apologies," Nysska replied. "Without you, none of this would be happening at all. We move on your timetable. Which means I need to be ready by..."

"Friday morning," Veronika Brooks said. "That's when the tour's set up."

Nysska sighed. They had just finished breakfast. It was Tuesday.

"All right," Brooks went on. "Where was I born?"

"Salazar." Nysska was ready for that one.

"And Salazar is where?"

"On the southern border of the Sung River Territory."

"Good. What were my parents' names?"

"Olivier and Masayo Brooks."

"Brothers and sisters?"

"That one's easy. You were an only child."

"At what age did I join the Cathedral?"

Nysska hesitated. "Seventeen. The normal age is eighteen, but your parents gave you permission."

Brooks's eyes narrowed a hair. "That hesitation sounded suspicious. Would you not remember what age you were when you joined up?"

Nysska rubbed her face with both hands. "Yes, yes I would. I'm sorry. I will know all of this by Friday."

Percy walked over, Flax and Jax trailing after him, and plunked down in one of the other chairs around the small table where Nysska and

Brooks were working. "I have a question," he said through his usual grin. "The fuck are you going to do about your voice?"

Raoul groaned. "Percy, that's not helpful."

His grin grew wider. "What? She sounds like a sethyd! Commander Brooks, do you normally have a sethyd accent when you talk?"

Brooks favored Percy with a look that struck Nysska as *I don't know what to make of you, but I find you entertaining.* "I do not, no. And call me Veronika."

Percy tapped the fingertips of his right hand on the tabletop. "Seems to me, Veronika, that all this background studying isn't worth a pile of warm shit if everybody realizes Nysska's a fake as soon as she opens her mouth."

Cam had risen from her chair in the corner and come to stand behind Nysska, where she rested her hands lightly on Nysska's shoulders. "We've been working on that," Cam said. "In between her teaching me the Tongue of Truth. We figured there might be some kind of situation at some point where she'd need to speak unaccented Plainish."

Raoul said nothing, but he drifted closer, paying attention. Percy leaned forward, blue eyes twinkling. "See, that's what I *figured.* You're a lot of things, Nysska, but dumb isn't one of them. Let's hear it."

Nysska wanted to shrink back into her seat. Maybe enough so that she could disappear altogether. She had conquered what little stage fright she'd ever had as a small girl, thanks to her priest-singer training, but this felt completely different. Clearing her throat, she dropped into her "non-sethyd" accent—which was really just an impersonation of Cam.

"I figure I'm going to say as little as possible," she said, keeping her lips and tongue stiffer than usual and being careful not to round her Os too much.

Percy clapped his hands and hooted with laughter. "Now *that's* what I fucking wanted to hear!"

Veronika Brooks tilted her head as she spoke to Percy. "You know, you don't have to be a giant fucking asshole about it."

Still grinning, Percy shrugged at her. "I kind of do."

Now Raoul put his hands on the table, intent on Nysska. "Say something else. Announce yourself."

Nysska closed her eyes, concentrating. "I'm Commander Veronika Brooks of the Thirty-Fourth Crucible. I'm a guest of Governor Vachs."

"Holy shit," Governor Vachs said. She and Morrin had also moved over near the table. "This might actually work."

Brooks waved her hands in the air. "All right, yeah, that was pretty good, but I've got a question. And forgive me if this comes off as too fucking sensitive, but—" She clapped a hand to her forehead and raised the fringe of curls, revealing her lined brown forehead. "What're you going to do about those *horns*?"

Nysska groaned this time, and slumped forward onto the table, the horns in question clacking on the polished wood.

"That's a sensitive subject," Cam said, and Nysska groaned louder.

The parlor door nearest the house's main entrance opened, and Princess Aschling came in, leading a petite, dark-skinned woman carrying a large leather bag. "She's here, everyone!" Aschling said, her grin just as broad as Percy's but lacking every bit of the mischief. "Meet Madam Okafor! The best lens-maker in the Empire!"

Nysska raised her head and turned toward the newcomer. Madam Okafor squinted at her. "All right, let me take some measurements." She shuffled forward, opening her bag. "First silver, now yellow? You people are all crazy."

Considering what they were about to attempt, Nysska didn't think she could disagree.

That night, Nysska and Cam walked hand in hand along a narrow gravel path through the woods. On their right rose the end of Cliffside proper, and the tower from which Nysska had fallen loomed above them. Cam's grip tightened.

"How're you feeling?"

Nysska had been speaking in her approximation of Cam's voice since that morning, and intended to keep it up until whatever happened at Fort Slade was concluded. Still in standard Plainish, she said, "Sometimes I see that tower in my dreams."

"Would it..." Cam weighed her words. "Would it help to go up there? Maybe shake off the memories?"

Nysska imagined climbing the spiral steps...walking out onto the balcony...gazing out over the ocean. As she did, an imaginary pain almost as sharp as the real one pierced her chest, and the world around her swayed and spiraled as the sickening sensation of freefall enveloped her. She stopped and closed her eyes, and Cam wrapped her in a hug. "I'm sorry. That was a stupid suggestion."

Nysska shook her head, her chin moving back and forth across Cam's scalp. "No it wasn't. It might be exactly what I need." *And yet...what if there's another boat out there? What if there's another Argonium Infantryman, waiting with an arrow nocked?*

"But not tonight." Cam released her, but went up onto her toes to plant a quick kiss on Nysska's lips. "Tonight you're facing trauma enough."

They continued along the path, and a few minutes later the trees opened up to reveal a massive stone barn. No sooner had they entered the ring of light thrown by a series of oversize lanterns on poles outside than Princess Aschling appeared in the door and all but danced out to greet them. "Hello!" she cried in Plainish. "I am so happy you have come to see me in my workshop!"

Cam murmured, "It's a good thing *she's* not the one trying to lose an accent."

Nysska had to admit that Aschling's Plainish was a good bit rougher than her Tongue of Truth, but that was to be expected, since she'd studied what she called Esperanto for years and had only heard her first words in Plainish when the Ninth rescued her and Kagan and Singer from the Gemini.

Aschling darted between Cam and Nysska and hooked her arms into theirs, guiding them along. "First I show you around, and give you little hint of big special secret project I work on! Then we decide how best to tackle your more immediate concern."

Nysska said, "By 'big special secret project,' you mean your flying ship, yes?"

Aschling's face creased with theatrical outrage. "How could you know about secret project? It is very much secret!"

Nysska grinned. "Because you told me yourself. Multiple times. When I was here before, it was all you could talk about."

Aschling frowned. "Hmmm. You might be right. Still! It is too big a secret to show yet!" She led them through the door and into the barn's interior, which proved to be a single massive room. Along two walls she had set up work benches with—Nysska scanned their contents—every single wood- and metal-working tool Nysska had ever seen. Aschling had saws, drills, vises, and dozens of other apparatuses Nysska couldn't even name.

The far end of the barn was taken up by something large and oblong and draped with a huge tarp. Whatever was underneath it looked to be about ten meters in length and three or four tall. Nysska had never asked

Aschling exactly how a flying ship was supposed to work, but she saw nothing here that looked like wings. Instead it looked like...a brick. Something long and brick-shaped, hidden from view.

Aschling threw her arms wide. "Here! There is the big secret! Aren't you crazy to know what is under there? Doesn't it just kill you not to see?"

Cam laughed, and pulled Aschling into a hug. "I swear, Princess, you are a better mood-lifter than a shot of whiskey."

Aschling hugged her back, but then turned to Nysska. "I do not know if I can lift your mood, considering what you are asking me to do."

Nysska took a deep breath. "The runes made my broken horn grow back in about three weeks. I don't see any reason to think they wouldn't do the same for this."

Aschling nodded. "All right. I know this is necessary for your Big Plan. And I am very careful. But you tell me if I hurt you, yes?"

"Don't worry."

Aschling's grin returned, and she danced over to one of the work benches. "Then come see my new grinding wheel! It is better even than one I had back in Borealis!"

Nysska followed her reluctantly, with Cam trailing after. Cam said, "Want to hold my hand while she does this?"

Nysska reached for her. "Yes, please."

23

Despite Morrin's assurances that they had bought from the best wig-maker on the eastern coast, Nysska doubted the quality of the thing attached to her head. It itched and, though it had been pinned ferociously in place, she felt as if it were moving in a way that would draw immediate attention. She disliked the wig's itching even more than she disliked the pain caused by the whisper-thin glass lenses currently in place on her eyeballs. Madam Okafor had given her a slender vial filled with salt water and instructions to moisten the lenses no less frequently than every half an hour.

Nysska rode up to the gate of Fort Slade along with Governor Vachs, Cam, and the half-dozen Cathedral soldiers serving as Galena's security, decked out in the wig and the lenses and the head-to-toe body paint. The visual part of the disguise, she'd decided while looking in a mirror earlier, was pretty solid. Which meant, if she were going to screw things up, it would almost certainly be because she let her accent lapse. Her heartbeat thumped in her neck.

The first of the security gates was set into a ten-meter-high stone wall, on top of which were stationed soldiers with crossbows. It reminded her of the gate at the entrance of Sergei Benitoff's estate, except more serious and even less likely to let intruders pass.

An officer greeted Galena with a crisp salute. "Governor. I was told you'd be visiting us today." He peered at Nysska and Cam. "And who are your companions, if I may inquire, ma'am?"

Galena gestured with one hand. "Commander Veronika Brooks of the Thirty-Fourth Crucible, and Sensor Camble Delakroy of the Ninth. Two of my most trusted advisors." She leaned down a bit from the saddle, going from governor-regal to impossibly-beautiful-woman-personal in a heartbeat. "I never make any big decisions without consulting them. You understand that, don't you..." Her eyes tracked to the stripes on his jacket lapel. "...Major?"

The officer looked to be about thirty—too old for Galena, in Nysska's totally unbiased opinion—with pale skin and reddish-brown hair. Two pink spots appeared in his cheeks as she fixed those sapphire eyes on his. "Of course," the Major said quickly. He scribbled on a writing board. "I just needed their names."

"And now you have them. If you'll let us through, please? My time is limited."

"Open the gate!" the Major shouted, and Nysska rode through the first checkpoint without having to say a word.

The road continued for three more kliks, with another checkpoint at each klik. Security tightened at each one, and at the last one two soldiers searched Nysska's saddlebags and had her dismount to be patted down. One of the soldiers' eyes lingered on Nysska's face, and for a moment she was certain that the Commander's band had slipped, revealing the black circles flush with her skin—all that remained of her horns. But the soldier broke the eye contact and stepped away, signaling that he had found nothing of note.

The trio rode another klik, passing through a narrow canyon, until they came out into a wide plaza. At the other end of the plaza loomed an enormous stone building fronted with massive columns that held up a roof façade rising to a peak in the center. The building had a single massive entrance. Nysska spotted crossbow slits in the walls on either side of the enormous door.

Soldiers came and led their horses away, leaving them to approach the door on foot. When they had drawn close, the six-meter-high door swung open and revealed a gray-haired man with skin the same rich, dark brown as Cam's. He was tall and handsome, and if he'd smiled he would have been dazzling. Nysska decided that he most likely never *ever* smiled.

"Governor Vachs," the man said. "My name is Lemuel. I will be your guide today." His night-black eyes raked over Nysska and Cam. Coldly evaluating. "I understand you are considering storing some of your personal items here with us at Fort Slade."

"That's right," Galena said, as smoothly and easily as if they'd been discussing what was on the menu for dinner. "Such a thing *is* possible, is it not?"

"It is, of course," Lemuel answered, gesturing for them to come inside. "We do not provide such services to the masses, but for a Territorial Governor, exceptions can be made."

Nysska followed Cam and Galena into what looked like the mother of all entrance halls. Polished marble floors led to marble columns, designed after the ones outside, that stretched ten meters up to an ornately coffered polished mahogany ceiling. Another gate stood in front of them, but this one was cosmetic—composed of narrow bronze frames holding up broad panes of perfectly smooth, perfectly clear glass. Four more soldiers were posted at the bronze-and-glass gate, and they saluted Lemuel as they pushed it open and let everyone pass through.

Immediately beyond the glass gate the structure expanded into a series of terraces, each one accessible from the one below via broad marble steps at each side. *A massive staircase. They built a massive staircase inside a mountain, then hollowed out the stairs.* An array of doors were set into each terrace, and Nysska recognized the architecture—this followed the same scheme, more or less, as the offices carved into the sides of the quarry at Coalgarden. The Cathedral was nothing if not consistent.

As if she'd read Nysska's mind, Galena Vachs said, "Forgive me for the observation, Lemuel, but this doesn't look much like a mine. This looks like a much larger version of my administrative facilities in Tember."

Lemuel gave her an odd little half-bow. "As you say. This is the part of Fort Slade that very, very few people ever get to see—the logistical affairs and living quarters." He pointed along the lowest terrace. "Down there is our mess hall. Despite the reputation Cathedral cooks have garnered, I dare say our chefs will please you when we dine there later."

Cam spoke up. "This is the part very few people get to see? As opposed to what other parts?"

Lemuel's face remained impassive. "As opposed to the actual mining and smelting of argonium that goes on in the parts *no one* gets to see. No one except for those actually assigned here." Again with the little half-bow. "You will understand of course, Governor, that the extent of your tour today will not reach into the forbidden areas. It's a matter of Imperial security. Nothing at all personal."

Galena waved a dismissive hand. "I care nothing for digging rocks out of more rocks. All I want to see is where my goods would be stored. *If* I should choose to store them here."

Cam moved closer to her and spoke in a low tone—but not low enough that Lemuel couldn't hear her. "Galena—I want to see everything!" She then made a show of realizing Lemuel *had* heard her, and turned to speak to him directly. "I'm sorry. It's just—" She gestured toward her eyes. "I've benefited so greatly from the Emperor's gift, and I've never seen where my runes truly came from. I know we can't go into the actual mine. I just want to see as much as I can."

Lemuel raised an eyebrow at Galena, who shrugged her shoulders indulgently. "If you have the time, sir, then yes, I suppose we would like to get the full tour."

Something that almost reached the level of a smile touched Lemuel's lips. "I have the whole day blocked off for you, Governor, and would be more than happy to show your friends around." He cut his eyes toward Nysska. "I trust your tall and silent companion feels the same?"

Nysska inclined her head, her heart suddenly pounding as she said, "I do," in perfectly unaccented Plainish.

"Very well, then. If you'll come with me, we shall start down here at the far end, work our way up one side, and then come back down the other to end in the mess hall for the evening meal."

For the next two hours Lemuel led them through room after room, suite after adjoining suite, crisscrossing the "non-forbidden" area of Fort Slade. It didn't take long for Nysska to realize two things: first, that her disguise was holding up better than she'd feared it would, and second, that Fort Slade was, in fact, its own self-contained town. And not a small town, either—more like a miniature city, on a scale only slightly below the likes of Coalgarden. The terraces visible from the main entrance were only the face of the fort's massive subterranean construction. From each of the terrace doors the separate levels spread far back into the mountain, a world of its own chiseled out of rock, containing on different terraces stores, a school, a small theatre, and dozens upon dozens, maybe hundreds, of livable apartments.

Nysska knew the kind of space an actual mine took up, though. If this was the part that select members of the public were allowed to see...how much else was there, deeper inside the mountain? What vast spaces would the public never witness, where the silver lifeblood of the Empire was hacked out of the rock and sent into the fires until it gave up its secrets?

At the far end of the uppermost terrace stood an imposing, solid bronze door with two soldiers stationed on either side of it. A sign on the wall read, in both Plainish and Estmani, *AUTHORIZED PERSONNEL ONLY BEYOND THIS POINT*. It took Nysska no more than a couple of seconds to realize, after reading the sign, that both of the guards were Argonium Infantry.

Her mouth went dry, her throat constricting, as the deep, reverberating sound of a heavy bowstring carried over water. She felt anew the impossible pain in her chest as the arrow punched through skin and flesh and bone and nailed her to the stone wall of the Cliffside tower.

Galena was talking to Lemuel, and Nysska said quietly to Cam, "I'll be right back," and executed her best saunter over to the two guards. Neither of them left their post, but they both watched her come the way straight men tended to watch attractive women.

"You're both A.I., aren't you?" she said, pleased with how naturally her unaccented Plainish had begun to flow.

"Congratulations, sweetheart," one of them said with an overt sneer. "Learned to read insignias, huh?"

The other one chimed in with, "How'd you get a Commander's band, askin' stupid-ass questions like that?"

Nysska decided to name the two men Lip Wart and Fat Nose. Lip Wart had spoken first, so she focused on him. "No need to get nasty." She tilted her head to one side, just a degree or two, and would have bitten her lower lip, but she was afraid of smearing the makeup that Morrin and Cam had taken such care in applying. "I've just always wondered how it felt. The runes, I mean."

Fat Nose frowned and gestured with his chin at Cam. "Why'n't you ask your curvy little friend over there?"

Nysska looked him up and down—and spotted a small, polished-tin Dragon pin peeking out from under his jacket, affixed to the collar of his shirt. Her brain spun. She had always wondered exactly who was behind the Infantryman who'd shot her from such a massive distance. The Church of the Great Silver Dragon, or at least the Northern Clutch, had more than amply demonstrated that they wanted her dead, but then so had a great number of other people throughout the Empire.

What if the Dragon Church's influence had spread further than she realized?

Nysska took a step closer to Fat Nose and dropped her voice to a husky, conspiratorial whisper. "She's got nothing but shit to say about the Dragon. I try not to talk to her any more than I have to."

Nysska's insides grew several degrees cooler as the truth of her suspicion bore out on Fat Nose's face. She looked over at Lip Wart, who wore a similar look, so she followed up with, "Glory to the Great Silver Dragon."

Both men whispered in unison. "Glory to the Great Silver Dragon."

Nysska favored them both with her most seductive smile. "I *knew* it. I knew the Infantry had their heads screwed on straight. Now I'm doubly envious."

Lip Wart's breathing had grown marginally faster. He said, "How long are you an' your group staying?" Nysska kept her face perfectly still as Lip Wart ran the tip of his tongue out and along his upper lip. "If you can slip away an' come to the barracks, we can have us a really good chat."

Fat Nose nodded. "Especially if others in the Thaumetallicon feel the same way you do." He looked over her shoulder, as if to make sure neither Galena nor Cam were within earshot. "We been lookin' to expand. The Thaumetallicon'd make a *sweet* addition to the Clutch."

Lip Wart hissed softly. "Hey. That's enough for now." To Nysska directly, he said, "What's your name, sweetheart?"

"Veronika. Commander Veronika Brooks."

"Which Crucible?" Fat Nose asked, and Nysska almost panicked in earnest, because of all the facts to draw a blank on, in that second she couldn't have named Brooks's Crucible even if someone had a crossbow aimed at her temple.

"I'm between Crucibles right now," she said, hoping she sounded believable. "Seconded to Governor Vachs as an advisor." Fearing that the Infantrymen would keep asking questions until she revealed herself, Nysska decided to take the easy way out. "Maybe," she said, a little breathy, and stepped forward to touch Fat Nose on the chest. "Maybe I can get assigned here."

Fat Nose's eyes went a little glassy. "Th-that'd be sweet," he said, and might have said more, but Nysska turned to Lip Wart.

"So perhaps I'll see you two in the barracks later. If I can slip away." She gave Lip Wart a wink, and he looked surprised enough that she hoped she hadn't overplayed her hand. "Now, if you'll excuse me."

When she rejoined Cam, out of earshot of the Infantrymen, Cam whispered, "What the *fuck* was that? Are you trying to get caught?"

"Sorry." Nysska risked a glance back at the two men and found them both staring at her, but not suspiciously. More like with a very basic hunger. "I just thought maybe I could learn something about this place."

Cam shot them a look as well before returning her attention to Nysska. "And did you? They're not charging over here with shackles, so I'm guessing you didn't ruin your disguise."

"I think I learned something pretty fucking important, yes." Lemuel and Galena approached them, so Nysska said, "I'll explain later."

"Ladies, if you'll come with me, our tour is at an end, so it is now time to proceed to the mess hall."

"What's back there?" Cam asked him candidly, pointing at the door the Infantrymen guarded. "Is that the stuff we're not allowed to see?"

"Quite." Lemuel did his half-bow. "Imperial security, you know."

Cam sighed, piling on the disappointment. "I know, I know. All right, well, I'm hungry. Who else is hungry?"

Nysska's stomach growled, and she patted her belly. "No comment."

Lemuel gestured. "Right this way, then."

Nysska sat beside Cam's bed, holding her hand and doing her best to look concerned, while Cam groaned and held her stomach and clutched at the sheets. At the doorway, Lemuel stood speaking with Galena. Every few seconds he cast a disapproving glance over her shoulder at Cam.

"This is highly irregular," Lemuel said.

"I know. I know because this is the twelfth time you've said that. I don't know what it was in *your* mess hall that affected Sensor Delakroy so badly, but I do know that if she's not better in the morning, I'm going to need the best Imperial physicians to come and attend to her. I assume you have some of those on staff?"

"Yes, of course, but—"

"Good. Now, if you'll leave us, we need to let her rest."

Lemuel's tone wavered between disapproving and sucking up. "Governor, I hope you understand, due to matters of—"

"Imperial security," Galena said along with him. It made Lemuel's face wrinkle up as if he'd just sucked on the sourest of lemons.

"Due to security matters, yes, I'm going to need to post a pair of guards outside your door tonight."

Galena made the dismissive gesture with her hand that she'd perfected. "Yes, yes, good idea—we need someone to make sure Sensor

Delakroy gets the rest she needs. So please come and get us in the morning."

"Very good, Governor."

Galena shut the door and came over to the bed, sitting on the edge of it across from Nysska. "All right." She kept her voice soft. "Where are we?"

The part of Nysska that enjoyed quippy responses wanted to say, "We're in one of Fort Slade's unoccupied apartments," but she thought it lacked the proper zing and kept quiet.

"Well, I took a look around as soon as we got in here," Cam said, speaking just as quietly. "Checking for spyholes and such. Of which I found none." She let out another convincing groan for whomever might have been outside. "I was hoping they'd put us at the very back of the level, so I could get a good peek through the wall and into the mine, but, well..." She spread her hands. Lemuel had situated them in an apartment on the second-to-the-top level, about halfway back from the terrace door.

Nysska said, "Were you able to see *anything*?"

Cam shrugged with her eyebrows. "Hard to say." She pointed to an air vent in the ceiling, a good five meters over their heads. "I was thinking that that might lead to an air duct, which maybe one of us could have shimmied through and gotten somewhere that way, but..." She frowned and shook her head.

Galena said, "But what?"

"But above the vent—above the ceiling—there's a void. I'm, uh—I'm not sure exactly what it is. There's just this empty space, and then I think the underside of the terrace above us? Maybe? Anyway, it extends in every direction. Sorry, I wish I could be more help."

Galena cranked her head back to look at the vent. It was bronze, with a honeycomb pattern to it, and had begun to corrode around the edges. "Not sure what good that could do us. It's not like there's a ladder in here."

Nysska stood and moved directly underneath the vent. She dusted her hands off on her thighs, activated the runes in her legs, and jumped straight up.

Her fingers jammed through the cutouts in the vent cover so hard that at first she was afraid her hands might have broken, but they still worked well enough, and she had enough presence of mind to grab onto the cover and yank. It came out of the ceiling with a sharp, distressingly loud *crack*, and as soon as Nysska landed she stretched out full-length on the floor and shoved the vent cover under the bed.

At once the door's latch turned over and, to Nysska's intense distress,

Fat Nose and Lip Wart appeared in the doorway. "What was that noise?" Lip Wart demanded.

Nysska slowly got to her knees and pushed up to her feet. "Sorry, fellas," she said, since neither Cam nor Galena had anything to say. "I tripped and banged my shin on the bed frame." Nysska went to the door and, since Fat Nose was closer, she reached out and laid a hand on his chest again. "No need for alarm." He spluttered as she slid her hand down to his side.

"I'll talk to you both later," she said. "Just as soon as my friend's feeling better. All right?"

Fat Nose and Lip Wart exchanged glances, the looks on their faces indicating a blend of frustration and eagerness. She figured as soon as they'd heard the group was staying the night, they had fallen all over themselves to volunteer for guard duty, not expecting all three women to be in the same flat.

"All right, then," Lip Wart said, and steered Fat Nose back outside. "Just let us know if you need anything."

"Thank you," Galena called as the door clicked shut.

Nysska came back over to the bed, where Galena said, "What was *that* all about?"

Nysska held up the small leather pouch she'd slipped out of Fat Nose's pocket. As Cam and Galena watched, she emptied its contents into the palm of her hand.

"Huh," Cam said. "Too bad you didn't get your hand on those sooner."

Nysska put the objects back into the pouch and handed them to her. "Too bad indeed. Hang on to them for me, will you?"

Galena looked up at the ceiling. Cam did the same, and said, "Can you get through that?"

"Maybe I should go," Galena ventured. "I'm the smallest of the three of us."

"No—I think I can do it." Nysska waved one hand in front of her forehead. "Wouldn't fit if I still had the horns, though. So there's that for a blessing." She went to Cam, still stretched out on the bed, and gave her a quick but heartfelt kiss. "If anyone comes in while I'm gone…"

"You're in the bathroom," Galena said. "With a touch of the same thing that affected Cam."

"Right then. Wish me luck."

Nysska ignited the runes in her legs, arms, and torso, took aim at the squared-off black hole in the ceiling, and jumped. The hole turned out to be the bottom edge of a short vertical shaft, about a meter in length, and if Nysska hadn't had the extra strength granted by the runes there would have been no way for her to gain any kind of purchase.

As it was—with the runes glowing red through the skin of her forearms—she pressed her palms into opposite sides of the shaft and pushed. To her astonishment, and not a small amount of delight, even that awkward placement held her weight.

Nysska walked her hands up the shaft and disappeared into the ceiling.

24

Nysska had been expecting to find herself cramped into a ventilation tunnel of some kind. There had to be an airflow system of one type or another, given how far into the mountain Fort Slade was dug, but she did not foresee the place where she now crouched. The "void" that Cam had seen turned out to be an open semi-level—a blank space between floors about a meter high, supported by regularly-spaced squat pillars and dimly illuminated by light coming up through other ceiling grates like the one Nysska had just climbed through. It reminded her of the observation floor of the Echo Box, back in Mount Stark—and made her wish she could stand up. Crouching, her shoulders hunched over, the top of her head still brushed the ceiling. Resisting the urge to grumble, Nysska dropped to all fours.

She had a brutally limited amount of time to find the truth about the poisoning in Slocum. Stuck there in between floors and gazing out over all of the shafts of dim lantern light, she was forced to admit that she had no idea *how* to discover the truth. She wasn't even sure which direction to head. Finally she decided to follow the faint flow of air over her shoulders.

First came the problem of moving silently. Nysska didn't know how much noise would carry through the stone to the apartments below her as she crawled, but she couldn't take the chance of *any* noise traveling. That led to her traversing the space in a kind of bear walk, balanced on her palms and toes, carefully placing each hand and foot as she went. She paused over one ceiling grate, but heard only the sound of two people she didn't recognize arguing about one of them going to bed too early, so she kept moving. Nysska had doubts as to how much valuable information she was likely to get from Fort Slade employees in their living quarters getting ready for bed. In any case, she couldn't waste time finding out.

After what felt like a solid hour, which Nysska suspected was probably only a few minutes, she reached the far end of the space and arrived at a wide bronze grate set into a wall. The air flow disappeared through it with a soft whistling sound. It was fastened in place by bronze rivets, and for anyone else this would have been a dead end.

Nysska pushed up her sleeves. The light from the metal in her forearms gave her extra visibility as her fingertips, impossibly bolstered by the red runes' thaumaturgy, found purchase on the edges of the rivets and slowly, carefully pulled them free of their moorings. The process produced a few pops and clicks and one metal-on-metal squeal, but she took enough time with it that she didn't think it should have alerted anyone. At least she hoped not.

Nysska repeated the process with five other rivets. She gently moved the grate aside and set it on the floor, then brought the power of the runes up a few degrees so that she could see into the coal-black tunnel in the rock the grate had protected. It appeared to end after a few meters, opening up into some larger space. Nysska took a deep breath, let the runes subside, and crept through the opening.

The space she entered looked like the opposite of the one she'd left—another gap between floors, but with the dim shafts of yellow light emanating from overhead instead of below. The difference in smells struck her too, the air permeated by something sharp and metallic and *familiar* in a way she couldn't quite place yet. Again moving slowly and deliberately, making zero sound, Nysska traveled from one weak beam of light to another, looking for a way up.

She passed one opening almost without realizing it. No light shone down and, when she gingerly rose and listened, she heard nothing. No breathing, no rustles of clothing. Nysska reached her fingers through the familiar honeycomb cutouts and, bit by bit, exerted energy and pressure from her runes until the grate popped free of the floor.

It didn't make as loud a noise as the one had in the room with Cam and Galena, but it did make noise, and Nysska pulled her fingers back through and let the grate rest in place, waiting while her heart pounded for footsteps to come rushing in.

She counted to fifty. When nothing happened, she set the grate aside and leveraged herself up out of the floor and into a dark, silent chamber.

It looked like a storage room, but one that had not been used in a long while, as dust covered every surface. Shelves lined the walls. A few buckets and mops and brooms lay scattered about. Nysska remembered the obvious footprints left on the floor of the bizarre dust-filled room in Solace Canyon, and how it had made her think that anyone who came in would know in a heartbeat that intruders had been there. Feeling foolish, Nysska grabbed a nearby broom and swept the floor free of dust. Maybe anyone casually poking their head in wouldn't notice a clean floor. Or if they did, maybe it would arouse less suspicion than sethyd-sized footprints.

I'm a priest-singer, Nysska told herself. *Not a spy.*

She held her breath as she opened the room's single door and peered out—but then forgot how to breathe entirely for several long moments.

Nysska stepped through the doorway onto what appeared to be the highest balcony encircling a vast, shadow-filled, abyss-like pit. Other balconies circled the pit farther down, spaced about ten meters apart, but the distance between her and the floor of the pit was so enormous that she couldn't even hazard a guess. It looked as though the entire mountain had been hollowed out, and along various platforms and terraces and broad ramps built and chiseled and dug into the stone, men worked. The ringing crack of each stroke of their pickaxes filled the air, saturated it with a brittle chorus, and as Nysska breathed that high, tuneless song into her lungs, she recognized the smell that came with it.

Argonium.

Everything she'd been told about this place was true. The heart of the Empire, the metal that let Emperor Valco impose his will through the Thaumetallicon and the Argonium Infantry, lay exposed here, mercilessly ripped and clawed out of the earth so that human will could be imposed upon it. The runes beneath her skin did not come to life with their ruby fire, but she felt them hum, breathing and sighing in sympathy.

A few people here and there moved about on the lower balconies, but the place was so vast, and the sporadic lighting so incomplete, that they looked like tiny shadows, and none of them raised their eyes to see her. Even if they had, her disguise was still in place, so they would only have seen a tall, gray-haired human woman. Not a sethyd wondering what the fuck she'd gotten herself into.

Something caught Nysska's eye. She squinted, looking again, and saw it once more: a flare of light from a chamber on the next balcony down and about halfway around the pit's perimeter.

A flare of *snow-white* light.

Nysska could never see what Cam saw with her augmented Sight, but she had listened to her carefully describe the white runes hiding under Emperor Valco's skin. Here, in this place—the place where argonium was mined and smelted and distributed to the Imperial Colleges for their runemasters to forge—could a flash of pure, snowy white light *not* be connected to the Emperor's mystery runes?

Nysska didn't think she could afford not to find out.

The balconies were connected by flights of steep metal stairs, but Nysska didn't want to take the chance that she might meet anyone in close quarters, so she picked a shadow-filled section of rough stone wall and climbed down, her rune-enhanced fingers digging into crevices and niches as she lowered herself the ten meters to the next level.

Nysska dropped the last couple of meters, landed softly on the balcony and, moving calmly but with what she hoped would look like the confidence of someone who was supposed to be there, walked the remaining distance to the door from which the snowy light had flared. It was unlocked. Nysska opened it just enough to peer inside with one eye.

On the other side lay a room not dissimilar to what she'd thought of as the "smelting chamber" at Solace Canyon. Big, about fifteen by fifteen meters, with smelting equipment taking up the far wall—a furnace that fed molten metal into a huge bronze cauldron, which was then tipped to pour into a series of molds. Men worked at the smelter—she counted four —and since the rest of the room contained a series of racks stacked with crates and boxes, Nysska slipped inside, silently closed the door, and hid in one of the corners behind the largest crate she could find.

As she peered out from around the crate, she once again appreciated how much easier this was without horns. It made her feel very slightly less naked and defenseless.

The smelting setup wasn't quite what she'd seen before. This appeared to involve a separate step—she couldn't see it clearly because of the humans in the way, and she wasn't familiar enough with the process to identify what she was looking at in the first place, but it appeared to be a broad, flat tray where the molten argonium collected before it went into the cauldron. She watched as the tray filled, and as one of the humans stoked the fire beneath the tray until it burned a ferocious blue-white...

Something about the molten argonium changed.

The tray tilted a few degrees, and liquid metal poured off of it, collecting in another cauldron Nysska hadn't noticed before. Watching it pour, the stream looked *darker* than it had a moment earlier.

The tray tilted back in the other direction and emptied its contents into the larger cauldron, which then moved along a raised track and poured the remaining molten metal into molds.

As it poured, the same brilliant, snowy-white radiance emanated from it in waves, filling the room and casting the starkest of shadows.

Nysska had never been intimately familiar with the workings and characteristics of argonium, but she knew for fucking certain that it wasn't *white*.

And yet the Emperor's runes were.

Nysska narrowed her eyes, mind spinning. The Ninth had never trusted Emperor Valco. Not really before they found out about the white runes, but definitely not afterward. Him with his murky motives and his willingness to deal with the Mountain Bulls. Here, witnessing this, Nysska knew she was about to learn something. She could feel it building in her brain, a shimmering, seething pressure.

The smaller cauldron, into which the darker material had poured, was mounted on a wheeled cart. One of the humans pushed it away and left it at the end of the row of racks behind which Nysska had hidden herself, next to another identical one. The man left it there, crossed the room, grabbed an unused cart, and set it into the place where the first one had been.

Nysska crept down to the end of the row, keeping out of sight behind other crates and boxes, and when all the humans had their backs turned, she rose and leaned forward to look into the smaller cauldron next to the one that had just been placed there. The metal inside had cooled and—she frowned, trying to understand what she was seeing—cracked and turned to a kind of dust.

A horrific wave of nausea washed over her as she recognized it.

The poison from Slocum.

The poison from Slocum, that Morrin had traced to Fort Slade, was a *by-product of argonium.*

Nysska backed away, trying not to gag, her eyes watering, and cracked her elbow against a pile of ingots on the shelf draped with a thin white cloth. She succeeded in not making any noise, but the action dislodged the cloth—

Revealing the edge of an ingot of snow-white metal.

Nysska's head pivoted, taking in the size and shape of the molds into which—

Into which the—

Her heart galloped in her chest.

Into which the *refined argonium* had just been poured.

Argonium. The inherently toxic metal.

Could be refined. Removing the toxin.

And what was left—the snow-white metal—the metal with *no toxic properties.*

That was used to forge runes for the Emperor.

Nysska crouched there in the shadows, doing her level best not to hyperventilate or scream with rage.

The door to the balcony swung open. A man she'd never seen before walked into the room with the kind of bronze-clad, rock-solid confidence that she had seen plenty of times in plenty of other human men, wearing a long black coat she recognized instantly. Its convoluted pattern of brilliant gold swoops and whorls labeled him as a high-ranking Imperial College runemaster. He sauntered across the floor to the cauldron filled with cooled argonium waste and simply stood there with his hands on his hips until one of the smelting crew noticed him.

The runemaster said, "Well?"

The smelter jumped as if a whip had just cracked at his feet, and said, "Apologies, sir!" and scrambled to a box on one of the rack shelves. He pulled out a metal scoop and a heavy cloth sack exactly like the one she'd taken from the cellar in Slocum.

"My time is more precious than yours, you realize," the runemaster said as the smelter hurriedly filled the sack with argonium waste.

"Here you go, sir." The smelter tied off the sack and handed it over, all but bowing and scraping in the process. The runemaster took it with a disdainful sniff, turned on his heel and walked out.

Once the door had closed, the smelter said, "Asshole," and went back to his work.

Nysska slipped out the door onto the balcony and caught a glimpse of the runemaster making his way toward one of the staircases. She looked around, saw no one near enough to pay her any attention, and slid over the balcony rail in a shadowy patch. Clinging to the stone wall again,

Nysska stayed in shadows as she descended, parallel with the runemaster, to the balcony below. That put her on the third balcony down from the unused room where she'd gained entrance to the mine. She hoped she'd be able to get back up there.

Instead of entering another room, the runemaster picked a spot on the balcony and simply waited. Nysska slipped over the balcony railing again, but instead of clinging to the wall, she moved along the balcony's underside, supporting her weight by gripping the exposed heads of bronze bolts. Such an action would have been patently impossible without the red runes in her arms. She grinned, just a little, as the strength flowed effortlessly through her, the red glow hidden by her uniform's long sleeves.

When Nysska reached a spot almost directly beneath the runemaster, she pulled herself up and onto a diagonal support beam tucked away in heavy shadow. No more than a meter separated her from the man.

Three or four minutes later Nysska heard footsteps approaching, and another man joined the runemaster. Nysska recognized standard Cathedral-issue boots, which meant he was regular army, not Thaumetallicon or Argonium Infantry, but she couldn't make out any further details.

The soldier spoke in a relaxed tone, but pitched low enough to make sure his words didn't carry. "You got it?"

The runemaster produced the heavy sack full of poison and handed it over without a word.

The soldier hefted it. "All right. This should do it for another month."

The runemaster spoke up. "Have you secured another courier?"

"Don't worry. The boys in Slocum were falling all over themselves to get another shipment." His voice tightened. "We're putting in better controls this time. The shit goes in a sealed and locked chest, for one. We don't need another demon losing her mind. No disrespect to Jinna."

"So it was the concentrated exposure, then? Producing the erratic behavior, I mean."

"Near as we can tell, yeah."

"But getting this into the proper hands will preserve our deal?"

The soldier clapped the runemaster on the shoulder. "Relax. We'll be skiing in the Crags while Valco's riding a fork in the middle of Caulspring."

That satisfied the runemaster. He grunted a goodbye and left, as did the soldier a moment later. Nysska stayed where she was, her mind bouncing off the insides of her skull. The realization that argonium could be refined to remove its toxic properties...and that Emperor Valco had the purified runes implanted under his own skin...

Did that mean other high-ranking nobles had the white runes as well?

She shuddered. *Fuck all that. And fuck whatever danger Valco's in from these...whatever they were. Revolutionaries.* What it *meant* was that Valco—as well as the Fort Slade smelters and who could guess how many runemasters—*knew* that argonium could be purified. *Had known* about it for...how long?

And they had the toxic runes implanted in every Sensor and every Infantryman anyway.

Nysska's gorge rose. All of the pain and suffering, all of the early deaths—the fact that no runebearer ever lived past the age of forty thanks to the runes' toxins—*none of that was necessary.*

Sensors didn't have to die.

She swallowed hard.

Cam didn't have to die!

Nysska let the strength from the red runes flow through her body and made her way back up to the unused storage room.

Nysska paused when she reached the shaft that led down to the room where Cam and Galena waited. She heard no unfamiliar voices and, after waiting a moment, *did* hear Cam say something softly, followed by Galena's answer. Since neither of them sounded panicked, she said, "I'm coming down," lowered herself until she hung by the shaft's lip and dropped into the room.

Cam flung herself onto Nysska and held her tight. Nysska returned the hug, but only briefly. "Here, we've got to get the grate back in place."

Cam nodded, and Galena came forward and asked, "How can I help?"

Nysska picked up the grate and eyed the opening. "I'm afraid neither of you is strong enough to wedge it back into place if I held you up. And I don't think the two of you together could support me well enough. So... hmm. Here." Nysska pulled the mattress off the bed, upended the bed frame, balanced the grate on one corner, and used the frame to push the grate back up into the ceiling.

As she set the frame back into place, Cam said, "Could you have done that without the runes?"

Nysska wanted to grin at her, and say, "Probably," but the weight of what she'd learned bore down too hard on her shoulders. She drew breath to speak, but Galena said, "Wait—some of your makeup's come off. Let's go into the bathroom and I'll touch it up."

Nysska followed after the Governor without question. It would not do at this point to be discovered. So it was there, in a cramped bathroom inside the Empire's most secure fortress, that in hushed tones Nysska told Cam and Galena everything she had discovered in the argonium mine.

When she finished, Galena rubbed her temples. "All right. All right. So —so we needed to come here...to find out exactly what the poison is and where it's coming from...so that we can stop the sethyds who have your mother held captive...because if we don't stop them, they're going to invade the Empire and do their best to wipe us all out. But now we know that at least *some* highly placed Imperial citizens are—what? Siding with the sethyds? They think—do they think the sethyds wiping us out is inevitable? And they're just trying to get on the good side of 'Yshtarra' to save their own asses?"

Cam had gripped the edge of the stone counter against which she was leaning. Nysska watched her fingers tremble. "It's to control us," she said in a voice no less dangerous for how quiet it was. "It's to keep us from fucking *taking over.*" She closed one hand into a fist and punched the stone. "How do you prevent thousands of incredibly powerful people from overthrowing an empire? You fucking *kill* them. While you and your inbred noble fucks live long, happy, healthy lives."

"We've got to tell people," Galena said, sounding not at all like a Territorial Governor. "We've got to tell *everyone.*"

"No." Nysska shook her head, staring holes in the floor, her mind still racing. "What we've got to do is *prove* it."

25

Fort Slade lay to the northeast of Coalgarden. Heavy Imperial traffic followed the Shima Highway, which stretched in as straight a line as topography would allow from Fort Slade to Caulspring, where the Erskine River connected the capital to the Salt Ocean. From Caulspring, turning north on Redbud Road, a day's further travel ended at Cliffside.

A morose trio occupied Governor Galena Vachs's coach along the Shima Highway. They had to return to Raoul's home as fast as possible and get everyone caught up on the... Nysska struggled for the right words to describe it. The heinous crimes? The unrepentant villainy? *The fucking horrifying bearshit,* she said to herself.

But once they got there and poured all the horror out for everyone to see, what exactly could they do about it?

Nysska shot looks at Cam, who sat beside her, and Galena, who faced them. Both of them appeared enthralled with the wood grain of the coach's doors. Nysska put her hand on Cam's. "How are you doing?"

Cam rubbed at her nose. "I think I'm done with the tears. For now, anyway."

Nysska peered across the narrow gap at Galena. "Governor."

Galena looked up. "You don't have to call me that."

"No. But you know what I have to ask you."

Galena's eyebrows lifted, but after a couple of seconds lowered again. "I knew nothing about this, Nysska."

"But you're from a noble family."

"Yeah, apparently not noble enough."

Cam held Nysska's hand as she spoke. "We're not trying to accuse you, Galena. All I want to do—again, for now, anyway—is just *understand* this."

Galena squeezed her lips to one side and nodded. "That makes sense. And I've been wracking my brains about it ever since you told us—you know how, sometimes you'll learn something, and it makes a lot of little things in the past suddenly add up, things you didn't pay any attention to at the time? Well, nothing like that's coming to mind."

Nysska said, "No cryptic conversations you might have overheard among family members? No odd little turns of phrase in correspondence you might have glimpsed?"

Galena shook her head. "No. Nothing like that. I don't know what kind of circle the Emperor has that he's supplying with the purified runes, but it *has* to be a small one."

Cam said, "Right now it doesn't matter. Because you hit the nail on the head last night, Nysska. If there's no way for us to prove this, then it doesn't matter what we know or don't know. Nobody's ever going to believe us, and if we get up in the town square and start shouting the truth to the masses, the Emperor will have us on forks within the hour."

"Right. Like trying to convince everyone in Slocum that the sapping sickness isn't real and Yshtarra is a fake. Without proof, I'd be killed before anyone even had a chance to consider what I was saying. ...Maybe *with* proof, even."

Galena stretched in her seat. "This doesn't even touch the original problem. Now we know what the poison is and how it's getting where it's going, but I don't know that that helps your mother, Nysska, in any meaningful way."

Nysska sighed. She had no other response.

Cam said, "You told us that 'Yshtarra' has every sethyd woman pregnant all the time now, right? Because they're building their numbers. But that's years down the road, isn't it?"

Nysska tilted her head back against the cabin's wall. "Not as many years as you think. You know that every sethyd pregnancy produces twins, yes?"

Galena blinked. "Seriously?"

Nysska focused on her. "Oh—you're unaware. Yes. Every single sethyd pregnancy always produces a boy and a girl. What you call 'fraternal twins.' That already makes our birth rate double that of humans. Well. Have I mentioned how long sethyd pregnancies last?"

Cam frowned. "Is it not nine months?"

"Eighteen weeks."

Galena had pulled her knees up to her chest, propping her heels on the edge of her seat. Now she wrapped her arms around them, eyes wide. "*Shit.*"

Nysska said, "Oh, but there's more. How old must a human be to pick up a sword and fight? Fight effectively, I mean. Defeat an armed enemy on the field of battle."

Cam gestured vaguely with one hand. "What, fifteen, sixteen? Maybe fourteen if he's big?"

"Ah—there. You said 'he.' Every human sent off to war is male, yes?"

Galena rested her face on her knees. "Shit. Shit. *Shit.*"

Nysska continued. "Every sethyd female is exactly as strong and fast and tough as every sethyd male, remember? If necessary, we could field our *entire adult population.*" She paused. "And a sethyd child can kill a full-grown human male at three years."

Galena lifted her head. "When do sethyd girls become fertile?"

"Ten."

Galena dropped her face to her knees again. "Dragon fuck me in every hole."

Nysska could see that Cam had made all the connections as well. The rich brown of her beautiful face had taken on a grayish tinge. She said, very quietly, "How many sethyds are there in Slocum?"

"We took a census. Once everyone arrived in the Crags. At that point —four years ago—there were about four hundred thousand of us. How many humans are there, Empire-wide?"

Without lifting her head Galena murmured, "Eight, maybe nine million."

Cam's mouth appeared to have gone dry. "Ten years and they can wipe us out. All of us."

Galena said, "Not even that long."

A short, joyless laugh escaped Cam's lips. "And to think, last year I was worried about the Empire rising up and killing all of *you.*"

"It could still happen." Nysska ran her hand across the space where her right horn used to be. "That's the thing we cannot ignore. If word of what Tylar and Randolf are planning gets out, Valco will send the Argonium

Infantry to the Crags, backed up by the rest of the Cathedral, and there will be mass casualties on both sides. On the other hand, if Tylar and Randolf are given time to finish assembling their army—once again, mass casualties. Mass suffering. Genocide. They will assemble a force that will end the human race on Kainos and, if they strike a deal with the Gemini, perhaps on Borealis as well."

Eyes and voice hollow, Galena said, "We've got to do something." But it was clear from her tone that she had no idea what.

Neither Cam nor Nysska spoke.

Galena stared out the coach's window. "I've had a plan. Since I was about five. You've seen it in action—act like an utter imbecile, let people underestimate me, gather all the knowledge I need, and then fucking take them out."

Nysska frowned a little. "You were going to get rid of Wendell Anwar? Your cousin?"

Galena waved one hand. "All right, maybe not him. He never really wanted to be Governor anyway, and now it doesn't matter. The point is that I was going to advance. Slowly, maybe, but steadily, and I was going to do it on *my terms*. You know how many potential husbands I've had to put off? A *lot*. All these men with their gray hair and their greasy smiles and their big knuckles, and I sussed them all out, every one of them. Read their pitiful little personalities and played them like pianos. Every one, I learned exactly what it would take to get *them* to reject *me*, and I was fucking subtle about it. No scandals coming my way. No talk of 'poor Galena, well, you know how she is.' I just got them all to leave me *alone*. I was headed for the Emperor's throne, I was, and well on the way." She paused. "And then *this*. Dropped in my lap. Dropped in all our laps. *Fuck*."

Nysska and Cam traded long looks as Galena's attention remained focused outside the coach, but neither of them could think of anything to say to that.

Another hour passed in silence. The sun dropped to the western horizon and the coach pulled up outside an inn on the edge of a town called Thrasher. Galena's driver climbed down off the bench and rapped on the door before opening it. "Horses need rest, Governor. This is a decent place to stay—I'm having the boys give it the once-over, then you and your friends can maybe get a night's sleep. We'll be back at Cliffside by tomorrow evening."

Nysska still had on most of her Veronika Brooks costume, but wasn't sure how well her skin had remained covered, so she pulled her hood up.

Since losing her horns, passing as a human had become *much* easier. She said, "I'm just going to stretch my legs," and stepped out of the coach, which creaked on its springs with the shifting of her considerable weight. They had come to a stop in the shadow of a three-story gray wooden building with a sign over the front door that read, "The Fatted Calf."

Nysska beckoned to the driver, a Cathedral soldier named Millis. He came to her promptly.

"Something I can do for you, ma'am?"

"How far is Caulspring from here?" she asked, keeping her face mostly concealed with the hood.

Millis took a moment. "It's about fifteen kliks, ma'am." He pointed. "Straight down the highway. We'll be passing right along the northern outskirts of it tomorrow—do you want to schedule a stop?"

She eyed the heavy clouds overhead that stretched horizon to horizon. "No, no. I was just curious."

Another soldier, one of the security escort that had been accompanying Galena since she left Tember, emerged from the inn and waved. Millis said, "That's the all clear."

Nysska hooked a thumb at the coach. "I'll tell the ladies."

That night, after Cam's breathing had grown deep and even, Nysska rose from their bed. Feeling a sense of déjà vu, she slid the room's window open, shimmied out of it, and hoisted herself up and onto the roof, a slender violet shadow rendered all but invisible in the darkness. In the past, this kind of skullduggery would have been precipitated by a clandestine visit from her brother Gerrit, or at the least accompanied by one of Percy's brilliant cats. Now Nysska moved by herself. She crossed the inn's roof, dropped down and sprinted into a line of trees, then turned east, parallel with the Shima Highway, and let her legs carry her through the forest.

The next morning, as Cam, Galena, and Nysska—her body paint refreshed and wig and disguise lenses firmly in place—sat at a table and worked their way through plates of badly scrambled eggs and scorched sausages, Cam quietly said, "I had an unpleasant dream last night. I dreamed that I woke, after the third moon had set, and that you weren't in bed with me."

Nysska glanced around before speaking—not only to make sure that no one was within earshot because of what she was about to say, but also to make sure no one had overheard Cam referring to the two of them sleeping together. She leaned in closer, which signaled Cam and Galena to lean in as well.

"It was no dream," Nysska said, and told them what she'd done.

Snow fell on Cliffside as they arrived.

Nothing like the blizzard conditions from Mount Stark. Not even enough to make the roads hazardous. But the ground had frozen solid thanks to multiple bitter cold nights, and what snow there was stuck to every surface, turning the house and the grounds into a stunning winter sculpture. When the coach pulled up to the portico, Nysska spotted Rosie in the side yard, running at full speed with her tongue hanging out and flapping in the wind, clearly enjoying herself. Morrin had been playing with her, but now ran to the coach and hugged Nysska and Cam as they climbed out. She paused when Galena appeared, caught between sticking out a hand and curtsying, but Galena gave her a brilliant grin and hugged Morrin herself.

Nysska said, "Are the cats not out playing with Rosie too?"

Morrin chuckled. "No, the cats have better sense than either the dog or I do. Come on, let's get you all inside. Everyone's waiting."

Morrin wasn't lying. Gathered in the kitchen were Raoul, Percy, Flax and Jax, Kagan, Singer, Aschling, and Veronika Brooks. They'd just finished a meal, and when he sprang to his feet along with everyone else, Percy erupted in a massive belch, which sent both him and Veronika into a fit of laughter.

Flax and Jax made their way to Nysska immediately, and Flax leapt up onto her shoulders, curling around her neck to purr in her ear. Jax looked up at Cam expectantly, and when Cam cradled her arms and said, "Well, come on, then," Jax jumped up into them and settled onto his back so that Cam could commence with the belly scritches.

"Are you hungry?" Raoul asked. "We've just finished round one, but judging by that belch, Percy's got room for round two now."

Percy patted his flat belly and grinned. "Damn straight! That just means 'half full!'"

"Dragon's backbone, yes," Galena said as she picked up a chicken leg off a silver platter and bit a huge chunk out of it.

"The Governor has spoken," Morrin said with a grin that mirrored Percy's, and Raoul set three extra places as Nysska, Cam, and Galena joined everyone at the table.

Raoul filled a bowl with a ladle-full of what looked like clam chowder. "Well? Tell us everything!"

Over the course of a meal consisting of excellent baked chicken, acceptable carrots, disappointing strawberries, and a dessert that more than made up for the fruit—Raoul said it was called "tiramisu"—Nysska told them everything, up to and including her midnight excursion from the inn.

The group as a whole understood the implications and realities of all of it just as well as Cam and Galena had.

Kagan's lips curled back away from his snout full of fangs as he poked disinterestedly at his plate. "This is danger to Empire. In many ways. And because of that, is danger to Borealis." Nysska translated for him, as she'd been doing since the discussion started.

Even Princess Aschling had lost her perpetual sunny smile, along with her appetite. She caught Nysska's eye. "It is possible," she said, "that we here in this room are only ones who can stop this—this—"

Singer finished the thought for her. "This *war*."

Before anyone else could speak, the door to the kitchen swung open. One of the servants said, "Many pardons, Commander Cullen, but there is an Imperial messenger here for you."

Raoul stood. "If you'll all excuse me, I'll be right back." He left the kitchen, but returned only a moment later, holding one of the ornate tubes that carried Imperial communiques. Raoul glanced back at the door. "Young man was in a hurry. He'd no more handed me the tube than he was back on his horse and gone."

"Well?" Percy said. "What's in it?"

Raoul opened the tube and slid out a rolled-up parchment bearing the Emperor's wax seal.

Nysska's eyes lingered on the seal as Raoul cracked it open. He held up the parchment, reading quickly, and his breathing grew shallow. "Oh fuck," he said, and then louder, "Oh *fuck*."

Galena said, "What? Tell us!"

Raoul lowered the parchment, staring at and through the assembled crowd. "Security at Fort Slade figured out there had been a break-in. They called in a Crucible, but couldn't get a pinpoint on who it was, thanks to Nysska's runes. But they *did* find traces enough to decide it was a sethyd who did it."

Nysska's stomach clenched, tight and sour, around her meal.

Raoul continued. "And since there weren't any sethyd visitors, they've decided it must have been a spy from the Crags." He swallowed hard and ran a hand over his scalp. "They've mobilized the Argonium Infantry. They're going to go straight to Slocum and demand that the intruder be turned over."

Galena said, "Why did they send a messenger *here*, though?"

Raoul waved the paper at nothing. "Because I've been ordered to report to Caulspring. Percy, you and Cam, too." To Veronika Brooks, he said, "I'd suspect you as well, Commander."

"If they knew where to find me," she murmured. "I'm on personal leave."

"Dragon's fiery shit," Cam breathed. "It's starting."

"But we've got to stop them!" Galena cried. "If they get up to the Crags, Yshtarra's people are going to consider it an act of war—right?"

Nysska nodded, her eyes squeezed tight shut. "That is correct."

Percy pounded his knuckles on the table. "There's no fucking way we can beat the fucking Argonium Infantry to the Crags! Not from here!"

Nysska turned to look, along with everyone else, at the sound of a throat being daintily cleared. "If I may," Princess Aschling said in Plainish as she rose to her feet, her smile back in place. "I've got something to show you all…"

26

Kelvin Dhillon stood at his post on the top floor of Yshtarra's Devotion House, working on the hilt of his favorite dagger. With a small knife he carefully peeled off another tiny strip of wood where the seasoned hickory wrapped the bronze tang. When he was finished, if he didn't make any serious mistakes, the pattern of the hilt should match that of his horns exactly. Not the same shape, of course, since his horns curled like a ram's, but the ridges and curves lined up and felt good in his grip. He had carved his initials at the top, just below the guard. *KD.* He took pride in those initials.

The humans had given him a different surname when he and his family landed. *Kelvin Saltharbor.* He understood why. Records of the ship's passengers were created there in Saltharbor, and this was the humans' dim, unimaginative way of marking each of them. But the name Dhillon held significance. His mother had told him it meant "one with a brave heart." The idea that he would willingly relinquish that for the name of a filthy human city appalled him.

Besides, Yshtarra had commanded him to reject the human name. She had commanded them all to do so, through her mouthpieces, Tylar Singh and Randolf Thakkur, and he followed her teachings gladly. Yshtarra painted a new picture of the world for him and for everyone else who heeded her message. Soon they would overrun the Valconian Empire, seize the land that should have been theirs by rights, and then turn their attention to the Estmani in the north and the Skahna to the south. Only one at a time, though. Yshtarra was wise, and did not wish to lose sethyd lives needlessly by fighting a war on two fronts.

Kelvin glanced up from his carving to look out the window, and his orange eyes snapped wide.

Beneath the heavy cloud cover that had blanketed the valley all day, a building half a klik across the city was on fire.

As he watched, flames splashed across the roof of another one a street away, and he heard shouting from outside—*was this another attack?* He had a good view of the broad thoroughfare that ran in front of the Devotion House, down which many of his fellow Yshtarrans sprinted toward the fires.

Kelvin sheathed his dagger and took a step away from the window—but paused. He'd been ordered to stay at his post no matter what. *No matter what.* After the would-be assassin Nysska Stonegate—he refused to think of her with her sethyd name—had breached the House, Tylar and Randolf had doubled the security, and told him and the others assigned to Yshtarra's safety not to abandon their posts under *any* circumstances.

Another roof ignited in hungry flames the same color as Kelvin's eyes. Nevertheless, he stayed put.

Not long after that he heard a soft thump from overhead.

It didn't sound significant. He'd heard clumsy squirrels make more noise. But then a second thump reached his ears, followed by a third, and Kelvin unsheathed his khopesh. He moved out of the sleeping room he'd been occupying and into the long hallway that ran the length of the Devotion House's top floor.

The first thing he noticed was that the trap door leading up to the attic was missing.

The second was the touch of sharp bronze against the back of his neck.

"Drop your sword. I don't want to kill anyone if I don't have to."

Kelvin moved only his head as it swiveled, letting him see from the corner of his eye the one person he'd been warned against. The sethyd who'd occupied his thoughts only moments earlier.

"Nysska Stonegate," he whispered. His eyes rose to her forehead, where her horns had been reduced to the barest of stumps. "I see you have dishonored yourself even further."

"Your hand still grips your weapon," the assassin growled. "Drop it and submit so that I don't have to spill any more of my brethren's blood."

Kelvin's hand tightened on the khopesh's hilt. "I am no more your brother than—"

He broke off when something huge and black and covered with fur dropped through the trap from the attic.

"I—I—what's—"

Kelvin's mind hitched. His eyes watered as the giant thing moved toward him, a thing that belonged on four legs but walked on two, but it didn't just walk, it *glided*, so sure and graceful were its movements. Kelvin screamed at his own brain for focusing on such needless details when he should have been either attacking or running for his life, but neither of those options seemed available to him as he stood and stared, legs trembling, feet rooted to the floor.

A dark-skinned human girl followed after the creature, and now Kelvin knew his mind had snapped in half, because the human girl's eyes were silver, silver just like those of the massive wolf-man whose muzzle had opened to reveal a red cave lined with white stalactites and stalagmites. When Nysska the assassin took the khopesh out of his hand he didn't resist.

"Thank you," the assassin murmured in his ear, as the silver-eyed human girl produced a length of heavy chain.

"We only do that a couple more times," Singer said quietly after they had left the sentry bound and gagged in an empty room. "Chains are heavy, and make noise."

Nysska led the way down the stairs. "I know. But I want to minimize casualties if we can." When they reached the second floor hallway an elderly house servant opened one of the living quarters doors and froze in place, staring with huge yellow eyes at Nysska and Kagan and Singer. Nysska laid a finger across her lips and whispered, "Go back inside. Stay there. You'll be safe."

The man did as Nysska said, his eyes locked on Kagan until the door shut. They heard a lock engage. Kagan leaned toward Nysska. "Scaring sethyds is fun."

Nysska said, "Then this might turn out to be the best night of your life," and beckoned for them to follow her as she headed down the stairs toward the ground floor.

At the far end of the ground floor hallway another sethyd stood guard, his back to them, keeping watch at the window. Nysska took a step toward him, but Singer put a hand on her arm and motioned her to stay back. Nysska frowned, but complied, and Singer produced a round black ball a little smaller than a hen's egg from a pouch at her belt. As Nysska watched, Singer hurled the ball and with a sharp, wet *crack* the sentry slumped to the floor.

Nysska covered the distance quickly and found the sentry unconscious and bleeding from a wound on the back of his head. Singer picked up the ball, wiped it on the guard's clothes, and put it back in her pouch. While Nysska bound the guard in more chains, she said, "Fucking hell, Singer, I think his skull might be fractured. What is that ball made of?"

"Lead," Singer answered. "Do not worry, I do not hit him *that* hard. He wakes up with a bad headache, he is fine. Maybe just bit of nausea. Some double-vision. I'm sure it passes."

"Stash him where?" Kagan asked.

Nysska gestured at a nearby door. "The cellar is through there. We might as well bring him with us. Can you carry him?"

Kagan picked the guard up with one hand and tucked him under his arm. "Lead on."

Nysska opened the door to the cellar just enough to peek through it. She saw no guards at the top of the stairs, but heard a couple of voices from below, and showed Kagan and Singer two fingers before pointing down. They both nodded, and Nysska opened the door wide.

Singer whispered, "You draw weapon, yes?"

Nysska shook her head. "I have to make sure they both go down fast. Need my hands free."

Singer shrugged and hung back.

Nysska descended the stairs, letting her runes ignite beneath her skin. That was how she had come to think of it—not *making* them wake up, but *letting* them. Over the last several days the thaumaturgic power of the runes had come to feel like some kind of vast red ocean beating against the alloy sea walls inside her body. As if the act of lowering those walls would let the power flood out of her and fill the world around her with splintering, tearing force.

At the bottom of the stairs, across the length of the cellar, two sethyds —a man and a woman—stood in front of the door to Simana's chamber. The woman was faster to draw her khopesh than the man, but the man said, "It's her! We've got to w—"

That word was probably supposed to be "warn," but Nysska never found out for certain, because the concussive red ocean channeled its power into her legs and propelled her across the cellar floor faster than the man could finish speaking. Nysska planted a palm flat against the side of his face and smashed his head against the wall behind him—not hard enough to kill him, she hoped, but definitely hard enough to keep him from warning anyone of anything—spun on one foot and stabbed down with her other hand, breaking the woman's sword arm and sending the khopesh clanging away amid the racks.

The woman recoiled and tried to scream. Nysska grabbed the front of her tunic and jerked her forward and, as the runes in her arms and chest flared magenta through her violet skin, slammed her forehead down on the bridge of the woman's nose. She crumpled in Nysska's grip.

Nysska looked around to see Kagan and Singer at the bottom of the stairs, the unconscious sentry still under Kagan's arm like some kind of floppy parcel. "Come on," she said. "We can put them all in my mother's room."

The rug from before had been discarded—probably because it was soaked with blood—and as they passed the hatch leading down to the underground river, Singer said, "I thought you would put them in water. That is where this goes, yes?"

"As I have stated more than once," Nysska replied, trying not to roll her eyes, "I don't want to kill anyone we don't have to. If we put them through the hatch, they will almost certainly drown. Plus, who knows what that would do to the water supply?"

Singer's face took on a *whatever* expression. "Is fine. I prefer enemies who cannot get back up, but this is your show."

Nysska unlatched the heavy door and pulled it open, half expecting another sentry to come lunging out at them, but their fiery distractions appeared to have worked. She stepped across the threshold and saw her mother collapsed across the bed, as if she had returned from a night of excess and simply lay where she had fallen.

"Mother?" Nysska said, rushing to her side. *"Panjo?* Are you awake? Can you hear me?"

Behind her, she heard Singer sound out the word. "Pahn-yo?"

Simana groaned and tried to roll over onto her back. Nysska helped her, gently, and put a pillow under her head out of sheer muscle memory. Simana's eyelids fluttered and opened, but only halfway. "Nysska." She swallowed hard. "You came back."

"Of course I came back."

"No, daughter—you—they –" Simana's eyes swam in and out of focus. "They knew you would. They have...laid a trap for you..."

"No, *Panjo*, it's all right. I'm getting you out of here. I—I'm able to do that now. Better than I could before." She slipped her arms under Simana's back and knees and lifted her off the bed. "Let's take you somewhere safe."

Simana weakly clung to her, but tears filled her eyes. "Oh, Nysska... there is nowhere safe now."

A sound reached her from out in the cellar—a heavy, crunching sound, and a cry of pain that did not come from a human throat. Nysska swiftly laid her mother back onto the bed and scrambled to the door, to see Kagan on the floor in a corner, holding one hand with the other, panting hard. Singer stood in the middle of the floor, crouched and fight-ready, a long, slim dagger in each hand.

At the other end of the cellar stood Tylar Singh, a wicked black khopesh drawn and ready—

With red runes glowing a brilliant magenta through his deep violet skin.

"What's that the humans say, Nysska?" Tylar said as he raised the khopesh. "What's good for the goose is good for the gander?"

The next half minute grew choppy in Nysska's mind. Fragmented—as if each second had become a world of its own, a separate battlefield, a distinct map of pain and bloody impacts. Tylar could not have had his runes as long as Nysska had had hers, and for half a heartbeat she hoped he wouldn't have complete control of them. That hope died as he launched himself across the length of the cellar at her. As if he disappeared from one spot and reappeared so close she could feel his breath on her skin. Her raised khopesh only partially stopped his as the curved razor edge bit into her shoulder and *clanked* against the rune beneath the skin.

Nysska drove the heel of her hand into Tylar's chin but he'd seen her attack coming and rocked back with it, his body swaying and looping as the grip on his khopesh shifted. Nysska sprang away from the blow but crashed against the door behind her as the blade sliced through her jacket and shirt and laid open a long thin line across her abdomen—

One of Singer's daggers flickered through the air toward Tylar's neck. His head snapped sideways as his brilliant white eyes tracked the blade. As his hand flicked up and caught it Kagan crashed into him and clamped his jaws down onto Tylar's thigh—

And Tylar screamed, the khopesh whipping around, but Nysska's own curved blade caught it before it could cleave through Kagan's neck. She whipped his weapon out of his grip and hammered a fist into the center of his chest—

Just as Singer landed on his back, her mouth stretching wide to reveal her own dagger-sharp fangs, and she buried those fangs in Tylar's throat just as he kicked Kagan in the ribs and sent him flopping and thudding away across the floor.

Kagan spat out a chunk of Tylar's flesh, ripped from his thigh, one of the red runes exposed there and grotesquely bent up out of the wound. Tylar's scream climbed higher as he reached up and grabbed Singer by the throat and hurled her over his head. She smacked against the wall to the right of the door to Simana's chamber and slid to the floor, leaving a trail of blood on the stone—

As Nysska's khopesh came around in a savage arc, her own runes blazing through her skin, light pouring from the seams of her clothes and through the cuts Tylar had made. The long curved blade caught his right arm at the elbow and sliced cleanly through the joint.

Tylar staggered backward, his breath frozen in his throat now, pale eyes fixed on the bloody, spurting stump. He didn't see Kagan move until the towering wolf-man seized Tylar by his remaining arm and one of his legs and heaved him off the floor.

Nysska said, "Kagan—" but if the Borealan heard her it made no difference. He went to one knee as he brought Tylar down with the force of a falling redwood. Nysska heard Tylar's spine splinter apart.

Kagan dumped Tylar on the floor and sprang across him to Singer, who was groaning and trying to sit up.

Nysska approached Tylar cautiously. He was still alive, and the blood from the severed stump of his arm had already begun to slow.

She thought about the wreck of her own body when the Gemini rescued her from the sea below Cliffside. How, even with the hole in her chest and most of her bones broken, the runes had brought her back. Allowed her to heal from damage that would have dragged out into an agonizing, unbearable death.

Tylar gasped and gurgled, staring up at her.

She said, "I don't want to hear it," and pressed the blade of her khopesh through his neck with a crunching, rocking motion that left his head rolling free from his shoulders.

She wiped Tylar's blood off her weapon onto his tunic and stood, turning to see Kagan helping Singer to her feet. "How are you two? How badly are you hurt?"

"I bang my skull," Singer said, touching the back of her head gingerly. "But I do not think it is broken."

Kagan raised the hand he'd been cradling earlier. "Maybe one or two bones break," he rumbled. "Will not slow me down."

Nysska gestured to his ribs. "What about there? He caught you with a pretty solid kick."

Kagan took a slow, deep breath, and grimaced. "Maybe three or four bones break. Do not worry. I do not cough any blood."

Singer gently took Kagan's helping arm from around her shoulders, steadying herself. "Do you not say you are only sethyd with runes?"

Nysska spread her hands. "I thought I was." She cast a baleful glance at Tylar's corpse. "They must have seen that I had them, realized that was an option, then taken steps as soon as I escaped."

Kagan sniffed the air above Tylar's corpse. "I do not like this. It takes three of us to beat one of him."

Nysska said, "He was like my brother Gerrit. A specially trained fighter. One of my people's elite warriors."

The door to Simana's chamber unlatched and swung open, and Simana almost fell out of it, clinging to the door frame. "I tried to tell you," she said, her voice weak and breathy. Her eyes wandered, unfocused for a moment before fixing on Nysska. "Now you have to listen to me. Will you listen?"

Nysska dashed to her mother and took her up in her arms again. "Of course, *Panjo*. What do you want to say?"

27

Nysska lay full-length, belly-down, on the edge of a grain storage tower's roof.

She had sent her mother with Kagan and Singer, getting her to safety, while Nysska had held a quick planning session with the rest of the group. Now, with the Borealans gone and Raoul, Cam, Percy, Morrin, and Veronika Brooks having stayed with Aschling, Nysska felt purely, painfully alone.

If she hadn't had her runes she never would have made it to this vantage point, having climbed the outside of the Devotion House as easily as would a spider and then leapt from rooftop to rooftop, following a circuitous route through the city that kept her from being spotted. But then, if she hadn't had her runes, a great number of things would never have happened.

My runes. She turned the words over in her mind, examining them from every angle. Did that feel right? Claiming them as her own, when she had spent so long wishing she could get rid of them?

The parade yard below her stirred. This was where Simana had told her to come. To see the truth. A teenage sethyd boy sprinted across the broad expanse of hard-packed earth to the barracks at the back of it, and seconds later lantern light flared from the room farthest to right. The door burst open, and she recognized Randolf Thakkur from the way he walked, stomping out and slamming his fist against each of the long line of doors facing the parade ground. She couldn't make out his exact words from where she lay, but it didn't take much intuition or imagination to see that the boy had been sent with a message from the Devotion House. In the time it had taken Nysska to sneak around the city, someone had discovered Simana's absence and Tylar's death.

Sethyds poured out of the barracks and assembled in front of Randolf. She counted, squinting. *Thirty-two...thirty-three...thirty-four including Randolf.*

That was Simana's hushed, urgent message. "There are thirty-four more just like Tylar."

Nysska wondered if Master Seeley, the man who had made her more than a sethyd, had also sold his services to the worshippers of Yshtarra. Or had Tylar and Randolf abducted someone else from one of the Imperial Colleges? Forced them to implant the red runes?

"Find her!" Randolf's words carried that time. "Find her and fucking kill her!"

The assembled Yshtarrans shouted something back to him, some kind of in-unison acknowledgement, and the red runes gleamed magenta through their skin.

Nysska rolled away from the roof's edge, came up into a crouch, and stole away into the shadows.

Franklun Simeon's house was dark when Nysska arrived at the back door. She had circled it twice, on the chance that someone had found out she'd been there before and decided to lie in wait for her. There was plenty of activity in the city, but as far as she could tell it was all centered around the now-all-but-extinguished fires that had served as their distraction for invading Yshtarra's Devotion House. That, and the seventeen pairs of roving runebearing sethyds who would take delight in nothing more than taking her to pieces.

Nysska didn't want to take the chance of someone hearing her knock. With a brief flash of magenta under her right sleeve she broke the lock out of the door and opened it just wide enough to slip through.

The house lay dark and quiet except for a sliver of light from the living room.

Now came the part that made her most nervous about approaching Franklun again. How did she know he was still on her side? Had Axel betrayed her? Would she be walking into multiple spear-points? She couldn't think of any way to know other than to try it and find out. "Franklun," she called in a loud whisper. "Franklun, are you here?"

Nysska heard a thump, perhaps like the noise made by not overly graceful feet hitting the floor, followed by a familiar creak, and a moment later Axel and Franklun appeared in the doorway of the living room, Axel pushing Franklun's chair again.

"I knew it," Franklun said. "I knew it had to be you causing this much chaos. Are you trying to burn down the city? Because lighting fires like this is a really fucking good way to burn down the city."

"I need your help," Nysska said. She moved closer to the two of them. "I hate to show up like this and start making demands, but—I truly mean this—I'm trying to stop a war."

Axel lit another lantern, but Franklun slapped at his wrists. "Put that out! We don't want anyone knowing we're awake!" As Axel abashedly extinguished the lantern, Franklun peered into Nysska's face. "You *do* mean it. Come, sit. Explain to me about this war."

Nysska didn't feel like sitting, but she was going to have to walk Franklun through each step if she hoped to convince him, so she turned one of the straight-backed chairs in his kitchen around backward, sank onto it, and started talking.

Twenty minutes later Franklun tugged on one of his horns, his lips pursed, his eyes focused on nothing. "It could work," he said. "You know, none of the Mountain Bulls ever spoke to me, and the Yshtarra crowd just pretends I don't exist."

"Well, I don't know exactly when the Argonium Infantry is going to get here, but I know they travel really fucking quickly."

A wolfish grin curled Franklun's lips and revealed his teeth. "I suppose it's worth a try," he said, and cranked around in his seat to look at Axel, who'd been lingering nearby the whole time. "You see any flaws in what she's asking for, boy?"

Axel licked his lips. With a nervous tremor in his voice he spoke directly to Nysska. "What about *you*?"

Franklun's face darkened. "Oh. There is that."

Nysska stood. "Don't worry about me. Just make it happen." Before either of them could protest, she turned and left the way she'd come in.

Nysska spent the next few hours hiding. She wouldn't have been able to pull it off, evading Randolf's runebearer squadron, if the night hadn't been so dark. The clouds persisted overhead, though, blocking out any trace of moonlight and making torches and lanterns the only sources of illumination. A few times she almost got caught, but the more she used her runes the steadier and more reliable they became, and she was able to spring from one rooftop to another, darting away before any eyes could settle on her.

When the dimmest, faintest gray light pressed against the clouds from the edge of the mountains at the eastern horizon, Nysska made her way to the Canyon of the Word. If her experience and Raoul's recollections proved correct, dawn would be the time to act.

Nysska entered the Canyon and scaled the wall, heading for the High Terrace. This she could have done without her runes. It would have taken her much longer.

When she reached the top, the caves which had been converted to the priest-singers' living quarters stretched away to her left and right, but she ignored them and turned to face the Pulpit. The rock outcropping that seemed to have been set there by the hand of some ancient architect. The place from which a priest-singer cast their voice into the canyon below, listening to it grow and swell and become something more than just sound produced by a sethyd's throat and lungs and diaphragm. In the Canyon of the Word, projected from the Pulpit, a priest-singer's voice became a living thing. A wave of love and harmony that filled every crack and crevice in the stone, as well as in the hearts and minds of those listening.

It made Nysska physically ill to think of the Canyon being used to catalyze anger and bitter hatred.

Which made what she was about to do—or at least try to do—that much more painful.

The sun had risen another few degrees. Slocum had begun to stir. Miners headed for the deep shafts. The few ranchers who lived in town making their way out to the small, rocky livestock fields. Weavers, merchants, cooks and cleaners, all starting their days.

Nysska strode out to the tip of the Pulpit, where an ornate bronze guard rail had been driven into the stone, took a breath that filled her lungs to capacity, and bellowed, *"People of Slocum! Yshtarra would speak to you! Come, gather in the Canyon of the Word!"*

Her voice filled the Canyon and flowed over its edges into the rest of the city. The effects of a priest-singer's song were at their most profound there at the site, but no Devotion ever passed that the entirety of Slocum didn't know about. Nysska shouted out the message again, and then a third time.

Figures appeared in the doorways of the priest-singers' quarters along the High Terrace. They stood there, motionless. Watching her.

As Franklun had asked them to.

Below, at the Canyon's entrance, sethyds of every stripe showed up. They were too far away for Nysska to make out individual faces, but she could see by their body language that they were confused. Tentative. *They're not used to this. Yshtarra doesn't address her followers herself.*

And yet, in the strengthening morning sunlight, the golden horns that Nysska now wore over the stubs of her own gleamed and flashed, signaling to the crowd. "Yes!" she shouted, her voice traveling to every corner, reaching every ear. "Your Exemplar wishes to speak to you! Come in! Come in and listen!"

Roughly a hundred sethyds had entered the Canyon, another hundred right behind them at the entrance, when Randolf charged in, seven of his runebearers flanking him.

Nysska's stomach clenched. This was another gamble. Would Randolf order any of his followers to strike her down, there in public, with hundreds of people watching? Would he consider being branded a traitor to the new Exemplar too great a risk to take?

She couldn't tell what he was saying to his people, but none of them moved to attack, so Nysska called out again. "Come in! Come in and listen, everyone!"

The crowd swelled, growing faster and faster, as hundreds and then thousands of sethyds filed in. There were no seats on the floor of the Canyon. Everyone was expected to stand, and stand they did, heads tilted, eyes of yellow and orange and white fixed on the Pulpit. Fixed on her.

When the floor had filled—with Randolf and the thirty-three other runebearers clumped together near the center—Nysska spoke.

"Children of Patrinomonto." She couldn't help but appreciate, even now, in this life-or-death moment, how glorious the Canyon's acoustics were. "We do not couch our meaning in flowery nothingness the way the humans do. We speak the truth. And the truth—has been withheld from you."

A murmur made its way through the crowd, a susurrating sound like whitecaps breaking on a beach.

"Pay attention now, because what I tell you affects every single sethyd living in Slocum. You have all been lied to. *There is no sapping sickness. There is no plague. You are being poisoned.*"

The murmur rose, grew abrasive, sharp-edged. Nysska half expected an arrow to sing out of the crowd and find its way to her, just as the one had at Cliffside, and she fought to keep her breathing even and her hands steady on the rail.

"Yshtarra never had the cure to the disease because, let me say this again, *there was no disease.* Her followers poisoned the water supply, and then treated you all with the medicine to create a debt. It was a *false debt.* They were *false followers.*" She took a deep breath and raised her volume: "Because *there is no Yshtarra.*" With that, Nysska whipped the golden horns off her head and held them up, gleaming in her violet-skinned fist.

No murmur rose from the crowd now. Instead came gasps, and shrieks, and cursing.

Nysska pointed straight at Randolf below. "That man. Randolf Thakkur. He and Tylar Singh created Yshtarra. Because they want *war.*" She let that word, *war*, echo around the Canyon's walls. "They want thousands upon thousands of sethyds to die, and for what? To kill the humans? To take their land? *Listen to me!* I have come here to tell you that there is a better way!"

Nysska heard a sound from the distance. Faint but clear.

Drums.

On the Canyon floor, Randolf screamed, *"Lies! She lies to you all!"* The acoustics were not as good in his location, but still good enough that every sethyd there heard him. "That woman is Nysska Kaur! Or maybe you know her better by her *human* name—Nysska Stonegate!"

The murmur returned with an ugly edge to it.

Randolf bellowed even more loudly. "Look at her! She has killed Yshtarra! She wants to let the humans kill all of us! Swarm her! Tear her apart!"

"I do not have to lie," Nysska said, and her words rolled over Randolf's and crushed them flat. "You have only to look in the cellar of Yshtarra's Devotion House. There you will find traces of the poison Randolf used on you, as well as the delivery point from which he contaminated the city's water. There you will find the place where they kept my mother captive. *She* was the Yshtarra you saw. Rendered helpless. Used as a figurehead. A puppet."

The drums grew louder. Now the sethyds on the Canyon floor heard them, too. A few heads turned. The murmur grew alarmed.

Randolf heard the drums and seized on it. "Do you all hear that? Do you? That is the Argonium Infantry! The Emperor only sends them in to act as the heel of his boot! They have come here to crush us—subjugate us—kill and enslave us!" He stabbed a finger at Nysska. "And they have come at *her* behest! She summoned the humans here because it is *she* who wants a war!"

The drums reverberated down the streets of Slocum. The Infantry had to be mere moments away.

"More lies!" Nysska slammed the words down at the black-horned crowd. "There is no need for war. Not when the humans will share every resource with us. I see a future for sethydkind—a future filled with *abundance*. A future in which we leave this desolate valley and settle in a lush forest. Only Randolf Thakkur and his followers stand in the way of that reality! They are determined to foment war no matter what—and to do so, they have implanted themselves with *runes*!"

No mistaking the sentiment this time. The crowd gasped as one.

Nysska forged ahead. "They have taken the creation of the humans and shoved it under their skin—just like the foul abomination I fought and killed in Tember!"

The crowd separated from Randolf and the runebearers. Moved back, away, leaving them in an isolated circle. Her words wouldn't have had as much power if the people of Slocum hadn't already been rendered susceptible to suggestion, but the advantage was there for the taking, and by Atiina, she meant to take it. Nysska shouted, "Who would you trust—a man who has lied to you, *poisoned* you, tried to play dictator with your very lives?" She thumped her chest. "Or someone who wants to save every sethyd life?"

Drums filled the canyon like the deepest thunder. The crowd parted again, spreading back and away from the entrance, as the one hundred members of the Argonium Infantry arrived, silver runes pulsing and gleaming through their skin.

Randolf and the other runebearing sethyds moved toward them. Slowly. Spreading out into a line two sethyds deep. The leader of the

Infantry stared at Randolf across the entrance of the canyon, an abruptly established no-man's land fifteen meters wide and forty across.

"We have come seeking the spy who invaded Fort Slade," the Infantry leader shouted. Nysska couldn't tell how old he was thanks to his helmet, but he stood tall and broad, a tower of deadly confidence.

"Listen to me!" Nysska bellowed. "This conflict is needless! We live in a world of humans and sethyds. The two can co-exist!"

The Infantry leader looked up, noticing Nysska at the Pulpit for the first time. "Who are you to make such a bold statement?" he shouted in response.

"I am..." Nysska shot a glance at the clouds. "Someone who can prove it!" She reached up, touched the Speaking Stone she'd been wearing tucked behind her ear ever since arriving in Slocum, and said softly, "Aschling. Now."

A thunderous, grinding roar came shattering out of the clouds overhead.

Nysska had never heard a sound like it before, and judging by the response from everyone below, human and sethyd alike, neither had any of them. The sound came again, louder, as if the bones of the planet itself were scraping together, shrieking in god-like rage. The clouds lit up from within, filled with bursts of fiery yellow-orange, and directly above the Canyon of the Word the clouds parted—

As something enormous descended from them.

A hundred meters long it was, a vast shape that *glittered silver* from hundreds upon thousands of scales.

The grinding, otherworldly, unnatural roar exploded into the air as the shape pivoted, revealing the wide, fang-filled *mouth* that took up one end of it—and above that, a pair of great brilliant red *eyes*.

The sethyds had frozen like a horde of violet-skinned statues, staring, many mouths agape. This was like *nothing* from their experience. None of them had anything close to a frame of reference. They stared, unable or unwilling to understand what appeared to be a vast silver beast slowly, majestically descending from the clouds.

Not so among the humans. Nysska heard a voice with a Caulspring accent utter the words, *"It's the Dragon..."*

Those words spread like flames among the bearers of the silver runes.

"The Dragon has come!"

"The Great Silver Dragon!"

"The Dragon has come to judge us all!"

267

Nysska touched the Speaking Stone again and murmured, "Do it."

From a dark structure on the Dragon's underbelly, burning globes came arcing out, balls of churning fire that smashed down into the unoccupied stretch at the Canyon's entrance, and Nysska heard a human scream, *The scales! The burning scales! The Dragon has come!*" while another Infantryman shrieked, *"No, Dragon, no do not judge me I beg you!"*—

Nysska watched from the Pulpit as the Argonium Infantry in its entirety turned tail and sprinted away as fast their rune-augmented legs would take them.

"Thank you," Nysska shouted again, this time with her face turned up, clearly speaking to the Great Silver Dragon. "Your work here is done for now."

With an echoing, menacing, prolonged *hisssss* the immense silver thing rose back up and disappeared into the clouds once more.

The crowd on the Canyon floor stared at her. Stunned. The silence that stretched out more deafening than the loudest of her bellows.

"We have a choice to make here today," Nysska called out. "We can side with Randolf and his pack of liars. Or we can choose peace. A peace which, as I have just demonstrated, is backed by powerful, undeniable forces. So decide! People of Slocum, decide! Children of Patrinomonto, *decide!*"

A voice from the crowd called out. "If we pick you, what will happen to these 'followers of Yshtarra'?"

Nysska spotted him, near the entrance. Franklun. Suppressing a smile, she answered him. "They will be dealt with."

Another voice, from halfway around the canyon—Axel. "Then I choose to align myself with you!" Other sethyds the boy's age called out as well, scattered throughout the crowd, echoing what Axel had said.

Slowly, but gaining strength and speed, a chant arose from the gathered sethyds.

Two syllables.

Nyss-ka

Nyss-ka

Nyss-ka

Randolf snarled and drew his khopesh. "You may have swayed these weak-minded idiots, but it won't stop me from taking your head off!"

Nysska leaned forward, over the guard rail, and put every bit of insistence into her words that she could muster. "People of Slocum! Children of Patrinomonto! If you value peace, run now! Leave the Canyon! *Go!*"

That stopped Randolf and his followers. Only for a few seconds, as they looked at each other, unsure what to do. But Franklun took the lead. "You heard her! We need to get out of the Canyon while she deals with these war-mongers! Come on!"

Axel appeared next to his grandfather and steered him out the Canyon's entrance—past the smoldering, scorched craters where the fire balls had struck—and into the street outside. That was all it took. The rest of the sethyds rushed to the exit, spilling out like sands from an hourglass bulb.

Except for Randolf and the followers of Yshtarra. They remained, and Randolf raised his khopesh and pointed at Nysska. *"Kill her!"*

Nysska drew another deep breath—the deepest she'd ever drawn—and *screamed*.

"That sounds like a massive risk," Cam said, wriggling on the uncomfortable wooden bench.

Nysska, standing at one of the view ports, wanted to agree, but she couldn't stop staring out at the night sky. The perfectly clear night sky, starlight falling on the carpet of clouds below. Finally she made herself break away and rejoined the group.

Nysska sat down with Cam, Raoul, Percy, Veronika Brooks, and Morrin James, all of them clustered in what Aschling called "the cabin." Aschling wasn't taking part in the discussion, but instead scampered back and forth and around and through the massive tangle of pipes and levers and gears that filled the cabin's far end, pulling and pushing and adjusting a great spoked wheel set into the floor. The cabin itself had struck Nysska more like a treehouse than part of a vessel, but the floor seemed sturdy enough, and Aschling promised it wouldn't fall off the bottom of the airship.

"All I can do is base it on what happened when I screamed into Lockridge's ear. I think what happened was because of his runes. I think there was some sort of resonance—like when someone strikes a tuning fork, and another tuning fork vibrates. Or when a soprano hits a high note and breaks a glass. This...what I'm talking about—it would be that. Just on a larger scale."

Scowling, Raoul said, "Lockridge was a Gemini. These aren't Gemini. You don't know that the same thing will happen. You don't know that it won't end up, I don't know, making them all stronger."

269

"Everything about this is a gamble," Nysska replied. "But I think it's a gamble worth taking. And I'm not asking anyone else to participate."

Aschling stepped away from what she called her "bank of instruments" and pulled one part of the Speaking Stone set Nysska had given her out of a pocket. "And this works? I am able to hear you through it?"

Nysska held up her own. "Oh, they work. I took them off an Argonium Infantryman in Fort Slade. Here, let's practice."

Randolf had taken a running step, but as Nysska's scream filled the Canyon, he stopped and covered his ears.

This was not like a Song of Devotion, or the impassioned speech she'd just given. Nysska held nothing back.

One by one, but joining quickly, the two dozen other priest-singers who'd been watching the whole time—the priest-singers Franklun had rallied at Nysska's request—joined her. A couple on the Pulpit, the rest around the edge of the Terrace.

All of them screaming.

All of them.

Screaming.

This was not what the Canyon was meant for. It felt like blasphemy.

She screamed even louder.

The sonic onslaught filled the Canyon like molten bronze filling a crucible. Every bit of glass in the priest-singers' quarters shattered. Small rocks on the ground below shivered and danced. Drops of blood fell from Nysska's nose into the emptiness below her.

She screamed louder still.

So did the others.

Randolf and his followers trembled and jerked and spasmed, all of them screaming as well but their voices lost in the crushing, obliterating sound as every living sethyd priest-singer roared their battle-cry.

Nysska watched, transfixed, as Randolf's skin split open. Cutting through tissue and cloth and leather like red-hot knives, the runes sliced and sawed their way out of the runebearers' bodies, melting as they emerged, searing violet skin. The runebearers collapsed to the ground one by one, bit by bit, limb by limb crumpling under the trauma and the agony. Nysska watched, unable to look away, as the ground below them grew dark red and steamed as blood and ruined, bubbling metal poured out onto it.

Finally Nysska ran short of breath.

She felt hands on her, pulling her back and away from the edge. *Something's wrong. Something's wrong with me,* she knew it, but couldn't pinpoint *what.* Then she was on the ground and looking up at Cam and Raoul and Percy. Nearby, Veronika Brooks slammed out orders. Nysska raised her hand and saw that the skin hung off her arm in tatters, that she had split apart *everywhere,* and Cam and Raoul and everyone and everything faded away.

28

Nysska moved slowly and painfully and very, very carefully as she and Simana passed through the ornate bronze-and-mahogany doors of the Emperor's receiving chamber. She didn't want to rupture any of her sutures. At the same time, she kept a steadying hand on her mother's arm, as the drugs Tylar and Randolf had forced Simana to take had not fully worn off, leaving her weakened. Simana's mind, though, remained as sharp as ever, for which Nysska felt immensely grateful. Franklun rolled in behind them. Between herself, Franklun, and her mother, she expected that at least one of them could lay things out in the proper way.

Atiina's wisdom, she hurt. *Everything* hurt. She could barely stand, let alone walk properly. If anyone had attacked her at that moment, her one option would've been to try to die gracefully.

It could've been much worse, she told herself. *I could've died. As Randolf and twenty-three of the other sethyd runebearers had.*

Much like the last time Nysska had met him, before he had sent the Ninth Crucible to investigate the mass sethyd murder at Summergray, Emperor Valco stood in front of the enormous fireplace with his broad back to them. The Cathedral soldiers who had shown them in turned and left, closing the huge door behind them.

"Do you know what you have done?" Valco said without moving.

Nysska shot back, "I stopped a war."

"You have sent the Church of the Great Silver Dragon into...I do not know what to call it. An 'apoplectic frenzy,' perhaps. I'm being told you commanded an actual silver dragon to come down out of the clouds and breathe fire! Such a level of, of *trickery*, however you accomplished it— Dragon *damn* it. Not to mention you've severely affected the readiness of my Argonium Infantry. That alone should seal your fate."

"I stopped a war," she repeated. "I never said the plan was perfect. Forgive me for leaving a loose end or two."

Valco pivoted slowly, the firelight deepening the lines and crevices of his face. His blue eyes raked across the three sethyds before settling on Nysska. "And here I thought you people were supposed to be *powerful*." He frowned. "What happened to your horns?"

"Long story."

His eyes narrowed a fraction of a centim. "And these are?"

Nysska gestured. "My mother, Simana Kaur, and a respected citizen of Slocum, Franklun Simeon."

Valco approached them, the grace of his movement and the bulk of his muscle beneath the royal garments belying his aged face and silver-white hair. A frown deepened the lines on his forehead. "Respected? How? He's a cripple."

Nysska took a step forward. Aware that the way she delivered what she was about to say could well determine whether the three of them left the Emperor's receiving chamber alive. Taking a deep breath, Nysska spoke softly but put bronze into every syllable.

"Watch how you speak to us, old man."

Valco recoiled as if she'd struck him with her open palm. "I beg your pardon?"

"You heard me. Keep a respectful tongue in your head while you listen."

Valco drew a breath. At one sharp word from him the crossbowmen waiting just outside would turn the three of them into bloody pincushions. But Nysska kept her yellow eyes on his, boring into his skull, plainly and utterly fearless. Valco let the breath back out before he took a smaller one.

"While I listen to what?"

Nysska waved a hand at one of the many plush chairs and couches in front of the fire. "Would you like to sit while we talk?"

Valco's mouth tightened. "No, I would like to stand right here while you spit out whatever it is you have to say."

Simana and Franklun still flanked her. She took strength from their presence. "Very well. We know about the refined argonium. How you remove the toxin from it." She dropped her volume just a hair, but increased her intensity. "We know about the white runes."

Valco's skin was pale to begin with, but as Nysska spoke his face turned white as rice. His knees might have buckled, just a little bit. He said, "Yes, yes, why don't we all make ourselves comfortable..." and drifted over to the biggest chair in the room.

By the time Nysska and Simana had taken seats on a couch across from him, and Franklun had wheeled to a spot near the fire from which he could see and hear everyone else, Valco appeared to have regained a measure of composure. Venom touched the edges of his words. "It was *you*. That's where the horns went. You're the one who broke into Fort Slade."

Nysska inclined her head.

Valco leaned forward. "But *how*? The security there is impregnable!"

"It is very plainly not."

He stared at her for a long moment. Then he sat back in the chair, one elbow propped on an armrest, and drummed his fingertips against his chin. "You would not have come here and told me this if you thought I would simply have you killed. Which I could. Effortlessly."

"True. But you won't."

"And why won't I?" He made a vague gesture in the air. "You can't—there is no—you can't *prove* anything. It's just your word against mine. Nothing more than a crazy story. The ravings of a sethyd gone mad. Most Imperial citizens already hate you and your kind, you realize that?"

Nysska allowed herself a tiny smile. "No one has to believe *my* word. It'll be *your* word that carries the truth."

Valco's frown returned. Deepened into a scowl. "I beg your pardon?"

"You spread your word by Imperial Decree. Every citizen of the Empire knows that when a Decree is made, that is law. That is *truth*. Once a messenger is handed one of your pretty little message tubes with a scroll inside—a scroll with the Imperial Seal on it—no one questions it. What is read off that parchment is the word of Emperor Valco himself. Yes?"

Valco slowly shook his head. "You're babbling."

"Hardly. If I want the truth to spread, I shall give the word. And Imperial Decrees go out all over the Empire."

The Emperor laughed. It sounded nasty. "On *your* word? Miss Stonegate, as you said, official Decrees bear the Imperial Seal. The one and only Imperial Seal. What do you hope to accomplish with obvious counterfeits?"

"'One and only,'" Nysska said, allowing a bit of derision to slide into her words. "We both know *that's* not the case." When Valco only stared at her, she went on. "You keep a spare. In case an accident should befall the one you use every day. Locked up tight, yes, but a spare exists." Nysska reached inside her jacket. "I wondered if you were going to notice it was gone before this was all over." She pulled out a large, heavy gold ring with an unmistakable design embossed on it and flipped it to Emperor Valco. "Here, you can have it back, I suppose. I won't be needing it anymore."

The ring thumped to the floor at Valco's feet. Once his gaping mouth snapped shut, Valco grabbed the ring off the floor and held it up to the firelight. *"How?"* He put his hands on the chair's armrests as if to stand, but then didn't. "How did you get this? Tell me how you got this!"

Nysska made a show of examining the nails of her right hand. "There are people—citizens—in your Empire, sir, who, not to be too indelicate, *worship* us. I met one of them a few months ago. A Scribe of yours. I killed him in the Imperial Archives."

Valco's eyes threatened to come out of his skull. *"That* was you, too?"

"People such as that Scribe believe we can destroy their souls. Free them from the inevitable horror and suffering brought about by judgement at the hands of the Great Silver Dragon. When I had the opportunity, I sneaked back into Caulspring, found a close associate of your dead Scribe and, to my lack of surprise, discovered that he shared his friend's beliefs. I offered to alleviate his suffering if he brought me the spare Imperial Seal."

Valco slumped in the chair, one hand covering his face. "My new Scribe. The one found hanging in his quarters."

"You should be more careful when deciding a person's cause of death. I broke his neck for him prior to hanging him up. He thanked me before he died."

Now Valco did stand, moving past Franklun to pose in front of the fire again. Franklun said nothing, but wheeled back out of Valco's reach. The Emperor said, "And what did you do, exactly, with the Seal while you possessed it?"

"I had thirty-five scrolls drawn up, precisely explaining the nature of the argonium runes, how you've always known the toxin could be refined out of them, how you're allowing runebearers to suffer and die needlessly, and how you and, presumably, the highest nobles are keeping the purified runes for yourselves." She sniffed. "The Thaumetallicon will be greatly interested in this revelation, I think, but they won't absolutely *fuck your life* the way the Argonium Infantry will. I should think a force of highly-trained, nearly unstoppable warriors might have a few things to say, once they learn you're letting them rot and die for no reason."

Valco hung his head. His voice trembled in a way Nysska hadn't heard before. "You don't understand."

"No? Explain it to us."

"I don't—*we* don't—the white runes aren't like the others. All they do is maintain our health. Grant us long lives, unmarred by disease or weakness. Heal us if we sustain damage." He spread his arms. "They are the reason I look like this. I am ninety-seven years old, Enforcer Stonegate. I could not rule the Empire effectively if I were confined to my bed, drooling and gibbering."

Nysska rose and went to him. He slowly faced her, bearing an expression she couldn't decipher. "But that's *worse*," she said. "That's worse than simply reaping the usual benefits from the runes without the toxic effects. To grant yourself longevity and health, while condemning all the others to a painful, early death? Do you see why that's horrible?"

"Enforcer Stonegate. Nysska. I…" He faltered. "What do you want?"

"I want all the runes removed from the runebearers. Then, if they so choose, they can have those runes replaced with purified ones."

"Were you not listening a moment ago? I already told you that the purified runes don't grant us the same kinds of abilities as the others!"

Her eyes narrowed. "Oh, but I think they *could*. I think your runemasters have fashioned the purified ones to do what they do so that you'll be *inconspicuous*. No one knows you have them and, this way, that's how it stays. But I'm betting those same runemasters could forge untainted Sense runes just fine."

He let a long, rasping breath scrape its way out of his lungs. "Say I make this happen. Just like that. I snap my fingers and it occurs."

"You *are* the Emperor."

He shook his head and went back to staring into the flames. "If I did that tomorrow, the Empire would collapse. Do you know the chaos, the riots, the mass destruction that would arise from that knowledge spreading wide? Is that what you want—the Valconian Empire destroyed? You said yourself that you just prevented a war. Do you now want to cause just as much, if not more, death and devastation?"

"Do I want more deaths? No, of course not. But this cannot continue.

You can no longer control those more physically powerful than you by *poisoning* them. By setting a, a, a *term of expiry*."

"And if I do not comply, you will have all your false Decrees released."

"Well, they're *not* false, though, are they? Everything in them is the unimpeachable truth. And even if you denounced them, the fact that they bear the Seal would force people to at least consider them. The truth would be out there, among the citizenry, and your hold on the runebearers—which equates to your hold on the Empire—would weaken and break. And you wouldn't be able to stop it."

In the smallest voice she'd ever heard him use, Valco said, "Can we not come to a compromise?"

Nysska hesitated. Into that pause, Simana spoke. "If I may offer a suggestion?" She rose and approached the fire as Nysska and Valco both turned to her.

Valco said, "So you *can* speak."

Franklun wheeled his chair half a meter closer. "Sethyds speak when we have something worthwhile to say."

Simana touched Nysska's shoulder. "Everything my daughter has told you is true. And if anything happens to her—or anyone she's close to—every one of those thirty-five decrees will be released. But you indicated you might be open to compromise. *What if*...what if you were to announce that your runemasters had made a breakthrough in their science? What if they discovered that it *might be possible* to refine argonium? What if their experiments needed subjects...experiments that might stretch out over, shall we say, the next five years or so...and begin with the runebearers closest to, as Nysska put it, their 'term of expiry'?"

"I know exactly who the first subject should be," Nysska said, nodding. "The white runes heal you if you're hurt, yes? There's a Scent Sensor in Mount Stark. A man named Olivette."

"Olivette. Mount Stark. Surely." Valco closed his eyes. "Five years? Five years to come up with a new system." He opened his eyes again and glared at Nysska. "Five years to replace what has kept our Empire strong for the last *three hundred*."

Nysska said, "Five years sounds like plenty of time to me."

Valco threw up his hands. "We don't even know if the purified argonium *can* be fashioned into the Sense runes! You're just guessing about that! And it's not as if we don't need defenses! The fucking Gemini are still out there, seeding the Empire with their fucking red runes and red dust and all this chervoxite bearshit! We can't be defenseless, Miss Stonegate!"

Nysska sighed. "I'm not asking you to be. Five years. Figure something out in *five years*. Your runemasters are smart. And we already know argonium and chervoxite can be alloyed to make new kinds of runes."

Valco blinked. "You cannot be suggesting what I think you are."

"Why not? Offer amnesty to the Gemini. *All* the Gemini. Prove you mean it. Bring them into the Empire. Offer them funding and land if you have to. You'll be making a precious new resource available as well as getting some very smart, *very* stealthy people to stop trying to kill you."

"Speaking of land," Franklun said, "we would like the Crags to be made an officially self-governing sethyd territory."

Valco snorted. To Nysska, he said, "And I suppose you want to go run it, don't you?"

She made a sour face. "Not even a little bit."

Franklun indicated Simana. "The two of us will."

Nysska surprised herself by putting a hand on the Emperor's arm and steering him away from the fire. "Look. You have the mother of all golden opportunities here."

"Oh I do, do I?"

"I'm serious. You do what we're asking, and do it the right way, and first off you'll be the Emperor who let runebearers live long, normal lives. Second, you're going to make an immensely powerful *ally* out of the Gemini. Can you imagine how effective a spy a Gemini would be? What if you had thousands of them?" Valco's eyes unfocused. "And third. *Our* people. You stop treating us like second-class citizens. Give us land charters throughout the Empire. You know what we can do. Don't you want the Valconian military to have sethyds fighting alongside the Argonium Infantry? Don't you want to have a combined force that will secure the Empire for centuries to come? Do all this the right way, and your subjects will *love* you."

Valco rubbed his temples with the heels of his hands. "Every human in the Empire thinks you're a bunch of demons."

"Not every human."

"Most humans."

"It's an obstacle that can be overcome."

His arms flopped to his sides. "How?"

She took a step back, frowning up at him. "Are you not the Emperor? You have to change the way your subjects think. So do it. *Guide* them.

Lead by example. Host a ball or whatever kind of celebration you want, and invite my mother and Franklun, and a Gemini woman named Bronna Smith." She gestured widely, taking in the territory beyond the palace walls. "Send theater companies out across the Empire and have them perform plays that show humans and sethyds and Gemini living and working together. Commission songwriters to write songs about how we're not literal demons, and how the Gemini got treated unfairly, and see that they're sung in taverns. Get some storytellers to tell new stories. It wouldn't be *that* hard."

Valco took a long moment, his forehead creasing and uncreasing. "And what do *you* want?"

"An open channel," she said without hesitation. "Communication. I want to be able to come and talk to you about matters of the Empire. There are things you need to know. Things to discuss." She tried her best to sound friendly. "Look, sir, I know we're blackmailing you, but you've got to see that it's all going to be *massively* to your advantage. This is going to make sure the Valconian Empire lasts for *thousands* of years, not hundreds. And it'll be filled with people who follow you because they love you. Not just because they're terrified you're going to send the Infantry in to kill them if they fuck up."

Nysska saw something in Valco's eyes she'd never seen there before. A glimmer of something...pure. Something like...hope?

He cleared his throat, projecting the demeanor of a grandfather who disapproves of a grandchild's actions but can do nothing to stop them. "I meant *you*. Personally. Nysska Stonegate. What do you want out of all this? To be the new head of the Thaumetallicon? Governor of a human territory? What?"

"I would like to return to the Ninth Crucible. Officially."

"That cannot be the end of the list."

Nysska let her lips curl up on one side. "I...do have one more request. Your Brilliance."

"Tell me."

Nysska, Simana, and Franklun exited the Imperial Palace and moved into a small courtyard where a tiny crowd waited for them. Raoul and Morrin hovered off to one side, talking quietly, until the sethyds emerged. Percy and Veronika Brooks stood together as well, but with their arms around each other's waists and the two blood lynxes at their feet. They both broke into wide grins when Nysska waved to them. Aschling and Singer, who had her disguise lenses in, had been kneeling and petting Rosie but sprang to their feet.

Cam broke away from the crowd and rushed to Nysska. "Well? How'd it go?"

Simana said, "My daughter told the Emperor to watch his mouth." She didn't smile when she said it, but the pride came through just fine.

Raoul and Morrin had moved closer. Raoul said, "She did *what*, now?"

Singer asked, "Do you talk about Borealis?"

Nysska shook her head. "Not yet. We *will*, and we'll do it soon, just not today."

Singer looked disappointed, but nodded. "People like Kagan take some adjusting for humans here, huh?"

Cam took Nysska's hands in hers and squeezed them. "So it went well? Truly?"

Nysska squeezed back. "It truly did."

"What about the, ah, special item we discussed?"

Nysska grinned just as widely as Percy and Veronika. "Well..."

After a clear, brutally cold night that led to a frigid, cloudless morning, Wallace Embry rolled out onto the street that ran past the Mount Stark infirmary. He would have much preferred to propel himself, but both of his arms were still in casts, as was his left leg. The vision in his right eye remained blurry as well, though that might have been getting better. As it was, his morning constitutionals were dependent on a huge, gray-haired woman named Lucia who never smiled but did enjoy the occasional dirty joke. Lucia had persuaded her brother, a carpenter, to build a special chair to accommodate Wallace's outsized physique, since she and the physicians all thought fresh air was an important part of his recovery. Wallace appreciated the generosity. He just wished it weren't so cold.

Lucia wheeled him along the street and around the corner into the broad square of the city center just as the sound of galloping hooves reached them. In a few seconds a rider appeared—an Imperial messenger —with the familiar ornate metal tube in one hand.

"Looks like he's headed for the posting board," Wallace said over his shoulder. "Could we go see what it's about?"

Lucia only grunted, but she gamely changed the big chair's course and approached the tall, broad board in the center of the square. It had an awning built over it, as most did, to keep the rain off any important announcements or Decrees. Thanks to the angle of the sun, Wallace couldn't make out any details of the parchment as the messenger tacked it up with a small hammer and a few nails. The messenger didn't wait for them to get there. He turned, cleared his throat, and shouted around the square in exactly the same way that every other Imperial Decree had always been delivered.

"Attention, citizens of Mount Stark and all surrounding areas! His Brilliance, the Emperor Valco, hereby decrees that the prohibition against relationships consisting of two men or two women is immediately dissolved! Such relationships, be they matrimonial or not, shall henceforth be awarded the protection of the Empire, and any actions taken to disrupt such relationships shall be met with the harshest of penalties! So declares His Brilliance, the Emperor Valco!" The messenger coughed lightly. "I shall make this announcement again at noon and at the eventide! Heed these words, all of you, for they constitute an Imperial Decree!"

As the messenger took his horse's bridle and walked it toward the nearest tavern—past a number of Mount Stark citizens, all of them standing there looking thunderstruck—Wallace twisted painfully around in his seat. "Take me back, Lucia!"

The big woman cocked an eyebrow at him. "Why? You got something important to do?"

"Yes!" Wallace said through an enormous grin. "I have to get a letter to Stockbridge!"

THE END

ACKNOWLEDGMENTS

This book would not have been possible without some talented, insightful, very very patient people. My heartfelt thanks to John Hartness, Sarah Adams, and Tuppence Van de Vaarst for guiding all the wild words home. To Susan Roddey for another spectacular cover. To Clint McInnes for his insight and unbridled enthusiasm. And to Tracy Jolley, without whom I would be hopelessly adrift.

ABOUT THE AUTHOR

Dan Jolley began writing professionally at age 19. Starting out in comic books, Dan has worked for major publishers such as DC (*Firestorm*), Marvel (*Dr. Strange*), Dark Horse (*Aliens*), and Image (*G.I. Joe*). He soon branched out into licensed-property novels (*Star Trek*), film novelizations (*Iron Man*), and original novels, including the science-fiction/super-hero *Gray Widow Trilogy*.

Dan began writing for video games in 2007, and has contributed storylines, characters, and dialogue to titles such as *Transformers: War for Cybertron*, *Prototype 2*, and *Dying Light*, among others.

His latest work includes *The Storm*, a mystery-thriller inspired by actual events in Dan's hometown, and the best-selling Audible Original audiobook *House of Teeth*.

Dan lives with his wife Tracy in northwest Georgia. Readers can learn more about him on his website, www.danjolley.com.

ALSO BY DAN JOLLEY

ADULT FICTION

The Gray Widow Trilogy:

Gray Widow's Walk

Gray Widow's Web

Gray Widow's War

The Demon-Sleuth Scrolls

The Runemaster Homicide

The Black-Horned Grave

The Runemaster Curse

The Storm

YOUNG ADULT BOOKS

The Alex Unlimited Trilogy:

The Vosarak Code

Split-Second Sight

True Chemistry

MIDDLE-GRADE BOOKS

The Five Elements Trilogy:

The Emerald Tablet

The Shadow City

The Crimson Serpent

House of Teeth (Audible Original audiobook)

FRIENDS OF FALSTAFF

Thank You to All our Falstaff Books Patrons, who get extra digital content each month! To be featured here and see what other great rewards we offer, go to www.patreon.com/falstaffbooks.

PATRONS

Dino Hicks
John Hooks
John Kilgallon
Larissa Lichty
Travis & Casey Schilling
Staci-Leigh Santore
Sheryl R. Hayes
Scott Norris
Samuel Montgomery-Blinn
Junkle

www.ingramcontent.com/pod-product-compliance
Lightning Source LLC
Chambersburg PA
CBHW020602110726
47899CB00002B/342